11B1 3.50

The Dying Light is the second novel in the *Evergence* trilogy following *The Prodigal Sun,* the American debut of Australian science fiction writers Sean Williams and Shane Dix. Their first collaboration, *The Unknown Soldier,* published in Australia, was hailed as "fast paced and thoughtful space opera" by *The Leading Edge.*

Sean Williams has been writing full time since 1990, with approximately 50 published short stories. He has won a prize in the 20th Writers of the Future Contest, been recommended by *Year's Best Horror & Fantasy* and *Year's Best Science Fiction* anthologies, and won Australia's two most prestigious SF awards. His first solo novel, *Metal Fatigue,* won the Aurealis Award for Best SF Novel (and also reached the top 15 in the Internet Speculative Fiction Database's Top Books of 1996). His second, *Resurrected Man,* received the Ditmar Award for Best Novel of 1998.

"An unusually fine story-teller . . . phenomenally prolific . . . one of Australia's hottest new science fiction authors . . . shows every sign of becoming the next successful writer to break out from Down Under."

—Dave Wolverton

Shane Dix has been writing since he was fifteen. His story "Through the Water that Binds" won the 1991 Canberra SF Society's short story competition. The story was also featured in the Australian landmark science fiction anthology *Alien Shores.* In addition to science fiction, he has had published mainstream stories, poetry, and articles about the state of SF in film and tele

D0204881

EVERGENCE

THE DYING LIGHT

SEAN WILLIAMS & SHANE DIX

ACE BOOKS, NEW YORK

If you purchased this book without a cover, you should be aware that this book is stolen property. It was reported as "unsold and destroyed" to the publisher and neither the author nor the publisher has received any payment for this "stripped book."

This is a work of fiction. Names, characters, places, and incidents are either the product of the author's imagination or are used fictitiously, and any resemblance to actual persons, living or dead, business establishments, events, or locales is entirely coincidental.

EVERGENCE: THE DYING LIGHT

An Ace Book / published by arrangement with the authors

PRINTING HISTORY
Ace edition / July 2000

All rights reserved.
Copyright © 2000 by Sean Williams & Shane Dix.
Cover art by Bob Warner.

This book may not be reproduced in whole or in part, by mimeograph or any other means, without permission.
For information address: The Berkley Publishing Group, a division of Penguin Putnam Inc., 375 Hudson Street, New York, New York 10014.

The Penguin Putnam Inc. World Wide Web site address is http://www.penguinputnam.com

Check out the ACE Science Fiction & Fantasy newsletter and much more on the Internet at Club PPI!

ISBN: 0-441-00742-2

ACE®
Ace Books are published by The Berkley Publishing Group, a division of Penguin Putnam Inc., 375 Hudson Street, New York, New York 10014.
ACE and the "A" design are trademarks belonging to Penguin Putnam Inc.

PRINTED IN THE UNITED STATES OF AMERICA

10 9 8 7 6 5 4 3 2

For Scott and Kerri

Darkness is looking forward and saying: "I do not know what to do next; I have lost my way and it is too late to find it now."

—*HUBERT VAN ZELLER*

The cruellest lies are often told in silence.

—*ROBERT LOUIS STEVENSON*

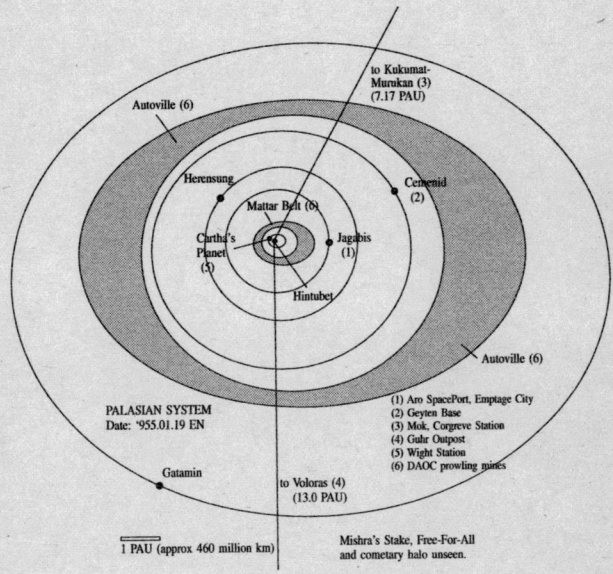
to Kukumat-
Murukan (3)
(7.17 PAU)
Autoville (6)
Herensung
Cemenid
(2)
Mattar Belt (6)
Cartha's
Planet
(5)
Jagabis
(1)
Hintubet
Autoville (6)
PALASIAN SYSTEM
Date: '955.01.19 EN
(1) Aro SpacePort, Emptage City
(2) Geyten Base
(3) Mok, Corgreve Station
(4) Guhr Outpost
(5) Wight Station
(6) DAOC prowling mines
Gatamin
to Voloras (4)
(13.0 PAU)
1 PAU (approx 460 million km)
Mishra's Stake, Free-For-All
and cometary halo unseen.

PART ONE:

PALASIAN SYSTEM

Prologue

Words could not describe what he saw; they could only approximate. And therein lay the terrible irony of his situation: that he, of all beings in the galaxy, who could see things as (perhaps) they truly were, was utterly unable to convey all but the vaguest of impressions to those few who wanted to know.

<Find . . .>

Thoughts flew at him from all directions—thoughts tangled with emotions, sensations, and subconscious associations. So entwined were they, so hopelessly meshed, that by the time they reached him it was often impossible to disentangle a single thought from the rest. Sometimes one stood out, or several in concert, but he was rarely their intended recipient. Only occasionally did they demand a response, and when they did, he tried his best. Even so, his efforts rarely satisfied the demands of the Cruel One's servant.

<Find me . . .>

He looked.

All beings perceived the galaxy by their own unique light—brightest in the young, flickering as age increased, ultimately extinguished with death. It was this light he saw, not what it revealed, and the more these individual lights overlapped, the clearer his vision became. Perceived reality reached him from so many perspectives, some of them conflicting or downright contradictory, that the overlap took on its own life and became a thing unto itself. The *essence* of reality dominated his world. Not what a rock looked like to one person, or what it was called, but what it meant to everyone who encountered it—what it *was* in the larger weave of minds.

Through his eyes the galaxy was recognizable: densely populated planets hung like bright galaxies spinning in gulfs of impenetrable dark. As attention wandered across the void, his all-pervading sense followed, lighting up a place, a person, an artifact, then moving on. What it did not touch was irrelevant, for according to the rules of his universe anything not sensed did not exist. Yet even at the very fringes of his senses, the voice was speckled by fleeting glimpses of life. Every experience was there for him to harvest, no matter how exotic, or how hidden.

Normally, at least, that was so. But the Cruel One had taken the galaxy away from him, and left only darkness in its place. The infinite abyss pressed in upon him, making him feel as if he were suffocating. Only a handful of minds occupied the space surrounding him. One major clump represented the installation that contained him, accounting for almost ninety percent of the impressions he gathered—maybe a thousand minds in all. The rest were scattered, their lights weak, solitary and frightened. All except one—the one the others wanted him to find.

<. . . the Shining One.>

Sometimes the voice would part and allow him a glimpse of the being he sought. Just for a second—but in that briefest of moments its brightness and elegance outshone all else around. Whenever the mind appeared to him, he received an impression of something magnificent and wondrous. Something that was almost . . . *chilling.*

<Respond!>

The Cruel One's servant was persistent. The voice hammered at him, wearing down his resistance. He struggled to orient himself within his body, fought the outward urge that tugged him into the void. His limbs trembled—unseen by himself, but registered by the people watching him. Even in this much reduced form, his influence extended many thousands of meters.

<Find me the Shining One!>

The muscles of his distant body twitched. Electrodes recorded the minuscule currents of electrons and fluid through his brain. Powerful computers dedicated to the task took these vague data and translated them into words.

: ANOTHER

: RESONATES

A moment passed while the listeners absorbed his response. He could feel their minds turning, reacting in a dozen different ways—some with surprise, others with relief, even a few with ill-disguised fear. None held the object of his quest in awe, as did he.

Then:

<Where?>

That question. Always the same question: *where?*

How should *he* know? Spatial orientations were things he barely understood; they were too easily confused with temporal or emotional impressions. What was space when measured against the combined input of so many disparate minds?

But he did his best. The Cruel One was impatient for results, and that made her servants anxious. They regarded their master with contempt, yet they feared her also, and when they feared her most, their contempt found an outlet in those farther down the chain.

The watcher in their midst absorbed their feelings without rancor. He knew his place; he knew where he fitted into the Cruel One's schemes. His usefulness was defined solely by his ability to locate the Shining One. If he failed to do so, then his usefulness was at an end. The Cruel One was not known to be tolerant of anyone who failed, especially those who did not belong to her own Caste.

Every being sees the Universe in their own unique light, but very few see themselves with such acute honesty.

<Find me the Shining One!>

He did his best. He always did his best. And if his reply displeased the Cruel One's servant, he was never to know for certain

<Where?>

: HERE

: SOON

1

IND *Ana Vereine*
'955.01.19 EN
0415

Alone but for the screaming wind, she fell. Her outstretched arms sought to find equilibrium, but to no avail. With nothing around for her hands to find purchase upon, her fall continued unchecked. The sickening sensation persisted in her stomach; the wind at her face and in her ears was relentless.

When exactly she had begun to fall she couldn't tell. Not that it mattered. Once she had been weightless, now she was falling; the only difference between the two was a matter of *destination.* Everything in the universe was just an orbiting body looking for something with which to intersect. If she had found her ultimate trajectory, then perhaps that was for the best. At least the waiting was over.

Suddenly from the darkness something touched her hand. She pulled away instinctively, sending herself into a spin. But the touch against her skin was persistent. It fluttered like a flesh-warm moth, moving along her wrist, her elbow, and finally settled on her upper arm.

She tried too late to pull away. Its grip tightened; slender, smooth digits dug deeply into her and tugged her forward. She called out in panic, but the blackness absorbed any sound she made.

When she flailed at the limb clutching her, her hand found skin. A hand. No fur, no scales, no chitinous exoskeleton; no claws, no suckers, no pinchers. It was a *Pristine* hand.

Cautiously, she explored the one that was falling with her. She moved her fingers along the person's wrist, elbow, and upper arm; her other hand found a smooth stomach, rib cage, and breast. Then, alarmed by the all too familiar terrain, she gripped the other person tightly. Wanting to push her away, instead she pulled her closer.

From the darkness she saw her own frightened face emerge; from the roaring wind she heard herself call out. . . .

Morgan Roche woke with a start and clutched her sweat-drenched sheets to her chest. A lingering vertigo made her giddy, and for a moment she didn't know where she was. The narrow bed, the dark room, the smell of deep-space service: she could have been anywhere, aboard any Commonwealth of Empires' vessel, on any number of missions for COE Intelligence.

Then, in the dull glow from the ceiling light, she saw the valise resting on a nearby table, and reality suddenly dispelled her confusion. She was in the second lieutenant's quarters of the *Ana Vereine,* a former Dato Bloc vessel now registered under her name, and she had no mission apart from the one she had given herself. Her indenture to COE Intelligence was a thing of the past—a memory returning to haunt her like the nightmare that had awoken her, and just as difficult to shake.

Rubbing at her arm, she vividly recalled the falling, the fear.

Then the flat echoes of an incident alarm wailing beyond

her room goaded her to full consciousness. Disentangling her legs from the sheets, she climbed out of the bunk.

"Full lights." Squinting in the sudden glare, she amended: "Half lights. *Half* lights!"

The glare dimmed as she stumbled to the cabin's small wardrobe. She grabbed the first shipsuit she saw. Standard dress for a Dato Bloc officer, it consisted of a unisex, form-fitting garment cut from rust-colored fabric, with black insignia at shoulders and waist. Active fibers tightened the weave around her limbs, guaranteeing a perfect fit every time.

As she dressed, she sent a subvocal inquiry via her implants to the transmitter on her left wrist:

<Uri? Box? What's going on?>

The voice of the Box answered immediately, the AI's neutral tones coming from the tiny speaker beside the bed:

"We have completed our final jump, Morgan. The *Ana Vereine* entered real-space fifteen minutes ago."

At the end of the sentence, the sirens ceased.

Roche glanced at the clock beside her bed. <Why? We weren't due to arrive at the Palasian anchor point for another three hours.>

"Indeed. That was our original schedule." The Box paused before adding: "There has been an unusual development. Cane thought it best that you were here on the bridge."

<What sort of "development," Box?> A knot of worry began to tighten in her stomach. <Is it the other clone warrior?>

"Nothing so dramatic, Morgan. Simply—perplexing."

She took a deep breath to hide her irritation. If the *Box* was perplexed, then she doubted she would be much help. What the most sophisticated artificial intelligence in the Commonwealth couldn't fathom, no mundane Human would have a chance of deciphering.

Still, tired or not, she had to keep up appearances. Sitting down on the bunk, she slid her feet into a pair of boots and fastened the ankle straps.

<Okay, Box, tell Cane I'm on my way. Are the others on deck?>

"Kajic and Maii are asleep. Haid is awake, but has not responded to my summons."

<Where is he?>

"In the rehabilitation unit."

<Break into the program, then. We need three on the bridge, just in case it turns out to be serious.>

"Understood." Again the Box hesitated, as though it was about to debate her assumption that it didn't rate as a crew member. But all it said in the end was: "I shall wait until you have arrived before taking any action."

<Good.> Boots on and fastened, Roche stood. At her approach, the door to her quarters slid open. She heard an airlock chime in the distance, ready for her to step into the ship's central transit corridor. <Give me two minutes.>

The *Ana Vereine,* first of the new Marauder-class combat ships to roll off the Dato Bloc production lines, was designed to hold a full complement of three thousand crew members. Its size reflected that—uncomfortably at times. Currently carrying a crew of just five, its labyrinthine holds were sealed; active life support was restricted to officers' quarters, the bridge and a handful of essential areas; major accessways were dimly lit and cool, filled with nothing but the gentle susurrus of hundreds of cubic kilometers of moving air.

Sometimes it seemed to Roche, as it did now, on her way to the bridge, that she had been swallowed by a vast, metal beast. That at any moment the ship would spring to life, shrug free of its carbon-based passengers and head off on its own adventure. And perhaps it would serve them right if it did; they were so far from realizing its true potential.

In the eighteen days since leaving COE Intelligence HQ, they had traveled a highly circuitous route. Fearing a double cross from Page De Bruyn, head of Strategy and Roche's former employer, the Box had plotted an untraceable course to Walan Third, where they had surrendered Makil Veden's body to the Commerce Artel. That small but necessary detour cost them time: although they remained at the Eckandi base for less than a day, their total on the run had already reached eight by the time they left.

From Walan Third the *Ana Vereine* headed toward Baeris Osh, a Surin territory, before abruptly changing course for the Handrelle System. Every time they completed a hyperspace jump, Roche half-expected to find an ambush waiting for them. The chances of De Bruyn second-guessing their path were practically zero, since it was impossible to predict the destination of a ship once it entered hyperspace, but the fear was hard to shake. Only on the last two jumps, when they finally angled back toward the border of the Kesh N'Kor Republic and their original destination, had Morgan begun to believe that she was actually safe, that she might yet outrun her past.

Still, there was always the future to worry about. If an ambush was what De Bruyn intended, Palasian System was the obvious place to stage it. Only a stubborn belief—based mainly on recent experience—that COE Intelligence would never do anything quite so obvious kept her from losing sleep over that possibility. Page De Bruyn had revealed herself to be a far more cunning and deceitful opponent than that.

Besides, it wasn't what she was running *from* that most concerned Morgan, but what she was running *to*. The Box had said that the alert had nothing to do with the Sol Wunderkind in Palasian System. A gut instinct told her that that was not the whole truth.

Rounding the last corner on her approach to the bridge, Roche felt the peculiar hopelessness of her dream return with a vividness that stung. She slowed her pace and took a few deep breaths, wanting to regain her composure before she stepped onto the bridge to join the others.

The last time she'd had that dream had been the night before taking the Armada entrance exam on Ascensio, many years before. But why had it returned *now,* on this, her nineteenth day free of COE Intelligence? She was at a loss to understand the connection. The dream spoke of her deepest fears: of failure, the future, and . . . *freedom*?

She shook her head to rid herself of the discomforting notion. She *was* glad to be free of COE Intelligence, wasn't she? She didn't like to think that even the smallest part of her might be having regrets.

When her mind was relatively still, if not entirely clear, she took another deep breath and stepped through the open portal and onto the bridge.

The bridge was not the largest room on the *Ana Vereine,* even though it felt as if it could have been. The main chamber was roughly heart-shaped, with a single holographic screen dominating the left lobe, more specialized displays in the right, and various officer stations sweeping in three arcs toward the rounded base. A smaller, circular room at the base of the heart was the captain's private chamber. This chamber, plus the shape of the bridge itself, lent the entire floor plan a passing resemblance to the Mandelbrot Set, with the captain's podium located at the intersection of X and Y axes. Except that on the *Ana Vereine,* there was no captain's podium. There was just a large hologram projector occupying its usual spot.

Tempering the bewildering array of displays and control stations, the walls bore the colors of late sunset with the occasional tapestry to blunt sharp corners. The lighting was muted, and brightened only under battle conditions.

One person occupied the vast area. He was leaning against the astrogation officer's station with his arms folded, the shipsuit he wore emphasizing his supple strength.

"Sorry to disturb you," said Cane, straightening as Roche entered. His dark brown skin and bald skull made him seem Exotic, subtly alien, and the little Roche knew about his origins didn't help shake that impression.

"That's okay," she said, wishing she could emulate his

alertness. Not for the first time, she cursed the modified genes responsible for his extraordinary resilience. "What's the situation?"

"We found something." Cane nodded at the main screen. "Or at least, the Box did."

She crossed the bridge to the first officer's chair as he talked. "Show me," she said, sitting.

"Well, that's the strange thing," Cane said. "There's nothing to show."

Roche, frowning, swiveled in her chair to face him. Before she could speak, Cane added: "At least, nothing *I* can see."

"The phenomenon we have encountered is not visible in the physical universe," explained the Box, its voice issuing from speakers at the base of the holographic projector.

Roche shifted her attention back to the main screen. The only thing it revealed were the cold specks of distant stars.

She sighed, impatience rising within her again. "Is someone going to explain what's going on here?"

"Of course," said the Box. The view on the main screen changed, became the route plotted by Roche and the Box while refueling at COE Intelligence HQ. "Our original course from Walan Third consisted of fourteen hyperspace jumps across the Commonwealth of Empires, culminating in one final jump to the anchor point of Palasian System. We traveled entirely without incident until this last jump." An arrow skittered through the depths of the screen, settling upon a point almost at the end of their route. "Here. Four hours into the jump, sensors aboard the *Ana Vereine* detected an anomaly in our vicinity."

The screen displayed complex diagrams representing the distorted topology of hyperspace—that strange realm where even the basic laws of physics could not be taken for granted.

"The disturbance lay directly in our path," the Box continued, "although its distance from us in physical terms was difficult to determine. My one attempt to change course around it was unsuccessful, perhaps because of the influence it was—and is still—exerting over our navigational data."

"What sort of influence?" Roche asked.

"A type I have never encountered before, Morgan. Our course became increasingly uncertain the closer we approached it. By attempting to go around it, we ran the risk of passing through it instead. Eventually the potential hazard became so great that I decided to return prematurely. We had nearly completed the final jump by that point, so I thought the loss in time would be offset by the chance to see what awaited us."

"And?" Roche watched in guarded fascination as the main screen changed again; n-dimensional mathematics was not her specialty, but she assumed the Box knew what it was talking about.

"The source of the disturbance remains a mystery."

"So? As long as we don't hit it, we can still make it to Palasian System, right?"

"If only it were that simple, Morgan." The screen returned to the picture it had displayed when Roche had entered the bridge: stars, none so close as to be remarkable, and nothing else within the external scanners' fields of view.

Nothing . . .

"Where's the primary of Palasian System?" she asked, frowning.

"We can't find it," Cane said. "That's the problem."

Roche's frown deepened. "We're *lost*?"

"If anything," said the Box, "it is the system itself that is lost." A navigation chart appeared on the screen. "If you study the data, you will see that we have arrived with the correct orientation one light-week short of the terminus of our original jump, two light-weeks from Palasian System. Star charts confirm this. What we are seeing is what we *should* be seeing, except for one important detail: Hintubet, Palasian System's primary, appears nowhere within the starscape before us."

"I find that hard to believe. It has to be here somewhere—"

"None of the stars in this region produce a spectral match. Neither do any within a fifty light-year radius." The Box paused before pronouncing its conclusion: "Palasian System is patently not where it is supposed to be."

Roche found her sense of fatigue quickly fading. "That's impossible. The disturbance must have knocked us more off course than you thought."

"Not by so great a margin as to lose an entire star, Morgan."

"Then the star charts must be wrong."

"They aren't. Apart from a few slight discrepancies, every other navigational marker in this region matches."

"Well, *what* then?" She shook her head in annoyance. To come so close to her destination only to find that it had been snatched away from her was like something out of a bad dream—another one. "A system can't just disappear without a trace!"

"I agree that it is improbable," said the Box, its tone mollifying. "But the only conceivable alternative is that it has been destroyed."

"How?" She automatically glanced at Cane. No one knew exactly what the genetically modified clone warriors made by the Sol Apotheosis Movement were capable of—possibly not even Cane, who was one of them. "Surely not even a Sol Wunderkind could do *that*."

"It would seem unlikely that the entire system was destroyed," agreed Cane. "But when you consider that the only alternative explanation is that it has been moved, you have to admit—"

"This is a rhetorical point," the Box cut in. "We lack data, Morgan. What measurements I can make from this distance are hampered by the fact that light from the region is at least one week old. I have found no evidence to suggest any sort of event sufficiently calamitous to destroy a star without leaving any trace of stellar wreckage—but I may be missing something. We need to go closer to find out."

Her eyes narrowed suspiciously. "I thought you said the disturbance posed too great a risk to navigation."

"Not necessarily. Long-distance jumps through this region of space are likely to be perturbed. I suggest instead that we approach the vicinity of where Palasian System used to be by increments, studying the anomaly as we go. Should the risk increase further still, we can come to a halt again and consider other courses of action."

Roche nodded, agreeing in principle with what the Box was saying. If the risk was only to navigation and the ship was in little physical danger, then there was little reason not to continue. The lack of information, however, made it hard even to guess how much danger they were in: if something *had* destroyed Palasian System, then they might be heading right for it.

Nevertheless, there was no other choice. They had to keep going. It was either that or turn around—and the latter was hardly an attractive prospect. With the possible exception of the Box, none of them had a home to return to any longer.

"What does COE Intelligence have to say about this?" Roche asked. "Is there any mention in the data they've given us?"

"Very little, I'm afraid, Morgan. We have the report transmitted by the battalion of Armada Marines before it was destroyed, including a vague description of the damage done to the system at that time. It describes Palasian System as quarantined or sealed, but nothing else."

"No updates since then?"

"Since the *Ana Vereine* disengaged from COE Intelligence HQ, reports have been intermittent at best."

So much for their agreement with De Bruyn, she thought sourly. Still, if that was the worst the head of Strategy had planned, then she should be grateful. Unless—

Again she shook her head. Not even Page De Bruyn would destroy an entire solar system to obtain revenge—especially not when the fate of the Commonwealth of Empires might be at stake.

"I agree with your analysis of the situation, Box," she said slowly. "We need to find Palasian System, but to do *that* we need information. We will, therefore, proceed with your plan: to approach the last known location of Palasian System more cautiously, by slow-jumping a little closer each time and taking stock as we go. That way we'll have a chance of staying on course and avoiding anything waiting for us."

There was almost an air of smugness to the Box's tone as it replied: "Very well, Morgan. I will begin plotting a new course immediately."

"Good. But don't perform any maneuvers until Uri is conscious and watching what you do. We don't know what effect rapid transfers might have on the ship. Defer to him if he thinks you should take it more cautiously."

"Naturally." The Box's smug tone had faded, and Roche did her best to suppress a smile of satisfaction. Although the uniquely self-aware AI had been programmed by its creators on Trinity to obey her orders, that didn't mean it had to enjoy the situation; any chance it found to assert its independence, the Box took it. She had learned the hard way not to give it generalized orders that were too easily evaded, or outright perverted, in order to meet its own hidden agenda—whatever *that* was. Where her own lack of experience made it difficult for her to be specific, she allocated an overseer to keep an eye on the Box's activities, just to make sure.

If that bothered the Box, all the better. She had earned this subtle form of revenge, at least, after the way it had manipulated her in the past and probably intended to in the future.

"Okay," she said. "You get started, Box. Cane, track down Maii and get her up here. We'll need her to search for life signs when we get close enough. I'm going down to rehab to see what's happened to Haid."

"Shall I rouse Kajic?" asked the Box.

"No," said Roche, levering herself out of the chair. "He'll be awake soon enough, if he isn't already. Let him come to you in his own time, when he's finished any status checks he needs to perform. We don't need to rush him. I want to take this slowly: we might not get a second a chance to find out what's going on."

Especially if the other Sol Wunderkind is *behind it,* she added to herself.

"I'll notify you when we are about to begin," said the Box.

"You do that," Roche said as she left the bridge.

The ship's rehabilitation unit was four levels down from the bridge, in an annex off the medical unit. On the way down, Roche was joined by a fist-sized drone that darted from a service hatch and assumed a position near her right shoulder. The jets of air propelling it sounded like a cough played at high speed. When the drone spoke, it did so in a tinny version of Uri Kajic's voice.

"What do you think, Morgan?" he asked.

Roche glanced at the drone without breaking step. "I thought you'd be listening in."

"And?"

"I think something strange is going on."

"Likewise. The sooner we find out what it is, the better." The drone skittered ahead, emitting agitated *fft*'s as it turned a corner. "I do believe the Box, though," he said, "when it says it doesn't know what the anomaly is."

"So do I, strangely enough," Roche admitted. "Otherwise it wouldn't have brought us out of the jump so suddenly."

"There's more to it than that, Morgan. I've studied the astrogation data. The Box mentioned a few 'slight discrepancies' but it didn't tell you what they were."

"Are they significant?"

"Perhaps. The stars in the direction of Palasian System appear to be closer than they should be. Not much closer, admittedly—a few billion kilometers or so—but closer all the same. It's as though a big chunk of space is missing from this area."

"The space containing Palasian System?"

"That would seem the logical conclusion," Kajic agreed. "But can you imagine the force required to achieve this? Destroying a star, or even moving it, is bad enough; taking the space surrounding it as well is a completely different matter."

Roche contemplated the possibility for a long moment. She had never heard of such a thing—indeed, she found it hard to visualize. Nothing could destroy space itself. Nothing she had ever heard of, anyway.

"All the more reason, then, to make our approach a cautious one," she said. "Will the ship hold up? *Can* it slow-jump as often as the Box would like?"

"I've looked at the basic plan, and it seems sound. We'll drop in and out of hyperspace once every ten minutes, traveling several million kilometers each time and accelerating between. At first we'll approach the anomaly in tangents, so we can look at it from a number of directions; that way we might be able to determine exactly how large it is. If things go well, we'll try getting a little closer to see what else we find." The drone bobbed as Kajic spoke. "The ship itself will be fine. Its engines are designed to function under battle conditions. In fact, it'll be good to have a really thorough workout. The last time we put it through its paces was back at Sciacca's World."

Roche nodded but did not speak. The *Ana Vereine* and a handful of raiders had made short work of the *Midnight,* the ship she had been traveling in at the time. Only the Box's decision to blow the frigate's antimatter reserves had prevented the Dato Bloc captain from capturing the ship, or destroying it himself. As a result, the *Ana Vereine* had yet to make its first kill.

Still, it had performed well in battle, and she accepted Kajic's opinion that it would survive the coming hours. It was only an old superstition that made her hesitant to place her faith completely in a new ship.

"We'll stick out like a beacon, jumping that often," she said, halfheartedly trying to pick holes in the Box's plan.

"True. But there's nothing we can do to avoid that." Kajic paused, then suggested: "We can camouflage the ship, if you like. Make it look like a freighter experiencing drive difficulties—?"

She shook her head. "Palasian System has been quarantined. Only a fool would try to get in, faulty drive or not. If we stumble across an Armada blockade, as unlikely as that is, they'll shoot us out of the sky regardless of what we look like."

"They can try." Roche heard the ghost of a grin in the thin reproduction of Kajic's voice. "Any other questions?"

"Only one." The one she had avoided asking herself: "What do we do if we can't work out what happened to the system? Where do we go from there?"

"Only time will tell us that, Morgan. Time, and the right data."

"I know, I know." Roche inhaled deeply, trying to center herself. "Just make sure the Box tells me if we *do* find something, okay? That'd give me one less thing to worry about."

"You have my word," said Kajic. "And don't worry, Morgan. You're doing fine."

Roche smiled. "Thanks, Uri."

With a staccato tattoo of air-bursts, the drone accelerated ahead of her and ducked into a maintenance closet.

Roche continued the rest of the way to rehab alone, genuinely reassured by Kajic's closing comment. Her relationship with the Dato Bloc ex-captain was still an ambivalent one. Although both had been betrayed by their respective governments, making them allies of sorts, Roche had initially felt uncomfortable having the ship's previous commander aboard. Removing or imprisoning him had never been an option, though: he was as much a part of the ship as the navigation AI or the engines. What remained of his body floated in a life-support tank in a little-visited section, plugged by an experimental neural interface into the workings of the vessel surrounding him. As much as she might have preferred, she couldn't have one without the other.

So it was just lucky that he had chosen to take her under his metaphorical wing and train her in the art of command. All her years in COE Intelligence had taught her how to obey orders, not how to give them. Already she had come to rely on his judgment in many matters, not just those to do with the ship; without him, these last few weeks would have been considerably harder.

Still, she could understand why others might be suspicious of a Dato Bloc captain in their midst with unlimited access to the entire ship. The situation begged betrayal of some sort—which is why she had instructed the Box to keep as close an eye on Kajic as *he* was keeping on *it*. She couldn't allow her own, possibly irrational, opinions to place her or her other companions at risk; she mistrusted all of them equally, had to do so in order to keep going. And if Kajic ever found out, she was sure that he would understand.

The Box's voice broke into her thoughts via her implants: <All is arranged, Morgan. We will proceed in ninety seconds, once the *Ana Vereine* has achieved the necessary velocity to slow-jump.>

<Good work,> she subvocalized. <The ship is in your hands and Uri's.>

<Understood.>

She increased her pace through the Marauder's glowing corridors. The entrance to the rehabilitation unit finally appeared on her left. At the same time, a warning buzzer sounded, alerting the occupants of the ship to an imminent hyperspace jump.

She had barely steadied herself when the ship's drives went to work. Reality flexed around her; space-time twisted in impossible directions. A wave of giddiness came and went, making her blink.

Then everything was as it had been a moment before—

except that the ship was no longer a part of the physical universe. It had entered hyperspace, and was accelerating at many thousand standard gravities relative to the normal universe. For all the effect the jump had on the interior of the ship, however, it might have gone nowhere. Which was exactly how it should have been.

The doors to the rehab unit slid open when she took another step forward. Yet another step took her across the threshold, into a world she rarely visited.

Rehabilitation, as the term was employed in most military organizations, was synonymous with cybernetic enhancement. Where more orthodox medical techniques failed to heal a wound, replace a limb or rebuild a broken mind—or if there was no time to employ sophisticated methods of healing—technology stepped in to breach the gap. Everything from artificial limbs to neuron patches could be provided by the best mobile rehab units in the Commonwealth of Empires, and those of the Dato Bloc were at least as advanced. The *Ana Vereine* in particular, given its recent manufacture, possessed facilities Roche had only heard about.

The large workroom was designed as an open surgery, with several adjoining chambers available for procedures requiring more sterile environments. Four long tables, uncomfortably like mortuary slabs, awaited patients in states of perpetual readiness, while close by hung numerous multi-jointed waldoes, medical scanners and replacement parts. Along one wall, screens could project views of any operations under way, or retrieve from memory similar situations to compare prognoses. Another wall boasted three holographic "cybercorpses"—human bodies composed entirely of replacement parts, from carbon-fiber bones to synthetic skin—with no single part repeated in any of the "bodies." Designed for reference, the cybercorpses rotated once every twenty seconds, as though performing a macabre pirouette. When Roche stepped farther into the room to look for Haid, six glassy, empty eyes seemed to follow her for a moment, then drifted away.

She found him in one of the auxiliary chambers, hard-wired into a simulation that was teaching him to use his new support biomesh. After their escape from Sciacca's World, an immediate priority had been to equip Haid with a body at least approximating the Pristine. Time had been against them, however. The surgery alone required for a total rebuild would have taken several weeks; recovery and readjustment at least the same again. Haid had opted instead for a basic overhaul: an eye to replace his empty socket, the support biomesh to compensate for his lack of an arm and to supplement the strength of his legs, plus new interfaces to control the lot.

The installation, undergone piecemeal, had taken seven days. Another five had seen him on his feet for the first time. The remaining seven had been spent in the simulator, retraining his reflexes to respond to new stimuli.

When Roche found him, he was floating in free-fall, twisting about his center of gravity in an ungainly manner. The glossy black mesh of the exoskeleton stood out against the gray of his undersuit, but perfectly matched the sweat-soaked sheen of his midnight skin. Despite years of abuse and layers of scar tissue millimeters thick, Haid still possessed the distinctive coloring of a Montaban native—along with the rugged good looks.

His eyes were uncovered, but Roche could tell that she was invisible to him—along with the rest of the ship. Placing her left hand on a panel flush to the door frame, she synchronized her own implants to the illusion in which he was enmeshed. The vision through her left eye went gray with static for a moment, then cleared.

With his feet anchored by magnetic soles to the hull of a spacecraft, Haid was trying to thread a gossamer-thin guideline through a moving eyelet. He was naked, apart from the biomesh, and very clumsy. The surface beneath his feet moved without warning, making his judgment unreliable, so every action with his new arm had to be carefully considered. In other simulations that Roche had observed, he had run over burning sand while carrying a glass of water, balanced on a narrow ledge with his old arm behind his back, and attempted to imitate the movements of garishly dressed dancers—all with the critical eye of the rehab AI grading every movement.

Roche gave him five minutes before actively interfering. In that time, he came close to tying a loop through the eyelet, but a sudden shift in the surface beneath his feet cost him his grip on the thread, forcing him to start again. His lips moved silently, cursing under his breath.

"Haid." Roche tried to keep her voice soft, but its incongruity broke the illusion instantly. "Ameidio, can you hear me?"

Haid sighed; his new skeletal arm, with its black mesh skin, sagged. "Yes, Morgan, I hear you."

"The Box said you weren't responding, so I thought I'd better check on you myself. Is everything okay?"

Ignoring her concerns, Haid said: "This rehab AI is a sadist. I *swear* this damn hole is getting smaller." His eyes gazed blankly into the distance, away from her. It wasn't just the simulation: he was exhausted. "Next time I'll get it, though. Next time I'll—"

"Something's come up," she interrupted, trying to keep her voice firm and level—a line dragging him back to reality. "We needed you on the bridge."

"I felt us come out of hyperspace," he said. "Are we there already?" He looked around him, as though waking from a dream, and frowned. "No, wait. We jumped again just a moment ago, didn't we? That wasn't planned."

"No, it wasn't." She outlined the situation as briefly as she could—that Palasian System appeared to have disappeared—not wanting to worry him, but at the same time reinforcing the fact that he hadn't been there when she *might* have needed him. If the ship had been under attack—

"I would have noticed instantly." His voice was calm but there was no disguising his indignation. "There would have been sirens, impacts, power fluctuations. Not even a wirehead could sim through something like that."

"But if you *had* noticed, it would've been too late for you to do anything."

"Like I could do anything, anyway, with *this*." Haid raised his new arm and flexed it. The movement was smoother than it had been even a day earlier but was still noticeably jerky.

Roche shook her head, even though Haid wouldn't see the gesture. "Your other arm is fine. And besides, you don't need coordination to help on the bridge. Not unless we're boarded—and I hope it'll never come to that."

"Likewise." He let the arm fall to his side. An instant later, the illusion collapsed around them, brought to an end by his mental command. The zero-g field relaxed, eased him slowly to the floor of the auxiliary chamber. His legs became rigid when they touched the floor, held him upright as his full weight returned. "But the fact remains that you need me in full working order—and that means as much deep-training as possible—"

"It also means getting some rest." She let go of the touch panel and took a step closer. "You look terrible."

He grimaced. "Thanks a lot."

"I'm serious. Take a shower, have something to eat and drink. Then meet me as soon as you can to discuss what's going on—"

A second wave of disorientation rushed through Roche as the *Ana Vereine* returned to real-space. She moved forward as Haid swayed, but he reached out with his new arm and steadied himself.

"See?" He smiled wryly at his own achievement. "Give me another week and I'll be wrestling clone warriors bare-handed."

"I sincerely hope not," she said, turning her back on him and walking out of the simulation room.

"Any news on that front?" Haid asked, moving stiffly after her. Picking up a towel from a bench by the door, he wiped the skin of his upper body dry, where the active fabric of his absorbent undersuit was unable to reach.

"None," she said. "We're still too far away."

"Unless the disappearance of the system is a related event." Haid put the towel aside. "Does anybody know how advanced the Sol Apotheosis Movement was? Maybe they found a way to camouflage an entire system."

"I doubt it," she said, although the possibility wasn't one she had considered. "If they'd possessed that sort of tech, they wouldn't have been destroyed so easily. They could have camouflaged their base and escaped the siege any time they wanted."

"Siege?" Haid shook his head. "A simple 'no' would have done, Morgan. You know history isn't my strong point."

"Nor mine," she said. "It took me days to find what little there was available. I've condensed it into a single file and placed it in the open datapool. You can access it later, if you want."

"Maybe." The ship rolled beneath them again. Haid's oddly mismatched eyes—one much like a monocle covering the entire socket, and the other, the recent addition, a crystal sphere where a normal eye would sit—lifted in surprise to meet hers. "The Box is not wasting any time, is it?"

"It's found something it doesn't understand, and doesn't like it."

Haid chuckled softly. "So trying to make me feel guilty about not responding is just your way of taking out on me your frustration with *it*."

Roche smiled in return, ignoring the gibe. "I'm heading back to the bridge," she said. "When you're ready, join us there. We could use your input."

The ex-mercenary nodded as she headed for the door. "At least it looks like we might have something to do, for a change."

Haid's parting comment pursued her after she left the rehab unit. Eighteen days on the run, fearing a COE Intelligence betrayal every step of the way; major surgery, followed by recovery and intense rehabilitation; a destination about which they knew little, except for the fact that it had nearly been destroyed by the deadliest warrior to grace the galaxy in two and a half thousand years—and Haid was complaining about being *bored*?

Roche didn't need that sort of excitement in her life. In fact, an uninterrupted sleep would have suited her much better.

A familiar mind-touch greeted her as she headed back to the bridge:

<Good morning, Morgan.>

Startled by the unexpected intrusion upon her thoughts, Roche missed a step. <Hello, Maii. Cane woke you, I see.>

<Yes.> The reave's voice carried with it a faint tinge of grief. Hardly surprising, Roche thought; the girl had had so little time to adjust to the death of her mentor, Veden. As his ward, she had earned the right to recite the ritual leave-taking during the ceremony on Walan Third, but she had declined, both reluctant to appear in public and conscious of time pressing.

<Did he fill you in?>

<He said that Palasian System seems to have disappeared. And while the Box tries to find it, you want me to check for life signs.>

<Near enough. See if you can detect anyone where the system used to be. An eyewitness would be good, but anyone at all will do.>

<I have already tried several times. From such a distance, resolution is poor.>

<I know.> Privately, Roche was amazed that the girl thought she could detect anything at all. <But keep trying. At least there's a chance you might be able to tell us something the Box can't.>

<Okay,> said Maii. <We're jumping at the moment, so I'll wait until we come out again. It's easier that way.>

<Whatever. You're the expert.> Roche walked on, trying to fight the weariness slowing her stride.

<You're tired,> observed Maii. <Cane woke you too?>

<I wouldn't have slept much longer anyway.>

<Another nightmare, Morgan?>

She nodded unnecessarily. <Yes.>

<I can help you, you know.>

As an accompaniment to her words, Maii sent a brief image of an underwater scene: a coral reef lit by mottled green sunlight with large gray fish lightly brushing against her body. Despite the constant motion, the endless cycle of life and death swirling around her, the mood generated by the image was one of peace and inner calm.

A healing dream, designed to ease the girl's own path through grief.

Roche hesitated before answering. As uncomfortable as she still was with epsense therapy, she had to admit that the offer was made with the best intentions. That made a flat "no" much harder to pronounce.

<I'd be happier to have breakfast,> she said eventually.

<Well, there's not much happening on the bridge at the moment. Cane and I can take care of things for a while if you want to grab yourself a meal.>

Even though she disliked being away from the heart of the action, the offer was appealing. It could be her last chance for a long while. <Thanks, Maii.>

<My pleasure.> A mental smile accompanied her next words: <And don't worry, Morgan. We'll keep you informed.>

Roche hurried to the officers' mess, two levels up from the rehab facility. There she ordered a nondescript breakfast and took a seat at one of the many empty tables filling the room. The dispenser provided her with a good imitation of eggs, cereal, and fruit juice. She forced herself to eat slowly, chewing each bite rather than gulping it down.

Every ten minutes the ship rolled as it moved from one universe to the next, edging closer to the anomaly each time.

She couldn't help but wonder what the Box was learning along the way, but she refrained from asking for an update. If anything happened, someone would be sure to call her. Until they did, all she had to do was relax.

After a couple more mouthfuls, she realized that she couldn't relax. There was too much at stake—and too little known about the situation to help her guess at what she had to do.

There was something she *could* do, however. Midway through the small meal, she routed a display through her implants and selected the file she had collated on the Sol Apotheosis Movement from the combined data resources of the Commonwealth of Empires and the Dato Bloc. Somewhere in the file, she hoped, was a clue regarding the technological prowess of her enemy.

Whether she would find anything useful was unlikely, though. The history of the Sol Apotheosis Movement was poorly documented until the time of its destruction. It had been founded early in the 36th millennium, '325 EN, by a visionary whose name was no longer recorded. The Movement's aim had been to achieve Transcendence by means of genetic manipulation and biomodification, rather than by downloading living minds into AI networks, as was usual. By bucking both tradition and common sense, its adherents were ostracized and banned by their native government—also unnamed—so they sought and found an empty system deep in the backwaters of their region of the galaxy. Acquiring the system by the expediency of simply moving in and adopting its name, they devoted their considerable energy to consolidating their position rather than taking their message any farther—for a while.

By '836 of the following millennium, they had established trade with the Eckandar Trade Axis which, along with the Commonwealth of Empires, had begun expansion into the area surrounding them. With trade came a new openness, and it wasn't long before biomodified prophets began to spread through neighboring regions, looking for converts.

Some of these prophets were early versions of the Movement's crowning—and most deadly—achievement: the Sol Wunderkind, a genetically modified combat soldier with abilities far superior to any known Caste. Word began to spread, and within decades their existence was well-known, as was the threat they represented.

Many attempts were made to discourage or disperse the prophets, but they persisted. Squabbles broke out when the Ataman Theocracy attempted to reclaim Sol System as its own—even though the system had been abandoned centuries before as an uneconomic prospect. Tempers flared; the Movement countered every attempt to take the system away from them. Eventually an alliance was formed between the Commonwealth of Empires, the Dominion, and the Ataman Theocracy—the three largest Pristine nations in the Movement's range—to wipe out the threat once and for all.

The largest joint military flotilla ever assembled by the three nations was dispatched to Sol System. There, they surrounded the main base of the Sol Apotheosis Movement and presented its members with an ultimatum: leave or be destroyed. The Movement refused to leave, so the leader of the combined Pristine forces ordered his ships to open fire.

Within seconds of the first shot, the main base of the Sol Apotheosis Movement self-destructed, taking with it ninety percent of the Pristine flotilla. The Sol Apotheosis Movement was utterly destroyed.

The name of the man who gave the order to fire was Adoni Cane. His fate was not recorded, but Roche could only assume that he had died along with the millions of others in the system.

Details beyond that point were particularly scarce. The Pristine alliance, although nominal victors of that bloody conflict, chose to erase the entire event from their various histories. Exactly why the Movement had chosen to commit suicide in such a dramatic manner was not explained convincingly anywhere that Roche could find. No one had postulated the theory that they might have considered long-term revenge.

Until now . . .

A lone Human with no memories apart from the name Adoni Cane had been recovered from a life-support capsule in a backwater region of the Commonwealth of Empires. In the time Roche had known him he had demonstrated extraordinary feats of endurance, intelligence, and strength. Plus he bore an uncanny likeness to the man who had shared his name two and a half thousand years ago. At roughly the same time, another such castaway, name unknown, had been recovered near Palasian System. Within days, the system had been in flames, and now appeared to have disappeared entirely. The Sol Apotheosis Movement, it seemed, was back. Why, though, was anyone's guess.

As far as finding out exactly how advanced the Movement had been, there were few indicators. With regard to genetic technology at least, they'd had no peer. The few researchers who had studied the history of the Movement all concluded that the COE was behind them in many ways, despite the intervening millennia. Any doubts Roche herself might have had regarding that claim were easily dispelled by the existence of the Adoni Cane she knew. No other mundane civilization in the history of the galaxy, to her knowledge, had the ability to craft such a superbly capable Human purely by manipulating genetic code. Only High Humans might possess that knowledge, and they had no reason to meddle in affairs beneath them.

In other areas, however, less was known. The destruction of the Movement's base in Sol System had been accomplished by means of an enormous explosion, the likes of which had never been seen before or since. The weapons systems employed by the earlier versions of the Wunderkind had also outstripped anything available at the time. And their defensive abilities must have been remarkable, to have held off frequent attacks for so long before their eventual self-destruction.

But did they have enough technological know-how to destroy or to hide an entire system? Roche might have accepted the possibility had the Sol Wunderkind that invaded Palasian System been discovered in a fully functional warship. With such a vessel, he might have been capable of anything. But he hadn't been in a warship. He had been removed from a life-support capsule similar—if not identical—to the one in which Cane had been found.

She skimmed through the data collected by the medical officers aboard the *Midnight.* Cane's capsule had been unique in that he had actually been grown from a zygote within it, but otherwise it had been empty. Its empty shell contained no obvious navigation or propulsion systems; the only life-support provided was the hibernation regulator that had kept Cane in stasis during the months until his discovery; only the most basic of AIs kept the whole system operating. If every capsule was the same, then the Sol clone warrior in Palasian System had woken up naked and unarmed, not better-equipped than most small armies.

Since then, however, he had somehow managed to commandeer at least one COE Armada vessel and attack no fewer than five semipermanent COE installations. And now he had effectively disappeared, taking the entire system with him.

So little was known about him—what his intentions were, how capable he was of fulfilling them, and exactly what he had done in the few weeks since his awakening. Even if Roche found Palasian System, there was no guarantee the clone warrior would even be there anymore. He could be light-years away, wreaking havoc on other outposts.

Then a new thought struck her. The clone warrior had awakened unarmed, but had immediately taken control of the nearest ship. Perhaps he had performed a similar feat in Palasian System as a whole. Given the right knowledge, he could have made his own equipment from the resources scattered across the system—if the right resources were present.

She checked the COE database. Palasian System contained a small Armada refueling base, one communications outpost, one town-sized colony, and a scattered handful of scientific installations, two of which were devoted to studying solar flares and xenoarchaeology. That was all, on eight planets and a large assortment of smaller satellites. Nothing stood out as possessing the sort of equipment the fugitive would have required to build a device capable of hiding an entire system. Of course, not knowing *how* the device worked made it hard to guess what was required to build it, and even more difficult to work out how to counteract its effect.

Before Roche could take her exploration of the files any further, the ship shuddered violently. She looked up in alarm as the bulkheads around her rattled.

<Box! What was that?> she asked via her implants, letting her spoon fall into what remained of her breakfast.

<A difficult translation, Morgan,> replied the AI. <There is no need to be alarmed.>

<If you're pushing the ship too hard—>

<I am doing nothing of the sort.> The Box sounded mildly offended. <We are simply coming closer to the anomaly. Disturbance is to be expected.>

<How much worse do you think it will get?>

<I am unable to answer that question at this point,> said the Box. <But I can assure you that the situation is being closely monitored.>

<Good.> Roche stood and put her plate into a disposal hatch. <I'm on my way, in any case.>

The Box said nothing more, perhaps sensing the renewed determination Roche felt—partly a result of the food, partly the refocusing of her attention on the goals they all shared. For the first time in the hours since her rude awakening, she actually felt alert.

When she reached the bridge, Cane occupied exactly the same position he had earlier, watching the expanse of the big screen with his arms folded.

Maii sat not far from him. A strip of white cloth covered her empty sockets, matching the loose shift she wore in preference to Dato Bloc shipsuits. Roche automatically sent a smile her way, and when she saw the Surin return it knew that the ritually blinded girl was using Cane's eyes for visual input. The only other person available to read was Roche herself—but that would have rendered the smile invisible to the epsense adept.

Aloud, Roche asked: "Any news, Maii?"

<None so far, Morgan. The area seems to be empty.>

She grunted acknowledgment of the fact to herself, then added: "What if the system was camouflaged? Would it be possible for the Sol Wunderkind to block epsense as well?"

Cane looked up. "The whole system?" he said. "Highly unlikely."

"But it *is* a possibility." She turned to face him. "A remote one, I'll admit—"

"What I meant was," Cane interrupted her, "if the system *is* camouflaged, then I doubt my sibling is responsible."

My sibling . . . The words made Roche's skin crawl. Sometimes it was hard to accept that Cane and the Sol Wunderkind that had effectively destroyed Palasian System were of the same breed—possibly even identical in every respect.

"Why not?" she asked.

"Because, tactically speaking, it makes no sense to be confined to a single system. If I were in his shoes, I would want to move on, taking with me only the resources needed to make my task easier at my next destination." Cane's shoulders lifted in a smooth and easy shrug, as though he were discussing a poor tactic in a barroom game, not the destruction of a whole system. "Also, to hide in such a manner would be tantamount to admitting defeat. Camouflaged or not, it's only a matter of time before the system is found—if not by us, then by someone else."

Roche nodded. "It could be a decoy, then. Something to keep us occupied while he slips away."

"A lot of effort for little reward. However he did it, *if* he did it, it must have been enormously energy-expensive."

"Maybe. But what if—"

Box's soft, controlled voice cut across her own: "There's

really no point even trying to guess until we have more data, Morgan."

"Okay, okay." Roche raised her arms in mock defeat. Sitting in her chair, she faced the main screen to check the status of the ship: it was about to emerge from the short slow-jump that had begun so awkwardly. Maybe when Haid appeared, they could discuss the situation in more detail.

<There is no known way to block epsense,> said Maii, continuing the conversation Cane had interrupted, <apart from at the source. Any thought that slips past a mental shield can be detected. No matter how small. The most powerful E-shield wouldn't even weaken it.>

Roche nodded, absorbing that fact without comment.

"Emerging from hyperspace in fifteen seconds," said Kajic, his voice issuing from the base of the holographic projector. Now that he had no crew to impress, he only occasionally bothered to manifest in physical form.

The ship groaned back into reality as noisily as it had left. Roche held onto the edge of her seat as the floor writhed beneath her, seeming to melt for an instant as space transformed. Somewhere nearby, something clattered. When the ship stabilized, she forced her muscles to relax, then looked around.

"Someone warn me next time," said Haid from the entrance to the bridge. He held a tray in his new hand and, bending, used his other hand to pick up packages of food that had spilled during the disturbance.

"Klaxons sound automatically prior to every translation," said the Box.

"Yeah, but who listens to them?" Haid finished piling the meal back onto the tray. "I thought this ship could handle anything."

"Not quite," said Kajic. "But close enough."

Haid's face lost some of its good humor at the sound of the ex-Dato Bloc captain's voice.

"Yeah, well," he said, taking a seat at an empty station.

"When the Box summoned me, I thought I'd bring breakfast up here. Hope that's okay."

Roche frowned, puzzled. She hadn't asked the Box to summon anyone. "Box? What's going on?"

"I have an announcement to make," the AI said. "The preliminary survey is now complete and, although much of the data remains to be processed, I have one confirmed observation to report. In accordance with your wishes, Morgan, I summoned Haid to ensure that the entire crew was present to hear it."

Roche didn't respond immediately. The Box wasn't normally so considerate of her wishes. It smacked of overcompensation, as though it was courting disapproval elsewhere.

"Continue," she said after a moment. If it *was* planning something, then she would have to wait until later to find out what it was.

The Box complied, calling up a number of complicated diagrams on the main screen. "At the heart of the region formerly occupied by Palasian System lies a radiant point-source."

"A singularity?" Roche broke in. She hadn't even considered the possibility that the system had been sucked into a black hole.

"No," said the Box. "The point-source appears to have zero mass and is radiant predominantly in the upper infrared spectrum. I have detected what may be a cloud of primordial gas surrounding the point-source, but will have to make more observations before confirming that suspicion."

"How close are we?" asked Haid, clearly as disturbed by the thought of a black hole nearby as Roche was, despite the Box's assurance of their safety.

"Twelve billion kilometers." The map on the screen highlighted points as the Box spoke. "The next slow-jump will halve that distance."

"Is that a good idea?" asked Roche.

"All available evidence indicates that the risk of undertaking such a maneuver would be small."

"The risk for whom?" said Roche. "Yourself or all of us?"

The Box hesitated before snapping: "Both, of course."

Roche smiled at the Box's apparent indignation. "Okay," she said. "Then I can't see why we shouldn't do it. As soon as you're ready—"

<I have something.> Soft but clear, Maii's words touched Roche's thoughts—as, she assumed, they touched everyone else's simultaneously.

Roche looked across the bridge, the discussion of the point-source instantly shelved. The Surin's face was blank, indicating intense concentration, as it had been since the end of the last jump.

"What is it?" Roche asked, leaning closer.

<Something strange.> The girl frowned. <Or an echo of something. I can't tell which. It's very faint. I've missed it so far because it's so hard to sense at all.>

"Describe it," Roche prodded.

<It's not a person—but it is alive.> Confusion deepened Maii's frown. <A great distance from here, yet close. I don't understand what I'm seeing.>

"Are you picking up any *thoughts*?" Roche pressed.

<None. Not even a base emotion.>

"Could it be an AI, then, or hidden by a very effective shield?"

<A shield would leak somewhere, and not even the Box has thoughts I can read.> The reave's body sagged. <Damn. Every time I think I've got a grip on it, I lose it again. It's like trying to catch air!>

Roche reached out with a mental hand to touch the Surin's straining mind and ease her frustration. "It's okay, Maii. Wait until the next jump. It might be stronger then."

" 'It' might be the anomaly itself," suggested Haid.

"Now there's a possibility I *don't* want to consider." Roche sighed as warning Klaxons began to sound again. "Box, any thoughts on that?"

"None that would not offend."

The rare joke from the Box elicited a chuckle from Haid, but one that was short-lived. The Box's sense of humor—usually at the expense of carbon-based life forms or epsense science—only reinforced its uniqueness. Roche also detected a faint hint of annoyance, as though it was peeved that the reave had taken the wind out of its sails, ruining the effect of its big announcement.

Maii emerged from her trance as the ship jumped in accordance with the Box's wishes. <I sensed no malice,> she said, her mental voice clearly audible through the groaning of metal. The slow-jump was easily the most uncomfortable so far.

"That's something." Haid folded his arms. "But I'd still feel happier knowing what we were heading for."

"A black hole doesn't have to bear us any ill will to be dangerous," agreed Kajic.

"It is not a black hole," asserted the Box.

"Famous last words," muttered the ex-mercenary.

"I agree with Kajic," said Cane. "Just because it's a natural phenomenon doesn't mean it can't still be deadly."

"At least we could go in with weapons armed," added Haid.

"Do it, then." Roche concurred with the ex-mercenary's unspoken message: sitting around waiting was only making them more tense. "Cane, work with him."

"Done." The two men crossed the bridge to take positions at the weapons station.

"Anything else to report, Box?"

"Some inconclusive findings," it said.

"Such as?" she persisted, silently cursing the AI's reticence.

"The steep flexure gradient in this region is suggestive of significant, and recent, spatial trauma."

Roche's eyebrows knitted. "That means nothing to me."

"Space-time has been warped on a massive scale," the Box translated. "The traumatized region occupies a disc-shaped area roughly seventeen billion kilometers across and two billion kilometers thick. The radiant point-source lies at the heart of this region, although I have been unable as yet to determine whether it is the cause of the flexure or simply another effect. It is conceivable, perhaps even likely, that the point-source and the anomaly are different facets of the same phenomenon. However, more research is required before I can be certain of that."

"How much more?"

"That depends on the result of this slow-jump," the Box replied. "We will be jumping to the very edge of what should be Palasian System, not far from the anchor point that was our original destination. It is my conjecture that the degree of flexure will increase sharply at this point."

"Proving . . . ?"

"Again, I hesitate to speculate until we have concrete data."

Roche grunted. "How long, then?"

"I estimate fifteen minutes before we arrive at our destination."

"So soon?"

"As a result of the flexure gradient, our relative velocity is greatly increased. In a sense, the anomaly has been drawing us toward the point-source."

"It sounds even more like a black hole, now," said Haid over his shoulder.

"The effect is only relative to real space," continued the Box. "In hyperspace, we are actually fighting an uphill battle: although our movement in hyperspace corresponds to greater than normal movement in the real universe, it is becoming increasingly difficult to move in hyperspace at all. I have consulted Kajic and arrived at a maximum output rating for the slow-jump drive—a rating which we will not exceed."

Roche nodded in satisfaction. Even though she didn't understand how progress could be easier in real-space but more difficult in hyperspace, at least Kajic and the Box were co-operating.

<I'm picking up that trace again,> said Maii into the break in conversation.

Roche glanced across the bridge. The Surin was frowning once more. "Where?"

<I'm not sure. It's always hard to tell from hyperspace. The trace is definitely stronger, but maybe no closer. There's still no sense of threat.>

"Can you at least tell if it's mundane?"

The reave looked troubled. <Part of me says it isn't, but that's just a gut feeling. High Human, perhaps, but I don't think it's that either. The source is something I've never come across before.>

A Sol Wunderkind? Roche wanted to ask, but didn't. Maii would have said if that were the case. Yet she couldn't quash the thought: something in hyperspace was pushing them away while in real-space drawing them closer. If not the fugitive, then what?

Roche folded her arms and watched the main screen as the minutes ticked by; the large number of unknowns made her want to scream out in frustration. She needed answers, not possibilities.

<If there *are* any answers,> put in Maii, <we'll find them when we find Palasian System.>

Before Roche could acknowledge the truth of the reave's comment, a low rumble echoed through the ship, beginning at the stern and fading to silence at the distant prow.

"Now what?" asked Roche, looking around in alarm.

"Uh—one moment," said Kajic.

"We had a flicker of red lights down the port hull," said Haid, "but they've cleared now."

"A slight disturbance," said the Box. "Nothing to be concerned about."

Roche bit her tongue until Kajic delivered his own report.

"No problems with the drive," said the ex-captain finally. "We must have encountered some sort of turbulence. Possibly a hyperspatial shock wave of some kind."

"The anomaly again?" said Roche.

"It seems likely."

"We are nearing the edge of the anomaly," said the AI. "Obviously there will be some turbulence."

"Aimed at us, perhaps?" suggested Haid.

"No," said the Box. "Describing what we are experiencing as a shock wave is peculiarly apt. The turbulence may be caused by the anomaly only in the same way that the presence of a large mass 'causes' gravity."

"Not deliberate then, but symptomatic." Roche ran a hand restlessly along the arm of her chair. "It's all the same from this end, isn't it?"

"Not really," said the Box. "If we can piece together a pattern to the symptoms, we should be able to deduce the nature of the anomaly that is causing it."

"Here comes another one," said Cane, his head cocked, listening.

The groan returned, as gradually as before but noticeably louder when it peaked. Roche, her hands pressed firmly into the chair's armrests, felt a faint buzz through her fingertips.

"Could it hurt us, Uri?" she asked.

"Conceivably, yes. The stress is caused by sympathetic vibrations in the hull. So far I have been able to dampen the resonance."

"Let me know if it gets too bad."

"I will. If we encounter it again."

Roche waited anxiously as the ship traveled onward. Barely two minutes later, a third shock wave rolled through the ship, this time accompanied by a sluing sensation to starboard and down, as though the ship were being dragged off course.

"Red lights again," said Haid.

An instant later, from Cane: "Clear."

Roche waited on edge for Kajic's report.

"No damage," he said finally. "But it was definitely more severe. The closer we get to the anomaly, the stronger they're becoming."

"Can we ride them for much longer?"

"If they continue worsening at this rate, no," said Kajic. "But we'll come close."

"Good enough." Roche swiveled her chair to face the main screen. Only a handful of minutes remained before the slow-jump was due to end. "Pull us out the moment we can't take it. I'll leave that decision in your hands."

"Understood."

As another groan began to build, Roche again gripped the chair's armrests, and held on tight. She felt as though a bell were tolling directly behind her head, a bell so large that its vibrations were absorbed by her bones rather than heard. Before it had completely faded, another swelled to take its place.

"Box," she said, raising her voice above the noise. "If you have *any* idea at all what that anomaly is, I want to hear it."

"I now have several theories, Morgan. Which is the correct one, of course, remains to be seen."

Roche opened her mouth to demand an outline of the various possibilities, but was cut off by a sudden lurch upward. Her stomach dropped, then rose again, into her chest.

"We're experiencing gravity fluctuations," said Kajic. "I can only keep us going another fifty seconds."

Roche studied the main screen, momentarily tempted to call a halt. Their planned arrival point was inching slowly closer. Given a further half-minute, they would almost make it. She decided to trust Kajic's instincts.

"There must be some way to dampen the shock waves," she said.

"I'll raise the E-shields, but I don't think that'll help much." The ex-captain's voice sounded strained.

"Whatever you can do, Uri."

The noise worsened, despite the shields, as did the rolling

sensation in Roche's gut. Maii, lacking eyes of her own and therefore more susceptible to balance problems, looked decidedly uncomfortable. Haid had taken the precaution of fastening his impact harness. Cane, behind him, was as steadfast as ever—but even he swayed when a particularly strong wave shunted the ship in an unexpected direction.

Roche watched the seconds counting down on the big screen: 21 . . . 20 . . . 19 . . .

The shock waves became inseparable, and the ship seemed to toss on the surface of a stormy sea. Red lights flickered on and off across all the boards, registering slight damage across the hull. Most would be repaired almost instantly by the tide of maintenance nanomachines swarming over every external surface of the ship, but the fact that they were occurring at all was disturbing.

Ten seconds remained.

Roche watched their destination creep closer. It was becoming increasingly difficult to hear over the prolonged groan surrounding them.

The lights flickered once, steadied, then flickered again.

"We have a standing wave in sectors G through K," announced Kajic grimly. "Preparing to abort the slow-jump."

Five seconds. Roche winced as the smell of ozone reached her nose.

Three seconds. On the main screen, the difference between the ship's current location and its destination was measured in millimeters.

Two seconds—

"Aborting now," said Kajic, the very instant artificial gravity ceased entirely. A siren began to wail a split second later. The lights flickered a third time as the drive drained power from the bulk of the ship to translate itself safely back into real-space. In the short-lived darkness, Roche actually heard the engines strain—a deep, regular thrumming coming from somewhere to her left. Their tempo was rapid but reassuringly regular under the circumstances.

Then the lights returned, unsteadily and noticeably dimmer than they usually were. Space twisted inside out, and the floor bucked under her feet. Her momentum tried to pull her forward, onto the floor and across the bridge. Gripping the chair's armrests even tighter, she resisted the impetus with all her strength. To her left, Maii lost a similar battle and skidded on her knees into a bank of instruments. Even Cane staggered, clasping Haid's shoulder to keep his balance.

The floor bucked again, this time in the opposite direction. Maii gasped in pain as she slid backward and collided with her seat. The bulkheads around them likewise groaned in protest.

"Uri!" Roche shouted above the racket. "What's happening?"

"We are experiencing difficulty emerging from hyperspace," said the Box, its voice amplified but calm—*too* calm for Roche's liking. "I will act as an intermediary between Kajic and yourself for the time being. The ship is his primary concern at the moment."

Another jolt almost cost Roche her grip. She reached behind and over her shoulder to fasten the seat's restraint harness. "Are we going to make it?"

"I should think so," said the Box. "The chances are very good that we will all survive."

Roche was grateful for the "all." The Box could endure almost anything, and had been known to assume the same indestructibility of its wards in the past. Cane, on the other hand, had already moved across the bridge to help Maii into her harness.

"We have damage," reported Haid from the weapons station, his voice raised to be heard. "Lost some banks on the starboard bow. I don't quite know what happened; looks like they've been sheared clean off. No pressure drops reported, though, and hull integrity's intact."

Roche concentrated on what he was saying. "What have we lost?"

"Hypershields in that area. Some A-P cannon. We'll be able to compensate easily enough."

"Good. We—uh!" The *Ana Vereine* swung to starboard, then down; Roche winced as her restraint harness cut deep into her chest. The thrumming of the engines rose in both pitch and intensity until it became a screaming—like the screaming of a mighty wind—

—she was falling—

—and nausea flared deep within her as the association with the dream made her feel impotent and therefore even more anxious.

The main screen flickered, attracting her attention. Abstract representations of their course swirled into increasingly complex shapes, then disappeared entirely, leaving nothing in their wake. White lines scattered across the screen, making Roche blink; then it went black again.

Without warning, the ship began to steady. Bulkheads settled back into place with a series of decreasing creaks. The screaming of the engines ebbed, losing the desperate edge that had contributed to Roche's anxiety. The groan of tortured space faded with one last rending sound, then ceased entirely.

In the sudden silence, Roche didn't dare ask the question.

She didn't need to.

"We made it," said Kajic, his voice from near Roche's right shoulder clear and relieved.

"Yes," echoed the Box, its voice oddly hushed. "We most certainly did."

At that moment, the main screen came back to life. Blinding light filled the bridge, dazzling Roche until she managed to bring an arm up to protect her eyes. Compensators cut in an instant later, reducing the glare to more manageable levels. Through the gaps between her fingers, Roche peered at what lay before them.

"What the hell is that?" exclaimed Haid, preempting her own initial reaction.

A blazing yellow-white oval filled the center of the screen. At first she thought it was a sun, but the shape was wrong: it was distorted as though giant hands had gripped it at each pole and stretched it lengthwise. In addition, there were no flares or prominences, no hints of corona or sunspots. Just light, bright and unceasing, coming from something far too close for comfort.

There was only one thing it could be.

"It's the point-source," she said, directing her words at the Box.

"Precisely," it replied, as she'd half hoped it would not.

"But we should be millions of kilometers away from it. I thought you were taking us to the edge of where the system used to be—"

"I did. Yet here we are, only a short distance from what appears to be the center. Remarkable, isn't it?"

Remarkable? Roche echoed to herself. She could think of words to describe it, but that wasn't one of them.

Before she could say anything, however, Haid's voice broke into the conversation.

"We have targets!" he called. "Someone else got here before us!"

"Where?" she asked, instantly turning her seat to face his station.

"Two behind us," he said. "One on the far side of whatever that thing is. Emissions suggest ships, probably Commonwealth, but it's hard to be sure. There's some sort of interference fudging our data."

"They've seen us," said Cane. "One of them is moving in to engage."

"Launch base-line probes and broadcast our ID," Roche directed, her heart pounding as she considered their options. To Kajic she added: "Uri, keep well out of their way until we know what they are and who sent them. We don't want to intimidate them unnecessarily."

"Don't worry about that," Haid shot back dryly. "I won't

be making *any* moves until you can prove to me there isn't a clone warrior on one of those ships."

Roche watched nervously as the view shifted on the main screen. Numerous tiny drones spread out in a circle away from the *Ana Vereine,* expanding their base line of observation and thereby improving the clarity and range of the picture. The third ship came into view, oddly distorted like the glowing object it had been hiding behind. It was hard to determine exactly what sort of ship it was, let alone where it hailed from; the image was of a warped white line, burning bright with reflected light.

"Box," she said, "can you figure out what's jamming us?"

"There is no deliberate interference of transmissions in this region," said the Box.

"No? Then—"

"Our sensors are being swamped by emissions from the point-source. It is extremely radiant in both infrared electromagnetic and Perez radiations."

Roche blinked, surprised. Perez radiation was a side effect of a crudely tuned hyperspace jump, not what she would have expected of a seemingly stellar object.

Before she could inquire further, the Box went on: "Try looking for transmissions on the Eckandi emergency band. It should be relatively unaffected."

Roche gestured for Haid to do as the Box suggested. Within seconds, a rapid pulse of sound from the speakers of the main screen indicated that the ship had detected a digital transmission. An instant later, text appeared on the main screen and the pulse became an audible voice:

"—ONLY WARNING. REPEAT: YOU ARE IN CONTRAVENTION OF THE COMMONWEALTH OF EMPIRES SECURITY ACT, SECTIONS 45, 63, AND 72. THIS AREA HAS BEEN QUARANTINED. LEAVE IMMEDIATELY OR PREPARE TO BE FIRED UPON. THIS IS YOUR FIRST AND ONLY WARNING. MESSAGE ENDS."

The voice spoke with the clear, crisp tones of a machine,

not a Human—but that hardly made its words any less appalling. Roche took only a second to absorb the implications of its message.

An ambush.

"Haid, Cane—move us away," she said, thinking furiously. "Don't do anything else unless I tell you. Box, signal that we wish to respond; see if you can initiate a dialogue—or even subvert the AI to let us go." Even as she spoke the words, she knew it was unlikely the Box would be capable of doing this quickly enough. Nevertheless, she had to at least explore the possibility. "Uri, continue with repairs. Get that down shield back up as soon as you can. And Maii, find out what they're doing here and who the hell sent them. I need to know whether or not we have a chance of convincing them to let us through."

From her seat on the far side of the bridge, the reave shook her head. <I can't,> she said.

"What?" Roche swiveled to face her. "Why not?"

<I can't read them.> The reave's voice was strangely muffled, as though her thoughts were coming from a great distance rather than only from across the room. <They're not shielded. I just can't pick them up at all. If I could, I would have detected them long before now. We would have known they were here before we arrived.>

Roche frowned. Maii's last comment was worryingly true, if perplexing. "Keep trying. I need to know how they found us and whether or not they knew we were coming. If De Bruyn sent them, we know we'll have to fight, no matter what they say."

"But if they weren't expecting us," put in Haid, "how did they know where we'd be? I thought we couldn't be traced through a slow-jump."

"They didn't need to," replied the Box.

Roche was reminded of the point-source on the screen, twisted as though viewed through a giant lens. The spatial distortion the Box had been monitoring was obviously even more severe than she had imagined: anything trying to enter the space where the system had been was forced to emerge at this point—the heart of the system, yet at the same time its edge.

"They just sat here and waited," she said. "No matter where we tried to go, this is where we'd end up."

"Precisely, Morgan," said the Box.

"And the only way to get away from them is outward, away from where the system should be." She slapped her hand palm down on the side of her chair. "Dammit. We can't leave now, not until we know what the hell is going on!"

"I have convinced someone to let you talk," said the Box. "The AI has put me in direct contact with the officer in command of the primary vessel."

Roche took a deep breath. "Open the line."

"Ready, Morgan."

Roche tried to calm her nerves, then began to speak:

"This is Morgan Roche of the independent vessel *Ana Vereine.* We are traveling as a peaceful envoy under the authorization of Page De Bruyn of COE Intelligence. Why are you harassing us, and by whose authority?"

The moment she finished talking, the automatic broadcast ceased and a Human female voice took its place.

"COE Intelligence has no jurisdiction here," said the woman. "I am Commander Bassett of the COE Armada vessel *Golden Dawn* with orders countersigned by General Ramage. My directive is to prevent all unauthorized vessels from proceeding any further into Palasian System."

"Further *where*?" Roche shot back. "The system's *gone.* And as for authorization, I just gave you mine. We've been sent by the head of COE Intelligence Strategy to study the situation here, and to offer what help—"

The woman broke in firmly: "Your help is not required. Should you not leave immediately, then *I* have been authorized to use whatever force is necessary to ensure your compliance. You have exactly thirty seconds."

The vocal transmission ceased, and was replaced by the automatic recording.

Roche sat stunned for a moment, unable to believe what she had heard. Treachery she had learned to deal with, but not this blind, military farce.

"We've got confirmation on the ID," said Haid. "It's the *Golden Dawn,* and it's an Armada vessel as she said. A destroyer, to be exact."

Not quite a match for the *Ana Vereine,* Roche thought to herself. But there were three of them.

"Maii?" she asked. "Can you persuade them to change their minds?"

<I'm still not picking up anything.> The reave's voice was steeped in apology and confusion. <A few shadows, but nothing definite . . .>

Roche rubbed her forehead. On the main screen, the three Armada ships moved into position around the *Ana Vereine.*

"All shields to full strength," she said, sitting upright in her seat. "Uri, how're those repairs looking?"

"Almost there," Kajic replied. "Another two minutes and we'll be optimal."

Roche glanced at the screen. The *Golden Dawn*'s half-minute deadline had expired twenty seconds ago.

"They mean it, Morgan," said Cane, watching the screen with naked fascination. "They're going to fire."

Remembering the uncanny way he had picked the decisive moment during the battle for the *Midnight,* she didn't hesitate.

"Uri, take evasive action. Haid, arm the disrupters. Cane, prepare to return fire on my command."

"You're going to fight?" asked the Box.

"Do I have any choice?"

"Of course you do," the AI said.

"Well, *what*?" Roche snapped.

"You can turn control of the ship over to me," said the Box.

Roche opened her mouth, then closed it again. "Why?" she eventually managed.

"There is insufficient time to explain, Morgan."

"Try me," she growled.

"I have deduced the exact nature of both the point-source and the anomaly, and in the process have verified the location of Palasian System. By giving me control of the ship, I can take you there in a matter of minutes."

"So tell us where it is and we'll get *ourselves* there."

"Impossible, Morgan. Not that I am underestimating your abilities; there is simply too little time to—"

Lances of energy flashed on the main screen; static momentarily scrambled the picture.

"They're firing on our drones!" announced Haid.

"Take reciprocal action," Roche ordered. Barely had she finished when Cane began destroying the Armada's own base line probes. Specks of light flashed in the space between the three ships, their brightness negligible against the fiercely burning point-source dominating the view.

"They're tightening shields," said Haid.

Roche's thoughts went into overdrive. Tightening shields was a standard tactic in close space warfare. Any moment now, the attack would begin in earnest: the three Armada ships against the *Ana Vereine*. Numbers were against them, but that didn't mean that they would necessarily be overcome. Apart from the *Ana Vereine*'s technological superiority, it also possessed a number of armed scutters and shuttles in its docking bays; she could order the Box to launch these smaller craft to assist in the battle, and have Kajic employ the camouflage to make them harder to target. With so many diffuse targets to aim for, the outcome the Armada expected was far from certain. Still, the *Ana Vereine* was bound to incur *some* damage.

And if it prevailed, what then? They would be unable to return to the Commonwealth for certain after destroying three Armada ships while on a supposedly peaceful mission, and the matter of Palasian System would still be unresolved. If the Box was right, then it had offered her a way to avoid the battle and to reach her goal—both with one decisive move.

She had seen more death in the handful of weeks since

meeting Adoni Cane than she had in twelve years of active service for COE Intelligence. The thought of still more on her conscience made the decision easier than she expected.

At that very moment, the *Golden Dawn* opened fire.

"Incoming!" Haid's shout echoed through the bridge, closely followed by a juddering wrench as a full volley of flicker-bombs impacted upon the ship's aft hypershields. Cane's fingers played the weapons board like a virtuoso as Kajic swung the ship to bear on its primary antagonist. As the exchange intensified, violent discharges painted the space between the two ships with fiery colors of death.

"Box!" Roche called out over the sounds of battle: the shouts, the explosions, the roaring of engines. "Whatever you've got planned, do it fast!"

"Thank you, Morgan." The AI's reply was more gracious than Roche had expected, considering the moral victory it had won. To Haid and Cane the Box said: "Maintain a covering fire across the ship on the upper left of your screens. On my command, prepare to release proximity mines to prevent them from following."

Haid frowned at the screen. The ship the Box had indicated was the one that had been hiding behind the point-source; even now, the white-hot object filled most of that segment of the screen. "Where the hell—?"

"Do it, Ameidio," Roche ordered, even though she felt less than certain herself.

"I have surrendered control of the slow-jump drive to the Box," said Kajic via her implants, "and I will obey its orders until you tell me otherwise."

Roche nodded dumbly, wondering what the Box wanted with the drive, and why it wanted sole control over the systems. So close to the point-source, massless or not, even the smallest slow-jump had to be risky.

"Prepare for acceleration," announced the Box. "Maximum reactive power in fifteen seconds!"

As though the commander of the *Golden Dawn* had sensed Roche's change of plan, the Armada ships drew closer in a sudden rush, two of them overlapping shields and forming a solid wall of defense. The third sent bolt after bolt of energy hurtling toward the *Ana Vereine*—an assault designed to weaken E-shields prior to the arrival of a second wave of A-P fire and flicker-bombs.

An instant before the second wave arrived, the *Ana Vereine* surged forward. Roche was pressed back into her seat as the view through the main screen rushed at her. The single ship the Box had targeted reacted instantly, obviously believing that the *Ana Vereine* intended to ram; its E-shield formed a narrow cone pointed at the hurtling ship, hoping either to deflect it off course or to spear through its hull.

The Box's intention was farther afield, however. The *Ana Vereine* changed course an instant before striking the shield. As the Armada ship flashed by, Roche began to guess where they were headed. At the same time, the two vessels they had left behind began to turn, accelerating in pursuit.

The sound of proximity mines being fired behind them rattled in her ears. Two caught the single ship by surprise, slipping through its weakened aft shields and impacting on its hull. Damage was minor, but significant. Cane focused more and more firepower on the injured ship until it was forced to turn away, leaving the chase to its more distant, but fitter, siblings.

Too late. There was no way now that any of the ships could intercept the *Ana Vereine;* its lead was too great, and its destination too close.

Roche watched numbly as the image of the point-source swelled in the main screen. Not even automatic compensators could dull its brilliance.

I hope you know what you're doing, Box, she thought to herself.

Haid stared mutely up at the screen, his fingers working the disrupter controls automatically. Then a hand fell across his own.

"It's all right," Cane said. "The E-shields can manage from here."

"No they can't," Roche said urgently, leaning forward. "We'll need everything up front. Kajic, what's the ambient temperature and composition of the region ahead?"

"Unknown," was the ex-captain's reply. "Our instruments are—"

"Prepare for imminent hyperspace translation," the Box broke in.

"What?" On hearing the AI's intentions, Roche instantly regretted giving it absolute control. "You can't be serious! We're too close—"

"Not close enough, actually," returned the Box. "But we will be in ten seconds. Fasten your harnesses, everyone. This will be rough."

Roche's hands gripped her seat as the point-source ballooned to fill the entire main screen. She was dimly aware of the others around her—even Cane—doing the same, and of the stubborn thumping of the Armada guns on their aft shields, still harassing the *Ana Vereine* from behind. Part of her recalled the way the Box had threatened a collision course with COE Intelligence HQ under similar circumstances; she could only hope that its timing and intentions were as critical now as they had been then.

White fire consumed the screen. Sirens began to wail. The ship jerked once; she thought she heard Kajic call something to her. Then:

Space flowered open before them, unfolding in a series of crimson waves that quickly and violently enveloped the *Ana Vereine.* The ship shivered from nose to tail, shaken by forces Roche could only imagine. At the center of the vortex, several tiny specks of light flickered into being—only to disappear again as the main screen went black.

Then everything simply stopped.

2

IND *Ana Vereine*
'955.01.19 EN
0805

The main screen was empty.

Roche stared at it for a few moments, expecting it to suddenly clear and fill with . . . *what*? She had no idea what she expected to see out there. She had no idea where the Box had even taken them.

When it became apparent that the screen wasn't about to change, she swiveled around to check the others on the bridge. Cane had freed himself from his restraint harness and was assisting Maii back into her seat, their movements in the unnatural silence oddly loud and unreal. When he stepped away from her, Roche saw that the girl's head was bleeding slightly from her fall. Haid, the hand of his new arm resting on a touch pad, was still staring quizzically at the view that Roche had just turned from.

Then it struck her: the drive was no longer audible. But the *Ana Vereine* hadn't completed its slow-jump. It had just . . . stopped.

"Uri," she asked, her voice booming in the quiet. "What's going on?"

The holographic projector in the center of the bridge flickered. Kajic's image appeared through the static, the light brown skin and black hair of his old body looking as composed as always. His expression was serious, but not concerned.

"Minor damage," said the ex-captain. "We weathered the stress well."

"How long until we can see where we are?"

"My sensors are gathering some unusual data. The Box is checking to see if the irregularities are due to instrument malfunction. When its diagnosis is complete, vision will be restored."

"I have partial telemetry readings," said Haid from the weapons console. After a moment he reported: "No targets. No sign of the point-source, either. We must have left them all behind when we jumped."

"We did jump, then?" Roche asked Kajic.

"Well, we certainly entered hyperspace," said Kajic.

"But have we *left* it?"

"I didn't think an open-ended jump was possible," Haid said.

Kajic's image shrugged. "You'll have to ask the Box. I just did as it told me."

Roche put her palm on the arm-link of her chair, intending to access the raw data herself, but changed her mind before she did so. Better to remain distant for a moment rather than dive in headfirst. She needed to maintain a measure of objectivity if a quick decision was required.

"There appears to be a planet nearby," said Kajic. "That much I can tell you. A medium-sized gas giant if its mass reading is accurate."

"Try cross-referencing it with the navigation records of Palasian System," said Roche. "A match would at least confirm where we are."

Kajic dissolved in a burst of static that lasted a few heartbeats. When he re-formed, he said: "There's a ninety-nine percent chance the planet is Voloras, the outermost planet of Palasian System. If so, that places us well inside the cometary shell and the third dark body halo."

Roche searched her memory for what she knew about the system. "Wasn't there a refueling base around Voloras?"

"Guhr Outpost," confirmed Kajic.

"Any signals?"

"Apart from some strong crackles on the hydrogen band," said Haid, "we aren't getting a thing on any frequency."

"Try elsewhere," Roche said. "This far out, we should be able to pick up hyperspace transmissions."

"Already tried," said Haid. "Nothing; not even the beacon of the local anchor point."

"That can't be right." Roche frowned. "We're near the N'Kor border, and the Kesh have warning stations every few light-years—"

"I'm telling you, Morgan," said Haid, glancing over his shoulder. "There's nothing there."

"How could *all* of those beacons be blocked?" Roche could feel her confusion gradually developing into frustration. "Uri, *could* it be instrument failure?"

Before Kajic could reply, the Box cut in:

"It *is* possible, Morgan. And the fact that it has happened confirms my hypothesis quite neatly." At that moment, the main screen cleared. "Welcome to Palasian System."

Roche studied the screen. Initially she saw nothing but darkness—not even stars. Then the view changed, and a single red speck slid into view. Increased magnification made the speck a bright circle. The image was too fuzzy to make out any detail, but there was no mistaking what it was: against the unnaturally black background, one solitary sun burned.

"It can't be," she muttered, standing. "Hintubet is a calcium star—"

"And should be on the green side of yellow," the Box interrupted. "I am aware of that fact, Morgan. The difficulty in reconciling the emission spectrum of this star and that which Hintubet's *should* be was the main reason I delayed giving you this information. Now that I have had time to collate the data and to extrapolate from historical records, I believe I can say with certainty that this *is* Hintubet, albeit with a wildly altered photosphere."

"The star has changed?" asked Haid. *"How?"*

"The precise method is unknown at the moment; the archives lack specifics in that regard, although the general principles are clear. Until we dispatch probes to study Hintubet in more detail, we are limited to the data we can scavenge from this distance."

"Which isn't enough," said Roche. She faced Kajic. "Uri, I want high-speed drones launched to the sun and any planetary bodies we can find." She turned back to the screen. "Speaking of which, any sign of Voloras?"

The red star shrank and slid out of view. Seconds later, the crescent of a large planet appeared, red-tinged due to the sun's baleful light. The image of the planet came to rest in the center of the screen, its dense atmosphere swirled with gray bands.

"I have dispatched a probe," said Kajic. "The base line is already large enough for us to detect four moons."

"Voloras has five," said Roche.

"The fifth may be occluded," said Kajic. "The sizes of the four we can see match COE records."

"How long until the probe can get a decent look at the base?"

"One hour and fifty minutes. Guhr Outpost is on the missing moon."

Roche nodded. "Until then, we can't afford to take anything for granted. Give us a heading that will take us by Voloras, with the option to use it as a gravity-whip if we decide not to stop. Leave a drone behind to relay the data from the probes. I want the ship camouflaged, too, just in case someone saw us arrive and is waiting for us there."

Kajic's image winked out as he went to work.

Roche slumped back into her chair with a sigh and rubbed at her temples. They appeared to be in Palasian System, just as the Box had promised they would be. But it wasn't quite what she had expected: no hyperspace transmissions, a profoundly altered primary, and no stars in sight.

The first and last details suggested that the system had indeed been encapsulated within some sort of barrier. But what? She knew of no process that could hide an entire system from view *and* account for the warped space outside.

Or did she? The change in the sun's appearance did ring a faint bell. A name she had heard back in her days on the moon of Bodh Gaya, when she had been studying for her Armada exams, returned to her . . .

"Asha's Gauntlet," she said aloud.

"I'm impressed, Morgan," said the Box. "I didn't think you would work it out so—"

"We're picking up a transmission!" Haid broke in.

"Where?" Roche swiveled to face him, automatically linking with the weapons system. If life remained in the system, the chances were good that it belonged to the Sol Wunderkind. And if he was signaling them, then he knew where they were.

"It's not directed at us." Haid was skimming through the various diagnostic tools that enabled him to enhance a weak signal. "It's a wide-beam microwave from in-system. I'm picking up echoes off several objects near the source; the slight delays should give us a fair triangulation."

Roche let herself relax slightly. The signal must have been sent some time ago, given the distance at light-speed to the inner system.

"What about the content of the transmission?" she said.

"It's in some sort of cipher," Haid told her, then shook his head. "Haven't broken it yet, which isn't a good sign. They either crack immediately or take forever."

"Box, have a go at it," she said. Haid's refinement of the signal's source proceeded while she watched. The area containing a probable location of the transmitter gradually narrowed on a diagnostic display, until a single point flashed once and turned green.

"Got it," Haid said.

Roche overlaid a navigation chart. "It's the same distance from the primary as Jagabis would have been. And Jagabis has moons."

Haid nodded. "That'd give us the echoes."

"Uri, do we have confirmation of a planet in this area?"

Kajic's image returned at the mention of his name. "Not yet. It's off to one side of Hintubet, and I haven't searched that area in any detail yet. Now that I'm looking, it shouldn't take long to find—" He stopped, smiled. "In fact, there it is. Give me a little longer and I'll be able to estimate its mass."

"It *has* to be Jagabis," Roche said. "Someone's alive there."

"The signal could be a beacon," Haid suggested.

"In cipher? Unlikely," said Roche. "Besides, Jagabis was the innermost gas giant in the system. If I remember correctly, the main spaceport and colony were on one of its moons."

"Correct," said the Box. "The moon is called Aro, the colony Emptage City."

"Right," said Roche. "So if there are survivors, that's the first place to look."

"I can get us there in two days," said Kajic. "Faster if we flyby Voloras."

Roche nodded. "Plot a course, but don't do anything definite until we decipher the message."

Cane stirred, speaking for the first time since their arrival. "It could be a warning," he said. "Or a trap."

Roche looked over at him. "For whom? It couldn't be us. We weren't even here when that message was transmitted."

"True," Cane said. "But I find it disturbing nonetheless. The impression I get is that someone is still fighting."

"That's a good sign," said Roche. "That there's the slightest resistance left in the system is something of a miracle."

"Which is precisely what bothers me." The bridge's light glowed in his unblinking eyes. "I would never have been so careless as to leave any survivors."

Roche met his calm expression uneasily, his words reminding her of the ruthlessness of the adversary they were hunting—and of Cane's ancestry.

"It's worth checking, at least," she said after a moment. Then, turning from Cane, turning from the thought, she said: "Have you sent a probe, Uri?"

"I have dispatched five so far," Kajic reported. "Three are under way to Hintubet, Voloras, and Jagabis; the other two are heading to Cartha's Planet, the innermost world, and Cemenid, the largest. There are four planets outstanding: Herensung, Gatamin, Kukumat and Murukan."

"The last two being the double world?" Roche asked.

"That's right. There are also some sizable rocks in the dark body halos that might be worth exploring, but they're not a priority at the moment. I'll let you know when we have the system mapped."

"Okay." Roche visualized the bulletlike probes crossing the system under accelerations that not even the *Ana Vereine*'s protective fields could negate, thereby traversing the empty space more quickly than they could ever hope to. Even so, it would be hours before they started getting any data. At light-speed, the lag across the system was appreciable.

"That transmission just ended," said Haid.

"Box?" Roche said. "How's the deciphering coming along?"

"Completed," said the AI. "However, the translation is proving difficult. It appears to be in a language with which I am unfamiliar."

"Show me."

Several lines of standard alphanumeric script flowed across the screen. Roche studied it for a moment before admitting that she too was stumped. "It's definitely a language, not another cipher?"

"Without sufficient text to analyze, I am unable to do more than guess."

"Fair enough. Keep guessing, then, Box, and let me know if you come up with anything."

"Certainly."

"Uri, how long until the Voloras flyby?"

"One hour and thirty-seven minutes."

Roche sat back with a weary sigh, running a hand through her cropped hair. She was already impatient with the delay in obtaining information. Being trapped in this system without any idea of what was going on or even where the clone warrior might be filled her with anxiety.

"I don't suppose there's any way you could hurry things along?" she said wryly.

"Not unless you know some way to circumvent the barriers of light-speed, Morgan," said Kajic.

Roche smiled tiredly.

"There is," said Cane.

Roche looked over to him. "What?"

"Thought is not constrained by the physical laws of the universe," said Cane.

Roche sat forward with a start. *Maii!* If the girl could contact the minds of the people behind the transmission, Roche would have the data she needed immediately.

Only then did she realize that the reave had neither moved nor spoken since shortly after the *Ana Vereine* had arrived in Palasian System. Roche turned to see what the problem was.

The Surin girl sat motionless on the edge of her seat with her hands clasped together in her lap. A thin line of blood had trickled down from the gash on her forehead, staining red the white material of her blindfold.

"Maii? Are you all right?"

There was no response.

Roche moved over to the reave, squatting down in front

of her to examine the small lesion on the girl's forehead. It seemed to Roche to be nothing more than a superficial cut, and yet . . .

"Maii?" Still no reply. She touched the girl's shoulders and tried again: "Maii, can you—?"

Startled, Maii jumped back in her seat, pushing Roche's hand away.

<Maii, it's me!> Roche fought to restrain the reave's flailing arms. <*Maii!* It's Morgan!>

After a moment, the girl's panic subsided and her breathing eased.

<Maii?> said Roche. <Can you hear me?>

<I—I am here, Morgan.> The words were barely a whisper in Roche's mind.

<Are you okay? You're very faint.>

<So are you.> There was an edge of confusion to her words. <I couldn't sense you at all. There was nothing. I was afraid you were all dead.>

Roche winced as a wave of images and emotions washed into her mind: fear, loneliness, darkness, panic . . . She concentrated, doing her best to hold the mental inrush at bay while trying to radiate reassurance to the Surin child. When the torrent of emotions ebbed, Roche continued.

<We've been here all the time, talking unshielded as we always do. Surely you picked up something?>

<Only Cane,> replied the reave. <But nothing specific. I just knew he was there—somewhere.>

Roche searched the girl's blank face. The blood on her cheek stood out against pale skin and hair. <Could it have been the blow to your head?>

<No. It's nothing like that. Your thoughts are being . . . smothered. It's like only the ones specifically directed at me can get through, and even then only if their source is nearby—as you are now.>

<Smothered?> Roche repeated. <By what?>

<I don't know.> Almost imperceptibly, Maii shrugged. <All I can tell you is that it started when we arrived at the

point-source. But it didn't become severe until we slow-jumped.>

<So whatever's causing it must be somewhere in the system with us.> Roche rocked back on her haunches as she considered the reave's words. Another ominous sign. <Is there anything I can do to help?>

Maii nodded slowly. <Physical contact strengthens an epsense link. If you were to keep touching me . . .>

Roche's understanding filled the void of the Surin's unfinished sentence. The thought of Maii locked in the darkness of the blind and deaf-mute easily overrode her reservations—even though it meant having the girl constantly at her side. The last person to have depended on her so totally had killed himself to save her—

She stamped down on the memory. The last thing Maii needed right now was to have both of them dwelling on Veden's death.

<Thank you, Morgan.> The girl half smiled. <I can read you clearly, but will respect your privacy.>

"Is she all right?" Cane called out from his station.

"She will be," Roche replied, then said to Maii: <Can you stand?>

<Yes.>

<Good. If we can't use you to hunt for survivors, then you can help me brush up on local geography instead.> Taking one of Maii's hands in her own, Roche raised the girl to her feet. Together, with Maii's hand on her arm, they moved across the bridge to Roche's seat. The reave remained standing when Roche sat, her hand resting on the older woman's shoulder.

<Are we really in Palasian System?> Maii asked.

<The Box brought us here after the Armada ships attacked,> said Roche.

<How?>

<That's a little hard to explain. Hang on. I'll see if we can get the Box in on this conversation. The others might like to hear, too.>

Triggering her implants, Roche spoke aloud: "Box, if you've got the time, I'd like to talk to you about Asha's Gauntlet."

"Of course, Morgan."

"We studied them under Weapons Conventions in Military College," she explained to the others. "The idea is to turn a star into a giant hypershield generator or something. Is that right, Box?"

"Essentially," replied the Box. "A primitive 'solar envelope,' as it was originally known, was designed by the Eckandar Trade Axis several thousand years ago. Two prototypes—called *K'mok ni Asha,* which translates as 'Asha's Gauntlet'—were built in the 38th Millennium by the Kesh government. They tested one on a frontier system, but the experiment was a failure. Because of the disastrous results the second prototype was never used. It was rumored to have been dismantled, although this was never confirmed."

"I remember," said Roche, nodding. "The Gauntlet was supposedly designed as a means of protection for a system against attack, but the one experiment they conducted ended up completely destroying the system." Roche looked at the screen, and the sky empty of stars—all but one; the reddened Hintubet now occupied center stage again. "And now it seems we're inside one."

"At first," said the Box, "I was reluctant to accept the possibility that Palasian System had been encapsulated in such a fashion—even though the data suggested as much. It wasn't until we arrived at the point-source—the external manifestation of the Gauntlet's boundary—that the evidence became too conclusive to ignore."

"How does it work?" asked Cane.

The Box explained: "By manipulating a star in precisely the right fashion, it is possible to create and sustain a Riem-Perez Horizon large enough to enclose an entire system."

"That's the same sort of shield COE Intelligence HQ uses, isn't it?" said Roche.

"Correct," said the Box. "And the *Ana Vereine*, and most other ships large enough to power one."

"But we couldn't see the system from the outside," Roche said. "A hypershield isn't the same as camouflage—"

"No; hypershields are used as barriers against hyperspatial attack rather than to hide something from view. However, scale comes into play for Riem-Perez Horizons greater than two thousand cubic kilometers in volume. Space-time can only tolerate such a disturbance on a small scale; any larger and the enclosed area is parceled off and lifted to hyperspace."

"Where we are now," finished Roche.

"Thus the area of space contained within the affected area cannot be seen, because it simply no longer exists in the 'real' universe," said the Box. "The anomaly—which is a boundary effect—is all that remains."

"That explains why the engines stopped in mid-jump," said Kajic. "The jump was literally open-ended—across the boundary and into the space within."

"In a sense, we are still jumping," said the Box.

Cane moved closer to the screen, studying the image with fascination. "It's a remarkable concept," he said. "To *move* an entire system—"

"No distance at all, really," said the Box. "It has no vector relative to the real universe, and will not travel in the same way this ship slow-jumps."

"So I assume it will return when the Gauntlet is switched off?"

"No," said the Box.

"That's where the original Kesh experiment went wrong," added Roche. "It *can't* be switched off."

"The process is extremely energy expensive," explained the Box. "The sun's fuel is exhausted in a matter of weeks, during which time the Gauntlet gradually collapses back to a point. The system is destroyed in the process."

Cane tilted his head. "Then employing a Gauntlet to defend a system would be a pointless exercise."

"Which is why the Warfare Protocol forbids its use." Roche nodded at the screen. "It's no use at all for defense, and would make too destructive a weapon."

<So why does Palasian System have one?> asked Maii, using Roche's neural implants as an interface between her and the Box.

"I can think of only one possible explanation," the AI said. "Any attempt to cross the external boundary of the Gauntlet without simultaneously slow-jumping back to the real universe will result in complete annihilation. Similarly, any attempt to use a hyperspace drive while within the space contained by the Gauntlet will render the drive useless."

"So if the Sol clone warrior has no access to a hyperspace drive," Haid cut in, "or doesn't know how to employ one properly in the Gauntlet, he'll be unable to leave the system."

"Exactly," said the Box.

"A trap, then." Cane nodded. "And one which is not immediately lethal. But why go to so much trouble?"

"And who laid the trap?" asked Haid.

"Whoever got their hands on the second prototype, I guess," Roche said. "Which could have been almost anyone, depending on where the Kesh stored it."

"At least we know one thing," said Kajic. "It probably wasn't the Sol Wunderkind."

"Don't be so sure about that," said Haid. "We're trapped in here, too, remember?"

"Not 'trapped,'" said the Box. "We can leave any time we wish, simply by crossing the boundary the correct way."

"But the boundary *is* shrinking, right?" said Haid.

"Yes—"

"And we can't signal for help if we get into trouble." Haid grimaced. "That makes us a little more vulnerable than I like to be."

"As long as we do not employ our slow-jump drive while inside the Gauntlet, we will be able to leave." The Box sounded weary of the argument. "And even so, the natural collapse of the boundary is relatively slow. Should something go wrong, we would have several weeks to find another means out."

"Your confidence is admirable," said Haid, "even if I find it slightly naive."

Roche decided it was time to change the subject. "Uri, how long now until the first probe arrives at Voloras?"

"One hour and fifteen minutes. That's when you can expect the first decent pictures, anyway."

"Good. I suggest we get back to work until then. We might need to move fast, depending on what we see."

Haid scratched his scalp with his new fingers as he swung back to the weapons console. "Chances are it won't be a welcoming committee."

For Roche, finding something to keep herself occupied while the probe was in transit proved to be easy. With repairs still to be completed, the transmission waiting to be translated, and small amounts of long-distance data still trickling in, there was more than enough work for a crew of several dozen. Even with the Box and Kajic both able to perform multiple tasks at once, running a ship the size of the *Ana Vereine* under such conditions would never be straightforward.

Nevertheless, Roche had the opportunity to double-check her memory of Palasian System's records against the data the ship-bound detectors had collected.

The COE navigation register had been updated during the last survey, in '850 EN. Since then, few changes had been appended to the record. Palasian System had never been fully colonized; given its lack of a planet with a breathable atmosphere, that wasn't surprising. The innermost world was a rocky ball boiling under the glare of the F2 primary and was home only to an automated solar research facility. The remaining seven planets were gas giants, two of them bloated with hydrogen. All possessed numerous moons; two had extensive ring systems, but it would take more than pretty scenery to attract colonists. As it was, only the system's proximity to a Kesh border had earned it an Armada base and a refueling station. Not even the presence of three mineral-rich dark-body halos around the sun had tempted more than a cursory mining presence, an arm of the same company that had run the operation—and the penal colony—on Sciacca's World: Dirt & Other Commodities, Inc.

Still, Roche told herself, almost half a million people had called Palasian System home—at least temporarily. And she had to admit that there *was* plenty to look at. In all her travels for COE Intelligence, she had never had the chance to see a double-jovian before.

Part of her had hoped that when Kajic finally located the pair on the far side of the system, it would look somehow different from the other faint blobs he assured her were planets—but it didn't. All she saw was another dot, tinged red by Hintubet's new color.

With Maii at her side, she returned to mapping the locations of the planets and planning contingency routes between them.

<The population was certainly spread thin,> the reave commented at one point. <It's hard to see how an army could have killed them all.>

<It doesn't make our job any easier, either,> Roche responded. <If survivors are unable to communicate, we'll have to turn the system inside out to find them.>

<Unless, as you think, they've regrouped at Jagabis. It would make sense to pool resources.>

<Or to present a united front.>

<One last stand?>

<Perhaps.> Roche shrugged, trying not to dwell on the ramifications of that thought: had such a battle been lost . . . ? <Whoever sent the message, Emptage City and Aro Spaceport are the first places we have to go, right after we flyby Guhr Outpost. If we don't find anything in either of these places, then we'll try the Armada facility around

Cemenid; Geyten Base would have been the next most likely place to mount some sort of counterattack.>

<What about the research station?> Maii asked, indicating with a mental prompt the installation orbiting the double-jovian.

<According to the records, Congreve Station was abandoned some decades ago. Unless that changed, it would have been empty when the Sol Wunderkind arrived.>

<What were they studying there?>

<I don't know, exactly. It says 'xenoarchaeological research' when I ask. But planetary evolution seems more likely.>

<I guess.> Roche felt the reave's attention drift elsewhere, studying the files vicariously through Roche's senses. <DAOC are here, I notice. Does Ameidio know that yet?>

Roche shook her head. <Not that I'm aware of, and I'd rather he didn't find out until it's necessary.>

Dirt and Other Commodities Inc. had been the main target of Haid's underground resistance movement on Sciacca's World. Roche would understand any lingering resentment he might still feel after so many years spent fighting them. At the same time she didn't want it to get in the way. She would attempt to rescue DAOC employees just as she would anyone else—if there *were* any remaining in the system. . . .

<The asteroid belt and innermost dark-body halo—the Mattar Belt and Autoville—were mined by prowlers, not people,> said Roche. <So chances are they won't be a problem. The others were untouched.>

<I've never liked prowling mines,> Maii said with a mental moue. <They're just a small step from planet-wreckers.>

<At least they're civilized, not like outriggers.>

<All robots are civilized,> said Maii. <I just don't happen to enjoy their company.>

"The probe's rounding Voloras," announced Kajic, breaking the silence on the bridge. Roche cleared the vision in her artificial eye and looked up. The screen showed a close-up of the swollen arc of the gray gas giant's banded atmosphere. Purple haze tinged the view as the probe used the planet's magnetic field to brake.

"Seen anything yet?" Roche asked.

"Not much," Kajic replied. "The other moons appear to be untouched. The change in Hintubet's radiation has raised a few storms in Voloras's outer atmosphere, and there's a little more rubble in closer than the records say there should be. But apart from that, the planet is as expected."

"Still no signals?"

"All quiet," said Haid. "I can try provoking something, if you like."

"Best not to at this stage."

"I've no problem with that." Haid absently tapped the console as he talked. "Nothing's obstructed the probes so far, but that's not to say it won't happen. They're not exactly subtle, the way they accelerate."

"As long as no one traces the tightbeams back to us, we'll be okay." Roche gestured at the screen. "How long until the moon comes into view?"

"A few seconds," said Kajic, his image facing the screen from the center of the bridge. "When it does, I've programmed the probe to begin its survey automatically. There's enough of a delay to make direct control tricky."

"So it might already be seeing the moon?" asked Roche.

"Or even have been destroyed," said Kajic. "Although I . . ."

He stopped before he could finish the sentence. "Wait. Here it comes. I'll enhance the image as much as I can for the screen, but it might be better through your implants."

Roche put her hand back onto the link and slaved her vision to the probe's data, at the same time shutting her right eye to prevent overlap. Instantly she found herself hanging over the surface of the gas giant, spearing through space with a magnetic storm roiling around her. Ahead and just over the bulge of the horizon, a reddish dot had appeared.

"That's it," said Kajic. "We're lucky it's not eclipsed by the planet; the image would have been much weaker."

"Can you make anything out yet?" Roche asked.

"Nothing definite. The albedo matches, except for a dark patch on the southern hemisphere. You'll see it as the probe gets closer. It doesn't appear on the maps, so it probably isn't a surface feature."

"It isn't the base itself?" asked Haid.

"Refueling bases are always around the equator," Roche answered. "Orbital tethers won't work anywhere else."

"Of course." Haid's tone was apologetic. "It's been a while since I last saw one."

The image sharpened as the moon came closer, becoming a gibbous disc. Its surface was smooth and gray, like its parent, covered with a thick layer of ice. The unusual patch Kajic had pointed out dominated the bottom left quarter: a drop of ink on a circular bloodstain.

"It looks like a shadow," said Roche.

"I think it might be," Kajic agreed. "A shadow at the bottom of a crater."

Roche took a deep breath at the implications of that thought. As the probe swooped closer for its first pass, the details became clear all too quickly. Something had struck the moon's southern hemisphere with the force of a large asteroid. The resulting impact had torn a sizable chunk out of the moon and rung its cold core like a bell. Deep fault lines ran from pole to pole, where the brittle, icy crust had fractured. In infrared, the heat at the shadowy bottom of the crater was obvious, glowing like a red pupil in a dead, gray eye.

"Whatever it was," said Haid, "it hit hard."

"Is there any way to tell how long ago it happened?" asked Cane.

"My guess would be sometime in the last six weeks," said Kajic. "But probably no earlier than a month."

"Agreed," added the Box. "The rubble the probe encountered in the orbit of the moon is clearly ejecta from the impact that has not had time to disperse; that makes the impact fairly recent. But the crater floor is no longer molten, indicating that some time has passed. Between four and five weeks ago is my estimate."

"Any idea what it might have been?" asked Haid.

"At this point, no," the Box said. "But my intuition tells me it was most likely a ship of some description. It would have been much easier to cause a ship to crash than to give an asteroid the vector required to make it impact in such a way."

"Is it worth looking for survivors?" asked Roche.

"No." The Box sent an icon darting into the view, pointing out details Roche had missed. "Here you can see the fallen cable of the orbital docking facility; this fragment here corresponds to part of the base itself. You can also see how a major fracture line runs directly through the site of the main installation. This last detail must surely have been fortuitous—no one could have predicted exactly how the moon would fault—but I doubt that anyone would have survived the impact alone, anyway. The seismic energy released must have been tremendous." The icon disappeared. "It would have been over in seconds. A very effective blow against the Armada presence in this system—both in terms of resources and morale."

"It was deliberate, then," Haid said. "It couldn't have been an accident—a coincidence?"

"Possible," said the Box. "But unlikely."

Roche listened to the Box with a growing sense of unreality. The destruction of an entire Armada refueling base was still something she could hardly believe possible—even though the scant reports COE Intelligence had received from the system had intimated far worse. And now she was seeing it.

The destruction of Palasian System was no longer a morsel of information to gain leverage with COE Intelligence; it had actually happened.

<The Sol Wunderkind did this?> asked Maii, her voice

relayed by Roche's implants and broadcast over the bridge speakers.

"We don't have any other suspects," said Haid.

<How many people were on the base?>

"Three hundred," Roche replied. "Plus whoever was on the ship when it crashed—if it was a ship, of course."

"Either way, that's a lot of dead people," said Haid grimly.

"Whether there was one person or a thousand, the actual number is irrelevant," said Cane. "The only thing of importance to the clone warrior was to ensure that no one was left alive." He glanced over at Roche. "Assuming, of course, we have correctly interpreted my sibling's motives."

Roche studied Cane through the ghost image of the planet in her artificial eye. "Even more important than the base's strategic value?"

He paused before answering, his features contorted as though he was fighting conflicting emotions.

"Yes," he said finally, then turned from Roche back to the screen. "The primary objective would have been to destroy as many people as possible as efficiently as possible. The drive for efficiency would have necessitated an early strike against this base, yes, but if it had been automated, that need would have been reduced. Where there are no people to command them, machines can be inefficient in battle."

"So he would have attacked Aro Spaceport first?" Roche asked.

"Yes, had the refueling base been uninhabited." Another pause. "I'm sorry," he said, again facing her. "I do not like thinking this way. It is too easy for me."

Roche nodded, even though she didn't truly understand how his mind worked and therefore could not empathize with his feelings. When he used his genetically modified abilities, he was terrifying to watch. That he had not used them against *her* was something for which she'd be forever grateful—and therein, she thought, lay the paradox. Of the two Sol clone warriors at large in the Commonwealth, only one was obeying its natural instincts. Cane was not. But *why*?

Because he doesn't want to. That was the only answer she could supply. He had said as much himself. And if the part of him that wanted to kill indiscriminately had been subsumed by the part of him that didn't—which perhaps not even the Sol geneticists could have suppressed entirely—then she hoped it stayed that way. Especially now that she had seen what he *could* have done.

She rubbed her eyes, breaking the link and killing the image of the planet in her left eye. Fatigue, which she had successfully kept at bay since her abrupt awakening, was numbing her limbs and pressing at the backs of her eyes.

She was sufficiently aware of her inner feelings, however, to suspect that something more than fatigue was at work.

"The base is dead," she said, letting the issue slip for the moment. "The how and the why can wait until later. Uri, set course for the Voloras flyby and get us on the way to Jagabis. I want to see what's left of Aro Spaceport before we start making any decisions."

"The probe will be there in approximately ten hours," said Kajic. "We'll be past Voloras in four, and well on our way by the time data arrives."

"Good. I'll leave that side of things to you and the Box. As long as I'm kept informed, the two of you can run the ship for a while."

"Where will you be?" asked Kajic.

"In my room, catching up on some sleep." To the others on the bridge, she added, " I suggest you do the same. In thirteen hours we'll have much more data on our hands than we have now, and we'll need to be alert to deal with it."

<I'll stay here with Cane,> said Maii, <if that's okay with you, Morgan. I can sleep on a couch.>

"Make sure she does, Cane," said Roche. "I know you probably won't need to rest, but she does."

Cane nodded.

"That goes for you too, Ameidio."

"I'll do so as soon as I've finished here," said Haid, his hands busy over a console.

"Okay," Roche said. "Unless something happens, we'll meet back here in twelve hours."

She stood and led Maii over to Cane. The reave's hands briefly linked Roche with Cane, and in that instant Roche received a mental flash of Cane's mind. The impression was short-lived, and carried with it no actual thoughts, but it left her with the impression of rapid motion. Even after the contact had been broken, she couldn't shake a mental image of a gyroscope spinning, perpetually on the verge of toppling over but never quite doing so.

"Wait," said Kajic as she started to leave. "I'm picking up another transmission."

Roche continued toward the exit. "I doubt we'll learn anything new," she said. "Unless we work out the language—"

"It's not from Jagabis, this time," Kajic said. Roche stopped and faced Kajic's flickering image. "We're picking up the fringes of a tightbeam, probably reflected off the source of the first transmission. Whoever's sending this one must be doing the best they can with a fairly low-tech outfit. Hang on—we'll see if we can decode it."

"It's not in cipher," said the Box. "It is a standard text message. No voice, no images."

"Display it," said Roche, curious despite her exhaustion.

The view of Hintubet faded from the main screen. Now in its place were several lines of text:

I DO NOT RUN FROM YOU,
BUT NEITHER WILL I RUN TO YOU.
I DO NOT REQUIRE YOUR AID.

WHEN OR IF I DO NEED ANYTHING THAT YOU POSSESS,

I WILL TAKE IT.
YOU WILL NOT STOP ME.

I AM NOT YOURS TO COMMAND.

Roche read it once, then again. "That's it?" she asked after a third and final reading.

"The same message is repeated twice," said the Box.

"And it's not encrypted?"

"No."

"But it *was* sent on a tightbeam."

"Yes."

"Then that tells us something. I'll bet the reason we're picking up the fringes of the beam is because it's been through a number of relays to prevent triangulation of the source. Whoever sent it was less concerned about the contents of the message than keeping their location a secret."

Haid nodded. "That would make sense."

"And judging by the content, I'd say there's only one person who could've sent it."

"My sibling," said Cane, meeting her accusatory stare.

Roche nodded slowly. "He's alive."

"And kicking," said Haid. "I'm glad I'm not in the shoes of whoever he's talking to."

"The fact that he's talking at all is interesting," Roche mused. "In fact, it sounds like he's bluffing."

"You think so?" said Haid.

She shrugged. "If he's hiding, he's vulnerable."

"I guess we'll find out soon enough." Haid returned his attention to the console before him. "I'll see if any of the probes picked up the signal and try to pin down a source."

"Good. Any more, Box?"

"The transmission has now ceased," said the AI.

She considered whether she should stay on the bridge to see if anything else came in, but decided against it. The communication from the Sol clone warrior was important enough to warrant further examination, but not informative.

Again, without further data, she would only be speculating wildly.

"The situation's unchanged, then," she said. "I'll keep my implants open for any further developments. Don't hesitate to call me."

"I won't," said Kajic. His image dissolved at the same moment Roche stepped from the bridge.

Back in her cabin, Roche lay on her bunk, going over the data they had collected so far. Detailed images of the ruined Guhr Outpost came as often as the probe—now orbiting the small moon—passed by. All that remained of the refueling base were fragments twisted beyond recognition. Sensors detected high levels of radiation in the heart of the crater, which supported the theory that a ship, not an asteroid, had crashed there, but no remains of the ship had been found. Given the force of the explosion, Roche didn't expect any. The ship must have been fully fueled to have caused such a blast. Only time would tell how greatly the moon's orbit around the gas giant had been disturbed.

The remainder of the probes, now on their way to every major body in the system, were still too far away from their destinations to provide any new perspectives. The earliest she could expect data would be from the probe heading to Gatamin, six hours away; the latest, from the probe aimed at Kukumat and Murukan, the jovian pair, at over twenty hours.

Determined not to let frustration get the better of her—there was, after all, nothing she could do to change the speed of light—she tried instead to focus her thoughts on what she *did* know about Palasian System.

First of all, the COE Intelligence data appeared to be accurate so far. There had been a battle of some sort that had cost the Armada at least a refueling base.

Second, the system was suspiciously silent, apart from one unintelligible signal emanating from near the major port around Jagabis and another whose source was in hiding.

Third, the sun had been transformed into a cosmic hyper-shield generator by a weapon used only once before, over a thousand years ago. The last government known to have had access to the sole remaining Asha's Gauntlet prototype was the Kesh.

Fourth, Maii's mind-riding abilities had been negated by a mysterious "smothering" effect.

Fifth, the system had been cordoned off on the outside by three Armada vessels acting under direct orders from General Ramage, commander in chief of the COE Armada.

And that was all. Roche was fairly confident that the Sol Wunderkind was trapped in the system, but beyond that she didn't want to speculate too far. It was tempting to write off the epsense-dampening phenomenon as another of his extraordinary talents, but that seemed unlikely. Apart from the occasional suggestion from Maii that Cane possessed a strong but latent epsense ability, there was no indication that he possessed any such talents. Nevertheless, Roche was wary of closing off any avenues of exploration too early. Not while the matters of the Gauntlet and the Armada flotilla were still to be explained, anyway. She had learned from experience that especially where conspiracies were concerned, the major factor preventing the truth's being discovered was the observer's unwillingness to explore connections between facts that on the surface seemed unconnectable.

She leaned back into the pillow, pushing her knuckles into her aching, tired eyes. There was, in short, enough to make her cautious, but not enough to provide her a definite focus for her fears.

And that, in a sense, only made it worse.

You will not stop me, the second transmission had said. Could she have stopped *Cane,* had he chosen to attack rather than to aid her? Was he even on her side? *I am not yours to command,* the message had said. The words made Roche wonder whether he had ever truly been. . . .

• • •

She didn't realize she had fallen asleep until the alarm on her door buzzed.

In the dream she heard the hiss of a predator. She jerked forward on her bunk and called out in the dark, clutching at the fringe of the dream even as she was wrenched from it. She had been back on Ascensio, trying to lure a viridant out of its burrow by offering it a dead rodent. The lizard-like animal had been suspicious, but she managed to encourage it by repeating the offer several times. She had no intention of giving it the bait, though; her only intention had been to gain its trust—and then to strangle it. Only too late had she seen the glint in its eye and known that *she* was the one being lured. Her hand had lashed out, and the viridant had snapped its jaws around it, pulling her into its burrow. . . .

The door buzzed again. She shook herself from a daze and spoke into the intercom:

"Who is it?"

"It's me," Cane answered. "The data from the probes are due soon. I would like to discuss something with you before then, if it's not inconvenient."

"Wait a moment." She ran her hands over her stubbled scalp and wiped her face. Her skin was greasy and coarse at the same time—a grim reminder that she was overdue for a shower. After a moment she said: "Lights; door open."

The room brightened at her command. Cane stepped into the cabin.

"I'm assuming it's not an emergency," she said, "or else Uri would've called first."

"Little has changed," said Cane. "We have received another transmission from the same source as the first, but that's about it. Kajic posted details of it to your buffer, marking it as a low priority. If you were asleep, you wouldn't have seen it."

She checked her implants out of habit; sure enough, the message was there. She also learned that she had been asleep for seven hours. It felt more like four.

She stayed on the bed and offered Cane the chair. "So, what can I do for you?"

"Everyone is resting," he said. When he sat he folded his hands in his lap, making him look uncharacteristically unsure of himself. "I thought I'd take advantage of the situation to talk to you alone."

"About?" she prompted.

"The transmission from Jagabis."

"What about it?"

"I can translate it."

She studied him suspiciously. "The Box said it wasn't in any language that it recognized."

"I know."

"But *you* recognize it?"

"I didn't at first," he said. "Only after reading through the raw text for some hours did it begin to make sense. And even then, not all of it."

"I'm not sure I follow you."

"I am not *certain* what it means, but I do understand it. I know how odd that sounds, but the situation is as confusing to me as it is to you. And that's why I wanted to talk to you first rather than the others."

"You've kept this from Maii?"

"She knows I'm hiding something, but she won't learn what it is unless I let her."

Roche nodded. "So what does the transmission say?"

"It is a call to arms," he said. "It is also a plea for help. And a request to negotiate. And an order to retreat. And an offer of assistance. And—"

She cut him off: "I don't understand. How can it be all these things at once?"

"The message is composed of fragments. Some make sense, but a lot don't. The bits that don't are just meaningless, but there is still a resonance in the words—as though they have been engraved in my mind, that I might never forget them."

She suddenly grasped the implication. "Are you suggesting that this is some sort of language used by the Sol Apotheosis Movement? That you've been *programmed* to understand it?"

"Nothing else can explain why I know what some of the fragments mean, and respond to them"—he put a hand on his stomach—"*here,* almost before I have time to realize."

"Are they dangerous? Could they make you do things you don't want to do?"

Cane shook his head. "Whoever is broadcasting the orders doesn't know what they are doing. The fragments that make the most sense are the most emphatic, of course, but they are often the most inconsistent, too. The fragment repeated most often, for instance, is a request to trade information that is not relevant in exchange for supplies that no one in this century would need."

"Why would anyone broadcast something like that?" Roche wondered. "And where did they find the code? It wasn't in any of the records I accessed."

"I don't know, exactly," Cane said. "Perhaps the source *is* a beacon, after all."

"One the Sol Apotheosis Movement left behind, perhaps?"

He shrugged. "It may have successfully summoned my sibling here, then malfunctioned."

"That wouldn't explain why he bothered to reply."

"Unless the beacon is an AI," Cane suggested. "Or we have it the wrong way around. Perhaps the Sol transmission is from my sibling, and the reply from someone else entirely."

Roche thought this over. The first transmission had come from Jagabis, their current destination. "If so, that means we're heading into trouble."

"I know." Cane's dark features remained expressionless. "It appears that being able to translate the transmission, even in part, has only made the situation worse."

"It's not your fault, Cane," Roche said. "This whole system is a mess." She rubbed sleep from her eyes with the heels of her hands. "Besides, you can't help what you are," she went on, sensing that he wanted something more from her than just acting as a confessor. "Your lack of motive worries me sometimes, but you've convinced me that you don't mean *me* any harm—for what that's worth. Just because you're a weapon, and you've been designed to do certain things that might harm a great number of people, that doesn't mean you will. There's a big difference between design and intent, after all; I try to keep that in mind."

Cane nodded slowly. "Thank you, Morgan. I was worried that the reminder of what I am might cause you to rethink our association."

She smiled vaguely. "I'm glad you told me. At the very least, we can get the Box onto it and see whether it can't translate the rest."

"You would like me to tell the Box?"

"I can't see why not. Having some understanding of a high-level Sol language will probably come in handy one day." She went on: "When you have the time, go over the text of the transmission, pull out the bits that you can translate and see what the Box can come up with. It may be no more of a linguist than you or I, but it must be able to run basic statistical checks. Something's bound to come up."

Cane stood, his muscles flexing smoothly with the movement. "We'll begin immediately."

"I'll be down to review your results soon." She stood, too, and followed him to the door. "But don't let it get in the way of mapping the system. That's our first priority at the moment."

The door slid closed behind Cane, leaving Roche with yet another mystery to ponder. She wondered how many more this system would throw at her before finally surrendering some definite answers. And how much longer she could juggle the conflicting trust and suspicion she felt for Adoni Cane.

When she made it to the bridge almost an hour later, the first wave of information had begun to arrive. The probe aimed at the sun had announced that it had data to send within moments of Cane's return. Since then, the Box, Cane, and Kajic had been fully occupied, paring back the packets of data to the ones most relevant or likely to contain answers to Roche's many questions. As a result, the mystery of the possible Sol transmissions had been placed on hold.

"Okay," she said, settling into her seat. Maii took a place next to her, apart from a hand on her shoulder keeping carefully unobtrusive. "Let's see what we've got."

"Pictures in visual spectra, mostly," said Kajic. "And, according to the Box, the mechanism underlying the Gauntlet."

"Show me."

The main screen blossomed to reveal a bloated red giant, magnified to fill one third of the view. Cooler patches had been dimmed by compensators to appear charcoal black, giving the star's surface a cracked appearance. Massive disturbances, clearly visible despite the blur of distance, flowed sluggishly from each pole to the equator, skewed east by the star's rotation.

Roche winced at the sight. "You'd never guess that until a month ago, *that* used to be a green dwarf."

"Precisely," said the Box. "The change in its composition goes much deeper than I thought."

"How deep, exactly?"

"To the core. Look closely, Morgan."

The view zoomed forward, closer to the star. Gases bubbled like magma from an unimaginable interior, casting a baleful red light through the bridge. A green ring stood out on the screen, highlighting a darker point. As the ring swung past, Roche realized that the point at its center was an object orbiting the star, deep within its chromosphere. She had no reference points against which to estimate the object's size, but the way it disturbed the gases around it, leaving a deep, roiling scar in its wake, suggested enormous size or mass, or both.

"That can't be a ship," she said.

"It isn't," said the Box. "It is one of sixteen quark breeders in high-speed orbit, firing pellets of strange matter into the heart of the star."

"You can tell that just by looking at it?"

"Not entirely, Morgan. If you watch carefully, you can see the pellets strike the photosphere."

Roche looked more closely at the image. Sure enough, every few seconds or so, a bright spark of blue light flared at the base of the wake.

"Why strange matter?" asked Haid.

"Strange matter is super-dense," Roche said before the Box could reply, "and it can be moved more easily and more precisely than neutronium. With it, you can alter the workings of a star's core. Once you control the core, you can play with its electromagnetic and gravity fields."

"This, clearly, is how the Riem-Perez Horizon is generated," added the Box.

"Overkill," said Haid.

"The Gauntlet is a grotesque example of just that," the AI agreed. "If its designers had stopped to consider what they were doing even for a moment, they would have realized that what they hoped for simply wasn't possible."

Haid shrugged. "You have to admire them for trying, anyway."

The quark breeder continued to plow its way through Hintubet's wounded chromosphere, as implacable as the physics that foretold the star's death.

"What would happen if we destroyed them?" Cane asked.

"Disaster," said the Box. "The nuclear processes inside the sun would spiral out of control until the reactions sustaining the Riem-Perez Horizon ceased. The boundary would become increasingly chaotic until, within a very short period of time, it collapsed entirely."

"Any idea who planted the breeders?" said Roche.

"Detail is sparse at this resolution," said the Box. "I cannot tell if the breeders display any markings. However, only one nation in this region manufactures breeders of the sort required for such a macro-project as this, and that is the Eckandar Trade Axis."

"Do you think they might be involved?"

"No. The devices have been available for many centuries; the array is probably that belonging to the original Gauntlet prototype, not one manufactured recently."

"That's good to know. I hate to think why anyone would build them today." Roche mused to herself for a moment. "If this is the prototype, and it's being used to entrap the Sol Wunderkind, then it must have been kept somewhere nearby. Allowing time for the weapon to be dusted off and programmed, then put into place and activated, that doesn't leave much for transport."

"Do we know when it was activated?" asked Haid.

"Not before the twenty-sixth of last month," said the Box. "That was when the Armada Marines investigating the system were ambushed. Presumably the system was open at that point."

"Is there any way to pin it down further?"

"I have been observing the rate of decay of the boundary. If we assume that it originally extended to cover Palasian System's cometary halo, then that gives us an activation date somewhere between the thirty-seventh and fortieth."

"So that means the people behind the Gauntlet had a little more than one week to get it here," Roche said.

"How would they have got it past the clone warrior?" asked Haid.

"One assumes the breeders were slow-jumped as close to the sun as possible with a large relative velocity," said the Box. "Once they were captured by Hintubet's gravity and safely inside the chromosphere, there would have been very little the Sol Wunderkind could have done to interfere with them."

"He wouldn't have known what they were, after all," said Roche.

"They would have demonstrated no overtly hostile behavior," added Cane. "And there may have been more pressing matters demanding his attention."

"That makes sense." Roche turned her attention away from the sun and the device crippling it. "What else have we found?"

"We have a probe orbiting Cartha's Planet," said Kajic. "Everything seems in order there. Wight Station—the automated solar research installation—has not been damaged."

"Because it was no threat," Roche said. "Go on."

"The same probe examined the Mattar Belt as it flew through," Kajic went on. "There is evidence of activity on several asteroids, although only one prowling mine was observed in situ. Likewise, it had not been interfered with."

"Any sign of people?"

"No. The inner system appears to be uninhabited, except by machines."

"Perhaps we can use them to our advantage, then. Box, as we get closer, I want you to make contact with the AIs on Wight Station and the prowling mines. They may have recorded information that will help us plot the movements of the Sol Wunderkind."

"I will do so," said the Box. "If other installations have been attacked in the same manner as Guhr Outpost, the explosions should have been noticed by one or more of these observers. We may be able to pinpoint the exact time each attack took place."

"Let me know what you find." Roche turned to Kajic. "Any news from Jagabis?"

"The probe will be in position, relative to us, in about an hour. All transmissions ceased from that region twenty-five minutes ago, corresponding almost exactly with our arrival in the system."

Roche mentally approximated the time it would take data traveling at light-speed to cross the system twice; as Kajic had said, it did match the time required for someone on Jagabis to observe the arrival of the *Ana Vereine,* then for the immediate cessation of transmissions to be observed by Kajic.

"So someone knows we're here," she said somberly.

"They knew where we *were,*" said Haid. "We've been camouflaged since we arrived, which still gives us some element of surprise."

Roche nodded. "Have the other probes found anything?"

"Two used Gatamin as a gravity-whip, but neither reported anything unusual," said Kajic. "Again, that planetary system was uninhabited."

Roche took a moment to study the images of the smallish, once blue-green gas giant, third most distant from the sun. Apart from its remarkable rings, it was easy to overlook.

"Herensung likewise appears untouched," Kajic went on, "at least from a distance. There were a few orbital communication relays that are now silent, but until the probe arrives we have no way of knowing what has happened to them."

"That leaves Cemenid, and the double jovian." Roche was curious to see both. Cemenid, the largest planet, had been home to a COE communications base; Kukumat and Murukan were simply mysterious, on the opposite side of the system.

"Cemenid is a couple of hours away," said Kajic. "The double will be at least another twelve."

Roche couldn't complain about that; she already had enough data to keep her occupied for days, and would soon have more. The double jovian was simply a bonus.

She applied herself to the information with a will and Maii's help, trying to find any evidence of the Sol clone warrior's passage. Occasional details surfaced from the growing files—wreckage of satellite here, an ion afterwash there—but no actual sightings. Wherever the Wunderkind was, he had been effective in hiding himself—so far. When the data from the other major planets arrived, she hoped to know where he was *not,* at least. Then it would become a more difficult quest, through the gulfs between planets or in the mess of dark bodies known as Autoville between Cemenid and Gatamin. She didn't like to think that he might have hidden any farther out than that; Mishra's Stake, the second dark body halo, extended in a band one and half thousand million kilometers wide almost as far as Voloras. If he was hiding in there, he would be impossible to find.

The only consolation was that if he *was* in there, he would be effectively unable to surprise them. Which is why Roche felt safe ruling it out. He would never have allowed himself to reduce his options so severely, assuming Cane's behavior was anything to go by.

<He will watch patiently until he has sufficient information,> said Maii, <then strike. It won't be in his nature to act unprepared, or to wait too long. As soon as he knows how to destroy us, he will do so without hesitation.>

<There's a cheerful thought,> Roche responded, still acutely aware of what had happened to Guhr Outpost.

<We just have to be ready for him, and make sure he doesn't force us into any mistakes.>

Roche pondered this. <We may already be making a mistake by rushing into the system before the probes have had time to report.>

<I don't think so,> the reave said. <Even in-system the distances are large enough to give us an edge, given the power of the *Ana Vereine*. And besides, where are we now?>

<Inside the orbit of Gatamin.>

<The inner system doesn't really start until Cemenid. That gives us plenty of time to change course if the remaining probes *do* find anything.>

<But between Gatamin and Cemenid is Autoville, and there could be *anything* in there.>

<True. Then we'll just have to keep our eyes open.>

Roche smiled at the irony in the blind Surin's words, but she kept the thought carefully to herself.

"We're picking up something unusual," said Kajic.

"From Jagabis?" Roche asked, pushing the data she had

been studying to one side and focusing her attention on the main screen.

"No. It's a tightbeam from roughly the same direction, though."

"Contents?"

"A request for ID on a COE band. That's all." Kajic paused. "The transmission is coming once every minute, and we're only picking up the fringes of it. Also, it's blue-shifted, indicating that the source is moving toward us."

Toward them? Roche stiffened in her seat. "A ship?"

"That seems likely, although I haven't detected any emissions yet."

"Keep looking. Show me the message in full."

A window on the main screen opened, displaying four brief lines of text:

VESSEL ENTERING PALASIAN SYSTEM 0805
ID REQUESTED
RESPOND ASAP
QUOLMANN

"Who's this 'Quolmann'?" asked Haid.

"It's not a who," said Roche. "It's COE Intelligence shorthand for 'Trust me; I'm an ally.' "

"And should we?" asked Haid evenly.

"That depends," said Cane. "If the code is common knowledge, then we should treat its use here with suspicion."

"It's not well known," said Roche. "Otherwise it would have been changed. But I'm disinclined to trust someone even if they *are* from COE Intelligence."

"So what do we do?" Kajic asked. "Ignore it?"

"We can't afford to," said Roche uneasily. "The message was sent to *us*. They may not know exactly where we are, given that we're only picking up the edges of the tightbeam, but they do have a rough idea."

"They could be sending the message to several likely locations," suggested Cane.

Roche quickly dismissed the idea. "No, the ship is still coming in this direction." She thought for a moment, then said: "We're being predictable. Uri, I want to change course slightly; swing us away from the sun and to a wider approach. I know it'll mean taking longer to get to Jagabis, but I think we have to do it—at least until we know how far away this ship is. At the same time, send a remote to reply to the tightbeam on our original course. Give it half an hour before sending our ID and the 'Quolmann' code word—that's all. Keep the probe on our old heading until it receives a reply. It can relay any messages without putting the *Ana Vereine* at risk."

"Consider it done," said Kajic.

Roche read the text of the message again. "It's almost as though they were expecting someone from COE Intelligence to come," she mused.

"And have nothing to fear from them," added Cane.

"That puts them in a minority," said Haid wryly.

"The Jagabis data is being processed," announced Kajic.

"Finally." Roche prepared herself for another inrush of information. "Okay. Let's see it."

The probe had inserted itself into a polar orbit around the innermost jovian world of Palasian System. Even under Hintubet's stark, crimson light, Roche was struck by the beauty of the planet. Its bands and vortices were manifold and varied, ranging from thick jet streams to thin wisps; its pole was a region of intense electromagnetic activity, the atmosphere constantly erupting with flashes of lightning. Its rings were small relative to those of some of the other planets, but they were there, framing a large number of moons—fourteen known, Roche recalled from the COE files. The largest of them, Aro, was also the largest solid body in the system; for that reason, plus its more hospitable distance from the sun, it had been chosen over Cartha's Planet for the system's permanent civilian base.

She studied the data intently, eager for—and yet simultaneously dreading—her first sight of Aro Spaceport and its close neighbor, Emptage City. Although she knew that the probe had sent this view some hours ago, she couldn't help but feel nervous about what she might see, as though she were more intimately involved than a mere observer. What if the Sol Wunderkind were to be attacking Aro at the very moment the moon came into view? What would she do? She fought to suppress the discomforting notion, because the truth was, there would be nothing she *could* do. They would be helpless to defend the base. . . .

The probe changed course as it crossed Jagabis's north pole. Its tiny but powerful thrusters fired to insert it into an equatorial orbit intersecting that of Aro. Roche waited impatiently as the minutes ticked by until, finally, the red dot of the moon appeared over the bulge of the distant horizon.

The dot became a disc. The probe's thrusters ceased firing; momentum and the pull of Jagabis's gravity would complete the maneuver. The last leg of its approach would be conducted with as few emissions as possible.

The disc swelled steadily. A hazy atmosphere, rich in methane and sulfur, softened its edges. The hemisphere facing the probe was mostly in shadow, making details hard to discern, and Hintubet's bloody glare in the background only complicated the matter. Roche watched as Kajic tried various enhancement routines on the image, methodically refining the picture.

"I can't see the orbital tower," Roche said.

"What's that in the southeast quadrant?" Haid pointed. "Another crater?"

"No," said the Box. "Remember the scale. An impact that large would have cracked the moon in two."

"The COE maps have two methane seas listed," said Roche. "That must be one of them."

"It's a little hard to make out at the moment," said Kajic, "but I think you're right, Morgan."

"We'll soon find out," she said.

The moon expanded until its shadowed image filled most of the screen. Red sunlight glinted on an object in orbit around it, startling Roche until she realized that the telemetry data was still empty of signs of technological activity. An abandoned satellite, she guessed. Or wreckage. Whatever it was, it caught the light twice more before vanishing from view. Kajic's display showed several other unidentified and inactive objects, invisible to her limited senses, also in distant orbits, and she followed them instead to pass the time. A similar display on Haid's console revealed that he too was tracking them, ready to respond if one of them made any move at all—or showed signs of life.

The probe slid neatly into a geostationary orbit above Aro Spaceport and turned its instruments downward.

"Radar has located the main launch field," said Kajic intently. "No other clear landmarks, yet."

"The main dome?" asked Roche.

"I have something that might be an outline, but . . ." He shook his head. "It's not clear. The dome might be down. There's no way to be sure until the sun rises."

"How long will that be?"

"Ten minutes or so."

"Try infrared," she suggested. "If there are survivors, they'll show up as hot spots."

"I'm not finding anything, Morgan," Kajic said after a moment. "It's uniformly cool down there. Even the launch field."

"No fires?" asked Haid. "Traces of explosions?"

"Aro has an atmosphere and weather," said Kajic. "Excess heat will dissipate relatively quickly."

"But there's no evidence of the sort of damage we saw at Guhr Outpost, is there?" Roche studied the image on the main screen in detail, clutching at anything that would justify optimism. "There might still be a chance."

"Underground," said Cane.

"The main dome was fully exposed," said Kajic. "In fact, it was built in the walls of an old crater, so it needed only a roof."

"But the spaceport might have subterranean facilities," said Roche.

"The only way to check would be to go down there." Haid glanced around the bridge. "Any volunteers?"

"Let's see if we can't contact them first." Roche swiveled away from the screen. "Uri, have the probe broadcast a brief message asking for ID. Use the 'Quolmann' code. There may be a connection between survivors here and the ship signaling us."

"The people speaking the Sol command language?" asked Haid.

"Speaking it badly," Cane put in.

"Whatever," said Haid. "I'd be wary of letting them know we're anywhere near them just yet—if they're even there at all, that is."

"I know," said Roche. "That's what the probe is for. Send the signal, Uri. Repeat it once."

"Done." Kajic's image shifted within the hologrid. "And now we wait. We'll see a reply in about five hours, if there is one."

"Damn it." Roche cursed the situation—and herself for forgetting the light-speed delay. "I guess that's all we—"

"Hold it!" Kajic barked as something flashed across the screen. "The probe—something's firing on it!"

Roche slaved her implants to the data-feed. The hazy radar outline of the spaceport jerked once, then disappeared entirely from view. In the visual spectrum, the view slued wildly as the probe fought to stabilize itself. Damage readings scrolled down the borders of her field of view, suggesting that the probe had been struck on one side.

"Uri? What the hell is—?"

"I'm getting a fix on something," Kajic interrupted. The probe steadied, its cameras pointing toward the horizon of the moon. Light flashed from something metallic. "It's a derelict."

The view zoomed closer. The ship had once been a freighter, but now had a hole in its side that could have housed one of the *Ana Vereine*'s scutters. It was traveling in an orbit above and at right angles to that of the probe.

A cloud of escaping gas flowered briefly from the shadow of the ship's hole. A second later, it happened again.

"I'm picking up very low electromagnetic readings," said Kajic. "Almost undetectable. Hardly a life sign, and nothing like any weapon I've ever seen."

The view jumped again. Red warning indicators began to flash in the probe's telemetry display.

"I can't tell what's hitting it," Kajic said with some frustration. "And neither can the probe."

"Why isn't it doing anything?" asked Haid.

"It doesn't know *what* to do," Kajic responded. "It can't even run without knowing what it's running from."

Roche leaned forward as inspiration struck her. "Does the probe have anti-meteorite shields?"

"Of course; they're standard in anything designed to travel at speed in-system—"

"What about when it's not 'at speed'?"

"They shut down to conserve power . . ." Sudden understanding stopped Kajic short.

On the main screen, the probe's cameras caught a glimpse of the derelict ship. Red sunlight flashed on its pitted hull more strongly than before. Dust was still puffing out of the shadow in its side, as regular as a metronome. Then the image shook and disappeared again, the probe clearly having difficulty maintaining its attitude with so much damage interfering with its systems.

"It's a gas-gun," Roche said. "Probably a chemical thruster modified to fire slivers of metal or plastic; they're not hard to jury-rig. All that's needed is a small amount of power to run a targeter or a receiver, and no one will ever know it's there—until it's activated, anyway. And then, before you know it, you've been hit by something with enough kinetic energy to punch a hole right through your hull."

"The presence of the probe must have been enough to set it off," said Haid, nodding. "Just being there. Imagine what would've happened if it had sent that signal."

"Are there other derelicts in orbit?" Cane asked.

"I have plotted the orbits of at least a dozen small masses," confirmed Kajic, "many in similar orbits to this one—high and at extreme angles to anything around the equator."

"Thereby maximizing the relative velocities of the slivers," said Roche.

"So it's likely that all the derelicts are similarly armed," Cane said.

"Why bother?" said Haid.

"It's a trap, " said Roche.

"But for whom?"

"For us, I guess."

"No," said Cane. "This would have taken time to prepare. There must have been another target."

The probe shuddered again as another of the slivers struck it toward the rear. This time, the damage was severe. The feed died for a second before flickering back to life.

"We're going to lose it," said Roche, cursing under her breath.

"Soon, yes," said Kajic. "But not immediately. The probe knows it's been profoundly damaged, but it has been programmed to complete its mission before allowing total shut down. See? It's already changing orbit."

Roche followed the changing telemetry data. "What *was* its mission, Uri? I thought it had already accomplished it by getting there."

"Not quite. We needed to know what happened to Emptage City; that's its ultimate objective."

The probe's trajectory steepened at a frightening rate, accomplished by the faltering push of its thrusters and the steady drag of Aro's gravity. Roche fought the urge to grip her armrests as the atmosphere of the moon rushed toward the probe—and *her,* according to her senses.

Then clouds were sweeping past, red-tinged with sunrise. The radar image of Aro Spaceport expanded to meet her just moments after dawn broke across the surface of the moon.

Roche started slightly as the probe struck and the screen flashed with high-speed bursts of data. Then it went black.

"The feed has ceased," said Kajic.

"What did we get?" Roche managed, breaking the link to her implants.

"A number of partial images," the Box said. "I am reconstructing them for you now."

The main screen scanned through a number of blurry views of the surface of Aro. The first three contained scenes that could have been anywhere—too dark to make out details—but the fourth was surprisingly sharp. It showed the landing field of Aro Spaceport with a resolution down to three meters.

There were three ships parked in its dry docks. All were lifeless and gutted, with black holes along their spines indicating that they had been fired upon from above.

"Orbital laser-fire," said Haid. "Or bombardment of some sort."

"Maybe more pieces of derelict ships," Roche agreed. The field itself was pockmarked with circles—craters left behind from shots that had missed. The buildings of the landing field had been similarly destroyed.

"There's nothing here," she said. "Anything else, Uri?"

"One other clear snapshot," Kajic said. "The probe managed a course-change before it crashed and flew over the edge of Emptage City. There's just enough light to pick out fine detail."

"Let's see it." The spaceport vanished. In its place appeared the curved rim of an eroded crater wall, its lip blackened and jagged. From the point of view of the probe,

Roche was unable to make out the dome that had covered the colony.

"Can we see any closer?" she asked.

The crater wall rose to meet them as Kajic magnified the image.

"We were fortunate, in a way," said Kajic, "that the sun had only just risen. The incident light was striking at such a low angle that shadows revealed details we would normally have missed from above."

"I see them," said Roche, her stomach sinking.

The shattered base of the dome stood out clearly in the image, as did the bases of the struts and girders that had once held it in place.

"He cracked it open." Haid's words were steeped in awe and disbelief.

"That's all he needed to do," said Roche. "He let the air out, and everyone died."

"No," said Cane. "See the area around the base of the dome? It's blackened, as though by fire."

"But it's a methane atmosphere—" Kajic began, then stopped.

"Methane burns in the presence of oxygen," Cane finished.

"He punctured the dome, then started a fire." Roche could picture it all too clearly. "Then he left it to burn. It might have taken days."

Roche detected a mental frown an instant before Maii's voice intruded into her thoughts. <Why didn't he finish them off when he had the chance?>

"Because he didn't need to, Maii," Roche explained. "The gas-guns in orbit would pick off anyone who managed to survive and get off-planet—along with anyone who tried to mount a rescue, for that matter. Before the dome over Emptage City finally collapsed, he was probably on the other side of the system, attacking somewhere else."

"A very efficient strategy," said Cane.

Roche glanced at him, but was unable to tell from his

expression exactly what he was feeling. Approval? Admiration? Respect? She herself felt nothing but sickened by the cruelty with which the warrior had acted.

"What are the odds that someone could still be alive?" she asked of no one in particular.

"Minimal," replied the Box. "There may still be airtight chambers in some of the buildings, or underground as Cane suggested; small numbers of people may have taken shelter within them. But how would we go about rescuing them?"

"The gas-guns are easily avoided—" Roche began.

"True. Without the element of surprise and against appropriate shields, they would be ineffective. We could even destroy the derelicts before assuming orbit, thereby neutralizing the threat entirely. But the problem lies in locating the survivors quickly enough to mount a rescue attempt—survivors who have no way to communicate with us and may not have even the most basic of pressure suits to survive exposure to the atmosphere. Any rescue attempt would be complicated, time-consuming, and risky."

"With the Sol clone warrior still out there," said Haid grimly. "Laughing at us."

"Or hunting us," the Box added. "We cannot allow ourselves to be distracted. Our mission is to track him down."

"I know, I *know.*" Roche sighed. "I just feel we should at least *try.*"

"It's an honorable thought," said Cane softly, "but not one we can entertain at this moment. It's what he will expect us to do. Perhaps later, when we have the time."

Roche straightened in her chair, trying to regain the appearance of the staunch commander. "Perhaps. For now, though, we've lost our probe at Jagabis. Uri, how long until another can take its place?"

"A few hours."

"Do it. I don't want any blind spots."

"Understood."

She stood. "I'll be in the captain's office for a moment."

Maii lightly squeezed Roche's shoulder. <I'll come with you,> she said.

Roche considered arguing, but knew it would create a scene—and that was exactly what she was trying to avoid. She couldn't meet Haid's eyes as she and Maii crossed the bridge and entered the smaller chamber at its rear. When the doors slid shut behind them, Roche let herself sink into a padded chair and put her head in her hands. Acutely conscious of Maii's thin-boned hand on her shoulder, she drew a heavy veil across her thoughts.

To no avail.

They're all dead . . .

<It's harder than you thought it would be,> said the reave, her mental voice a gentle breeze blowing between their minds.

<Much,> said Roche, kneading her temples with her fingertips.

<There is too much unknown, and too much at stake,> Maii continued. <You have to confront the Sol Wunderkind before it escapes this system and destroys another; but how can you confront it without sufficient information to guarantee that you will not fail like the others who tried before? The more you look, the more death you see, and the less likely it seems that you will ever succeed—but that only makes it all the more important that you keep trying. You might be all that stands between the clone warrior and the rest of the Commonwealth.>

<Look, Maii,> said Roche sharply, <I don't need this right now.>

<No,> the reave soothed. <You don't. And yet you continue to torture yourself with it.>

Roche smiled to herself. <I suppose I do, don't I?>

<I don't know,> said Maii. <I'm guessing, not reading.>

Roche removed the girl's hand from her shoulder, and held it in her own. <Maii, this is the first thing I have ever tried to do on my own. And I guess I'm just a little . . .

scared. Not of the Sol Wunderkind escaping or anything, but of—>

<Failing,> said Maii, finishing what Roche was reluctant to express.

<I mean, I know I'm not really on my own, with you and the others around to help me, but COE Intelligence isn't there issuing the orders for once, and that makes it so important not to screw up in any way at all . . .> She stopped, realizing that she was close to babbling, and sighed. <I just need time to get my head straight.>

<I understand,> Maii said. Her face was expressionless but the waves of sympathy she offered were real. <There have been many moments since Veden died when I wondered how I could even think of going on without him. But here I am. I have no choice *but* to do so. The alternative, as they say, is far worse.>

Roche smiled. <And better to try and fail than to go back to COE Intelligence or give up entirely. At least it's *my* failure, not theirs.>

<I'm sure they'd be keen to contribute,> said Maii, her words stained with amusement.

<I'm sure they would.> Roche's mood sobered as an image of the ruined city on Aro returned to her. No doubt the killer of almost half a million people would have something to say, also.

With a *fizz,* a full-size image of Kajic appeared, standing opposite them with his hands respectfully behind his back.

"Apologies for intruding, Morgan. I have detected the emissions of a vessel on an intercept course with the relay probe we left to follow our previous course."

Roche took a deep breath. "The ship that hailed us earlier?"

"I assume so. It's still several million kilometers away, and I am unable to discern its class or origin, but I can tell you that it's small. Maybe a mini-shuttle or singleship."

"Occupied, I presume?"

"It is accelerating within the physical tolerances of a living being, yes."

The ghost of a thought came from Maii: <But what kind of being is it?>

It was with some unease that Roche realized that the Surin's words echoed her own suspicions: A singleship. One person. Who else *could* it be?

"Send something to meet it. An armored—and armed—probe, this time."

"To destroy it?"

"Not yet. Just to let the pilot know we're not taking any chances."

With a slight nod of acknowledgment, Kajic's image disappeared, leaving Roche alone with Maii once more. She could feel the girl's hand on her shoulder, but couldn't decide whether the firmness of the grip was an attempt at reassurance or an indication of Maii's own fears.

PART TWO:

GALINE FOUR

INTERLUDE

At the bottom of the pit, two suns now burned. He found it hard to sleep, their light was so bright. With tiredness came lack of focus and inability to concentrate. The latter especially was dangerous when the Cruel One's servant was in the room.

<Tell me!>

Sensation crackled through nerve-endings left vestigial by his species for good reason. It wasn't exactly pain; more a driving ache. His body strove to respond—from the tips of all five of his limbs to deep, primal points in his brain—but his being was elsewhere. He was dreaming awake. He was watching the two suns burn.

One hung far away, turning in odd spirals among several dozen much fainter lights. This Shining One was not diminished for being afar; if anything, its magnificence attained a proper perspective in the distance. It was an uncanny thing: made, yet not-made; Human, yet un-Human.

<Talk to me, *irikeii,* or I swear General Darkan will seed your planet with dusters designed to tear carbon bonds apart! We'll reduce your so-called Grand Design into a puddle of slime!>

The words formed involuntarily at the mention of the Cruel One. His body was learning new tricks of survival quite beyond the care of his conscious mind.

: THEY
: DANCE
<*Dance?*>
: THEY
: MOVE
<Where do they move?>
: FURTHER
<Further *where*?>

He could not answer the question. Again, the meaninglessness of spatial references confounded him. Movement was enough, surely. Why this endless concern about *location*?

Something—an electrode, a chemical, a laser—touched a point deep within him, a point they had not touched before. This time, it truly hurt.

He writhed. Visions assailed him. Not true eye-sight but mind-visions: of the Shadow Place on Hek'm, his accommodation since birth; of the minds of his attendants, and the minds of his family; of the web of minds unfolding around him, Olmahoi and others, all tangled in a knot of near-infinite complexity; of the simple AI drones who had smashed unseen through this web and snatched him from his people; of the Cruel One who had brought him *here,* wherever *here* was, where the knot was barely a tangle in a handful of threads, where two minds as bright as only a handful of others he had ever been permitted to see struck him like noontime sunlight streaking down a very deep pit . . .

He strove. Past the Cruel One's servant—with his complex web of lies and suspicions and delicate manipulations—

and the others who served him. Outward . . . Not to the distant ones, barely visible against the one who accompanied them. Nearer. He had studied these minds before, and recently too—relieved to have found someone new to look at. They too were dwarfed by the one they traveled with, of whose brilliance they had only the barest inkling, yet he found them intriguing.

Two crippled, yet strong; both possessing extraordinary stories, yet not unprecedented.

Another, piercing like a knife. This one he avoided. Her mind burned differently from those of the Shining Ones, although she too had a made quality. She was an abomination.

The fourth and last was . . . an enigma. Under other circumstances he would have studied this one exclusively. There were secrets here, secrets that might prove in the end to be unfathomable but would, he was quite sure, be worth the attempt.

Pain.

He concentrated.

: CLOSER

<Which one?>

: CONTACT

: MADE

<Ah . . . good. Some progress at last. Is it the same as the other?>

: YES

<Interesting, but not unexpected. Perhaps the situation isn't as unlikely as it seemed.>

He sensed the satisfaction of the Cruel One's servant arising from his immediate misunderstanding, and hastened to explain.

: SAME

: BUT

: DIFFERENT

<In detail yes, it would be. One can only replicate an n-body so far. Experiential discrepancies will necessarily fa-

cilitate operational divergences between the clones. To expect otherwise would be naive. It's their internal structure I'm concerned about—their mental architecture, if you like. Are they fashioned from identical plans, using identical materials, for identical purposes?>

He pondered this. It was something he'd not considered before. The Shining Ones had a *purpose*? He had thought they just *were,* like most intelligent beings he encountered.

Despite having had his life mapped out for him almost from the moment of conception, he did not believe in destiny. There was no guiding hand ruling the cosmos; he understood this better than most people.

There was only one way he could answer the question.

: SAME

Yet it was not enough. He could sense an impossible truth lurking in the bright points that marked the beings his captors sought. But how to express it? And what to do about it, even if he could?

: IRIKEII

<Yes? I know your name.>

: IRIKEII

<What do you mean?>

: IRIKEII

Words always failed him in the end. No matter how much the Cruel One's servant ranted and raved, he would never be able to explain any better.

: IRIKEII

: TOO

3

AVS-44
'955.01.20 EN
1110

"Welcome, Morgan." The transmission came from the singleship via standard COE communications channels: encrypted and on a tightbeam, but otherwise unremarkable. "I knew we were expecting someone from COE, but had no idea it would be you!"

"Not now, Myer." Roche looked up at the face in a corner of the scutter's main observation tank and was pricked again by its unexpected familiarity. "We're docking in five minutes, and I need to concentrate."

Mavalhin smiled the smile she remembered so well. "Okay," he said, "but remember, I'm right behind you, so don't cock anything up, all right?"

Roche didn't bother to reply. She knew him—or, more accurately, had once known him—well enough to realize that such comments were symptoms of his own insecurity. Whenever he'd needled her in the past, it had been because he felt threatened by her and needed to bring her down a peg or two. Nothing, it seemed, had changed.

Beside her at the helm of the scutter, Haid killed the audio link between the two crafts.

"The station has indicated that we are to dock at their main facility," he said. "So far, everything seems aboveboard."

Roche looked at the navigation display. The mini-station hung like a vast, gray stone in the dark-body halo the natives of Palasian System had called Autoville. Like most mini-stations, it had a spherical external framework almost a kilometer across upon which hung such hardware as thrusters, shield generators, docking bays, and communication dishes; on the inside huddled the modules required for unsuited habitation, packed piecemeal together and connected to the shell by a semi-rigid lattice. Much of the shell's interior was empty, apart from what appeared to be a small scout-ship docked in an internal gantry; as a result, the mini-station seemed incomplete. But Roche could tell just by looking at it that it had seen many years of service. Its one identifying feature—a black *R* painted on the end opposite the main engines—had faded from long exposure to space dust.

No lights were visible on the shell or in the interior. Whoever it belonged to, they were taking the job of hiding seriously.

"Bring us in slowly," Roche said. She would have liked to pilot the scutter herself, but preferred to give Haid the opportunity of flying with his new prosthetics. The bay they were aiming for was outlined in green, courtesy of the navigation AI. "Are we still clear, Box?"

She waited a second for the AI's reply. The *Ana Vereine*—along with Cane and Maii—was waiting camouflaged as a COE raider a safe distance away, resulting in a slight communication lag.

"I detect no suspicious emissions," said the Box eventually. "Apart from the singleships and a handful of drones, there are no other vessels in this vicinity. The station is communicating with several distant sites by tightbeam, but I have been unable to overhear their conversations."

"So far so good." Roche watched the mini-station grow steadily larger in the display. "Still, I'd be happier if they'd tell us who they are."

"They probably feel the same way about us," said Haid. "Our ID tells them nothing, and you've avoided mentioning why we're here. Trust works both ways, Morgan."

Roche nodded. "I know. But who makes the first move?"

"I guess they already have, by inviting us here." Haid adjusted the scutter's trajectory with a quick burn on the thrusters. "I'm not saying we should let down our guard entirely, but we have to give a little in order to get what we want."

"That doesn't sound like your normal line, Ameidio."

He smiled. "Just trying to see it from their perspective."

She supposed she should do the same, although it was hard to remain impassive following the shock of seeing Myer Mavalhin again. Any fear she had felt over the occupant of the singleship had vanished the moment she saw his face, in 2-D monochrome and highly compressed from the tightbeam transmission aimed squarely at the probe they had sent to follow the *Ana Vereine*'s path. Those dark eyes set deep in a broad, clean-shaven face; the black hair with its graying swaths about the temples . . . There was no mistaking him.

No mistaking, either, the warning he had sent:

"If you're heading to Aro Spaceport, then change course *now,* while you still can. A hostile agent unlike anyone you've come across before has been contained within this system, and we're unsure of his whereabouts. I urge you to turn and leave immediately."

She had already seen enough for the advice to carry real weight. Only the smallest hint of hope had kept her from seriously considering the option of leaving.

"If for any reason you are unable to escape the system,"

he had continued, "or if you're in need of repairs, then follow me to the coordinates 63 plus 4 degrees, 2 point 6 PAU. But maintain radio silence. We don't want to risk exposing ourselves with unnecessary communications."

We, he had said, as casually as only he could under such circumstances. *We.* There was someone else alive in Palasian System.

The yellow landing lights of the station's main docking facility winked invitingly to life as the scutter broached a minimum distance. No doubt the light was coherent and aimed directly at them to reduce the risk of anyone's overseeing. There would still be scattering off the scutter's hull, but Roche suspected the risk of anyone's detecting *that* was small. Precautions were sensible only to a certain degree; beyond that, they were symptomatic of paranoia.

Which is why, she guessed, she had taken Mavalhin at his word. He was not an unknown quantity, like everything else in the system; she couldn't entirely trust him, based on past experience, but at least she knew that he was only mundane and could deal with him if necessary.

Myer Mavalhin . . .

"You said you studied with this guy," said Haid, breaking into her thoughts.

"Huh? Oh, yeah . . ." Roche felt again that sudden rush of unreality as the fact that he was *here,* in Palasian System, struck home. "At COE Military Cottage."

"How well did you know him?"

"Well enough." She shrugged, and hoped the flush spreading across her face wasn't visible. "We took the same classes and were often buddied on smaller projects. We were regarded as a sort of team."

And it had been a very good team, she remembered. For a while. Maybe a year. Then it had been unbearable, prolonged by the fact that the College tutors had still expected them to continue working together. If not for Mavalhin's eventual expulsion from the College, she might well have left herself, just to get away from him. It had been that bad.

But here she was—part of her almost glad to see him again, after all this time, while another part of her still yearned to stick him in a blast tube and press Purge.

Roche had already discussed some of the facts with the others on the *Ana Vereine,* although she hadn't felt comfortable delving too deeply into her past. Even when the station had been located at exactly the place Myer had indicated—measured from Jagabis's location and plane of ecliptic: 63 degrees closer to them, 4 degrees above, and just over two and half times as far away from the sun—she had avoided talking to Mavalhin directly, for fear of exposing scar tissue she would rather have kept hidden. She had simply ordered the *Ana Vereine* to rendezvous with the station and sent a brief text reply indicating to him that she would be willing to talk terms.

But she could feel Maii's curiosity brushing at the edges of her long-term memory. And Haid knew her well enough to know that she wasn't telling the whole truth.

"I don't get it," he said. "You're prepared to take this guy at his word when he says he and his buddies want to work with us, but you'll hardly talk about him, let alone *to* him. Who is it you don't trust, Morgan?"

"I'm not sure," she said frankly, half-smiling in the gloom of the scutter. "I don't know what I'm thinking at the moment, which is why I'd rather not think at all for a while."

"That's not very reassuring, Morgan."

"I know, but . . . Look, I'm sorry. Let's just dock, and see what they have to say."

"Now I know why you left Maii behind. With her here, I'd at least have been able to dig a little deeper."

She was about to snap back that the reave would never have betrayed her confidence in such a way, but caught his grin in the fluorescent glow from the displays in time to realize he was joking.

"It'd take more than Maii," she responded evenly, "to make sense of this mess."

"So it seems," he said, returning his attention to the navigation display.

The scutter docked with a slight jerk. Within seconds, environment displays indicated that an external feed needed authorization before the physical link could be completed. Roche advised the scutter's AI to wait.

"A little rough," said Haid, leaning back in his seat and flexing his new hand. The matte-gray digits wriggled as fluidly as organic fingers did, defying their appearance.

Roche patted him on the shoulder, and levered herself out of the copilot's chair. "Nothing a bit of practice won't fix."

"I guess." Haid followed her into the scutter's empty passenger bay.

She reached into the shoulder bag she had brought with her and produced two Dato side arms, giving one to Haid. The holster of the other energy weapon she clipped to the belt of her black expedition uniform—again, a standard Dato make but not distinguished by insignia. Haid's weapon hung at his side like an extension of his biomesh.

"Ready?" he said, shifting the side arm into a more comfortable position.

"Not quite." Roche keyed her implants and linked them to the scutter's communications systems. <Box, are we still in contact?>

The lag was shorter this time. The *Ana Vereine* had assumed a more immediate position once the scutter had docked.

<Yes, Morgan.> The AI's voice was a whisper in her head. <Your audiovisual feed is clear. There has been no interference from the station.>

<How about you, Ameidio?> Roche asked, directing her attention to the man standing next to her.

A small window appeared in one corner of her vision. Haid's more basic implants were not designed to carry sensory data, but could transmit and receive text messages translated from speech by the scutter's processors.

FINE, he said. AM I COMING THROUGH OKAY?

Roche nodded. <Let's keep in touch regularly. If they cut us off, we pull out immediately.>

UNDERSTOOD.

<Given the power at my disposal aboard the *Ana Vereine*, I am confident I will be able to contact you at all times,> said the Box. <Should your return feed be interrupted, I will notify you.>

Roche nodded again, satisfied that she had covered that particular base as thoroughly as she could. The station would know that they were broadcasting to and from the scutter, but without cracking the Box's cipher, eavesdroppers would not know what was being said.

That was fine by her. Just because Myer and his friends probably weren't working for the clone warrior didn't necessarily make them allies.

Speaking aloud, she continued: "We'll wait for them to make their move. It shouldn't be long; they'll probably want to attach an umbilical to keep us under control. In fact, I'm hoping they will, because that'll give us easier access to the bay security systems. The Box is more likely to find useful data poking around the datacore than we are on a guided tour."

"Undoubtedly," said Haid. "It handled COE HQ easily enough, so—"

A clunk on the hull interrupted him. They both turned to face the airlock. A red light began to flash.

Roche cued her implants for an external transmission. "This is Morgan Roche," she said. "I'd like to speak to the person in charge of dock security."

"That would be me," came the immediate reply. "Gered Disisto at your service. We're trying to attach an umbilical, but your ship won't comply. Is something wrong?"

"I will release the airlock when I am satisfied that we'll not be harmed."

"Your caution is understandable, Commander," Disisto said. "And I give you my word that you are in no danger from myself or anyone under my command."

"Not good enough." She was tempted to correct the erroneous use of "Commander" but decided to let it go. "I'll allow the umbilical to be attached, but I'm not leaving this craft until you and one other officer arrive to escort me from it."

There was a slight pause, then: "I'll be down in a moment."

Roche instructed the onboard AI to proceed with the link-up. The sounds of faint movement came through the hull as the umbilical locked tight around the external airlock and equalized pressure. At the same time, fuel and data lines sought their respective sockets and clicked home. The sounds ceased at the same time the airlock display indicated that the umbilical was sealed.

"You there, Disisto?" said Roche.

"I'm here," said the dock security head not long after. "Outside and waiting."

First making certain her side arm was within easy reach, Roche stepped back from the airlock and cued it to open.

The outer airlock opened with a hiss and two men stepped inside, one tall and dark-skinned, the other short and fair, both wearing gray uniforms. When the outer door had sealed behind them, the inner opened and they stepped inside, bringing with them a pocket of heavily scented air.

"Disisto?" said Roche, looking to both men.

"That's me." The tall, dark-skinned man nodded, extending a hand to Roche, which she took, and shook. His face, like his frame, was lean without being thin, as though he exercised regularly. "Roche, I presume?"

"And this is Ameidio Haid." Haid bowed slightly.

Disisto indicated the other man. "Torr Synnett."

Synnett glanced at both of them in turn, but was otherwise impassive.

"I figured you'd want us unarmed," he said, gesturing at

Haid's side arm. "So this puts us at something of a disadvantage." When neither Roche nor Haid made any effort to remove the weapons, Disisto shrugged and said: "Well, now what?"

"Now we follow you out of here," said Roche. She indicated the airlock. "After you."

The four of them filed into the small enclosure and waited for the doors to cycle. The smell of spices was stronger closer to the two men, and Roche resisted the urge to ask what it was. Cinnamon, perhaps, with a hint of cloves, plus something more pungent, less familiar.

KESH, Haid said via his implants.

Roche glanced at Haid. <What do you mean?>

CAN'T YOU SMELL IT?

Roche tasted the air again. She had met Kesh agents while in the COE's employ, but always under Pristine-controlled circumstances. Never had she been in an environment that was home to any of that particular Caste for any length of time. If Kesh was what Haid said he smelled, then she would have to take his word for it.

"Welcome to Galine Four," Disisto said as the outer door opened. "No doubt you'll be unfamiliar with the layout of the station," he went on, ushering them along the umbilical. "But it won't take long to get your bearings. Until then I'd be more than happy to act as your escort. Or I can make other arrangements. It's up to you."

"You'll do fine," Roche said, moving forward to stand next to him. The ribbed plastic swayed slightly beneath their feet as they walked. "But I'd like to meet your commanding officer as soon as possible."

Disisto nodded amiably. "I'm taking you there now."

"Good," said Roche. "There are a lot of questions I'd like answered—such as what you're doing here in this system."

"I'm sure he'll be asking you the same things," said Disisto.

"And I'll be happy to answer him," said Roche. "Once I'm certain of his intentions."

At the far end of the umbilical, they stepped onto a metal platform which led to a flight of steps. The door behind them was the second of three along one wall of the main docking bay's disembarkation point. The scutter lay hidden behind the pressure-wall, which also possessed larger airlocks and umbilicals designed for the transfer of freight. None of the other doors was in use.

A dozen people occupied the disembarkation point, three of them dressed similarly to Disisto and his sidekick—obviously security officers like them. Above and on the far side of the chamber was a glassed-off observation floor which held still more gray uniforms. Even with so many people watching her, Roche felt alone; the disembarkation point was large enough to hold five of the *Ana Vereine*'s scutters.

The acoustic properties of the room lent a booming quality to their footsteps as they descended the stairs.

"Not much of a reception," Haid joked.

"You'll have to understand that we're a little busy at the moment," said Disisto earnestly. "If one of our scouts hadn't been in your vicinity, we probably would've let you go on your way rather than risk our necks talking to you."

"Speaking of which," said Roche, remembering Mavalhin. "Will that singleship we spoke to be docking soon?"

"It's just coming in now. Why?"

"I studied with the pilot some years ago. I was wondering whether I'd get the chance to catch up with him later."

"Well, he has debriefing and decon before he'll be allowed to mix with the rest of the crew, but I'll make sure he knows you asked about him, if you like."

Roche felt a mixture of relief and regret rush through her. "Thanks."

Disisto led Haid and Roche toward the main exit, with Synnett bringing up the rear. Roche glanced behind them just as the seal around one of the other umbilicals flared green, indicating that someone—presumably Mavalhin—was about to disembark. The three other security guards in the disembarkation point moved up the steps—and it was only then that she realized that the guards hadn't been there to greet her and Haid at all.

<Odd,> she commented to Haid. <So much for being cautious. They don't seem to give a damn if we're here or not.>

FEELING PUT OUT, MORGAN? Haid shot back.

<No, it's just not what I expected.>

The corridors and open spaces they passed through were uniformly drab: gray walls and floors, with minimal lighting; clearly a work area and not intended to look pretty. The few people they encountered were busy performing errands and took no notice of Disisto and his entourage.

"So," she said after a while. "What exactly is it you do here? The station, I mean."

Disisto faced her with a smile. "Research," he said. "But beyond that I'm not authorized to say. That will be up to the chief to explain."

"And just who is this 'chief'?"

"Professor Linegar Rufo," said Disisto. "He's in charge of Galine Four."

"That's the name of the station, I take it?" Disisto nodded without breaking his stride. "Is there a Galine One, Two or Three anywhere around?"

"Not that I'm aware of," he said. "There may have been once, but I've never heard of them."

"You've worked here long?"

"Five years."

"A long time to be cooped up on a station like this," said Haid.

"It beats a lot of the other jobs I've had."

<Box,> Roche sent via her implants, <look up Galine Four in the COE register and see what you can find.>

<Already checking,> replied the AI.

Haid picked up the conversation, grilling Disisto about his previous employment—which seemed, for the most part, to have been for the Traders' Guild or independent merchants. Roche followed the exchange with half an ear while continuing her discussion with the Box.

<Let me know if you find anything. Any luck breaking into the station's security system?>

<On a superficial level, the task was absurdly simple,> the Box replied. <But I have not yet managed to obtain anything more interesting than basic hardware specifications. There is obviously a secure cache I have not yet penetrated.>

<That's odd.> It wasn't like the AI to be so easily thwarted. Still, Roche had no doubt that, in the end, the Box would obtain the information she needed. <How about Galine Four? Found anything yet?>

<An advertisement in the xenoarchaeological sites of a science forum for a privately owned, mobile facility with permanent research staff on board.>

There was that word again: *research.*

<Xenoarchaeology, huh? Strange for such a vessel to be here, considering the ruins are recent and the builders Pristine.>

<Perhaps not, Morgan. There *was* an archaeological outpost in the system around Kukumat and Murukan.>

<So the station might have been visiting there when the clone warrior attacked,> said Roche. <Because it doesn't appear on any of the COE registers as a permanent facility, it would have been overlooked.>

<That seems plausible.>

<But why hasn't it left, then? That would have been the sensible thing to do.>

<Because it cannot. From my observations taken as the scutter approached, I can state with certainty that this station possesses neither anchor nor a slow-jump drive.>

Roche absorbed the fact with interest. <They're trapped here too?>

<So it would seem.>

<Is the *Ana Vereine* powerful enough to slow-jump both itself and the station out of here?>

<Unlikely,> said the Box. <But it could certainly rescue the station's occupants. I estimate a crew of roughly five hundred to a thousand—well within our carrying capacity.>

<Then at least we have something to bargain with.> Roche smiled inwardly. <And they know it too. No wonder they're playing it cool.>

<Unless they don't understand the danger they're in . . .>

Roche returned her attention to Disisto. The security officer was describing how they had sent manned singleships to every occupied point in Palasian System, and how they had found only destruction everywhere. If he knew anything about the perpetrator of the attack, he was hiding it well.

"And you've seen no evidence of life at all?" Roche asked.

"Only outriggers, here and there," Disisto said. "A spine or two must have moved in a few years ago without registering; they certainly don't show in the system stats. Most of them are in the belts the prowlers haven't already mined, although some have come in closer. We saw a couple attempt to intervene on Aro, but not very successfully. A piece of the Spaceport's orbital tower was rigged as a trap; cut them clean out of the sky."

"Our probe in that area found gas-guns in the derelicts—"

"Yeah, we ran into those when we put the tower out of action. It was about then we decided to cut our losses and get out of the way. Not that there's anyone left to rescue on Aro, anyway."

"Or anywhere else, it seems," said Haid.

"Except for this station," put in Roche. "Doesn't that strike you as a little odd?"

"Not really," said Disisto as they approached a transit tube. He pressed his hand onto the ID scanner, then turned to Roche. "We've been very careful, keeping emissions to an absolute minimum and staying put. We're not a battleship, and we're smart enough to know it. This warrior took out an entire Armada base, so we certainly wouldn't stand a chance against him."

<He's lying,> said the Box.

<About what?>

<About 'staying put.' The station's reaction engines have been operational for an extended period in the last few days.>

<How can you tell?>

<Every attitude vent and thruster is radiating heat, and I am detecting a poorly dissipated ion wash in this vicinity.>

<Enough to tell where it leads?>

<No. Just that Galine Four has traveled a large distance recently, and not hidden in Autoville as Disisto would have you believe.>

Roche chewed her lip thoughtfully, but she didn't have time to dwell upon the matter for very long: the transit cab had arrived and Disisto was ushering them inside.

"We're leaving the outer levels behind us," he said, punching a destination into the cab's control system. "If you experience any giddiness, it won't last long; a few ambient g-fields overlap between here and the Hub. In the center you shouldn't have a problem. You'll get used to the transition if you're here long enough."

"Seems like you could use a competent engineer," said Haid.

"Perhaps." The door slid shut, and Disisto moved to place his back against the far wall. "But as I said, you get used to it."

The cab descended with a sudden lurch that just as quickly reversed, leaving Roche feeling as though she was going upward. Haid lost his balance and scrabbled with his artificial hand for purchase on the wall. He missed the support rail, and fell to one knee.

Roche reached out to support him; he righted himself with a grunt.

"A little unsteady, there," observed Disisto. "Sorry about that."

"I'll be okay," Haid muttered, embarrassed. He wrapped his good hand around a support. "You did warn us, I guess."

"How much further?" Roche asked.

"Not far, once we arrive at the Hub." Disisto cocked an eyebrow. "You in a hurry?"

"Just don't want to keep our host waiting." The floor beneath them shifted again, but this time Haid managed to remain steady. "So aren't you interested in what we're doing here?"

Disisto shook his head. "It's none of my business. My concern is security only, and you've had the okay from the chief. I'm curious, naturally, which is why I volunteered to be your guide. But I won't push the matter unless . . ." Something shifted behind Disisto's calm façade, as though there was a question he wanted to ask. Just then the cab shuddered. "We're almost there," he said, changing the subject. "Our gradient should be nice and smooth from here on in."

The sensation of motion faded almost entirely. Within thirty seconds, they came to a halt and the doors slid smoothly open.

Disisto disembarked first. The first thing Roche noticed was the noise: voices, footsteps, whirring machinery—so different from the near-silence of the *Ana Vereine*. The second thing she noticed, once she had left the cab, was that the dull gray decor had been left behind; here, in the Hub of the station, the walls were white and the light dazzling. The corridor ceilings were laced with vines and other unobtrusive plants. The air was fresher too, although still thick with the smell Haid had identified as belonging to the Kesh Caste.

Several people walked past as Roche waited for Haid to leave the cab. Not all were Pristine: Roche spotted two Mbata talking animatedly in their native tongue, and one Surin walking alone. Some wore uniforms similar to Disisto's, but different in color; a substantial proportion, however, were casually clothed. A couple eyed them with curiosity, but didn't stop.

"Which way?" Roche asked, indicating the four corridors that branched from the tube's exit.

"Down here." Disisto pointed along the rightmost corridor. "Don't touch anything or talk to anyone unless I say so. We're all a little jumpy and I'd hate for there to be a scene."

Roche nodded, noting that the inhabitants of Galine Four's Hub did seem a little tense. No one met her eye, and Haid's radical biomodification aroused ill-concealed suspicion in one or two.

Disisto led them along the corridor, then to an accessway that curved gracefully into the distance. One hundred meters farther on, they passed a window, and Roche stopped to stare through it. On the other side was an enormous chamber filled with plants growing in free-fall. Long tendrils rose from spongelike vats of nutrients; moss and vines covered every flat surface; occasionally among the ubiquitous green was a speck of color—probably a fruit or vegetable doing its best to remedy the imbalance.

"Commander Roche?" Disisto stood waiting for her while Haid and Synnett continued on their way.

"Huh?" She turned toward him. "Oh, sorry. I was just admiring your garden."

Disisto smiled. "I try to spend as much time in it as I can. Rank, as they say, has its privileges."

"Sometimes."

"Yes, sometimes." His smile slipped, and Roche found herself missing it immediately. "Let's go," he said.

They followed the other two along the sweep of the corridor and to a semicircular antechamber where two armed guards in black waited by a sealed double door.

"He's expecting us," said Disisto to the nearest guard.

The guard nodded and the doors sighed open. Disisto marched between the guards, waving for Haid and Roche to follow. Synnett brought up the rear, as implacable and silent as a cloud's shadow.

They found themselves in a short corridor, facing another

double door. The space was empty and dimly lit, and warmer than the antechamber had been. Once they were inside, the door shut behind them.

"Where—?" Roche began.

Disisto raised a finger to his lips. "Wait."

"Place your weapons on the floor," boomed a voice from the ceiling, its non-Pristine mouth lending a slight lisp to the fricatives.

I TOLD YOU, sent Haid.

<That you did,> Roche replied. The voice belonged to a Kesh.

"Relax," said Disisto. "It's nothing sinister. The chief just won't allow arms anywhere near him."

Roche glanced at Haid. "What happens if we refuse to comply with his wishes?"

Disisto shrugged. "Then you don't get to meet him."

<I advise diplomacy at this point,> said the Box via Roche's implants. <Refusal may cost us more than acceptance would.>

<That's easy for you to say,> Roche shot back. <You're not here.>

Even so, she loosened the clasp on her holster and placed the side arm on the floor by her feet. Haid, after a moment's hesitation, did likewise.

"The cyborg will be placed within a restraining field," said the voice when both weapons were on the floor. "Sudden movements will not be tolerated."

Haid grunted and went to raise his hand, but was unable to. Gritting his teeth, he attempted the movement more slowly, and this time his hand inched up to his chest.

Disisto watched him in alarm. "I'm sorry." His concern and surprise were genuine. "I had no idea they would—"

"Just as long as there are no other surprises waiting for us," Roche said with some anger.

Disisto glanced at the door. "I hope not."

Haid's hand clenched into a fist. SONOFABITCH.

The lock clicked.

"You may enter," said the voice.

The door slid open, revealing a room as large as the bridge of the *Ana Vereine*, but far less cluttered. An expansive, circular desk, cut from polished white stone and adorned with shimmering holographic tanks, occupied the center of the room. The ceiling was also circular, and stepped around this central point, like an inverted amphitheater. The walls were comprised of dozens of inactive screens, and off to one side, was one large window through which could be seen the green of the station's gardens.

Disisto nudged Roche forward, and she stepped inside. Haid, moving cautiously so as not to activate the restraining field, did likewise.

Her first impression upon entering the room was of spaciousness and grace. Her second was of clinical efficiency, as though the room served as a laboratory when not used for meetings. Her third was less analytical, relying mainly on the data her sense of smell provided.

Cylindrical light fixtures suspended between the floor and ceiling cast a pure, white light on the room's three occupants.

"Greetings, Commander Roche," said the first, a Pristine standing on the far side of the desk. His hair was white, where he had hair at all. He was so small and his skin so waxy that Roche guessed his age to be over one hundred standard years. His movements, though, were far from infirm.

"You would be Rufo," said Roche.

The professor raised an eyebrow in mock surprise. "I see Gered has briefed you." His eyes then fell upon his security head, who shifted uneasily beneath the stare.

"Some," said Roche, noting Disisto's discomfort. "Nothing of consequence."

"Anyway," said Rufo grandly, "I welcome you to my home."

Roche eyed the two Kesh standing to either side of Rufo; neither looked particularly welcoming, even for a Caste not given to pleasantries. Both wore formal uniforms of office, with leather surcoats and boots over black bodysuits that bulged with muscle.

"Your home?" said Roche.

Rufo moved around the desk to greet her. At close range, he seemed even smaller. "I finance and run this establishment. My employees are under no illusion as to who pays their bonuses—although I like to believe that I am a fair taskmaster." His piercing, bright blue eyes darted to Disisto. "Would that be a fair comment, Gered?"

The security officer nodded smartly. "More than fair, sir."

Rufo smiled and moved back around the desk. "Introductions, then. Morgan Roche, your name we know, and that of your companion, Ameidio Haid; Gered filled me in as well. But you two have not met all of *us,* yet." He stopped upon reaching the first of the Kesh, and reached up to place a hand on one massive shoulder.

"This is Lieutenant-Doctor Haden B'shan, my second in command."

The Kesh officer bowed, his hairless head catching the light; his tough skin was predominantly yellow, but with blotches of blue and purple in symmetrical patterns, like ink blots, scattered across every visible surface. Where ears would have been on a Pristine, two dark-colored membranes a thumb's-width across were visible.

"I am honored," he said in a surprisingly high-pitched voice.

Unable to think of anything appropriate to say, Roche bowed also. She was slightly surprised by his words: Kesh were not normally so gracious to members of other Castes, particularly ones they hardly knew.

Haid on the other hand, slowly placed one fist on his chest and said: *"Do-tri'sk en sh'ante ruk."*

B'shan smiled, the moist inner lips of his mouth appearing for an instant. "*Du.* Impressive."

"Some time ago I served with a squad of Kesh commandos on Nirr," Haid explained.

"Which family?"

"G'rodo."

B'shan nodded. "They were a noble lineage, prior to their excision from the N'Kor Republic."

"I always felt the Dictatrix could've shown leniency in their case."

The other Kesh made a noise in his throat that sounded like gravel underfoot. B'shan nodded again, this time with solemn dignity. He stepped back to draw attention away from himself, the soles of his leather boots squeaking on the floor as he did so.

"And this," Rufo continued, "is Field Officer Shak'ni."

Shak'ni was taller than B'shan, but thinner. His face was etched with fine birthmarks in a bright shade of red, like veins. This time, the bow was begrudging, barely a nod. Shak'ni's eyes met Roche's only briefly as she returned the gesture, his contempt for her as palpable as the smell of his Caste filling the room. He didn't waste nods on a greeting, and Haid too said nothing.

Moving back around the table, Rufo returned to a position directly in front of her and Haid.

"Together," he said, "Haden and I have been scouring this system for evidence of the warrior that wrought such destruction upon it."

"I guessed as much," Roche said, glad they'd finally arrived at the topic that most concerned her. "I'm keen to analyze your data."

"And I am keen to analyze yours." Rufo's stare held hers firmly. "I presumed that's why you had came here. Crossing the Gauntlet is a feat not undertaken lightly."

"You know about that?"

"Of course. The various technological experiments performed by advanced Castes prior to Transcendence were a fascination of mine during my youth." Rufo stopped, as though a thought had just struck him, then continued: "But it would make more sense to explain from the beginning. Please, take a seat."

He waved a hand, and five white chairs rose out of the seamless floor in a ring around the circular desk. Roche hesitated for a moment, then took the one nearest her. Haid sat beside her; the two Kesh sat opposite them.

"Gered, if you would be so good as to wait outside, I will summon you when Commander Roche is ready to leave."

Disisto nodded, turned and left the room. Synnett followed close on his heels.

"Now." Rufo took the remaining seat. As he did so, the holographic tanks lining the walls and on the desk flickered to life. Color and movement surrounded them: scenes of distant worlds and stations, only a handful of which Roche recognized; strange texts in unknown hieroglyphs; the faces of dozens of people of all Castes and types, lecturing silently.

"I have many interests," said Rufo, "but foremost of them all is the past. History and the flotsam by which we gauge it has fascinated me ever since I was a child. From the age of four, I devoted my life and, upon my father's early death, a considerable fortune to the pursuit of such knowledge. But for such relics, and the resources my father left me, many of my childhood dreams would have gone unrealized.

"For instance—" He stood abruptly, pointing at the ceiling above the desk. From the center of the roof descended what appeared to be a sculpture no larger than Roche's hand, or a fossil cast in amber. Roche was unable to tell what it was, exactly, even when it had come to rest a meter above the desk.

"Give us a hint," said Haid, his artificial eyes focusing closely on the object.

"This," Rufo went on, his hands held out before him, "is my most prized possession. It was plucked by these very fingers from the wreckage of a spaceship ten times older than any of the existing civilizations in this region."

<It's the Gil-Shh'ana Fiche,> said the Box. <The cornerstone of all that is known about Primordial civilizations! Its location has been a mystery for twenty years.>

"It is a data-storage device built by none of the known

Castes, past or present," said Rufo at the same time. "The information it holds has never been fully translated, but it contains words written before even the most ancient Caste is known to have inhabited the stars."

"How is that possible?" Roche asked when she had the overlap straightened out.

"Clearly there are gaps in our knowledge," Rufo explained. "At least four Primordial Castes precede the earliest confirmed records we have. We call them Castes A, B, C and D, for even their names are unknown."

"But they *are* Human?"

"Of course, Commander. It is an established fact that no other intelligent species ever conquered the stars." Rufo spoke as though to an ignorant child. "Apart from this, all we can say for certain is that these Castes disappeared many hundreds of millennia ago. There are relics scattered here and there for those who care to look, but not enough to build a coherent picture of what their societies were like; not even enough to convince most universities to teach the facts that we have uncovered. I have devoted my life to expanding that pool of knowledge, and a few others along the way."

Realization dawned on Roche, then. "You've found some ruins, haven't you?"

"I was led to believe so," Rufo said. "Mok, the only moon of the Kukumat-Murukan double binary, is said to hold a fabulous collection of artifacts that have yet to be catalogued. Regrettably, the unfortunate business in this system has prevented us from examining the site. You see, I am not so involved in my work that I will ignore Human suffering when it occurs in front of me."

"And what exactly have you done about it?" asked Haid with a hint of skepticism.

"As much as you, so far," Rufo replied, clearly resenting Haid's reproving tone. He faced Roche. "I have removed my station to a safe place and dispatched smaller vessels to survey the damage."

"And you haven't intervened?"

"How could I do anything other than study what has happened here? That is the area in which my skills lie; I am neither tactician nor warrior. I decided that the long-term interest of the region would be best served by intelligence rather than valor."

"And what *have* you found?" Roche asked.

Rufo sighed and returned to his seat. "I have seen things in these last two weeks, Commander, I never expected to see. Things that . . . Forgive me." Visibly distressed, he leaned back in his seat and signaled for B'shan to continue.

The Kesh stood. "Understand, Commander Roche, that we on Galine Four are not allied to any military service. Therefore, if at any point during what I am about to tell you, your training suggests an alternate interpretation, please do not hesitate to interrupt. We will welcome your input."

Roche nodded, not wanting to discourage his mistaken assumption of her origins: while the *Ana Vereine* was camouflaged as a COE warship, it was safer to reinforce that impression. "Your rank is honorary, then?"

"A title, no more, left over from my adolescence in the service of the Dictatrix. I am an academic first and foremost, now." Noticing her glance at Shak'ni, he added: "My fellow Kesh is acting as a liaison between Galine Four and the N'Kor Republic. Prior to our arrival here, we were researching several sites in non-Pristine territories."

"Understood," said Roche. "Please, continue."

B'shan moved closer to the table. The Gil-Shh'ana Fiche retreated back into the ceiling as a large display flickered into life. In the tank appeared a scale map of the orbits of the five innermost planets of Palasian System.

"You are no doubt aware how it began. A COE courier, *Daybreak,* en route to Gorund Sef picked up a single life capsule not far from here and disappeared shortly thereafter. Two days later, it reappeared on a course for Guhr Outpost, broadcasting an emergency beacon. The outpost's commanding officer sent a tug to intercept *Daybreak* and bring it in for repairs. Subsequent to that, the base reported being under attack, then it too fell silent."

"Yes," Roche interrupted. "A battalion of Marines was sent to investigate. The pictures brought back by the one surviving ship showed the inhabited bases in Palasian System in flames."

"By the time *Daybreak* was recovered, it was already too late," said B'shan grimly. "The emergency beacon was a distraction; the crew had been dead for a day before it was even sent. The . . . *person* responsible commandeered the tug sent to intercept it, and, in conjunction with a small asteroid he had already diverted from its orbit, destroyed Guhr Outpost before its commanding officer could realize what had happened. The asteroid collided with a medical vessel parked in a refueling orbit, and sparked a chain reaction that resulted in the ignition of the outpost's entire fuel reserves."

Haid whistled. "No wonder the crater was so big."

"Bear in mind that much of this is supposition extrapolated from the small amount of evidence left behind at the scene, plus flight data from several of the derelicts we recovered and some faint observations recorded by various installations scattered through the system. We can't even tell how many people were involved in the attack. But given that only one person was rescued from the life-support capsule, and that the chain of events begins at that moment, we have assumed that this single person was alone responsible for what happened here. I know this seems unlikely, and we have no images of this person to prove any of it—or even ascertain his identity. Unfortunately, we can only work from the data we have, and that isn't much. I would hate to give you the impression that we know exactly what occurred, when at best all we can offer you are theories."

Roche nodded, indicating for him to continue.

"From Guhr Outpost we have traced the tug's movements to Gatamin, where it changed course and headed further in-system."

"How did its pilot know where to go?" Haid asked.

"The tug, naturally, contained detailed navigational charts showing every settlement in Palasian System. Relevant targets were easily located." B'shan rotated and expanded the map of Palasian System. "Geyten Base was hit next. The Armada base knew that something had happened to Guhr Outpost, but didn't have enough details to react in time. Barely had they readied two ships to investigate, when the enemy struck."

"We received pictures from Cemenid just before we arrived here," Roche said. "We were unable to locate the Armada base at all; the moon appeared to have disappeared."

"Precisely." The view in the central tank changed to show Cemenid—a bloated gas giant almost half again as large as Jagabis, with a violent atmosphere that appeared orange in Hintubet's red light. Three visible moons were ringed in green, plus a dark patch in the cloudscape. The image became grainy as the view zoomed in to focus on the dark patch. "This scar in Cemenid's atmosphere does not appear in any navigational records; the fact that you did not notice it suggests that it is no longer visible at all."

"Are you suggesting . . . ?" Roche began.

"That the image here"—B'shan pointed at the dark patch in the central tank—"is the impact site of the moon which was once the home to Geyten Base."

Roche glanced at the Kesh: his expression was serious. "The whole *moon*—?"

"Disturbed from orbit and sent into the atmosphere." B'shan changed the view again, this time to one showing wreckage in orbit around the gas giant. "We have discovered a large number of fragments corresponding to plate-armor commonly used to protect prowling mines from major impacts. It's my opinion that at least two were conscripted by the pilot of the tug on his way through the innermost dark-body halo. They are massive enough to shatter a small moon, or to deflect it from a stable orbit. Furthermore, their security is light and their AIs are simple to reprogram."

Roche pictured the prowling mines—each larger by a significant factor than Galine Four itself—barreling down on the unprepared Armada base. At that speed, little would have stopped them. The base personnel would hardly have had time to evacuate, let alone save any valuable military hardware. The destruction of the base had, once again, been conducted with chilling efficiency.

B'shan added: "We suspect that this incident is related to the ambush of the Armada battalion sent to investigate the distress call broadcast by Guhr Outpost sixteen days earlier. The Marines had been in the system for a week, as best we can tell, but disappeared around that time."

Roche nodded. That made sense. It fit in with the little COE Intelligence had told them, anyway.

"So where did the tug go from there?" she prompted.

"Actually, it probably wasn't there at all. Once the mines had been reprogrammed, there would have been no need for its pilot to have been present. That explains why, only a short time after communication with the base was lost, it caused an alert at Aro Spaceport when it tried to land without authorization."

"I can't believe they'd let it land after everything that had just happened," said Haid.

"They didn't. Port authorities destroyed it when it refused to respond to a third warning."

Roche frowned. "They destroyed it?"

B'shan nodded. "But the pilot was no longer on board. His tactics were uncanny: he was never where anyone expected him to be, always one step ahead. He skipped from *Daybreak* to the tug when there was only the slightest chance that Guhr Outpost might have guessed he was aboard; then, barely after the authorities on Aro had learned about events at Voloras and Cemenid, he'd already left the tug and sent it to act as a distraction while he went about his real business."

"Which was what?" Haid said.

"While Aro Spaceport mopped up the debris of the tug—believing they had destroyed the threat to the system with it—the pilot was using two prowling mines and the resources they contained to set up the next stage of his attack. It must have been during this time that he built the gas-guns and the targeters left behind in the derelicts; he certainly would have been hard-pressed to do it later."

"That makes sense," Roche said. "It also gave Aro Spaceport time to let their guard down."

"It would seem so." B'shan called up a map of the orbits around the major moon of Jagabis. "What he appears to have done in the end is to bring one of the prowlers into close Aro orbit by swinging it past Jagabis on a tight, elliptical orbit that kept it well out of view until the last minute. Then, once it was in place, it fired cutting lasers onto Emptage City, shattering the dome. It also used a flotilla of scavenger drones to attack the ships docked at the midpoint of the orbital tower. At the same time, the second ship came in by a different route and severed the orbital tower entirely."

"How?" said Haid.

"Simply by colliding with it," said B'shan, "and wrenching it out of its moorings."

Roche concentrated to follow the icons moving through the main screen. "The aftershocks of the collision would have destroyed any ships still attached to the tower. Hence the derelicts."

"And the added angular momentum would have carried much of the tower into a higher orbit, where it appears to have been cut into fragments. These fragments served as windmill-style devices designed to keep interlopers away. The cable is very thin and hard to detect; the end of each spinning segment was moving fast enough to cut a ship in two."

"And that's what happened to the outriggers," Haid said.

"So it appears," said B'shan. "We subsequently cleaned out the upper orbits of the windmills before you arrived, but there wasn't much we could do about the gas-guns. We balked at destroying the derelicts entirely, for fear of destroying evidence, but didn't want to risk our observers by sending them in to deactivate the traps one by one."

Hearing that, Roche thought of Mavalhin: he would have been grateful to be relieved of that duty, she was sure. Although cowardice wasn't exactly his style, neither was bravery.

"We detected several transmissions from that region shortly after we arrived," she said. "Did your observers detect them also?"

B'shan waved a hand and the screen filled with Sol command hieroglyphics. "They appear to be in some sort of code. We've had no luck cracking it, though."

"We also picked up another one from a different source, this time in plain text via tightbeam."

B'shan nodded. "The source of that transmission is in the vicinity of the Kukumat-Murukan double planet. We believe it to be either a decoy or an entirely innocent message not meant for our ears."

She raised an eyebrow. "A decoy? Why?"

"Because there have been no attacks since the destruction of Emptage City shortly before the closing of the solar envelope surrounding this system. It is tempting to assume that the person responsible has escaped."

"So why are you hiding out here?" said Haid.

"Cautionary measures," said Rufo softly. "It would be foolish to assume that we are safe until we have proof."

Roche leaned forward, addressing B'shan. "You said it might be an innocent message. From whom?"

"Other survivors, like us, who are also trying to avoid detection. Until we are able to leave this system, we are all denied the option of escape; better to wait until rescue arrives than to advertise our presence."

"What other survivors?" Roche pressed. "The base on Mok was supposed to be empty."

B'shan shrugged. "The source of the transmission has only been approximately pinned down. It is 'near' Mok in the sense that it is within an area several million kilometers across containing the double planet. It may have come from a lone outrigger drifting past, on its way elsewhere."

Roche granted him that. "And what about the Gauntlet? You must have seen it arrive."

B'shan glanced at Rufo. "The quark breeders entered the system twenty-one days ago."

"Do you know who brought them?"

"If we did, then we might at least know who to expect when rescue arrives," said Rufo.

"They entered the system from deep space," explained B'shan, "and aerobraked in the sun's atmosphere. Aro Spaceport was under attack at that point, so by the time we knew they were present they were already in position. From that point, the process was rapid: within twenty hours, the Gauntlet was activated and the system enclosed."

Rufo looked up, and spoke softly: "We assumed it to be you, at first—that you were a vanguard for a much larger recovery operation."

Roche nodded, uncomfortably aware of the unspoken questions behind his words: Who sent you? How much longer do we have to wait? *Will* we be rescued at all?

She could say nothing to allay his fears, but she had to say something. "Perhaps between the two of us we can build a more conclusive picture of what's going on here."

"I hope so," said Rufo, with a slight smile. "Anything you can add would be appreciated."

"You've been very open with your own data," said Roche. "I guess it's time I returned the favor."

Before she could begin, however, the Box spoke up:

<Wait, Morgan. There is something I need to discuss with you.>

She frowned. <Is it important?>

<Potentially.>

Conscious of Rufo and the two Kesh waiting for her to continue, she raised a hand. "One second," she said, then, to the Box: <Okay. What is it?>

<A small problem,> said the Box. <I am unable to penetrate this station's datacore.>

<Are you serious?>

<It would appear that there are two levels of security operating on Galine Four. The first, and least secure, is the one I have already penetrated; this allows me access to low-level information, such as visuals of corridors and some holds, air-flow analysis, water recycling figures and so on. The second level is completely separate, and cannot be accessed from the first; it covers at least half of the inner private chambers, including the room you are currently occupying, and every single datum relating to navigation and recent movements. It also covers Rufo's private files, and any others that might confirm or deny what he and his assistant have said.>

<And you've tried everything you can to get at this information?> Roche asked.

<It's not simply a matter of gaining access to them, Morgan. I don't even know where they are. It's as though the two security systems are completely separate, and bear no relation to each other whatsoever—which is, of course, impossible.>

<But we need access to this data before we can even think about trusting them.>

<I know. I must explore the station in more detail. The low-level security system is too limited to give me a clear enough overview of exactly what's going on. In order to get that overview, I need a physical link in the station.>

<Meaning you want me to go exploring?>

<I need you to gain access via palm-links to as many diverse outputs as possible. If one of them allows us into the inner security system, or at least near it, then we will be that much closer to knowing what is actually going on here.>

Roche nodded to herself. <You hear that, Ameidio? Feel like going for a tour?>

I CAN'T, Haid sent back. I ONLY HAVE A TEXT LINK, REMEMBER?

<I didn't mean it like that. It has to be me, and you're coming along. I'm not leaving you here alone—not with that damned restraining field. You'd be too vulnerable.>

SO WHO'S GOING TO DO THE TALKING?

<The Box, of course. I'm sure it's capable.>

She returned to the opulent brightness of Rufo's office. He and the two Kesh officers were watching her expectantly, B'shan still standing while Shak'ni watched her with ill-concealed suspicion. Roche wondered belatedly if the latter could read minds—then discarded the thought. If Maii couldn't use her epsense abilities in Palasian System, no reave could.

"I apologize for that," she said aloud.

"Talking to your crew?" Rufo asked.

"That's correct. Something arose that required my attention."

"Nothing too serious, I trust?"

"Crossing the Gauntlet appears to have been more stressful than I realized. We've discovered fractures on our anchor drive housing that will require maintenance before we leave. We can repair the damage ourselves, of course, but it would be much easier—and quicker—if we had access to a dry dock."

"Our facilities here are fully equipped," Rufo said. "You are welcome to use them."

"I wouldn't want to impose—"

"Think nothing of it," the scientist interjected. "I am happy to offer whatever services I can, free of charge. In return, when your drive is repaired you might consider taking some of my crew with you when you leave Palasian System."

"When the time comes, we'll take as many as we can." Roche smiled inwardly; he had risen to the bait with very little prompting on her part. "I suggest, then, that Ameidio and I view your facilities to determine if they're suitable. My information officer can fill you in on our discoveries so far, and evaluate them in the light of what you've shown us. That would not only save time but would also ensure that the most appropriate talents at our disposal are put to the task."

"That makes sense." Rufo beamed at her. "But please, do not put yourself down. It takes great skill to command a vessel of war for the Commonwealth of Empires."

She returned his smile, although his flattery felt forced, and opened the connection to the Box. <Got that? You're my information officer, and you'll be dealing with them direct. For that you'll need a face—like the one you faked when we took over the *Ana Vereine*.>

<Understood, Morgan. I am opening a direct communications link as we speak.>

<Just remember, I want to know *everything* that's decided at this meeting, so make sure I have a recording available for later.>

<Morgan, your mistrust pains me. I can only assure you again that my best interests lie entirely with yours.>

<Yeah, but the moment they don't . . .> Roche swallowed the comment; now wasn't the time to dredge up old arguments. <Just see what else you can learn from them, okay?>

<I will.>

"There is a request for a direct line coming from your vessel, Commander Roche," said B'shan. "I presume this will be your information officer?"

"Yes. Her name is Lieutenant Gold. Will the line be secure?"

"Naturally. No one outside of this room will be aware of what is said within it."

"Good." She stood. Haid did likewise, moving stiffly through the restraining field. "If you'll arrange someone to show us the way, we'll get on with our work."

"Gered will be your guide," Rufo said, joining B'shan at the central desk. "But one other thing, before you leave. You have not mentioned whether you have a reave in your crew. Can I assume then that you haven't?"

Roche hesitated, unsure where he was heading. "Not necessarily," she said.

"Well, if you have, then you'd be aware of the epsense-dampening field that has enveloped this system. We've encountered it ourselves, and are close to neutralizing it. Two of my three reaves have regained at least a measure of their normal abilities." Rufo smiled. "So if you *do* have any on your ship, I'd be happy to assist you in any way I can."

"Thank you." Even if what he said was true, Roche would need a lot more convincing of his motives before she let Maii into his clutches. "I'll certainly take it into consideration."

The doors to the office opened and Disisto led Roche and Haid through. Glancing back, Roche saw the main tank flicker to life, revealing the face of a white-haired woman in COE uniform, with the usual blue-black interior of a COE ship behind her.

<You, I presume, Box?>

<Correct.>

<You look familiar . . .>

<I modeled the features on yours, as you may look in fifty years.>

<*What?*>

"Greetings, Professor Rufo," was all she heard the woman in the tank say before the door closed on the meeting.

Galine Four's dry docks were situated inside the spherical framework that formed the exterior of the station. A circular hold laced with retractable mesh allowed access to the dock from the outside; massive gantries and many-limbed cranes lined the dock itself like the limbs of a giant anemone.

The *Ana Vereine*'s scutter wasn't visible from the pressurized observation platform Disisto took them to, but a couple of other ships were, one of them a small courier vessel that had suffered slight damage along its flanks. Roche studied it with casual interest while she accessed the specifications of the dry dock via her palm-link. Her other hand rested lightly on the butt of the side arm Rufo's guards had returned to her after she left the station's sanctum sanctorum.

Haid stood not far away, discussing the finer aspects of navigation with Disisto. Synnett watched coolly from the entrance to the observation deck.

The letters of the courier vessel's ID code suddenly fell into place. Although the complete sequence was impossible to make out, she could at least tell that it had once belonged to COE Intelligence.

<Well, well, well.>

<You have something, Morgan?> asked the Box.

<Only *Daybreak* itself,> she said. <What do you suppose it's doing here?>

<That I do not know. Rufo has yet to mention it in our conversation.>

Roche filed the information for future reference. <How about at your end?>

<Still nothing, I'm afraid. The dry dock is on the same security level as the main docking facility. We'll obviously need to access something in the heart of the station.>

<You said there are black spots you can't see. Would it help if we could get into one of those spots?>

<Possibly, but—>

<Give me the location of the nearest; I'll see what I can do.>

<The closest is one of the docks—probably the one holding *Daybreak*—but that is bound to be guarded. There are others within walking distance.>

The Box sent a map of the station with black spots marked, which Roche studied for a moment. A small black spot lay almost directly between her and the main docking bay. She turned back to Haid and Disisto, keeping the map in one corner of her eye.

"Hey, Disisto," she said. "I need to get to the scutter."

"Is anything wrong?" asked Disisto. His concern seemed genuine.

"No, I just need some specifications from the maintenance AI. I can probably find my own way, if you want to stay here and talk."

Disisto's expression relaxed into a smile. "I think we'd better stick together, Commander. That'd be safest for all of us."

"As you wish."

She headed for the exit at a brisk pace. Behind her, Haid cursed under his breath; his artificial limbs were getting the better of him, it seemed.

HOW'S THAT? he sent.

<Fine,> she replied. <Keep it up.>

Synnett fell back to help Haid while Disisto—his long legs equal to Roche's—did his best to keep up with her.

"You're in a hurry," he said as they turned into a broad access corridor lined with branching portals every ten meters. Technicians moved aside as they approached.

"Restless," she replied. "I've been stuck on the ship for too long."

"The raider? It doesn't look that cramped."

"It isn't really, I guess. It just feels like it at times. The walls close in, the roof starts to cave, the air begins to stink. There are moments when I'd do anything to be somewhere else, just for an hour."

"Which is why you came here to meet Rufo, I suppose." He glanced sideways at her. "I was wondering about that. It seemed odd for an officer to relinquish command so readily—especially given the circumstances."

"Just because I'm not on the ship doesn't mean I'm no longer in charge," she retorted.

"You have a good relationship with your crew, then. They obviously know where they stand."

If Disisto was trying to unsettle her by implying her crew couldn't be trusted, then he was hitting uncomfortably close to home.

"I trust them," she said steadily, not wanting him to see her ruffled by the comment. "That's all anyone can ask."

He nodded. "A big crew on a raider, then?"

"Moderately."

"Haid won't tell me where he fits in, exactly. My guess

is weapons systems or security. Is he tight-lipped, or won't you let him talk?"

She shook her head. "You're full of questions, Disisto."

"It's part of my job."

"Is Rufo making you ask them?"

"Not exactly." He pulled a slight moue. "I report to Field Officer Shak'ni."

"Really?" That surprised her: both his answer and his candor. "I thought he was just a guest."

"You're full of questions too, Commander," he said, grinning. "Under different circumstances I'd be happy to tell you everything, but as it is . . ."

He let the sentence hang. Roche didn't mind. She had reached the turnoff for the black spot.

"Let's go this way, shall we?" She quickly ducked down the corridor before he had chance to object.

"Hey, wait!" Disisto hurried after her, surprised by the sudden turn. "You can't—"

"Why not?" she shot back. "It's quicker."

"How could you possibly know that?" He grabbed at her shoulder, but she dodged aside.

"I have a good sense of direction," she lied. "You said it wouldn't take long for me to get my bearings, didn't you?"

He stopped in his tracks. "Okay," he called after her. "Okay, we'll go this way. But can we at least wait for the others to catch up?"

She slowed, watching him over her shoulder as she did so. He seemed to mean it. When she came to a halt, she put her hands on her hips and looked around.

They were standing in a corridor no different from any other in the outer levels of the station. There was no indication of any sinister activity: no strange noises, smells, or sights.

<Well, we're here, Box. Can *you* see anything?>

<Not as yet. There are doors ahead. Maybe through one of those.>

<Maybe.> Swinging her legs as though to flex her mus-

cles, she strolled ahead until she was in front of the first door. It was open. Through it she saw an unoccupied terminal, complete with palm-link, against the opposite wall.

<Tempting,> she said.

DON'T, Haid sent. YOU'RE PUSHING YOUR LUCK AS IT IS.

She turned, saw Haid and Synnett at the end of the corridor. She folded her arms and waited for them to catch up. Disisto stood next to her, a distant look in his eyes suggesting he was communicating with someone via his implants.

<What's he going to do, arrest me?> she asked Haid. <He's not even armed. And besides, we have something he wants: a way out of here.>

IT ISN'T DISISTO WE SHOULD BE WORRIED ABOUT.

Movement to her left caught her attention. Turning back to the room containing the terminal, Roche realized it was occupied. As she watched, a large figure moved slowly into view, obviously heading for the desk. Although clad from boots to gloves in a dark-colored uniform made of some exotic leather, it was clear from the woman's exposed scalp that she was a Kesh. In one hand she carried a steaming goblet of something that smelled very much like *vukh.*

When the Kesh noticed Roche watching her, she snarled and shut the door.

"You certainly have an eclectic crew," she commented to Disisto.

"This is an accommodation area reserved for some of the more sensitive members, which is why we shouldn't be here at all. But we have the okay from the chief to proceed." His voice was relaxed, but his eyes scolded her. "I know you're curious, Commander, but you need to be more considerate."

"Careful, you mean?"

"That too." Haid and Synnett reached them, and Disisto indicated the corridor ahead of them. "Shall we keep going? At a more leisurely pace, this time."

The walk to the main docking bay revealed little. Doors that were open only revealed empty rooms, and Roche was unable to gain access to a palm-link. By the time she reached the scutter, she had decided that entering the black spot had given her a moral victory only.

<He may have been telling the truth,> she said from within the scutter, while pretending to obtain the data she required. <It could just be an accommodation area for crew members who prefer the quiet of the shell to the Hub.>

<It is certainly possible,> said the Box. <But we have no proof either way.>

She left the scutter and joined the others. "Where to now?" she asked Disisto.

"Back to the dry dock?" he suggested.

"Actually, the walk has left me thirsty. How about a drink? You must have a recreation deck here. I'll buy you one, if they accept COE credit."

Disisto studied her for a long moment, then said: "Okay, if that's what you want."

Roche was unable to read his expression. "When Rufo and Lieutenant Gold have finished, we can join them then."

Disisto nodded as he began to walk. "The main bar is back in the Hub."

Roche followed, no longer trying to provoke him. There was very little else she could do until they reached the bar. After the disappointment of the one black spot they had entered, she didn't see any point in trying to access others. There were too many, to begin with, and Disisto would undoubtedly put a stop to it before long.

The bar was deep in the heart of Galine Four, occupying a large space between protein vats and the plant-filled central chamber. It consisted of three rooms connected to a central chamber by wide accessways. In each of the three rooms there was a semicircular bar and numerous tables. The lighting was dim, as befitted a bar, and the sound of voices and glasses clinking along with occasional spurts of

Roptio ur-music added to the ambience. The central area comprised a quarter-size dueling field, surrounded by seats.

A fight was in progress as they entered. The supporters of each combatant had clustered in groups to watch the hologram, cheering and jeering in equal measure.

Roche hooked a thumb at the scene. "A recording, I presume?"

"Must be something they pulled out of the archives," said Disisto, "because we haven't received any transmissions from outside the system for ages. Anything to keep the hardcore fans happy."

Roche glanced at Haid, caught him staring at the game in curiosity. "Ameidio?"

He turned to her. "Sorry. I wasn't paying attention."

She smiled. Haid had been confined to a penal planet for more years than he cared to remember. Dueling was a pleasure he had missed, and he had spent several days catching up on it upon finding freedom aboard the *Ana Vereine*. Even now, he obviously felt its call.

"What do you want to drink?" she asked.

Haid shrugged. "Anything that's not too strong."

"Disisto? Synnett?"

"We're on duty," Disisto said. He nodded to a doorway beyond the dueling field. "We can order through there."

He led them past the fight and into one of the side rooms where it was quieter and less crowded. A number of patrons were Exotic, and clearly appreciated the space. They found a table and sat: Haid and Roche on one side, with Disisto and Synnett facing them.

There was an awkward silence.

"So," ventured Roche, "how *do* I order?"

"There's a palm-link on your chair, if you want to use that. Otherwise, I can call an attendant."

"The link will be fine." She found the pad on the arm of her chair and placed her hand upon it.

<Do your stuff, Box,> she said. <Fake a COE credit ac-

count for me and, while you're at it, order a Montaban ale and three Dahish.>

<Certainly, Morgan.>

<How's the meeting going, by the way?>

<Smoothly, although there still has been no mention of the Sol Apotheosis Movement or *Daybreak.* It seems Linegar Rufo is less susceptible to an attractive woman than I had hoped.>

<Despite what you might think, Box, not all Humans are slaves to their biology. Nevertheless, keep working on . . . Oh, hell.>

She had spied someone crossing the room toward her.

"Morgan!" called Myer Mavalhin. "Fancy meeting you down here. I thought you'd be up with the big shots for sure."

Roche stood. "Hello, Myer."

Disisto glanced behind him. "Mavalhin?"

Mavalhin's step faltered upon seeing the dock security head. "Oh, it's you."

"What the hell are you doing here, Myer? I'll be having words with the ingress team about letting you out of decon so early."

"Hey, don't go too hard on them," the pilot protested. "It wasn't *their* fault."

"Then I'll be talking to *you* instead."

"In that case, it was *entirely* their fault." He winked at Roche. "But seeing as I'm here, I might as well stay, right?"

"Don't look at me, Myer," said Roche. "I'm only a guest."

Disisto shook his head and sighed. "Just remember you're on probation, all right?"

Mavalhin pulled up a chair and sat. "So, what're we drinking?"

Roche hid a smile. Nothing had changed. "I'll get this round," she said, "but after that you're on your own."

Myer smiled appreciatively. "I'll have a snifter of Old Gray."

Roche relayed the order to the Box just as an attendant

arrived with her first order. Haid nodded approval at the long-stemmed glass containing a murky brown mixture, and Roche raised her own colorless drink to her lips and toasted Disisto. Synnett drank without acknowledging anyone.

Sipping the cool, clear liquid made Roche realize just how thirsty the meeting and the walk had left her. She swallowed gratefully, then sipped again.

"It's a long way from Bodh Gaya," she said to Mavalhin after a third sip.

"But here we are," he said. "I heard you stayed with COE in the end. Looks like you've done all right with them."

She was careful to hide her true feelings. "I can't complain. It does get boring at times, but I prefer the security of a regular job. And it's not that restrictive. I spent a few years in Intelligence before transferring to active command. It's been fun, mostly." She did her best to maintain an air of self-composure and confidence. "You?"

He lifted his shoulders slightly. "Tried the Eckandar Trade Axis for a while, then a private freight company out past Tretamen. The bottom went out of the market and the company folded, and that left me in the lurch. I worked as a freelance courier for a few years, before finally signing on with Galine Four."

Disisto snorted. "Courier, eh? I heard you were on the run from Olmahoi creditors and needed cash to avoid gray-boot retribution."

Mavalhin gestured dismissively. "Exaggeration and rumor. Yes, money was short, but it never got *that* bad."

Roche could tell by the tightness around his eyes that it probably *had* been that bad. Rufo would have been able to purchase his services at a bargain price. Regardless of his personal flaws, Mavalhin's credentials would have been impressive; few people left the COE College so close to finishing, and their services were desired in many quarters of the region.

"So what is it you do here, anyway?" she asked.

Mavalhin opened his mouth to reply, but caught Disisto's

reproving look. He stopped, smiled, and said: "I'm just a pilot, Morgan. Nothing spectacular. I gave up on the dream of making something of myself. There's a place for everyone, I've learned, and I guess this is mine."

"That doesn't sound like the Myer I once knew."

"Well, I've changed, I guess."

Roche laughed. "Now that *really* doesn't sound like you!"

He fixed her with a disarming smile that lasted almost ten seconds. "Everyone changes, Morgan. You should try it sometime."

Roche smiled, but the accusation made her feel uncomfortable. "You'd be surprised, Myer," she said after a while.

"Really?" He beamed. "Go ahead, then. Surprise me."

An attendant brought his drink, and with it a welcome interruption in the conversation. Roche was even more thankful when the Box intruded before they could resume their talk:

<Morgan, I'm afraid that link at your present location is as isolated as the rest. We will need to gain physical access to other black spots in order to determine what is occurring within them—or try to locate an access point to the inner security shell.>

Roche fought to contain a rising sense of frustration. <We've already tried that, and Disisto didn't give me the chance—>

<I have a plan,> said the Box. <The *Ana Vereine* contains a variety of covert surveillance devices designed to infiltrate an enemy vessel. Some of them are microscopic in size and self-replicating; a small amount placed at any location in Galine Four would quickly spread to cover the black spots. I could even reprogram a pseudospecies to allow me terminal access.>

"Morgan?" It was Mavalhin.

She quickly raised a hand to silence him, then closed her eyes, shutting out her immediate surroundings so she could concentrate on what the AI was saying. <That's just fine,

Box, but they're on the *Ana Vereine*. How are you going to get them here?>

<Quite simply, and without raising suspicion. Rufo has repeated his offer to treat any ailing reaves we might have on board. All we have to do is agree, send Maii with a packet of surveillance bugs on her person, then instruct her to release them at the first possible moment. Or the bugs could be suspended in the atmosphere of the scutter itself. They would disperse through the air conditioning system when the atmospheres merge.>

Roche thought about it for a long moment. <I don't like the idea of putting Maii at risk.>

<We could send Cane with her. He would be a more than adequate bodyguard.>

<True.> That would leave the *Ana Vereine* empty except for Kajic and the Box, but she kept that concern to herself. <They don't know anything about Cane, so he could pass as an ordinary crew member. Is there no alternative you can think of?>

<None, apart from firing a swarm of bugs at the hull of Galine Four and hoping some sneak through its anti-meteor shields. The odds are against more than a few managing to get inside.> The Box paused before continuing: <Of course, there *is* the possibility that everything is exactly at it seems—that we can trust Rufo implicitly in everything he says. The high security might be standard for Galine Four and the other discrepancies we have noted nothing more than unfortunate coincidences.>

<You've talked with him longer than I have. What do *you* think?>

<I am not totally convinced,> the AI said. <But that doesn't mean that *you* have to—>

<Okay, okay.> Roche opened her eyes and reached for her glass. <We have to know what's going on here, and if this is the only way to find out . . .>

<It is.>

She took a deep draft of her drink. <Then you have my approval to proceed with this plan, Box.>

<Understood. I have notified the main dock that the scutter will be disengaging in five minutes. Prior to its departure, I will finalize the details with Rufo. I will bring the *Ana Vereine* closer to minimize transfer time. If there are any changes, I will let you know.>

<How long do you think?>

<Thirty minutes. Cane assures me he will be ready to disembark in ten minutes.>

<Good. Tell him to be careful—and, if you can, make sure he's wired somehow. I don't like the idea of being out of touch with them.>

<Regardless of what happens, the bugs themselves will enable us to keep an eye on them.>

<Okay, Box. Keep in touch.>

She put the glass down on the table. Mavalhin was watching her curiously.

"I'm sorry about that," she said. "Just some business that needed attending to."

He smiled crookedly but said nothing.

"No rest for the wicked, eh?" said Disisto. Before she could say anything, he raised a hand to his ear, his head tilted as though straining to hear something above the general noise of the room. "Your scutter has requested permission to disengage," he said to her. "It's leaving without you?"

"Temporarily," she explained. "I've decided to take you up on your offer; you see, we *do* have a reave on board, and she needs help."

"So you've decided to trust us now?"

"Decided we have no choice," said Roche. "She needs the treatment."

Disisto nodded. "I understand," he said. "Is everything else in order?"

"It seems to be," she said. "For the moment, at least." Again she sensed something in his stare that belied the calmness of his face, but she could do no more than wonder about it. "Anyway, what were we talking about?"

"About how much you've changed," said Mavalhin with a smugness that irritated Roche.

"Shut up, Myer," she said.

"What?" He laughed. "I didn't say anything!"

"I don't have to prove anything to you," she said. "So let's just change the subject, shall we?" She picked up her glass and sat back, looking over to Disisto. "Let's talk about *Daybreak* instead."

It was Disisto's turn to smile. "You spotted it, then?"

"I'm not blind," she said. "Where did you find it?"

"It drifted in from the outer system five days ago. One of our scouts discovered it and hauled it here once he was sure there was no one aboard."

"And that scout was you, Myer?" she said.

Mavalhin grinned. "Sorry, Morgan. Can't help you there. I was over Aro Spaceport at the time."

She shrugged. It had been worth a try; Mavalhin would have been much easier to pump information from than the security officer. "*Was* there no one aboard, then, Disisto?"

"Apart from the bodies stacked in the hold, no, there wasn't. The pilot had abandoned the vessel long before we found it."

"That would be before he attacked Guhr Outpost in the tug, right?" put in Haid.

"I guess so," Disisto said. "Once he had no use for *Daybreak,* he must have discarded it."

"That surprises me," Haid went on. "In every other instance he's used the vessel he had just vacated to act as a distraction. But not this time. It would have been more sensible to destroy it. Any guesses why not?"

Disisto opened his hands in apology. "That's something you'd have to ask the chief. I'm not privy to all the information we've uncovered."

"The fact that he didn't bring it up makes me even more curious," said Roche.

"I'm sure it does." Disisto's smile hadn't faded; if anything, it had grown wider. Roche received the distinct impression that he was enjoying her attempts to probe the station's veil of secrecy.

"She's always been like this," said Mavalhin, leaning forward to put his empty glass on the table. "A troublemaker, too. Did you know that she hacked into the College Head's private datacore to reprogram his secretary AI? For a week, it would speak only in an obscure Mbatan dialect Morgan had unearthed in an archive. Because only a dozen or so people on the other side of the Commonwealth could speak that language, it was a whole day before the Head could get any sense out of it. It brought the Academy to a halt—and all so she could miss a Tactics exam she hadn't prepared for."

"Hey, that's a lie!" Roche protested with mock indignation. "*You* were the one with the exam! I did it so you could get out of taking it."

"Ah yes, that's right," he said. "You would've done anything for me back in those days, wouldn't you?"

Roche conceded a wry smile and shook her head. "I'd forgotten what you can be like, Myer," she said. Oddly enough, she enjoyed the banter almost as much as it annoyed her—which was a fair summary of her feelings for him, now *and* then. "But you won't catch me off guard again, that I promise you."

"That sounds like a challenge."

"You can take it any way you like."

"Accepted, then. Where shall we start?"

Somehow he drew her into a one-on-one conversation, against her better instincts. While Haid and Disisto listened, occasionally talking to each other or interjecting with observations, she and Mavalhin sparred as smoothly as they had years before. It amazed her how easily the old ways returned: she had never met anybody since him who knew just how to antagonize her. The reverse was also true. Despite the fact that they had both experienced much since they had last met, the mental processes that dictated the flow of conversation remained unchanged.

"Look, I'm sorry to have to break this up," Disisto eventually said, "but if you want to meet the scutter, we should start heading down to the docking bay."

Roche was surprised. "So soon?"

"Well, it's a bit of a walk there," said Disisto. "Besides which, we have to drop Myer off so he can finish his debriefing decon."

"Oh, come on, Disisto!" said Mavalhin.

But Disisto and Synnett were already standing, the latter tugging Mavalhin to his feet. Haid finished the contents of his glass and stood; Roche did likewise.

"Changed man, eh, Myer?" Roche scoffed.

The pilot ignored her.

On the way past the dueling field, Haid nudged her with one angular elbow and indicated the hologram with a nod. Roche looked, and had a quick glimpse of armored, robotic figures toiling with ferocious weapons on an open playing field. Nothing looked out of place.

<What?>

I THOUGHT I RECOGNIZED THE GAME AS WE CAME IN, he sent. IT'S A REPEAT OF THE GRUDGE MATCH BETWEEN ALEMDAR QUICK AND THE PREVIOUS CHAMPION, VOID 34.

<So?>

THE GAME WAS PUT ON IDNET SIX DAYS AGO. BUT PALASIAN SYSTEM WAS ENCLOSED *TWENTY* DAYS AGO. THERE'S NO WAY THEY COULD'VE RECEIVED THIS GAME FROM IN HERE.

Roche stopped to look at the game with renewed interest, but Synnett urged them forward irritably.

<Are you sure?>

POSITIVE. I WATCHED IT IN THE REHAB UNIT WHEN MY IMPLANTS WERE INSTALLED.

She thought it through carefully, while following Disisto and Mavalhin out of the bar. <That means they've had at

least one communication with someone outside. But how? I didn't think anything could cross the Gauntlet.>

<Nothing but a ship,> said the Box. <Or a drone designed to carry information.>

<A message drop? From whom?>

THAT'S THE PRIZE-WINNING QUESTION, ISN'T IT?

She frowned. <There's something really odd going on here—and the sooner we get Maii up and running again, the better. How long until she's here, Box?>

<The scutter has been cleared to dock and is moving into position. Should be only a few minutes at most.>

Disisto, ahead of Roche, halted at the entrance to a transit corridor.

<Good. We shouldn't be far behind,> said Roche. <By the way, I don't suppose you've run a search on Shak'ni? He seems an odd choice for head of security of a Pristine-run station.>

<No, Morgan, I have not. The only high-level security files from the Kesh governments I have access to are those gathered by COE Intelligence and the Dato Espionage Corps. But I can try if you'd like me to.>

<Do it. You never know what you might find.> She waited for confirmation from the AI. Technically it wasn't required to respond to every order she gave it, but it usually did, if only to have the last word. After a moment of silence, she said: <Box?>

Again, no response. Then:

<Morgan?> The Box sounded concerned.

<I hear you, Box.>

<The scutter has docked and an umbilical is being attached. Cane and Maii are preparing to disembark. Please respond, Morgan.>

Roche felt a terrible dread radiate from her gut.

<Ameidio, we're being jammed. It's a trap!>

Haid didn't respond either, but his worried eyes met hers just as the transit cab door opened to reveal Shak'ni glaring down at them. Another Kesh stood there also, along with three Pristines in gray security uniforms. All were armed, and their weapons were pointed at Roche.

"The reave and the clone warrior have disembarked," Shak'ni said to Disisto. "This charade can end now."

4

Galine Four
'955.01.20 EN
1575

Roche reached automatically for her side arm, only to encounter the hand of Synnett standing behind her. The silent security guard wrenched the weapon from its holster before she could even touch it. At the same time, the other security guards pointed their weapons at Haid. The Kesh standing behind him disarmed him before he could resist.

"What's the meaning of this?" Roche said, trying hard to keep her voice level. She aimed her words at Disisto, but he wouldn't look at her.

Field Officer Shak'ni stepped into the ring of security guards facing them.

"Morgan Roche and Ameidio Haid," he said with barely concealed satisfaction, "you are jointly charged with violating restricted space in contravention of quarantine laws. You are also charged with conspiring to compromise the safety of the region, including the N'Kor Republic. This charge is punishable by death, and any attempt to resist arrest will be seen as an admission of guilt and *will* result in your immediate execution."

"You can't be serious," Roche managed.

He stooped to thrust his face into hers. "We are, Commander," he said, the red markings under his eyes inflamed with repressed anger. "By the time we arrive at the docking bay, the creature you call Adoni Cane will be firmly under our control. We will not make the same mistake as those who have already died in this system—the mistake of underestimating his capabilities, or his destructive potential."

Clone warrior, Shak'ni had said. She groaned inwardly. They had known all along who Cane was.

"This is crazy," said Haid. "We should be working together, not—"

"Quiet, cyborg!" Shak'ni rounded on him. "Pristines are bad enough. Their puny attempts to improve themselves only fill me with disgust."

Haid's biomesh rippled, and one skeletal hand lashed out to strike the Kesh. Before the blow could fall, however, the guard behind him rammed the butt of a gun into his back.

Haid's hand withdrew, but he kept his eyes locked on Shak'ni's.

Mavalhin edged closer to the door, visibly distressed at the turn of events.

<Morgan?> called the Box. <Morgan, I've managed to raise a weak signal from your implants. I know now that you are still alive and can probably hear me. Don't do anything rash. I will assist you in a few moments.>

<Box!> She raised the output of her built-in transmitter to its maximum level. <What's happening to Cane and Maii? Tell me!>

Shak'ni faced Roche with a slight sneer creasing one corner of his mouth. "There is no use calling for help, Commander. We are safe from your meddling AI in here."

"I don't *understand.*" Frustration and the smell of the Kesh made her voice shrill. "How do you *know* all this?"

"That is not your concern. It suffices that we know how you attempted to deceive us."

"Don't be a hypocrite, Shak'ni," Roche snapped. "What you've done is no different—"

"What *we* did, we did in the interest of security. We gave you enough opportunities to reveal the truth, and your failure to do so demonstrated the maliciousness of your intentions." Shak'ni's features tightened into a mask. "Were you lucky enough to have been born a Kesh, you would be dead already."

From the corner Roche could make out Mavalhin staring at her. Even without returning his stare she could tell that he was nervous. And understandably so; he was just an innocent bystander caught up in what could easily become a major diplomatic incident. In fact, she sympathized.

Then:

<Morgan,> said the Box. <I still cannot receive detailed information from your implants, but I can download to them. I have prepared an indirect link which will bring us into contact via Galine Four's external security shell—to which I still have complete access. All you have to do is locate a data-input point, and I will be able to locate you.>

Easier said than done, Roche thought. She looked around, trying to find a palm-link. The only visible one lay on the far side of the cab, adjacent to the pad used to key destinations manually. It was only two meters from her, but Disisto stood in the way.

The cab shuddered beneath her feet as it neared the outer shell of the station.

A thought struck her. There *was* another link in the cab; all she had to do was gain access to it . . .

Haid swayed as the cab crossed another boundary mismatch. She reached out to steady him, ignoring the jab the guard behind her delivered to her shoulder blades.

"His balance is poor," she said, gripping Haid's shoulder tightly.

"It's true," Disisto said evenly. "Let her be."

The guard behind her relaxed slightly, and Roche dug her fingers into Haid's biomesh, pulling him minutely toward her. Their eyes met. Although it was impossible through his artificial lenses, she thought she saw a look of understanding pass through them.

The cab reached the point at which he had stumbled the first time they had made this journey, earlier. It shuddered right on cue.

Haid's legs gave way beneath him, sending him lurching into Roche. His shoulder along with the weight of his biomods acted as a battering ram, forcing her away from him and across the cab. She grunted, reached out to break her fall, and sprawled untidily at Disisto's feet.

Shak'ni hissed impatiently.

"Sorry," said Haid as he tried to regain his footing. Roche kept her legs carefully out of the way as he did so; the guards also avoided his artificial limbs, wary of a potential trap. He made it onto his hands and knees, and made a great effort of almost standing up before slipping back down onto one knee.

While the guards were busy watching him, Roche reached out to Disisto with her left hand. He reached out with his, to help her upright.

The moment their palm-links met, she triggered her implants and spoke as quickly as she could:

<Box? Box! We're in a transit cab heading to the main docking bay, and I can't hold this link long. You have to do something! Try and provide a distraction so Haid and I—>

<I have you now, Morgan. The cab will arrive in twenty seconds. Be ready.>

The link broke as Disisto let go of her hand. She blinked, realized that she was on her feet again.

"Thanks," she said. "I was a little dizzy there for a moment."

Looking down at his hand, he frowned and shook his head. "So was I," he said. "The weirdest thing . . ."

Haid was also on his feet. She made no move to stand next to him; being together would only make it harder for one of them to break free. The motion of the cab beneath her feet had slowed dramatically; it was already difficult to tell whether it was moving or not.

Be ready, the Box had said. But for what?

The doors opened on an empty corridor. Disisto stepped out first, closely followed by Mavalhin. The pilot looked around him, and backed quickly out of the way.

The guard behind Roche nudged her in the back. She stepped through the doors with her escort close behind. Haid and Synnett came next.

For a brief moment, Roche thought, the numbers were almost manageable. If they were going to break free, their chances were never going to be better.

She tensed. <Come *on,* Box!>

Then, as Shak'ni, the remaining guard, and the Kesh moved to exit the cab, the floor lurched and a sudden gust of wind swept past them.

"We've been holed!" Disisto shouted over the sudden wail of alarms. "The area's being sealed off!"

Roche froze, her space instincts taking over.

Behind her, the doors to the cab slid shut, cutting off Shak'ni's shout of protest.

Before anyone could even contemplate overriding the seal, Roche spun on one leg and knocked aside the pistol of the guard behind her. A second kick knocked the wind out of him and sent him back into the doors of the cab.

Beside her, Haid had Synnett in a wristlock, the narrow fingers and strength of his new arm provoking a hiss of pain. The security officer's weapon discharged a single bolt of energy that earthed harmlessly into the wall. One blow with Haid's free hand made Synnett drop the pistol, and Roche was there to scoop up the weapon and point it at Disisto.

Two side arms faced one for a split-second, until Disisto dropped his to the floor and raised his hands.

"That was fast," he said over the wail of the siren. "I don't know whether to be impressed or annoyed."

"I don't care either way," said Roche, approaching him while Haid covered Mavalhin and the one conscious guard. "Just give me your hand. Your *left* one."

He held it out to her, and she gripped it tightly. Making certain the gun was placed firmly under his chin, she activated her implants again.

<Okay, Box, what the hell have you done?>

The reply was instantaneous: <Fired the scutter's main engines while it was still in the dock, breaching the hull of the station at four points.>

<Are you *insane*?> she gasped.

<No. Merely in a hurry.>

<But you could've killed us all!>

<I was careful to direct the afterwash into the main facility itself, away from your position.>

<But what about Maii and Cane?>

<I made sure they were at a safe distance first.>

<And the scutter itself?>

<It has been severely damaged. The explosion triggered a chain reaction in three of its four fuel cells.>

<How the hell are we going to get out of here now?>

<There was no other option, Morgan. I had to split your party, and this was the only way open to me.>

<In the short term, yes. In the long run, we might as well have handed ourselves over.> Roche thought quickly. <Where are Maii and Cane?>

<In an emergency medical cocoon on the far side of the dock. Cane was gassed and overpowered as soon as he left the scutter. Maii was shot with a Xarodine dart. The surveillance devices were neutralized by microwaves. There was nothing I could do to prevent any of it. We had no reason to suspect that such an ambush was awaiting them.>

The Box sounded defensive, as well it might, Roche thought. She fought the urge to curse her decision to bring Maii to the station; regret was worse than useless.

The siren was getting on her nerves. The sooner they were on the run again, the better. They would have to move as soon as the pressure doors opened around them.

<We could escape in *Daybreak,*> she reasoned. <Can you override the secondary dock?>

<Perhaps. I have not tried that avenue as yet. Also, the link with the courier is sealed to me. I am unaware how badly it has been damaged.>

<We're a little short on alternatives,> Roche snapped back.

<Then I recommend you bring Disisto with you,> the Box went on. <His palm-link gives us access to a deeper level of security than before.>

Roche looked at Disisto's face, twisted in pain from the gun digging into his chin. She hadn't realized she was pressing so hard, but she did nothing to relieve him.

<I'm not leaving without Maii,> she said.

<A rescue attempt at this time would be foolish,> the Box protested. <Quite apart from the fact that both Cane and Maii are unconscious and would need to be carried, they are also being closely guarded. Furthermore, Shak'ni has alerted security that you have escaped detention; you would be recaptured well before—>

<All right,> she snarled, hating herself for seeing the sense in the Box's words. <We leave them behind—*for now.* But as soon as we have a way of getting them back, we do it. And I don't want any arguments about this, Box.>

<There will be none, Morgan. With Disisto's access, we may yet unravel the security net of Galine Four.>

<I hope so, for your sake.>

Disisto flinched as she pulled the gun out from under his chin.

"We're leaving," she said, keeping their palms together.

"But—"

"Don't argue. Just do your best to keep up." She turned to Haid. "You catch all that?"

"Yes," he said. "Give me a moment to tidy up and I'll be ready."

He used his pistol to knock the second guard unconscious, then turned to face Mavalhin. The pilot backed away with hands raised.

"Morgan!" he said "Please—"

"Sorry, Myer, but we don't have time for this."

"But I—I want to come with you!"

Haid hesitated; Roche frowned. *"What?"*

"Well, you'll need to get off the station, right?" Mavalhin's words came out fast. "I can help you do that."

"We already have a ship. *Daybreak* was a COE courier; if it'll fly, I can use my old overrides to assume command."

"Oh, I'm sure it will fly," he said. "But you don't expect to be able to just blast out of the docks in one piece, do you? I mean, how will you disengage?"

"He's just wasting time," muttered Haid, raising his pistol.

"No, wait," said Roche, remembering the Box's uncertainty and the fact that it still did not have high-level access to the station's systems. "What are you suggesting, Myer?"

"That I use my codes to get you away."

"In exchange for . . . ?"

"Passage, that's all. A chance to get out of here."

"Why?"

"It's time to move on, time for a change, and . . ." He hesitated slightly. "And other reasons."

Beside her, Disisto spat on the floor at Mavalhin's feet. The pilot flushed red, but did not respond.

"Don't trust him," Haid said.

"But he does have a point," she replied. "We might need those codes."

"We don't know whether his codes will even work!" said Haid. "Once they know he's with us, they could just change them."

She thought a moment longer, then finally dismissed

Haid's objections with: "Okay, Myer, take us to *Daybreak*. But don't push your luck."

Mavalhin grinned. "Thanks, Morgan. I owe you one for this."

"Just get moving."

Haid indicated the corridor ahead with the pistol, and Mavalhin headed along it, checking once to make sure they were following.

"You're crazy if you think you can get away with this," Disisto said to Roche. "You'll hardly leave the dock before someone fires on you."

"Tell me something," she said. "Are your implants programmed to monitor your well-being?"

"No."

"Then bear in mind that I don't need you alive," she told him. "Now shut up while I concentrate."

His lips whitened. She felt sweat trickle from her left hand, and wished she could let go of him, if only for a moment.

Within seconds they reached a sealed blast-door. It slid open as they approached, before she could wonder how they were going to get through it, and closed behind them.

<I am in the system that far,> said the Box. <I can ensure that the way ahead is clear, and that no one will sneak up on you from behind. The secondary dock itself is occupied, however, and you will have to deal with that in order to gain access to the ship.>

<Give me a view of the dock.> Instantly, an overhead perspective appeared in her left eye, revealing two technicians and three security guards standing in a spacious control room.

<What's that in the background?> she asked the Box. <The airlock?>

<*Daybreak* is connected by an umbilical to the dock. There is only room for one vessel at a time, and there are facilities for just one connection. The airlock leads directly to the umbilical.>

<Is it open?>

<No. It is locked.>

<Open it, if you can. Do you have the right codes?>

<Disisto has a priority access code, but to use it now would only forewarn them that you are coming.>

Roche nodded. <How about communications between the dock and the rest of Galine Four? Can you interrupt them?>

<Yes, although they already know that you are at liberty aboard the station.>

<Then we'll have to play it carefully.> She paused as another pressure door slid aside. The map the Box had given her indicated two more doors between them and the secondary dock. <If Shak'ni guesses where we're headed and manages to get a squad in before us, we'll be cut off.>

<That won't happen. I will self-destruct what remains of the scutter and create another hull breach if necessary. Decompression takes precedence over security problems; not even Shak'ni can change that.>

<At least they've got their priorities in order.> Roche smiled grimly, and thought about Maii and Cane, captives of Rufo. <I only wish I could say the same about us. . . .>

The secondary dock lay five meters past the final pressure door. As they passed through it, Roche tightened her grip on Disisto's hand.

"You so much as raise an eyebrow without my say-so," she said, "and I *will* shoot you. Okay?"

Disisto grimaced slightly. "I never doubted for a moment that you would, Commander."

"Good." She waved Mavalhin and Haid ahead of her. "We need to whittle their numbers down. Myer, I want you to go first and tell them you've come to get help from the main dock. The Box will kill communications, so they won't be able to check. Tell them a fire's responsible. Reinforcements have been cut off, and all hands are needed to help put it out."

"And if they don't believe me?"

"They can't afford not to. A fire in the main dock will spread quickly, regardless of pressure doors."

He nodded at Haid. "Where will he be?"

She pointed at a corner past the entrance to the dock. "But I'll be watching, Myer, so don't even think of trying anything."

He grinned uneasily. "As trusting as ever, I see."

Roche pulled Disisto around the corner, with Haid not far behind. <Okay, Box. Kill communications, and get ready to open that airlock.>

<At your command.>

From her overhead perspective of the dock, Roche watched as Mavalhin hurried into the control room. She couldn't hear much of what was being said, but Mavalhin's animated behavior along with the responsive body language from the guards themselves gave her an idea of what was happening. Two of the five personnel seemed skeptical, but the others appeared to accept his story. After a few moments two of the security guards, along with one of the technicians, followed Mavalhin out of the room, moving up the hallway toward the open pressure door. The guards and technician stepped through the door a second before Mavalhin, but instead of following, he jumped back.

The door slid shut, cutting them off.

Roche tugged her prisoner out of hiding. "Okay. We go in. Haid, you first, then Myer. I'll be right behind you."

The remaining security guard looked up as soon as Haid ran into the room, and in a moment his pistol was up and firing. Haid rolled behind a desk, out of harm's way, but Mavalhin caught a bolt in the shoulder that sent him flying, screaming in pain.

Roche rounded the door at the same instant, dragging Disisto with her. Her opening fire caught the guard in the chest. He collapsed back into a chair, his gun still firing. The weapon discharged noisily into the ceiling six more times before his trigger finger fell slack.

The lone technician backed away with his hands raised and a look of terror on his face.

Haid appeared from behind the desk. "Thanks, Morgan. Guess my reflexes are still a little rusty."

"Don't mention it," she muttered, keeping an eye on the technician and Disisto, while at the same time trying to determine exactly how seriously Mavalhin had been hurt.

<Box, open the airlock.>

The door slid open with a hiss, revealing a standard umbilical corridor on the far side.

<Can you seal the entrance in here?> she asked.

<I can do my best.>

<Let's hope it's enough.> She waved her pistol at the technician, gesturing for him to lie facedown on the floor. "Haid, knock him out."

Next Roche checked on Mavalhin. The pilot had been shot in the left shoulder. Blood leaked from between his fingers where he clutched the wound. She forced him to let go, and pulled the charred edges of the hole in his uniform aside.

The wound was deep but cauterized enough to keep blood loss to a minimum, otherwise he would already be slipping into shock. His eyes, when they met hers, were full of panic.

"Glad you came with us, huh?" Her smile was intended to allay his obvious fear. Despite his pain, he managed a half-smile in return. Roche stood, wiping her hands on her black uniform. "When Haid's ready, we'll board *Daybreak* and be on our way. Once we're out of here, we'll see what medical facilities we have and patch you up, okay?"

He nodded and struggled to his feet. Disisto followed obediently as Roche guided the pilot to the umbilical.

"I'm done," said Haid, stepping over the technician.

"Right. Through here." She prodded Disisto to go ahead of her. <Box, once we're in, seal the airlock.>

<Yes, Morgan.>

The umbilical was only half as long as the ones at the main dock. At the far end, the courier's airlock was sealed shut. Roche let go of Disisto for a moment, and placed her palm-link against it, hoping that she remembered the emergency COE codes well enough to fool the onboard AI.

After a moment of rapid dialogue, the airlock hissed and slid open. Taking hold of Disisto again, she entered the courier vessel.

Daybreak was little different from the many small cruisers she had flown in her years with COE Intelligence. It had room for a crew of eight and forty-two passengers, plus a small cargo hold at the rear. The bridge—cramped to Roche after her time on the *Ana Vereine*—was at the rounded nose of the craft and held crash-seats for five. The interior was dimly lit and purely functional. A standby screen glowed at the pilot's station, but otherwise the controls were dead.

Haid helped Mavalhin into an empty couch and strapped the brace tight, ignoring the wince of pain it provoked. Roche put Disisto into the copilot's position and lashed his hand to the palm-link. Sitting next to him, she opened her own link to the vessel's command systems, and thereby back to the Box. The craft accepted her COE overrides without complaint.

<Was Myer telling the truth?> she asked. <Will it fly?>

<All systems are green—except for the slow-jump drive, which is dead, and weapons systems, which are nonexistent. I am initiating a start-up sequence which will have the ship flight-ready in six minutes.>

The main screen showed a forward view of the dock, past the dry dock and a section of the outer shell. Lights began to flicker on the consoles. Roche tried to follow them, but the Box worked too rapidly.

Within seconds the reactor began supplying power to the main thrusters, preparing them for rapid burn, and as it did, Roche was touched by a sense of déjà vu.

The situation reminded her of the time she and Cane had escaped from the *Midnight* with Maii and Veden captive. Then, as now, the Box had been in control of the craft—and much more besides, it had turned out.

<This time,> she warned the AI, <*don't* blow anything up.>

The Box did not respond immediately.

<Box?>

<I'm sorry, Morgan,> it finally said. <The *Ana Vereine* is receiving fire from cannon on Galine Four. We are camouflaged, but are hampered by the necessity to remain nearby in order to assist your launch.>

<You can't destroy the cannon?>

<I am attempting to do so as we speak. However, there are many of them, and I am hesitant to damage the station too much while Cane and Maii are within.>

She checked the countdown on the main display. Only a minute had passed.

<How long can you hold off the attack?>

<Long enough. But you will need to launch with haste.>

<Understood.> She turned in her seat. "Myer, what are those codes? *Myer*?"

The pilot stirred. "What—?"

"The codes! What are they?"

"Oh . . . 16433051: Cold Sleep."

She turned back to the main console and fed the sequence into the main AI. It accepted the code without protest, and relayed the command to the secondary dock. Twenty seconds later, the umbilical disengaged and retracted into its housing.

<Okay, Box. We're clear at this end. As soon as the drives are able, we can leave.> She began preparing the navigation systems for departure, plotting a route from the main dock to a potential rendezvous with the *Ana Vereine*.

<There is one other thing,> the Box said.

She didn't stop working. <I'm listening.>

<I am picking up a broad-band distress signal from the xenoarchaeological base on Mok.>

She stopped. <The double-jovian?>

<Yes.>

<What does it say?>

<The message is very brief, repeated every fifteen seconds. It states only that assistance is urgently required.>

<Does it carry an ID tag?>

<A generic civilian code commonly used by independent mining collectives.>

Outriggers. Roche absorbed the detail with interest. Rufo had suggested that they might be active in the vicinity of the double-jovian.

<I don't have time to deal with this now, Box, but we'll need to check it out as soon as possible. If there *are* other survivors here, they're bound to be more help than Rufo.>

<Agreed.>

The timer showed two minutes remaining before launch.

"This could be rough," she said, directing her words at Haid but intending them for Disisto and Mavalhin as well. Getting out of the dock was only half the problem; if Galine Four was firing on the *Ana Vereine,* it would probably try the same on *Daybreak*—and the courier had neither shields nor weaponry.

An alarm began to *ping* on the main console. She glanced at it, and realized that someone was trying to hail them.

<Dock security is aware of your present location,> said the Box.

<Inevitable, I guess,> she said. <There's nothing they can do, though, is there?>

<The secondary dock is still sealed, and their movements are restricted by pressure doors to—>

"Morgan." Haid's soft voice carried with it a warning that made her look up immediately. He was pointing at the main screen.

Two figures in pressure suits were climbing onto the lip of the dry dock, carrying a swivel-mounted energy weapon between them.

"Damn!" Roche glanced at the clock again. One minute. If the security officers managed to place the weapon in time, they would have a clear shot at *Daybreak* as it passed overhead.

"Maybe we could gain time by answering the hail?" suggested Haid.

Roche shook her head, continuing to ready the ship for launch. "That won't stop *them.*" She nodded toward the two figures. "And I sure as hell don't need the distraction right now."

The thrum of the thrusters grew louder. Normally she would have used attitude jets to move the ship away from the wall of the dock, giving it a less cluttered path and minimizing damage in its wake—but this would forewarn the guards of the ship's imminent departure. Neither did she care how much damage she left behind.

The countdown clicked to single figures just as the gun was mounted.

Roche nudged the ship forward, ignoring the rough trajectory she had plotted and flying purely on manual. Attitude jets turned it slightly to present as small a cross-section to the gun as possible. Behind it, the guards moved into position.

When the counter reached zero, she directed *Daybreak* as fast as it would go straight for the impromptu gun emplacement.

Acceleration pushed her back into the seat, hard. Beside her, Disisto braced himself against the arms of the crash-couch. Mavalhin moaned at the pressure on his injured shoulder.

Light flashed in the main screen, and two muffled cracks pierced the roar of the thrusters. For the briefest of moments the gun loomed large in the main screen as the ship raced toward it, then Roche wrenched the ship to her left, away from the wall. Behind them, the energy-wash from *Daybreak*'s thrusters left a thick black scar on the dry dock. Nothing remained of the two guards.

<The station has launched interceptors from emergency egress bays,> the Box said.

<Singleships?> Roche asked, although she already

guessed the answer. The interceptors couldn't be large to have come from escape-launchers.

<Yes.>

<How many?>

<Fifteen.>

Daybreak cleared the lip of the outer shell, and suddenly all ahead was black: no stars, no navigational clues at all apart from the distant reddish sun. Roche swept the courier in a tight arc away from where the Box's telemetry data indicated the *Ana Vereine* was positioned; predictability in battle was a trap she had learned to avoid.

Two specks of light visible over the piecemeal curve of the station instantly moved toward *Daybreak*. More converged from the far side.

Roche cursed silently to herself as she counted the incoming ships. Half their number alone would have been a problem. The tiny, dartlike craft had none of the brute force of the *Ana Vereine*—were, in fact, less powerful even than *Daybreak*—but they were far more maneuverable. Armed, they could play a significant part in any battle.

In a matter of moments, the singleships reached firing range, and began to pepper the space around the courier with energy. The shots that struck home jolted the ship, provoking more protests from Mavalhin. Roche watched the damage board closely as she flew, but so far nothing crucial had been hit.

<Can't you destroy them?> she asked the Box.

<I will, once I am in position.>

The ship lurched as cannon fire struck it from the rear. Roche grunted and sent it angling away from its previous course, spiraling erratically to reduce the chances of being hit again. Luckily the damage was minor: a sensor or two, a small percentage of hull integrity; nothing life-threatening.

But the cannon fire was intense. It was only a matter of time before she miscalculated—or the targeters behind the cannon had a stroke of luck—and the courier was seriously damaged. If that happened, they would be dead.

Roche had no time to consider attempting to dock with the *Ana Vereine,* or even determining its location. She just kept her attention focused behind them, on the bobbing singleships and flashing cannon emplacements. Behind the flashes of light narrowly missing the courier, Galine Four loomed like a malignant, worm-eaten moon, much too close for comfort and receding only slowly.

Then something dark blotted the station from view. The black shape angled between *Daybreak* and the singleships harassing it, effectively acting as a shield against the cannon fire. From within the blackness came a barrage of retaliatory fire, destroying first one singleship that attempted to pass it, then another.

Not wasting the opportunity, Roche spurred the courier onward, putting all available energy into increasing their velocity away from the station. <Perfect timing, Box!>

<Save some of the credit for me, Morgan.> Roche smiled at the sound of Kajic's voice in her head. <It's a team effort, you know.>

The *Ana Vereine,* camouflaged black, thrust itself into close engagement with Galine Four. Although considerably outsized, it had been designed as a weapon of war, and looked it. Its angular outline was visible through the camouflage like a many-legged shadow blotting out the station's gray. The sheer power of its weaponry outshone that of the dim, red sun, casting the scene in a variety of short-lived colors, each blindingly bright.

<We will cover you as long as we can, Morgan,> said the Box. <I suggest you maximize the distance between yourself and Galine Four while the opportunity exists.>

<Already doing so,> she replied. <What about you?>

<When you are a sufficient distance away, we will disengage. We can outrun any vessel at their disposal, and will use the camouflage to its maximum advantage.>

<Are you taking much damage, Uri?>

<Medium to light,> Kajic replied. <We can last a few minutes longer before it becomes a problem.>

<Are you sure? I don't want you to do anything too dangerous.>

<I won't, I assure you. Remember, I'm the one getting hurt here. If I was going to risk serious damage, it would have to be for something a bit more noble than just letting you escape.>

<I suggest you continue along your current trajectory,> said the Box. <We will hold here as long as possible, then flee in another direction. I have already sent drones to disrupt your afterwash. That way, they will be unable to follow you—assuming, of course, they do not detect your drive emissions directly.>

<I'll feather the wash as soon as you leave,> she said. <That'll reduce the chances of them spotting us. But what about communications? Even on tightbeam, there's a chance they'll overhear.>

<A good point, Morgan. I suggest we maintain radio silence for three hours, just to be certain.>

<Agreed. Unless there's an emergency, I'll speak to you then.> She took one last look at the *Ana Vereine*. <Take care of yourselves.>

<We will, Morgan.> Kajic's voice sounded alive with the thrill of battle. <Speak to you in three hours.>

The line went dead, and Roche returned her attention to slipping away from the station.

Only after Galine Four become barely a blip on the courier's rear scanner screen did Roche finally feel safe enough to let *Daybreak* fly itself. Programming it to follow a course through the relative cover of Autoville—where, this far out in the system, a solid body every million kilometers constituted a crowded environment—she unlocked her harness and stepped out of the crash-couch.

She stopped beside Disisto. "I'm locking the ship to my implants," she told him. "You so much as touch those controls and I'll know about it. Understand?"

The security officer nodded slowly. "Given my situation, I'm hardly going to take any risks."

She held his stare for a few seconds before moving off to check on Mavalhin. The pilot was unconscious in his seat, blood spreading across his uniform from the wound in his shoulder. When she unlocked his harness, her fingers came away sticky.

"He's in a bad way," said Haid, leaning from the other side of the couch to help her lift him out of it.

"If there's an autosurgeon aboard, we might be able to help him." She gritted her teeth as they swung him upright. He was heavier than he looked. "The corridor we passed on the way in—the surgery should be along there."

Together they manhandled him to the courier's small medical facility. There, they laid him on a plastic stretcher and positioned the autosurgeon over him. The machine came to life with a slight humming sound as it began to take X-rays and ultrasound images of the wound.

Roche took a step back, turning her attention from Mavalhin to Haid. She noticed her friend's distraction as he quietly surveyed the room.

"What's up?"

"Huh?" His gaze came back to her. "Oh," he said, "I was just thinking. It's kind of weird to realize that the clone warrior was actually here, in this ship, only a few days ago."

"I know what you mean." She nodded at the stretcher where Mavalhin lay. "This might have been the very place they revived him when they removed him from the life-support capsule."

"Do you think he's left the system?"

"I don't know what to think." She folded her arms and leaned against a waste-disposal unit. "I just don't know how far we can trust the information Rufo gave us."

"Well, most of it made sense," said Haid. "At least, it fit what we've already learned."

"*Most* of it, yes. But I can't shake the feeling that he left the most important bits out."

The humming from the autosurgeon faded as it finished its examination. Roche read the diagnosis from the small screen: Mavalhin had a shattered collarbone and punctured left lung, and had lost a dangerous amount of blood. The recommendation was for surgery to correct the gross injuries, and a week's recuperation to reach full health and mobility.

Roche instructed it to begin the operation, and immediately surgical lasers flashed, cutting away the remains of the pilot's bloodstained and burnt uniform. She told the autosurgeon to notify her when the procedure was finished; then, with a pat on the back and a gesture toward the door, she ushered Haid out of the room.

"Rufo didn't mention that Galine Four had moved shortly before we rendezvoused with it," she said as they headed back to the bridge. "He also didn't mention that he'd had contact with someone outside Palasian System within the last week. And he definitely gave us no reason to suspect that he knew who we were, or that he knew about the Sol Apotheosis Movement."

"We should've guessed the last bit sooner," Haid said. "He did say he was an expert on history. He could hardly have missed the Wunderkind."

"I know." She felt bad about that, but there was nothing she could do to change the past. "He was also reticent in other areas, like the transmissions we picked up coming here. If Myer was near Jagabis when the Sol code was sent, you'd think he would have traced its source."

"Maybe he did." Haid shrugged. "Maybe that's why he was heading out of there when we ran into him."

"Well, we'll find out when he's awake, I guess."

Haid paused before speaking, his artificial eyes and midnight-black features unreadable. "I still don't trust him, Morgan," he eventually said.

"Neither do I, but he *did* help us back there."

"He helped himself."

"Perhaps. But it amounted to the same thing."

"This time."

Back on the bridge, Disisto sat in resigned silence.

"How is he?" he asked, looking up.

Roche leaned against the main console to face him. "You almost sound like you care."

Disisto looked offended. "Because we're on opposite sides, I can't be concerned? You have a monopoly on these emotions, Commander?"

"Not at all," she said. "Just wouldn't have thought it was a required trait for someone working under Shak'ni, that's all. I mean, he doesn't strike me as someone who cares about others terribly much."

Disisto's face clouded. "We agree there, at least."

"What does *that* mean?"

Disisto said nothing, but didn't look away from her.

"Listen," she said, "I don't know what you think we are, or what you think we've done, or even what you think we *will* do, but I can assure you that you're wrong about us. I'm not your enemy, and I don't regard you as mine. It's the clone warrior we should be worrying about, not each other. If he's still out there, none of us are safe, and fighting each other will only make the situation worse."

"Or perhaps he thinks we're working *with* the Sol Wunderkind?" Haid's words were to Roche, but his gaze was fixed firmly upon the security officer.

Disisto's expression was defiant. "That's what we were told," he said. "We were warned to expect another one—another clone warrior—and that he would be coming with an ex-COE commander called Morgan Roche in a ship stolen from the Dato Bloc."

Roche frowned. "Who told you that?"

"The chief, of course."

"And how do you know he was telling the truth?"

"Why would he lie?"

Disisto's blind acceptance of what he had been told exasperated Roche. "Did it ever occur to you to ask *how* he knew?"

"Why? He was right, wasn't he?"

Roche shook her head. "So no matter what we told you, you wouldn't have believed us?"

"There's no reason why I should." His eyes dropped away from Roche's. "No matter how much I might want to."

"What?" She leaned in closer now. "What is it you're hinting at? Why not just come out and say what you want to say?"

"I can't." The words were so soft, they could have been mistaken for a sigh. "Rufo has treated me well in the five years I've worked for him. I can't betray him now."

Roche glanced at Haid, who lifted one artificial shoulder in a tiny shrug.

"Okay." Roche stepped back, slipping her hands into the pockets of the shipsuit. "So you don't want to betray Rufo's confidence, but he's clearly doing something you disapprove of. Or—" She stopped as a thought struck her. "Or *allowing* something to happen?"

He said nothing, but the muscles in his neck tightened.

"That's it, isn't it? Shak'ni and B'shan are up to something, and you don't like it."

He looked at her again. "Not Haden B'shan. He's been with the chief longer than I have."

"Shak'ni, then. That doesn't surprise me. So tell us what he's doing, and perhaps we can stop him."

When Disisto didn't respond, anger surged from deep within Roche's frustration. "Dammit, Disisto, *talk* to me! I've got better things to do than play guessing games with you!"

"Why the hell should I trust you?" he said, throwing her anger back at her. "I've been told that you're dangerous, and *nothing* I've seen contradicts that! You don't even try to deny what's been said about you! The fact is, I don't even know who you are." He paused for a moment, leaning forward slightly and fixing her with a cold stare. "So tell me, Commander, just who *do* you think you are?"

Her hand closed into a fist, but she managed to subdue the impulse to strike him. Her anger had little to do with his attitude. In fact, if anything, she understood his point of view. Who *was* she to demand that he compromise five years of faithful service to Rufo? No, her anger came about from what had happened to Cane and Maii.

She let the tension drain from her, leaving just the residue of frustration in her clenched fist. A moment later she released this too, and sighed.

"Look, Disisto, I can't deny what you've heard about me, because most of it's true. Yes, one of my companions does appear to be a clone warrior, and yes, I did steal my ship from the Dato Bloc."

Disisto raised an eyebrow, surprised by her sudden frankness. "And the super-AI you held COE Intelligence HQ to ransom with?"

She nodded. "And Haid here is one of the few people ever to escape from the penal colony on Sciacca's World. You're in distinguished company, you know."

"That *is* the truth," said Haid, grinning.

Disisto looked from Roche to Haid. "I'm sure you think it is," he said humorlessly. "But that still doesn't mean I can trust you."

Roche reached down and unlocked the clasp of his harness. "I guess it all depends on how you look at it."

"Morgan!" Haid cautioned uneasily.

"Come on, Ameidio," she said. "He's not going to betray us—at least not until he's sure we can't help him." She unlooped the strap holding Disisto's left hand to the palmlink. "Besides, he can't stay tied up forever."

Disisto sat up, rubbing at his wrists. "Thank you," he said, with more than just a hint of sarcasm.

She shrugged. "I can tie you up again, if you like. Or you can quit with the attitude and come down to the mess where we can discuss things civilly. It's your choice."

He offered a half-smile and said: "The mess will be fine, thanks."

"Good," said Roche. "But remember that both Ameidio and I are armed and we'll be watching your every movement."

Disisto nodded, standing slowly. "Now *that* I can believe."

In the mess, the three of them sat at one of the many tables scattered about the room. Roche picked at a dish of reheated noodles while she sketched the details of how she had come to be in Palasian System. Disisto listened carefully, occasionally glancing at Haid when the ex-mercenary added a detail Roche had left out.

By the time they brought him up to date, an hour had passed and Disisto had hardly said a word.

"Well?" Roche prompted.

"I'm not sure," he said. "I think you've been honest with me, but . . ."

"But what?"

He pushed his plate aside. "Well, the business of Cane himself. If the clone warrior in Palasian System could cause so much destruction, then why hasn't Cane?"

Roche shrugged. "That's one of the reasons we're here: to see what makes them tick. But so far we've only seen two, and that's hardly a representative sample. For all we know, Cane could be the norm, not the exception."

Disisto looked down at his plate for a long moment, then back up at Roche. "There's another one."

What little appetite Roche had instantly vanished. "What? *Where*?"

"Hetu System. We received news of it a few days ago." He held up his hands before she could press him for more details. "That's all I know, Roche. I'm not privy to that kind of information. What little I do find out is on the sly. "

She forced herself to let it go—for the moment. Hetu System was on the far side of the COE, on the fringes of the region. There wasn't much she could do about it even if she wanted to.

"You heard about this other clone warrior a few days ago?" Haid said. "How was that possible? I thought you were unable to leave here."

Disisto looked tired, as though his decision to answer questions had come at great personal cost. "Seventeen days ago we were brought here on the back of the *Sebettu,* a Kesh destroyer. They brought us to the edge of the system, just inside the Gauntlet, and from there we traveled under our own power."

"So the Gauntlet was in place at that point?" said Roche.

"Yes."

Roche nodded, noting one lie from Rufo so far. He had said they had been trapped when the solar envelope had encapsulated the system.

Disisto went on: "Ever since then, we've received a communications drone from outside the Gauntlet every six days or so. I presumed they came from *Sebettu,* but if you didn't pass it on the way in, I guess I might be wrong."

That explained the recent duel Haid had noted in the bar. "All we saw was a blockade comprised of Armada ships. Were they there when you came in?"

"Yes. But they let us through once they were sure who we were."

"Really? Doesn't that strike you as a bit odd? I mean, we had a hell of a time getting past them."

"Not really," said Disisto. "As I understand it, the COE Armada wanted to seal the system once they had an idea what was inside it. The only way they could do that quickly was with something like Asha's Gauntlet. They did a deal with the N'Kor Republic, which had the only remaining prototype. At the same time, they contacted the chief and commissioned the services of Galine Four. The Gauntlet beat us here by a few days, so *Sebettu* ferried us in. Once we were inside, they left us alone to begin our work."

"Which was?" said Haid.

Disisto turned to him. "To study the actions of the person responsible for the destruction of the system."

"That's it?" Haid asked.

"What else do you suggest we do? *Fight* this person? The most we could hope for was to work out *how* he operated, in order to stop his doing it again elsewhere. Anything more would've been asking for trouble. If you ask me, it's risky enough just being here."

"Rufo agreed to be dropped in here without any means of defending himself?" Haid's expression was highly skeptical. "No means of escape? No way of letting the outside know if you might be under attack?"

"Not quite," said Disisto. "We do have communications drones of our own that we can send if we need to. But it was risky, yes. A drone takes at least ten hours to get out of the system. If we *did* get into trouble, by the time help arrived we'd have been dead. We haven't sent any yet, and I hope we don't have to."

"So why did Rufo agree to do it?" Roche asked.

"Lots of reasons, I guess. It's hard to know exactly why, because he doesn't explain himself to his employees as often as we feel he should." He managed a small smile. "I think it was because the COE applied a little pressure to make him agree. That, and they told him the person we would be looking for was probably gone anyway."

Roche's laugh was derisive. "And that you would basically be conducting an autopsy on a completely dead system?"

"Something like that," said Disisto.

"But it hasn't turned out that way, has it?"

Disisto shook his head. "The traps around Aro could've hurt us, and there could be others we haven't encountered yet."

"Not to mention the clone warrior himself," Haid pointed out.

"I doubt he's still here," said Disisto.

"Really? Why?"

"It stands to reason, doesn't it? We've been wandering around the system for almost two weeks, and we haven't been attacked. We've been careful, sure, but he would've spotted us eventually. And if he did, why didn't he attack us? We're the only major target left in one piece in Palasian System. It doesn't make sense that he would let us roam free—especially not when we're actively looking for him. He's not stupid."

"And this is what Rufo believes?" said Roche.

"No, Rufo is convinced he's still here," Disisto said. "But take my word for it, he's long gone by now."

Roche wasn't taking his word on anything, but was prepared to watch him entertain the thought. "Where to? Hetu System, perhaps?"

Disisto shrugged. "Maybe. Or maybe he's still in transit. It depends what sort of transport he's in, and what he's looking for. The nearest system is only a few light-years away, but it's not much more than an outpost. He might be looking for more of a challenge."

"I wouldn't call Palasian System much of a challenge," Haid said.

"What if this was just a trial run?" said Disisto. "Or just an opportunity to do some damage? Remember: he only made his move when the crew of this ship brought him out of the life capsule. Not only was Palasian System the closest port at that time, but *Daybreak* was already heading there. It would've made sense to go with the flow, to take what he could from here, then to move on in the direction he actually wanted to go."

Roche nodded. "I agree. It matches what Cane said. He's not going to waste time or opportunities; every decision he makes will be to maximize his return—however he measures it. Palasian System was just a means of making himself stronger.

"But where do *we* fit into this?" she went on. "You said someone from the outside warned you that we were coming. Who was it? And *why*?"

"The Armada, perhaps," said Disisto.

"You don't sound very certain about that," said Haid.

"I'm not," he said. "The last drone we received told us to expect you. I have no idea who sent it."

"Word must have leaked from Intelligence," said Haid, facing Roche. "Someone might have taken exception to there being another Sol Wunderkind on the loose."

"Maybe," Roche said. She could believe Page De Bruyn setting her up like this. "But why not ambush us properly? There's no way we could have withstood a destroyer or two at the edge of the Gauntlet, where they knew we were going to arrive sooner or later. Why leave it up to a nonmilitary installation inside what is basically a war zone?"

"Less risk?" Haid suggested. "Containment would be easier in here, if something went wrong."

"Not when we have a working slow-jump drive. Supposing Cane did go berserk, all he'd have to do is take over the *Ana Vereine* and fly it back out again."

"Do you think he's capable of doing that? Without Kajic or the Box, the ship would be difficult to control for a hundred people, let alone one."

"I'd hate to rule it out," Roche said. "Every time Cane reaches a hurdle, he seems to find a way over it."

"Until now." Haid turned to Disisto. "So what did you hit him with, anyway? Ferozac?"

"Diprodek-2, actually," the security officer said, unable to hide a hint of satisfaction. "It was the fastest-acting neurotoxin we had in store, *and* we had an antidote. All we had to do was hit him with a blast, catch him when he fell, then clear out the poison before it did any serious damage. It worked, too. I was receiving updates before the scutter activated its engines—and afterward, too, through the feed your Box tapped into."

Roche leaned forward. "What did you see?"

"Everything went as planned. The whole thing was handled by remote to ensure no one would get hurt. The scutter docked, and automatics attached the umbilical. When pressure equalized, the airlock opened. The clone warrior stepped through first to check things out, then he went back in to get your reave. They walked out together, and that's when we hit them. Just prior to that, we shot your reave full of Xarodine to stop her picking anything up—"

"Why did you do that?" said Roche, unable to keep the bitterness from her voice. "She couldn't read anything. That's why she was there, not to spy. It was Rufo who suggested we bring her in to see your medical team in the first place!"

"We had no way of knowing you were telling us the truth, Commander."

Roche shook her head in disbelief. "And I don't suppose you have any epsense adepts on Galine Four either, right?"

Disisto frowned. "None that I know of. Why?"

"Because Rufo told us you had some on board with similar problems." She glanced over at Haid. "Another lie," she said.

"Well, try to see it from his point of view," said Disisto. "He'd been warned about you; he had to take some sort of action."

"Why?" Haid asked. "We hadn't done anything to him."

"But for the sake of the station he had to assume that you *might*."

"Oh, come on, Disisto!" Roche snapped. "He never intended to trust us, and you know it! Stop trying to defend him. He lured us to Galine Four with the sole intention of neutralizing Cane. He didn't even give us a chance."

Disisto didn't deny it. "If that's the case, then he was pressured into doing it. It's not like the chief at all to take such risks."

"What do you mean?" said Roche.

"Well, whether he's in the system or not, we'd already managed to evade one clone warrior; we're pushing our luck putting ourselves in direct contact with another. The chief knew that, and at any other time he would have simply let you go by and not take any risks. But he sent Mavalhin to contact you, knowing full well what you would bring with you. And I guess he lied about our epsense adepts to get Cane on board. It's not an acceptable risk, in my opinion."

"You blame Shak'ni?" said Haid.

"And whoever's behind him, yes."

"So why didn't they do it themselves?" asked Roche.

"Shak'ni is a bigot," said Haid, "like a lot of the hardcore Kesh. Maybe it amuses him to watch Pristines making trouble for each other."

Disisto shrugged. "That's possible. I don't know, though. It bothers me that the chief isn't acting his normal self, and hasn't ever since we came here."

Roche sighed. "Okay, so what happens to Cane now?"

"Nothing," said Disisto. "He's powerless, and the chief knows it's best to keep him that way. Linegar may be under pressure at the moment, but he's not stupid."

Roche nodded. The idea of Cane bound in chains didn't sit easily with her, but there was some consolation in what Disisto said. While Cane was incapacitated, he was safe. But it was the image of Maii, locked in the perpetual darkness of her own skull, that bothered Roche the most.

Again, determination to rescue the girl flooded through her. Too many people had let *her* down recently; she refused to do the same to anyone she knew. There was too much mistrust in the galaxy as it was.

"If Rufo's so damned smart," she said, "why can't he see that we all want the same thing? Why are we fighting each other?"

Disisto met her gaze squarely. "*Do* we want the same thing?"

"I thought we did. Or hoped so, anyway." Roche shook her head. "I need to work out what your boss is doing, and why. Will you help me do that?"

Disisto took a deep breath. "If it means betraying his confidence, no, I won't."

"Then we have nothing else to talk about. For now."

• • •

Responding to a message from the autosurgeon via her implants, Roche stopped at the surgery on the way back to the bridge, sending Haid and Disisto ahead of her. By the time she arrived there, Myer's unconscious body had been wrapped in a bioactive blanket and strapped to the plastic bed. His left shoulder, chest, and arm were completely encased in a thin layer of translucent bandages that allowed enough red through to indicate just how severe the damage had been. He seemed peaceful, however, and Roche was content to leave him there for the time being—until either the autosurgeon pronounced him fit enough to walk or she needed him on his feet regardless.

She had been there only a few minutes when another message came through her implants. This time it was from the bridge: *Daybreak* had received a tightbeam transmission encrypted in high-level COE code. She quickly left the surgery, instructing the autosurgeon to keep her posted on Myer's progress.

She arrived on the bridge just as the courier's AI completed deciphering the transmission.

Haid looked up from tying Disisto back into his crash-couch as she entered. "That'll be the Box, I guess," he said.

"I hope so." She sat in the pilot's seat and instructed the AI to play the message.

"Morgan," said the Box, its voice brisk. "This message will reach you exactly three hours following our last communication. In that time, the *Ana Vereine* will have disengaged from Galine Four and headed in-system. We are currently leading a flotilla of seven pursuit vessels along a powered approach that will take us past Jagabis, through the Mattar Belt and close to Cartha's Planet. At perihelion, in twelve hours, we will adopt a neutral camouflage and power at maximum thrust to a different orbit. If you wish to choose a rendezvous point, please indicate so in your reply, before the delay becomes too great."

"We left a furious mess behind," the recorded voice of Kajic broke in. "There are singleships buzzing around everywhere, looking for any trace of you. The Box self-destructed a drone, hoping they'd mistake the wreckage for *Daybreak*, but I don't think they were fooled. It looks like they're getting ready to move elsewhere, just in case you come back in a hurry."

"I recommend strongly that you do not do that," said the Box. "*Daybreak* is unarmed and poorly defended; any attempt to breach their security will surely fail. Better to wait until we join you and use the combined resources of the two ships."

Roche nodded to herself; there was nothing she could do for Maii in a clapped-out courier.

As though reading Roche's mind, the Box went on: "You might be interested to know that Cane and Maii are unharmed. I was able to install a leak via Disisto's implants while I was connected to the secondary security shell of Galine Four, and through this leak, I have been monitoring their condition."

Roche smiled. *Thanks, Box,* she thought to herself. Disisto appeared to be telling the truth on that score.

"They are currently being held in separate cells in the station's outer levels," the Box went on, "and are closely guarded. Preparations are being made to move them to the Hub, but where exactly I do not know at this stage. Chances are, however, that it will be to a zone I will not be able to penetrate, even with my improved access.

"Lastly, a drone was launched from Galine Four within fifteen minutes of our departure. I was able to track it as far as the orbit of Gatamin, at which point it was accelerating rapidly for the edge of the system. If you have not already interrogated Disisto on this matter, you should do so immediately. Any information he can provide, willingly or otherwise, will be to our benefit."

Roche felt a brief flicker of self-satisfaction—Disisto had mentioned that they hadn't sent any drones out of the system—but quelled it. Although it was good to have preempted the Box in one instance, to dwell on it was obsessive.

"That is all for now, Morgan," it continued. "The drone following you is maintaining a fixed position with respect to *Daybreak* and will relay to me any message you send in return. It will be necessary for you to reply soon, though, for the delay between our communications will increase rapidly over the next twelve hours. Once we have a rendezvous point established, we can begin planning how best to use it to our advantage.

"Also, I will require you to perform a diagnostic check of *Daybreak*'s slow-jump drive. The result of that analysis will affect any plans we make. I will await your reply before taking further action."

The message ended abruptly, catching Roche off guard for a moment.

After a while she said: "What do you think, Ameidio?"

Haid shook his head. "We haven't got a lot of options, have we? It's unlikely they'd even stumble upon us out here, so the sensible thing would be to stay put."

"I agree." Roche slipped into the pilot's crash-couch and called up the communications systems. The tightbeam had come from a point in space not far behind them; she directed the systems to send her reply in that direction, once she had recorded it.

"But staying put is exactly what they'll be expecting us to do," she continued. "It's too obvious, too predictable. And it wastes an opportunity to do something useful. Instead of heading straight back to rescue Maii and Cane, we'd be better off looking for answers."

"Where from?"

"Kukumat and Murukan." She called up a map of the outer system. "Twice, now, we've received signals from near the double-jovian; Rufo can't or won't explain them, and that makes me suspicious. It's also the only obvious hiding place in the system we haven't investigated. None of the drones we sent there ever reported back."

"You think there might be survivors?"

"I don't know what to think. I'd rather keep my options

open until we arrive. Which should be"—she scanned a navigation chart and performed rough mental calculations—"about fourteen hours, if we go by Hintubet along the way. And if we do, that'll keep our transmission times to the Box at a minimum."

Haid nodded. "It also increases the chances of the pursuit ships seeing us."

"Marginally. They'll be tracking the *Ana Vereine,* not looking for us. By the time the Box loses them, we'll be gone."

Disisto had followed the exchange in silence up to that point. "What signals?" he asked. "I was told there was no one near the old base."

Roche turned to face him. "If that's what Rufo told you, then that makes me even more interested in having a look myself."

"I agree," said Haid. "It worries me what we might be heading into, but yes: I'm also curious to know what Rufo is up to. If he's lying to his own security staff, then something serious must be going on."

Before Disisto could respond, Roche turned back to the communications systems and began to record a reply for the Box. She had already checked the maintenance systems of the courier and determined that the slow-jump drive was dead; that was why the clone warrior had ditched it: after attempting to leave the Gauntlet and failing, destroying the drive in the process, he had had no use for the courier. It had become a liability, in fact, due to its inevitable association with him. He had abandoned it and gone elsewhere. Now she was hoping to find him in it; the irony was not lost on her.

But it did confirm one thing: he was in the system with them. Anyone who said otherwise was either wrong or lying.

She keyed their new course into the navigation systems. As the courier's thrusters began a long, steady burn, she settled back into the crash-couch and let g-forces erase the worry from her mind. For now, there was nothing else she could do.

PART THREE:

MOK

INTERLUDE

The enigma dissolved into the background, obscured by the intensity and close proximity of the light.

He strained desperately to follow her; the Cruel One's servant would be annoyed if he let her slip away. But he had no choice. He could either see her or he couldn't, and within moments she had completely disappeared. He let her go with a feeling of apprehension mixed with something not unlike relief. He had enough to do as it was.

Bathed in the light of the Shining One, he examined his options.

One: he could do everything the Cruel One asked of him, where possible.

Two: he could do only those things that he felt comfortable doing and feign ignorance or lack of understanding with the others—although the Cruel One's servant had an uncanny knack of recognizing his deceptions, and previous attempts had led to torture, both physical and mental.

Three: he could do nothing at all and endure the consequences.

Following the enigma was, already, one request with which he could not comply. Studying the Shining One was something he was happy to do, if he was able to. But neutralizing the abomination . . . Wasn't he already doing that just by being here? What more could be asked of him?

He wanted nothing to do with the awful child and her piercing, painful mind. His people would have killed her had they known she existed—or at the very least extracted a terrible price from the Surin Agora for allowing her to exist. That in part was what the grayboots were for: to prevent such things from coming into being, to stamp them out when they did, and to keep all knowledge of their existence secret lest others try to replicate past experiments.

But he didn't have the means to kill her, and he knew from the Cruel One's servant's mind that she was safe here in that respect. Her frail body was considered a threat by no one. It was her powers alone he was supposed to quash, as if that were possible. He was being asked to stop a wasp from stinging without damaging the stinger *or* the wasp. And the fact that this particular wasp was not even a natural creature only made the task that much more preposterous.

He could already feel her stirring, despite an intensive regimen of epsense-inhibitors. Xarodine worked on most Castes—including those possessing epsense naturally, like his own—but its efficacy decreased with extended use. The initial doses given to the girl would have worn off hours ago and been topped up several times since; her powers would be returning soon. They could keep her unconscious—perhaps—but nothing would stop her from dreaming. And even asleep she could be dangerous. Should she erupt, he might not be able to contain her, let alone neutralize her. Those nearby or linked to her in other ways would be in peril.

He briefly imagined what would happen to the Cruel

One's servant under such circumstances, but he dismissed the fantasy. That was why the servant had servants of his own. They stood between harm and the hearth; they bore the brunt of any such perils.

He said:

: SAFE

: SLEEPING

And that would have to do. The girl was probably harmless for a few hours yet. Eventually he would have to decide what to do with her, but for now . . .

The Shining One.

Its glow, he now realized, was a defensive measure designed to fool anyone encountering it into believing it to be evidence of profound epsense ability. As a camouflage it worked well; few people would penetrate its structure or decipher the giddying motion at its core. It was complex and amazing enough; why imagine that there would be more?

But there was. Behind the façade lay a much more interesting possibility, the same one he had suspected before but could not explain to the Cruel One's servant. Behind the shine and scatter lay a speck of unfathomable black. The speck haunted him; he could hardly drag his attention away from it. Part of him was afraid it would not be there when he looked—afraid the blaze would cover it again, this time forever. He and the Shining One had something in common, it seemed.

What that was, though, he still lacked the words to explain. *No one* had the words. Only a natural reave would understand.

Epsense theorists—some of them reaves, most of them not—likened a world empty of thought to a flat plain, in the same way that physicists described empty space-time as a rubber sheet. This plain they called "n-space." The addition of a thinking being—an "n-body"—added a small spike to the flat landscape. Reaves were spikes surrounded by small mounds that spread across the surface of the plain, joining the spikes together.

On first inspection, the Shining One was a peak so high, its foothills buried all the n-bodies around it.

Races of natural reaves, like the Olmahoi, warped the surface of the plain itself, creating valleys and peaks and, sometimes, holes. He was one such hole; without him at its heart, and others like him before, the Grand Design of his people would have unraveled millennia ago. He depressed n-space, disconnected n-bodies from each other even if there were reaves present, absorbed stray thoughts no matter where they came from. That was why he'd been kidnapped and brought here: to gather data for the Cruel One's servant. All things eventually found their way into the Olmahoi *irikeii.*

A closer look at the Shining One revealed the hole in its core—a hole so deep he could not find its measure. If it had a bottom, he never touched it.

He could sense it, though. And what he sensed both disturbed and fascinated him.

Something old.

Something that should not exist.

Something that seemed, impossibly, to be studying him back.

Yet through the eyes of those examining the Shining One, he saw just another Pristine Human, one of many hundreds of trillions scattered across the galaxy. Why would anyone go to so much trouble to bring such a thing into being and hide it in so ordinary a vessel—not just once, but several times? What could possibly be served by such a deception?

He saw in the minds of those around him—through the all-pervading nimbus of the Shining One—that some thought it a weapon made to wreak vengeance on Pristine Humanity. A weapon that could hide among its intended victims, striking with surprise and efficiency. That made sense, even though the evidence was tenuous at best, and sometimes outright misleading. And in the mind of the Cruel One's servant he found a nagging doubt that nagged at him in turn. Could it be so simple?

He hoped it was. The only other possibility to occur to him was too horrible to contemplate . . .

Knowing it was probably futile yet needing to try, he cast his mind outward, as he had done on only a few occasions before, to the very limits of his senses. There, normally, he sensed strange, superior intelligences, watching from their arcane removes as the lower Castes went about their business. The High Humans were like people watching ants; they saw the swarming, the building, the clashes between hives, but few if any ever stopped to notice the lone ant waving its antennae in the hope of catching their attention.

Still, he had communicated with High Humans before. They used means as far above epsense as epsense was above normal speech, and they tended to be reticent. But sometimes unintended data slipped through, as though the sheer bandwidth of the High Humans' media meant that their speech could not be effectively dammed. Some of it was incomprehensible; most of it was useless, relating to Castes or times far distant; but just one useful piece of data made the effort worthwhile.

He needed their help now. If what he suspected was true, even they could be in danger.

But there was no reply. He sensed nothing lurking at the fringes of the void. There was no one to whom he could turn for advice.

He was suddenly homesick. He missed his people: he missed their minds, their song, the tapestry they wove around him and in which he knew his proper place. Here, he had no one to commune with. Few even knew he existed, and those that did were unable to communicate properly. He was trapped by mundanes in a plot that, under ordinary circumstances, might only tangentially concern him.

He wondered how his people coped without him. Did

chaos reign, or had the keepers of the Shadow Place found a way to correct the imbalance? Was the racial mechanism that had brought him forth when his predecessor had died already conceiving his replacement? What would happen if he returned? Could the Grand Design tolerate *two irikeii*?

Perhaps he would have to remain in the void forever, trapped with only a handful of minds to watch until his own was extinguished! Except he knew from those around him that the void was impermanent: it would collapse upon itself within weeks. So perpetual imprisonment was not an option: it was temporary at best.

Then there were the Shining Ones to consider, and the Cruel One. Regardless of whether he was right or wrong about the former, of one thing he *was* certain: the Cruel One and her servant had no intention of letting him live after his mission here was complete.

For a brief, bitter moment he envied the enigma. Whoever she was, whatever she represented, she was freer than he could ever hope to be.

But there was comfort in knowing that he was doomed, he guessed. Once all hope was gone, there was nothing left to fear except fear itself.

And if he could take the abomination with him, all the better. . . .

5

COEI *Daybreak*
'955.01.21 EN
1390

From a distance, Hintubet's bloody, red light was insufficient to allow the courier's basic sensors to gather much detail about the double-jovian system: a blurred, overmagnified image of two red balloons tied together by a twisted silver string was all Roche could see, little different from the pictures the Box had procured from the orbit of Gatamin. No doubt the probes dispatched earlier would be sending remarkable pictures to the *Ana Vereine,* wherever the ship was, but only as the courier drew nearer did Roche have the chance to appreciate the uniqueness of her destination.

Individually Kukumat and Murukan might once have been unremarkable gas giants, both roughly a quarter the mass of Jagabis; together they formed a dynamic partnership as mysterious as it was fascinating. The most obvious detail separating the pair from the other planets in Palasian System was that it followed a retrograde orbit around Hintubet. Planetary scientists generally agreed that the pair had probably arisen out of a near collision between two previously independent worlds, one natural to the system and the other an interstellar wanderer. Although no actual collision had occurred, each planet had captured the other, and the shared momentum of the two had cast the pair into an entirely new yet stable orbit.

Under normal conditions, Kukumat would have been a brilliant, white-streaked yellow. Storms considered enormous even for a gas giant raged from equator to pole, the constant flashes of lightning through the thick, turbulent atmosphere casting weird strobelike patterns across the face of the planet. Now and then Roche imagined she could sense a pattern forming in the inconstant light, as though some unfathomable machine at the heart of the planet was trying to communicate with her.

Murukan, though only marginally larger, was radically different. Regardless of the light that fell upon it, the gas giant presented a deep, bloody red face. Instead of the thin streaks and whorls boasted by its brilliant neighbor, Murukan possessed massive upwellings of heavy gases, spewed high into the atmosphere by unknown processes deeper within. These upwellings bloomed like flowers at their peak, spread in overlapping petals that changed color and smeared laterally as the gases comprising them slowly reached the apex of their explosive rise, then began to descend.

Roche didn't doubt that the extreme atmospheric activity of the two planets owed much to their proximity; on close examination she could see tidal bulges many kilometers high sweeping across the face of each planet as it rotated with respect to the other. It amazed her to think that the situation was stable at all. But it was, had been for hundreds of thousands of years, and would have been for many more had not the Gauntlet arrived to change the system irrevocably.

By the time the courier managed to locate Mok—the single moon of the double system—the system's other unique feature had attained a tantalizing prominence. KM36 was an ion bridge linking the magnetic fields of the two planets. Although the link itself was constant, it arced—and was therefore visible—only once every thirty-six minutes. Each arc lasted approximately seventy seconds, and Roche was fortunate enough to catch an entire event broadside-on, from the best possible perspective. The ion bridge looked like a lightning bolt strung out between the two planets, flickering and snapping almost too quickly to follow in close focus, yet undulating like a plucked wire in slow motion from a distance. Its light was so bright it cast a shadow on Mok, lending it, briefly, a silver-white face.

Watching it, Roche was reminded of why she had joined COE Intelligence in the first place. It hadn't just been to escape from a difficult upbringing, but for sights such as these.

And perhaps, she thought, that was enough to explain the dream. . . .

She was standing, cold and wet, on the foredeck of an oceangoing vessel made entirely of stone. The mass of the ship was so great that she felt no movement beneath her as it cut through the choppy waters, and the surety of its progress made her feel as safe as though she were standing on solid ground.

The stars above were as icy as the wind, however, and although the spray from the waves never struck her, she was soaked to the skin and trembling.

"Are you frightened?" A man's voice came from behind her, scented and hauntingly familiar.

She turned. The man, clad in white, his skin ashen and dry like dust, stood at the starboard rail of the foredeck.

"No," she said, clutching herself. "I'm cold. Aren't you?"

"No. But we could both be lying," he added, the glint in his yellow eyes like the lightning in Kukumat's alien skies.

"I am neither cold nor afraid," came a second voice, this time from the port rail. "But I *am* here."

The newcomer was dressed in red; his complexion was ruddy, his skin moist. A fat-petaled flower protruded from a buttonhole of his greatcoat. And again, a familiar odor, but this one different from the first.

They know each other, she thought, with some surprise.

"In a manner of speaking, yes," the red one said, as if answering Roche but looking at his white counterpart.

"Although I suspect we have less in common than I once thought," said the white man.

"Appearances can be deceptive," said Red.

"Perhaps it's time to end the pretense," said White.

"Do we have any choice?"

The red man nodded ahead of them. "We'll find out when we get there."

The brief exchange had changed them: the one in white had become paler, his skin drier, while the red one had begun to exude blood. And the smells, once disparate and only vaguely familiar, suddenly merged to become something all too familiar to Roche. Now she could smell death; she could smell *war* . . .

The two men faced each other, a silent but tense confrontation. They retained only the shape of Humanity, now; the essence of their true beings was almost too much even for that.

Roche backed away until her spine made contact with cold, wet stone. Two huge masts towered above her like giant antennae, visible only as silhouettes against the sky. The tremendous momentum with which the prow cut through the waves remained unchecked, only now it seemed a matter for concern.

She looked again at the two men and realized just how alike they really were. Despite their differences, they could easily have been mistaken for brothers. Or even twins . . .

• • •

The anxiety induced by the dream had stayed with her upon waking. No matter how hard she tried, she simply couldn't shake free of it, and she longed for Maii's gentle touch. The epsense adept could have soothed her, eased some of the dread and foreboding that filled her. But the reave was far away, left behind on an unfamiliar station, captive of a man who had somehow outthought them all.

For a moment, she felt despair. How had she come to this? *She* certainly wasn't responsible. It must have been COE Intelligence, or the Kesh, or the Sol Apotheosis Movement, or . . .

No. There was no point assigning blame. She just had to keep moving, to do her best to rectify the situation and find a way out of this mess. Find a way to rescue Maii and Cane and—

"Morgan?" said Haid.

She turned from the image of the double-jovian at which she had been blankly staring, and faced Haid. It was only when she did that she realized it had been the third time he had called her name.

"You okay?" he said.

She nodded, but felt it was unconvincing. "What's up?"

"We're detecting radio emissions."

Immediately focused, Roche took a step toward Haid. "Where from?"

"Mok. They spike every time the ion bridge flares, as though someone's using the discharge to cover emissions."

She concentrated on his explanation; it made sense. "Any idea who this 'someone' might be?"

Haid shook his head. "The transmissions are coded to look like static, and I can't translate them without the Box's help. If I had to guess, though, I'd say it's the outriggers talking among themselves."

"And the two spines haven't moved?"

Another curt shake of the head. "They're still in orbit around Murukan."

While still some distance from the jovian pair, they had

detected the muted navigation beacons of two outrigger spines—spindly structures comprising little more than intra-system engines and fuel tanks shaped like bare-boned trees with lots of branches for waldoes to cling to. The spines appeared to be undamaged, but, apart from the beacons, showed no signs of life.

Roche had never encountered outriggers before, but had heard the stories of whole tribes of people crossing the gulfs between stars on the backs of such flimsy vessels. Their only protection was an "all-suit," essentially a miniature spaceship in its own right within which each member of the tribe would spend his or her entire life. Although outriggers came from many different Castes, they were a society completely unto themselves, separated from the rest of the galaxy by the time-debts they accrued by traveling at relatavistic velocities; some had wandered so far and for so long that they were rumored to be thousands of years old. Outriggers earned a living mining systems considered uneconomic for prowling mines or other large-scale automated means. That explained what they were doing so far out from the primary of Palasian System, where solid bodies were few and very far between but the total mass of unexploited minerals was considerable.

Beyond that, Roche knew little. What the spines were doing so close to a large planet—the sort of gravity well outriggers normally avoided—remained a mystery.

Similarly, there had been no repeat of the distress calls that had brought them to the double-planet. She was resigned to traveling closer to find out what had happened.

"How long until we reach Mok?" she asked Haid.

"One hour."

"Okay," she said. "Show me the pictures we're getting."

Disisto chuckled quietly from behind Roche. "It's probably not going to be what you're expecting."

"How do you mean?"

"See for yourself," he said.

Disisto was right. The little moon was highly unusual:

in size barely a thousand kilometers across and consisting of dark-hued dusty rock, with no atmosphere and a relatively low specific gravity. There were craters, Roche observed, but these looked suspiciously regular and similar in size, as though they were holes or tunnel-entrances rather than ancient impact sites. Between them stood odd protrusions resembling curved spikes or giant hairs growing out of the rock—as though the moon were covered in a large-scale version of Velcro. Each of the "hooks" was over ten meters high.

"Weird," she mused. "Are they artifacts?"

"Unknown. I've never seen anything like it before." Haid stared intently at the images filling most of the available screens and tanks. "There's no movement, so the chances are they're not alive."

"They might once have been," said Disisto. He was still on the couch where Haid had strapped him hours earlier. "The sun's changed; the difference could've killed a photosynthetic plant, for instance."

"The light would always have been poor out here," Haid said, shaking his head. "My gut says that they were made, but I have no idea what purpose they'd serve."

"Or even who made them," said Roche.

"Exactly," Haid agreed. "Those ruins are *old.* They could be the remains of a Transcended civilization, or even a dead High Human. You looked into the history around here, Morgan. Any records of such a thing in this area?"

"No, but it wouldn't hurt to look again."

"The chief was hoping the ruins might contain something related to Primordial Humanity," said Disisto. "An old base or colony, perhaps, with records intact. We have so little information to go by with respect to Humanity's origins. Any scrap at all could be helpful. If we'd known it was something like this, we would've come much sooner."

Haid looked back at the security chief. "I didn't know you were such a history buff."

Disisto shrugged. "Work with the chief long enough and it rubs off, I guess."

Roche didn't respond. His casual banter hid the underlying tension between them. Neither had forgotten their last conversation, when he had maintained his allegiance to Linegar Rufo. She couldn't afford to forget, though. Although she knew he meant well deep down, that they were forced to work on opposing sides made it all the more frustrating.

"Congreve Station?" Roche prompted Haid, keeping them on the subject at hand.

"There, at the pole." One image ballooned to reveal a low, blister-shaped installation near the moon's equator. "It's cold. Looks like no one's touched it for years."

KM36 chose that moment to flare. White light radiated from the screens as the ion bridge crackled into life.

Roche and Haid watched the instruments for more signs of concealed signals coming from Mok.

"Almost nothing, this time," said Haid. "Just one pulse at the beginning."

"I saw it. Like a warning tone, telling everyone to shut up."

Haid looked over at Roche. "They know we're here," he said.

Roche nodded. "But we still need to talk to them anyway." She pointed at a rough map of the moon's surface. "According to the instruments, the pulse came from that crater."

The image showed a black hole leading into the moon, not far from its equator.

"Deep," commented Haid. "Could hide anything."

"No different from the others, though. A simple jaunt to look wouldn't hurt."

He glanced up at her. "And who gets to do the honors?"

"I do, of course. Unless you fancy an EVA with your new implants?"

Haid smiled. "Well, I'm game."

"Yes, but you're not stupid," she said seriously. "You know I'm the best choice."

Haid nodded. "But you *are* going to try talking to them first, right?"

"There's no point. They're obviously in hiding; they're not going to want to talk to anyone, no matter what we say. Best to go knocking and see if they'll let us in."

"And if they blow you out of the sky?"

"Then they'll become targets for retaliation."

"We could send *him.*" Haid jerked a thumb at Disisto.

"Would you trust him?"

"No," said Haid. "But it wouldn't bother me so much to see him blown away, either."

Roche glanced at Disisto. The security head's expression was blank, neither offended by nor laughing at what might have been a joke.

"Don't think it would bother me too much, either," she said. "Nevertheless, it still has to be me that goes down. Give me half an hour and I'll be suited up and ready for the drop."

Roche waited in the airlock as Haid completed the final checks and brought the courier into the optimum position. Her suit was sealed and ready to go: armored, powered, and equipped with enough thrust to repel the moon's low gravity for several hours in total. The courier would drop her high above and at some distance from the target crater. Using gravity and the thrusters when necessary, she would approach with all due caution under cover of the ion bridge.

She carried a number of weapons at the ready, plus several concealed in the thigh and underarm compartments of the suit. If she encountered trouble, she would be as prepared as she could be.

"Drop in two," said Haid. "No activity. Arc due any time now."

"When you're clear, assume a geosynch orbit and wait for instructions. I'll switch on my beacon once you're out of the area." During preparations for the jaunt, she'd reconsidered her decision to go in completely unannounced. Broadcasting a navigational pulse would let anyone in the area know she was coming without giving too much away. If the worst she was facing was a bunch of outriggers, the suit would be able to take care of her; if not, not even the courier would be much use. "Maintain radio silence once I'm off-ship."

"Understood. One minute to drop."

She inclined her head so Haid's view through the airlock camera's included her face. "And don't do anything rash while I'm away, okay?"

A slight laugh filled her helmet. "Trust me, Morgan," he said. Then: "The bridge is arcing now. Thirty seconds. Hold tight."

Roche braced herself against the frame of the airlock, more out of habit than necessity, since the chamber had already been evacuated. A chronometer inside the helmet of her suit counted down the seconds. When it hit five, a series of dull clunks traveled from the bulkhead, along the rigid structure of the suit, and to her ears, then died as she let go and allowed herself to drift.

The outer door slid aside as the chronometer hit zero, and she kicked the thrusters to life and shot out of the airlock. A minute later, she switched on her beacon.

Her attention was focused on eyes-up navigation displays in her visor and artificial sight as she accelerated away from the courier; she barely glimpsed the red-tinged, craggy surface of the small moon rolling beneath her. The courier's engines fired the instant she was at a safe distance, propelling it precipitously away from her. For a brief, disorienting moment, she had no idea where she was.

Then the moon swung into view, and she rolled herself about so that her legs were pointing in a rough approximation of "down." She let herself fall, following the navigation prompt rather than trusting her own instincts. Orbital mechanics was difficult enough to calculate without the view she was diving into acting as a distraction.

Mok . . . the ion-bridge flashing . . . Kukumat and Murukan looming impossibly large nearby . . . and no stars to be seen, apart from one hanging blood-red in the distance. . . .

For a second she felt very small and insignificant, and momentarily regretted her decision to investigate the signals alone. But the feeling was irrational. She knew outriggers would prove a vital source of information on what had happened in the system, before the arrival of Galine Four and after. She had to approach them on their own terms, not cozy and safe within the courier. In their shoes, she would put her faith in nothing less.

The surface of the moon approached, and she changed her heading until she was flying through near-vacuum above its mottled surface. The ambient temperature, at 125 degrees kelvin, was higher than expected. The forest of hook-trees, or whatever they were, marched without apparent pattern or function over the disconcertingly close horizon. She was tempted to drop lower and examine one at close quarters, but forced herself to concentrate on her mission. One puzzle at a time.

Five minutes into her flight, she changed course to avoid flying over another crater but didn't veer so far away that she couldn't see into its interior. It truly was a shaft, not a crater, about five meters across; radar pulses failed to return, so she had no way of telling how deep it was. The walls seemed smooth, as though machined, but there was nothing else to suggest that the hole served any purpose. There were no ramps or ladders, no elevator shafts or windows, no doors or platforms; it was just a hole, lipped slightly at the top, with nothing inside it. Nothing that she could see, anyway.

It took her fifteen minutes to reach the target crater—dubbed Shaft-1 on the map produced by the courier's sensors—which looked identical to the one she had flown by ten minutes earlier. After circumnavigating the edge of the hole and learning nothing new, and feeling slightly bored at her lack of progress, she decided a flare would be her best option. The next arc was due in twenty minutes; she didn't want to wait that long.

Backing away and arming the first of six flares her suit was equipped with, she primed it to ignite in a way that would offset the dull red light cast by Hintubet, then fired it from her suit.

Moments later, a sustained burst of light came from a point high above her and to her right.

Finally, some color. In the shaft she could make out gray-brown walls descending into the moon, polished smooth by some unknown process. Nothing stood out: no detail of any kind. Swinging the suit higher to get a better view, she eased herself closer to the edge of the shaft and used scanning algorithms to analyze the view in more detail. Almost immediately, she had a result.

A segment of the visor formed a separate screen and zoomed closer, revealing a glint of reflected light under the lip of the shaft opposite her. Too small and too far away for her to identify, she quickly tagged the location of the object so she wouldn't lose it when the flare faded.

She lifted herself higher still, in order to look into the shaft while she could. The walls seemed to narrow as they fell away into the depths of the moon, but she knew that to be an illusion. She was certain now that the shaft was artificial: nothing naturally formed could descend so perfectly straight. As far as the light reached into the shaft, she could make out no deviation, no variation at all. Only at the very edges of shadow, deep in the moon, did she suspect that something changed, but even then she couldn't tell if it was an end to the shaft, an opening off it, or just an optical illusion.

Then the flare flickered and faded, and all was red-tinged darkness again.

With the gain on the eyes-up display on high, she flew

by instruments around the shaft to where she had noticed the glint of light. When her eyes had completely adjusted, she eased herself slowly over the lip of the shaft. Her suit lamps were no substitute for the flare, but the object was barely hidden at all, and she had no trouble catching a second reflection off it. It consisted of a silver device barely larger than her palm, attached to the rocky inside of the shaft.

Extending a slender probe, she touched it from two meters away, eliciting no response. Moving closer to touch it with her suit glove, she discovered that it was stuck to the wall by little more than a tacky gel, suggesting it wasn't a permanent fixture. A simple tug pulled it free, exposing instrumentation on the underside. Roche knew what it was immediately: a simple relay designed to confuse anyone listening in the area, and presumably planted there by the outriggers. Instead of being the source of the transmissions, Shaft-1 was just a decoy.

As such, it was something of an anticlimax. Nevertheless, it did provide tangible evidence that someone was in the area—someone who was transmitting to others and making at least some attempt to remain hidden.

"Morgan?"

Haid's voice over her suit-speakers startled her.

"Don't reply unless you have to, but I'm moving to encrypted channel thirty-one in two seconds."

The line went dead abruptly, and she shifted her communications channel to the one he had indicated, wondering as she did why he was calling.

"I know I'm supposed to keep quiet," he continued, his voice fuzzy from compression, "but I thought you should know that we're picking up a faint signal from deeper in-system. It's in that code Cane recognized—the Sol Wunderkind command language. I can't work out what it's saying, and Disisto says he can't either. But the weird thing is, it's being beamed right at us, from roughly where Galine Four was when we left it. I'd say someone's trying to communicate with someone else out here, and I'd hate to think what they might be saying . . ."

Haid's voice trailed off into silence as a chill swept over Roche.

Linegar Rufo was a specialist in antiquities. He knew about the Sol Apotheosis Movement. He knew a Sol Wunderkind was loose in the system. He had mentioned that transmissions had been received from near the jovian pair. He hadn't actually *said* the transmissions were from survivors of the Wunderkind's attack. If he had found some reference to the Wunderkind language in a forgotten archive, and if he suspected that the source of the transmissions would understand it . . .

Rufo was trying to talk to the Sol Wunderkind. Not only that, but he believed the Wunderkind was hiding somewhere near Mok.

Roche thrust herself up and out of the crater, alert for any sign of activity on the moon's surface. There was none, but that didn't reassure her. If Rufo was right, then she had more to worry about than just a motley bunch of outriggers.

She vacillated for a moment over whether to return to the courier or not. Haid would know she was still alive, so there was no need to reply to the signal. To return might just place him and the others at greater risk. And they were *all* at risk, just from being in the area. If the Wunderkind got his hands on another ship . . .

That brought her up cold. What would he do with the courier? He had already abandoned it once. Its slow-jump drive was slag, so he couldn't use it to escape the system. Likewise with the outrigger spines and Galine Four; no vessel in the system had a working slow-jump drive, except the *Ana Vereine*—and that, she vowed, would be kept well clear until she was absolutely certain it was safe.

Potentially, then, the Wunderkind wouldn't want to make himself vulnerable by exposing himself. That didn't make her feel much safer, though. An attack on a courier would undoubtedly be noticed; an attack on a single person, however, was something else entirely . . .

She decided that it would be best if Haid picked her up. That way they could explore the moon from orbit without risking anyone's life. And if she was right, if the Wunderkind wouldn't attack the courier itself, they would all be safe—at least until they actually found him.

She turned the suit around in a slow arc, angling upward. At the same time, she opened the encrypted communications channel.

"Ameidio, it's me. Work out a rendezvous. I'm—"

An ear-splitting squeal cut her short. The channel was swamped by noise, overriding her signal and any Haid might be trying to send. She hunted for a source of the interference, and after a moment realized it was the transmitter she had left behind in the crater.

Rather than fly back, she armed the suit's impulse weapon, targeted and fired. The relay was small and the distance increasing, but with the help of onboard systems, the projectile crossed the gap easily, impacting with a short-lived flash of light.

The interference didn't cease entirely, but it did ebb enough for her to hear Haid call:

"Behind you, Morgan! Behind you!"

As long as she lived, she knew she'd never forget her first sight of an outrigger all-suit.

It loomed over her like a biomechanical starfish with a ribbed halo surrounding it—almost thirty meters across, drooping slightly in the moon's low gravity, resembling the frills of an angry lizard. Toward the center were dozens of instrumentation spines and jointed waldoes, all directed at her. In the center was nothing but light: a powerful laser dazzling her despite her suit's protective visor. An ion beam lifted the all-suit above her, its spray of white fire disturbing the moon's surface in an angry manner.

She retreated, and it followed. Her sensors registered an

incoming transmission, superimposed upon the jamming signal.

"Identify," was all it said, its tone coldly artificial.

She aimed numerous weapons on the laser source. Behind it, instruments made out the shape and location of the central thorax, a pressurized pod large enough to contain a single Human and the equipment it needed to survive for a lifetime in space.

"Identify *yourself*," she replied.

Movement to one side caught her eye: another all-suit, its extensible antennae unfurling as it approached. It too fired a laser at her location, this one at a slightly different frequency to the other.

"Identify!"

Roche's suit issued a warning as a third laser hit her—this one from farther up. The three combined lasers were threatening the integrity of her faceplate; much more of this and she would have to opaque the helmet, or risk being burned and possibly even blinded.

"Identify!"

Roche sighed resignedly. Surrounded by three all-suits, she was hardly in a position to be defiant.

"Morgan Roche," she said, "ex-COE Intelligence and commanding officer of the independent vessel *Ana Vereine*."

"The Dato ship?" asked a voice that was hostile but at least Human.

"By design only. It no longer serves the Military Presidium."

"How do we know you're telling the truth?"

"You should've asked yourself that before you asked me anything at all."

"Indeed," chuckled a second voice, a female contralto. "So, why are you here?"

"I'm looking for survivors."

"Why?" The voice of the third outrigger was male and sharp with suspicion.

"We picked up a distress call."

"We didn't send one."

"Well, someone did." Roche suppressed an urge to snap. "Regardless, I need to know what happened in this system so we can stop it happening elsewhere. You can help me do that."

"How very commendable," said the first voice. "Your superiors must be proud of you."

"I told you: I'm independent. I don't have any superiors."

"You come looking for us in a COE Intelligence courier vessel, wearing a COE Intelligence suit, and you expect us to believe that you no longer work for them?"

"I don't care what you believe," said Roche. "And really, does it make any difference who I work for?"

The waldoes on the third all-suit shifted. "I think we should space her," said the accompanying voice.

"Private channel, you idiot," said the second outrigger, all humor gone.

For a moment the outriggers ignored her, only the slight motion of waldoes and antennae betraying the fact that some sort of interaction was taking place. Clearly the all-suits acted in much the same way as normal bodies for their inhabitants, with a peculiar form of body-language to match. Only the lasers didn't shift, aimed squarely at Roche through the helmet of her suit.

After a minute of silence, she opaqued her faceplate and had the suit display the view artificially. Haid was pinging her, sending her a repetitive signal through the interference to let her know he was watching and ready to act if needed. That was reassuring, but she wanted to keep him out of it if possible; she had to earn their trust on her own, without using force.

The outriggers shifted around her. She tensed, ready to defend herself if attacked. Instead, two of the lasers dimmed, then snapped off. After a few moments, the third did likewise.

"We're taking you to a quorum," said the second outrigger.

"I'm not going anywhere until you tell me who you are and kill the interference so I can talk to my crew."

"You're in no position to make any demands," said the third outrigger.

"For the last time, Yul," said the second, "shut up and let me do the talking. She's here to *help* us."

"I'd like to," Roche cut in. "Insofar as I can, at least; if you'll let me."

"Exactly. I'm Idil, and this is Yul and Eli."

Now the lasers were off, Roche could see the all-suits properly. Idil's was painted entirely in a color that might have been orange but looked pink in the light; Yul's had four silver bands around its midriff; Eli's was angular, almost rhombohedral in shape.

"We're from Long Span spine. Auditor Byrne says you can talk, but the ship you came here in is not to change its orbit. If it comes near the spines, we'll retaliate."

Roche grunted as the interference faded. She used the same encrypted channel Haid had requested earlier.

"Ameidio? You there?"

"Yeah," came Haid's voice. "You okay?"

"Fine. They're taking me somewhere to negotiate. I don't want you to do anything else but wait until I come back."

"How long?" he asked.

She relayed the question to the outriggers.

"A couple of hours," Idil said. "Or never. The quorum may decide it doesn't need your help. And if so, it might not let you return to your ship at all."

Roche privately doubted the outriggers' ability to damage her suit, but wasn't keen on testing her theory just yet. "Give them three hours, Ameidio, then use your judgment."

"Will do."

"And if you hear from the Box, tell it to stay away. We don't want the drive falling into the wrong hands."

"I understand," said Haid. "And should anyone make a

move on me, I'll get the hell out of here, but I'll try contacting you first. Any idea where they're taking you?"

"To one of the spines, I guess. They haven't said."

"Well, I'll keep the channels open."

Roche turned her attention to the outriggers. All three suits were oriented toward her, their antennae spread wide like eyes watching her intently.

"Okay," she said, readying her suit to take her up into orbit, toward the spines. "Let's go."

But instead of up, they took her down.

She lost direct radio contact with Haid the moment she followed Idil into the shaft. She could still hear the regular *ping* broadcast by the courier, but only as a series of faint and highly peculiar echoes, as though the shaft was absorbing the signal, interfering with it, then broadcasting it back at her from a dozen locations at once. She didn't know what would happen if she tried to contact him. Maybe nothing out of the ordinary, or he wouldn't hear her at all.

It was too late to worry about that now.

She followed close behind Idil, watching as the antennae of the outrigger's suit were enfolded to prevent damage to fragile components. The other two, somewhere behind Roche, were no doubt doing the same. The shaft itself was lit by the searchlights of the three all-suits and her own suit, giving her an intriguing glimpse into the moon's interior. The shaft's smooth rockface faded after a hundred meters or so; beyond that it shared the color and albedo of bronze, although it could easily have been something else. At one hundred and fifty meters, the shaft doglegged, first upward with respect to Roche, then to her left, then down again, then twice to her right. The turns were always at right angles, but the distances between them were irregular. Navigation was tricky, using thrusters and the occasional limb—or waldo, in the outriggers' case—to correct miscalculations. After several more such turns, Roche started to feel disoriented, as though trapped in some bizarre cosmic plumbing.

They passed a tunnel opening to her left, unlit and with the same radius as the shaft they were traveling along. They passed two others before moving "upward" into a fourth. From the inside, it was the same as the one they had left. She could see no markings, no fixtures, no artifacts of any kind. Nothing but endless tunnels, crisscrossing through the heart of the moon.

Only then did she realize that she had literally lost all sense of up and down—and so had her suit. It was obtaining readings consistent with being in free-fall, regardless of which way they traveled. Something in the tunnel walls, or elsewhere, had dampened the low gravity of the moon to nothing. Why, or how, she couldn't imagine.

Ahead of Roche, Idil began to slow. The all-suit issued a burst of white noise, and a hole in the pipe-wall opened to one side. No, not opened, Roche corrected herself; it had always been there. The holographic generator concealing it had simply been switched off.

Idil led the way through the hole, into a spherical chamber one hundred meters across, from which many other such openings led. Otherwise, the walls were smooth, ranging in color from the bronze of the tunnels to a deep cherry-red at the points farthest from the holes. The walls radiated light of a frequency not dissimilar to that of Hintubet.

The space within the chamber contained a thin atmosphere, held in place by some sort of boundary-field across each hole, and a further seven outriggers drifting in free-fall. Each was slightly different from the others. With instruments retracted, they looked like escape capsules, capsules made by ten different companies for ten different Castes; when instruments did appear, they did so in unique configurations and combinations. There were no portholes, no indications as to the appearances of their occupants at all, but it was easy to tell them apart.

Idil, Yul, and Eli dispersed once they were in the room,

and the seven others seemed to rearrange themselves slightly to accommodate the newcomers. Within moments Roche was the only thing moving in the center of the chamber; the outriggers had, perhaps by instinct, arranged themselves in a way that maximized the space between them.

"We want to know why you came here, Morgan Roche." The signal came from an outrigger whose all-suit was shaped like a teardrop, tapering at its aft end to a menacing point. Even this close and in an atmosphere, the outriggers still communicated by radio.

"I came here to find you," she answered. "Survivors, anyway. We were picking up signals from this region."

"Not from us, you weren't."

"No. I know that now." She paused for a second, then asked: "Why are you hiding down here?"

"Because we don't want to die, like the others," said one, his suit marked with concentric green triangles.

"You saw what happened?"

"Wide Berth spine lost almost a full complement over the spaceport on Aro. All hands of Long Span remained at a distance, and so we survived." This voice, thickly accented, came from an all-suit striped diagonally in black. The effect it had upon Roche as it slowly rotated was dizzying. "We came down here when the Galine station arrived because we suspected we would not be safe near it."

"We will never be safe in this system," said the green triangle outrigger in sharp disagreement. "We've already lost seventeen since we've been here."

"The short term is all that matters—"

"The short term is all you ever think about, Lud. When the one who killed the clan on Wide Berth comes looking for us, he will find you sitting here still, the easiest target in the galaxy."

A babble of argument broke out. Clearly the quorum was divided on what to do about the Sol clone warrior, just as Idil, Yul, and Eli had been about Roche.

She smiled to herself. This was everything she'd hoped for. If she could only keep them talking . . .

She caught a flash that might have been leakage from a private laser communication, then the teardrop all-suit spoke:

"We shouldn't squabble within the clan," she said. Her voice was firm, and resembled Idil's in inflection if not pitch. "We came here, Morgan Roche, to escape Wide Berth's fate. We have watched events in the system carefully since then, awaiting any sign that the one behind the attack on Wide Berth was coming here. So far, there has been no such sign. Your arrival caused a moment of concern, but it's clear that you are not the one. Your approach was too open, too blatant. I fear that the one we anticipate will be upon us before we even suspect."

"The data you collected—" Roche broke in. "May I—?"

"Access it? Certainly."

So easy? Roche couldn't help but be suspicious.

"Why?" she asked. "I thought *you* wanted to interrogate *me*?"

"We do. But the clan teaches that all answers lie in the questioner's own heart. If we exchange information, perhaps you will see for us what we do not."

Roche nodded. "Perhaps," she said.

"What do we have to lose?" The teardrop's blunt end unfolded like a flower, peeling back shielding to expose delicate machinery within. "You are not the one we feared. I therefore put my trust in you, Morgan Roche. I have faith you will not abuse it."

Roche was slightly taken back. "Just who are you, anyway?" she asked.

"My name is Byrne, auditor of Long Span spine. In situations such as these, when time is of the essence, I am the one that makes decisions."

"So their lives are basically in your hands?" said Roche.

"As mine is in theirs," she replied. "We are one, even when we disagree."

"You are their voice," said Roche.

The blunt end of the all-suit began to close. "I am also the one that asks the questions, and right now I would ask again: Why are you here, Morgan Roche?"

Roche was still a little stunned by the odd turn of events, but she knew that if she was going to get anywhere with the outriggers, then she was going to have to talk to Byrne, and that meant answering anything asked of her. So she outlined her reasons for coming to the system and what had happened to her since arriving. No point was covered twice, until the end, when Roche was asked to recapitulate her relationship with Adoni Cane. Many of the outriggers assembled for the quorum were hesitant to trust someone who had links with another Sol Wunderkind—albeit one who seemed less destructive than the one who had destroyed Palasian System. Roche could understand that.

"The other spine, Wide Berth," she said, fishing for information of her own. "What exactly happened to them over Aro?"

"We received distress signals," said Byrne. "A number of small pods, possibly escape capsules. Wide Berth decided to attempt a rescue. We advised against it, and suspected that the one behind the attack on the domed city—the Sol clone warrior, as you call him—was still in the area. Whether he was or not, we never did find out, but the pods were a trap. An orbital whip decimated the main body of those who went to investigate, while gas-guns picked off the survivors."

"We were unable to assist them in time," Lud's bitter voice broke in. "And those observing from the Galine station did not intervene."

"You saw the observers?"

"Yes."

"But you've had no contact at all with Galine Four?" said Roche.

"We hailed them when it arrived, but they ignored us," said Byrne. "This is not uncommon, of course, as outriggers are often overlooked. But when they also ignored the plight of Wide Berth, we knew its disinterest was more malevolent than usual."

Roche absorbed this. The ferocity of the attack on the Wide Berth outriggers didn't necessarily mean that the Sol clone warrior was personally directing it; automatic systems could have done as well. But Aro was the last location he'd been known to be; the chance of an eyewitness report was worth following up.

"No one survived the attack?"

"One," said Byrne. "The youngest of the clan, a boy named Yarrow. His role in the spine was observer, so he was removed from the focus of attack. We found his all-suit breached and drifting a day later. His emergency systems lasted barely long enough to return him to Long Span, where his all-suit was repaired."

"Could I talk to him?"

"That is impossible," said Byrne.

"He might have information—"

"He can tell you nothing," said Lud firmly.

"I'd still like to ask."

"His peace is more important than your wishes!" spat Lud.

The softer voice of Auditor Byrne filled the quiet following Lud's anger: "Yarrow has not spoken since the attack on his clan. You are welcome to try, but I don't like your chances."

"You're sure it *is* him?"

"Of course," said Byrne. "I oversaw his healing myself."

Roche wondered whether Byrne had actually seen the boy in the flesh or operated through his all-suit. She also wondered how Byrne could be so sure he was who he said he was since he'd come from another spine. It would be all too easy to hide in an all-suit and pretend to be someone who was actually dead.

But she decided not to push the issue any further, for now. Byrne seemed convinced of the boy's identity. Instead

Roche promised herself she would try to talk to the boy herself, later.

"Is there nothing new you can tell me about the Sol clone warrior's activities?" she said.

The spinning of Lud's striped all-suit slowed. "No."

"He speaks the truth." Byrne's voice was regretful. "By the time we knew something was wrong, the clone warrior had gone into hiding; and before we could escape, the system was enclosed. We are trapped here as surely as he is."

"Perhaps not any more," said Lud.

"True." Byrne's tone was thoughtful. "Morgan Roche, although I have said that I trust you, that does not mean that we will help you freely, or at all. The clan as a whole needs to consider everything you've told us. Your actions and those of Linegar Rufo could be interpreted many ways, and I must consult with my people before making any decisions."

"How long will that take?" Roche asked.

"Several hours. The debate will be thorough, with as many attending the Plenary as possible. You may attend the summation, if you wish."

"Thank you. I'd like that." Roche was curious to see how the outriggers would attain consensus on such a complex issue in so short a time, and was naturally concerned that its outcome would be in her favor. "But first I'm going to have to contact my ship from the surface. I told my crew that I would report in."

"Idil and Yul will escort you."

"I have no intention of escaping."

"I believe you, Morgan Roche," said Byrne. "They will act more as your guides than your guards."

Nothing was said, but Byrne's words still carried an implicit warning. Mok's labyrinth was extensive and difficult to navigate, and should Roche choose to attempt to elude her guides, she knew she would quickly become lost. If that happened, it was possible they would not be able to find her again. If they even tried.

To Roche's nominated guides, Auditor Byrne added: "Perhaps you could show her the central chamber on your return." Roche neither saw nor heard any kind of acknowledgment from either Idil or Yul, yet something seemed to be conveyed to the auditor. A second later she said: "Excellent, then you can join us from there."

With that, the outriggers led Roche out of the chamber, while the quorum assumed its former configuration, only with Auditor Byrne at the center and the remaining seven around her.

Roche's guides took her along the corridor outside at a more sedate pace than before. Roche couldn't tell if they were retracing their steps. The many turns and lack of reference points had her thoroughly confused, substantiating Byrne's unspoken warning.

"How do you know where you're going?" Roche asked.

Yul's gruff voice answered: "Breeding."

"Our internal guidance systems are highly specialized," Idil chipped in. "Much more sophisticated than yours. You could sever us from all our senses and take us anywhere across the system. Set us adrift, and we could find our way to within a kilometer of where we started."

"What's that got to do with breeding?" Roche asked.

"Some of us are third- or fourth-generation clan members," said Idil. "We gestated within and were raised as part of our suits; its systems are ours, although naturally the interface is not perfect. With every generation, however, we improve."

Roche was reminded of Uri Kajic. This wasn't so different. The ancient Dato Ataman, for whom the Marauder was named, might've saved herself a lot of trouble if only she'd talked to outriggers before launching the Andermahr Experiment.

But traditionally no one talked to outriggers. Did business with them, yes, but did not converse as equals. They were regarded with the same sort of suspicion and contempt as nomads were on some backward worlds. That they were capable of great technical skill didn't especially surprise Roche, but their sense of honor and integrity did. Auditor Byrne and Idil had both demonstrated clearheadedness and willingness to trust under difficult circumstances—something Roche's former colleagues in COE Intelligence were not renowned for.

"How many of you come from outside the clan?" she asked.

"About half," Idil replied. "We see a lot of disaffected types as we travel. Jaded combat soldiers; criminals looking for somewhere to hide; sociophobes. Most we reject out of hand. The ones we keep are those who demonstrate an ability to maintain group integrity over vast distances. It's a difficult thing to manage; some never do come to terms with the isolation. But once accepted, the lifestyle does have its rewards."

"Do you give preference to those who come from the same place as others within the clan? Or to groups of applicants? I notice that you and the auditor have a similar accent."

"We do, but our relationship is not what you might think. I joined Long Span as a teenager when it passed through the fringes of Gwydyon seventy-eight subjective years ago—one hundred and twenty of yours. My all-suit used to belong to the woman whose clan name I took after my tenth year as a member. She died of old age six months before I joined. In my twentieth year I elected to have a child, conceived parthenogenetically from my own tissue. I gave her the name of my mother, back on Gwydyon, and designed her all-suit myself. Auditor Byrne is my daughter."

Roche pondered this as Idil and Yul led her toward the surface of the strange, alien moon.

"I'm sure it's okay, Ameidio."

"Damn it, Morgan!" The annoyance was obvious in Haid's voice. "You're taking an awful risk."

"Only because I need to. You know that. I'll be away a

few hours longer, and the suit will need a top-up. If I had a choice, I'd let you come down, but I don't trust Myer and Disisto alone in the ship. So you'll have to send Disisto with everything I need."

"Why don't you just come up here? You can be here and back within an hour."

"Because it's not just about supplies. I might need someone else down here if the decision doesn't go our way. They've said we can trust them, but I'm not willing to believe everything they say just yet."

Haid was silent for a second. "Besides which, you want to have a look around, right?"

Roche smiled to herself. "You got it."

"I guess I can't blame you, Morgan. From what the suit recorded, I can't say I've seen anywhere like it before."

"Disisto will be interested in it too, given his association with Rufo's work. Another reason to send him down. And maybe I can work on him a little, get him to change his mind."

"Okay, okay," Haid said with a mix of resignation and levity. "Besides, it's getting a little crowded up here. Mavalhin's awake, and if I hear one more complaint out of him, I swear I'm going to put him in the airlock."

"Any particular issue?"

"He wants to talk to you."

"Naturally. But if it's not important, he can wait."

"That's what I keep telling him. Unfortunately, I've run out of reasons to keep him under sedation, and he gripes about being tied up."

Roche chuckled to herself. She could sympathize, but there was little else she could do. "Any other news?"

"A tightbeam from the Box arrived not long ago, bounced off a drone near Herensung. We have an ETA with the *Ana Vereine* in five days. The Box says we'll be able to contact it safely in twenty-four hours. It'll send us coordinates before then."

"That's progress, I guess." Since their last exchange of

messages to arrange the rendezvous point, they had maintained strict radio silence. "Good to know the ship evaded capture."

"The Box never seemed to have any worries."

"It wouldn't." Roche scanned the sky for any sign of *Daybreak,* but it wasn't visible. "Myself or one of the outriggers"—she forwarded him the unique frequencies Idil had given her—"will stay on the surface to wait for Disisto. The sooner he leaves, the better. Call me if there are any problems."

Haid signed off and Roche returned her attention to the world around her. She was resting in the very low local gravity near one of the hairlike spikes protruding from the surface of the moon. The soil below her seemed to glitter faintly—an effect magnified by the crackling of the ion bridge high above her. When she bent to touch it, she learned that it was only a centimeter or two deep; below that was black rock, inert to all the suit's sensors.

"You'll find it difficult to chip," said Idil, balancing on her main thruster not far away. "Some of us tried to analyze it when we arrived, but didn't have much luck. It might be some sort of artificial material we haven't come across before. Designed from the molecules up."

"Any idea who made it?"

"That's hard to say. There are living quarters off one of the central chambers. We can't get into them ourselves, but we managed to get some of our remote probes in."

"Did you find anything? Any reason why the builders left? Any bodies that might help identify the Caste?"

"Nothing. In fact, the quarters were never inhabited. They were possibly intended as a shrine, or a museum perhaps."

Roche considered this. An ancient, unknown Caste, close enough to Transcendence to no longer need its hereditary form but not so removed to have lost all affection for it, might have modified or built the small moon for purposes that had become meaningless over time. Mok might have drifted far from its origins before being captured by the double-jovian, or—and this was an area Roche hardly dared venture into—the entire arrangement could have been artificial. The two gas giants, the ion bridge, and the single moon were an unlikely combination to have formed naturally. Although the possibility was daunting, the universe had a capacity for surprise far exceeding Roche's own imagination and she knew better than to base any opinions on what she considered normal.

The aspirations and achievements, and even the whereabouts, of the Caste responsible for the artifacts were as impenetrable as the artifacts themselves. And that only made her more curious. Assuming the outriggers joined her cause, she would have days before the Box arrived. Which would be plenty long enough to have a decent look around.

Disisto complied readily with her instructions, and was suited and able to go within the hour. Half an hour after that, he had joined Roche on the surface with a utility containing the requisitions her suit needed to remain operating for an extended period. While it looked after itself, she introduced him to the two outriggers.

Idil's voice was frosty. "You're from the Galine station?"

"I run dock security."

"How much say do you have regarding policy?"

"None, really. That's all handled by the chief."

"Linegar Rufo?"

"Yes."

If Idil was appeased by that, Yul was not. "Your people stood by while a clan was murdered."

"That's simply not true—" Disisto began.

"You deny that you had observers in the area of Aro when the spine was attacked?"

"No, but—"

"They did *nothing*."

"What *could* they have done? They were only a handful. If your people couldn't do anything, how could mine?"

"At least you could've talked to us afterwards," said Idil. "Traded information."

"To have broadcast like that would have given away our location!"

"You're lying," said Yul. "You broadcast regularly on the old channels."

"Through relays."

"Exactly. That must be safe enough. Whoever it is you're talking to can't be any less dangerous than us."

Roche noted the comment. It seemed the outriggers also suspected Rufo of trying to contact the Sol warrior.

"This is all irrelevant," she interrupted. "Disisto is here because he's interested in the ruins you've found. He's not here as my ally, or yours. Far from it. If you object to his presence, I'll happily send him back."

Yul grunted, the waldoes on his all-suit twitching uncertainly.

"We will suffer his presence," Idil decided. "But if he gets into trouble, don't expect us to help."

"At least we know where we stand." Disisto's voice was stiff and formal.

Roche didn't trust herself to comment. "Shall we get on with it?" she suggested.

They descended into the moon, this time via another shaft. Roche had no way to tell this one from the rest, apart from its map coordinates. Again she had to rely on the outriggers to navigate for her and Disisto as they zigzagged through the tunnels.

"There are four thousand two hundred seventeen entrances on the surface of Mok," Idil said as they traveled. "The tunnels themselves extend for many thousands of kilometers within the moon. We haven't even come close to mapping them all. Some go nowhere or loop back on themselves; others end in chambers like the one you saw earlier; still others lead to museums, or what might be machines of some kind. It's hard to tell. But I get the feeling that we haven't touched upon the stuff that actually matters. It's hidden in some recesses of this moon we haven't discovered yet."

"You think this is just a smoke screen?" Disisto asked.

"It's a possibility. A labyrinth designed to make it difficult for intruders to get in."

"Or out," Roche added quietly to herself.

"They could've built a door out of the crust material and kept just about everything out," said Yul.

"Perhaps that wasn't enough," Idil ventured. "Depends how fearful their enemies were, I guess."

"It seems like you picked a good place to hide, then," said Roche. "Too good, almost."

"When the clan of Wide Berth died," said Yul, "it was an obvious place to seek shelter: distant, relatively secure, and belonging to no one else. We were hoping we'd go undetected." The outrigger's all-suit rotated slightly on its axis. A shrug, Roche intuited. "We have ruins similar to these recorded in the spine's archives. Other clans have found them and passed on the knowledge. This one was unrecorded because we are the first outriggers to come here. Until DAOC announced that they were seeding the inner belts with prowling mines, the system was never considered worth looking at. It wasn't until Thin Trunk spine passed on the word that there was a vacant turf large enough for two spines, and Wide Berth was free at the same time as us, that we decided to come. . . ."

Yul talked on, but Roche let her mind wander. She was less interested in why the outriggers had come here than how they could help her. No one had mentioned it yet, but she was probably their only hope of leaving the system. If the Kesh destroyer that delivered Galine Four didn't stop to pick them up—which was unlikely—they would be destroyed along with the ruins they inhabited. And while Roche wasn't keen to use blackmail to get the help she needed, she would do so if it was the only option left to her.

It wasn't just the matter of information on the Sol warrior she wanted. If the outriggers were working with her, the chances of rescuing Maii and Cane improved. The only question was, still, *how*?

When Yul had finished, Roche broke in with: "How heavily armed are you?"

"That depends," Idil responded.

"On?"

"If you want to know what weapons we have, the answer is *none*. But we do have cutting lasers, ion drilling cannons, spectrometry bombs, nano seeders, seetee crust-rippers—"

"Ah." Disisto suppressed a chuckle. "The smuggler's toolkit: weapons that never show up on customs declarations, but always appear when you try to haul them in."

"These are not weapons," Idil said coolly. "We would only use them as such if we are attacked."

"Why didn't Wide Berth spine do that on Aro?"

"They did, but . . ." Idil hesitated. "They didn't know *how* to retaliate. We are not trained at war."

"What about the stories I've heard about dust-shoals and booby-trapped asteroids?" said Disisto.

"All retaliatory," Idil insisted. "If one of our kind makes the mistake of broadcasting the discovery of a rich deposit, it is not uncommon for that deposit to be taken away from us. We can't prevent a system's owners from moving us on; even if we have a legal licensing agreement for the territory, the fact that they technically own it works against us. We are regarded as scavengers, or worse, by most people. Most of the time, we lose everything we have worked for, and that is all. But if we are expelled by force, we feel it to be our right to retaliate. So we leave reminders that we have been there, and that we are angry at being robbed."

"It's ironic," said Disisto. "The Sol clone warrior used some of your own tactics against you, over Aro."

"But his motives are decidedly more malicious than ours," said Yul. "Or yours."

"True," said Roche. She wanted to move the subject on,

but before she could, her suit signaled that she was receiving a tightbeam from a source nearby.

"Disisto? Is that you?"

"Yes. Haid gave me this frequency if I needed to talk to you in private."

"Good thinking." She glanced at her instruments; none of the outriggers seemed to have noticed the private conversation. "What do you want?"

"To explain what happened back on Aro. You seem to agree with the outriggers that the chief is at fault."

Roche sighed. "You want to defend Rufo?"

"There really was nothing those observers could have done to save anyone."

"You don't know that. And *they* certainly didn't know that at the time."

"They were only there to observe—"

"What if they'd *observed* survivors on the ground?"

"They didn't, did they? Listen, Roche: if one of our observers had been captured, the location of Galine Four could've been traced. That would've placed all our lives in danger."

"I thought you said the clone warrior had left the system."

"That's what *I* believe, not the chief. And it pays to be safe rather than sorry."

"What *pays* isn't the issue here. I'm talking about basic Humanity: helping people in trouble."

"I'm sure Rufo would have allowed the observers to intervene," Disisto said, "but the fact is hours would've passed before signals from the observers reached the station and our replies went back. By then, the attack would've been over. There was nothing those observers could do—except watch."

Roche didn't respond immediately. Disisto's last point was probably true, but it didn't allay her doubts. And there was something else, something he wasn't telling her. . . .

"You can ask Mavalhin if you don't believe me," he said

into her reflective silence. "He was one of the senior observers of the Aro attack."

"Well, that explains why they didn't use their initiative," said Roche. "Or follow their conscience."

He was quick to reply: "Exactly."

The sharpness of his voice startled her, but she had no time to ask him what he meant. The outriggers were slowing again, and—now that she was paying attention to her environment—she became aware that she was feeling gravity. Gently at first, but becoming stronger, her sense of up and down was returning.

The only problem was, it was coming at right angles to where it should have been. She let the suit orient itself properly against the field and scanned ahead to see where they were headed.

Not an exit, as she first guessed. The tunnel around them ballooned outward until it reached almost ten meters across, then joined another to form the stem of a Y. Two more joined, one after the other, and Roche began to feel as though she were swimming through the veins of an enormous beast.

"We're approaching the heart of the maze," said Idil. "Be careful. Gravity does odd things ahead."

Roche was grateful for the warning as, moments later, *up* suddenly became *down,* then began to corkscrew rapidly around her. Her inner ears complained at the disorientation, and for one horrible second her gorge rose in a manner she hadn't experienced since her early days of training. Only when the sensation subsided did she become aware of Disisto's chuckling.

"Neat trick," he said.

"What's that?" asked Yul, his voice as surprised as Roche felt.

"The only safe way past that point is to fly past," Disisto explained. "It'd be impossible to walk without bouncing off the walls."

Roche cast an eye behind her, studying the width of the tunnel. "Another defense?"

"That's the only thing we can think of," said Idil.

"What were they hiding?" asked Roche.

"I don't know," said Disisto. "But can you imagine the technology required to construct all of this?"

"Opaque your visors as we go through this next bit," Idil interrupted, a mandible waving toward the end of the tunnel. Ahead of them a cerulean membrane seemed to ripple as they approached. "Don't worry. It's quite safe. Just better to see it cold the first time."

Roche's stomach felt full of water as she took the outrigger's advice and let the instruments in her left eye guide her through the membrane.

There, rotating oddly in the center of a spherical chamber easily a kilometer across, was a pinch of space that defied Roche's best efforts to describe. It was hard to see directly, appearing almost as a shimmer in her view of the walls behind it. But it was more than a mirage. Much more. It had its own structure, its own definition—yet it wasn't anything at all. In a strange way, it reminded her of the anomaly they had passed through in order to enter Palasian System.

"Is that what I think it is?"

"It might be," said Idil. "It's hard to tell from within the Gauntlet, but we've found no reason to doubt it."

"An anchor point—*inside* the moon?"

"Why not? There's no particular law that says they have to be in open space. The vacuum's as perfect as it can be in here. Even the atoms and particles spilling off us somehow disappear into the background flux. As long as it doesn't bump into the walls, or anything else, it's quite safe."

"But an anchor point is fixed to the space-time grid, not the things around it," said Roche. "The ones near systems have to be taken apart and rebuilt regularly or else they drift. To try to fix one in place while the moon orbits Kukumat and Murukan *and* Hintubet would be impossible, surely."

"And yet there you have it," said Idil. A waldo waved

at the odd patch of space before her. "It doesn't work, of course."

"Because the whole system is in hyperspace," Roche said. "The only way out is through the external boundary, and even then only by slow-jump."

"It cost us lives in Free-For-All figuring that one out," said Yul.

"But an anchor point is a weakness in space-time," said Disisto. "What's *this* a weakness in?"

"Good question," said Idil. "If you find the answer, let us know."

A thought struck Roche: that if the anchor point was fixed, and the system revolved around it, then that would explain why it could be contained in such a way. But that didn't make sense either. Her mind hurt just thinking about it.

"Why did you bring us here?" she said after a moment.

Neither Idil nor Yul replied immediately. She looked around at the outriggers. They were floating motionless in the vacuum. She repeated the question.

"Sorry," said Idil. "The Plenary has begun. We would all like to attend, so we've brought you here to keep you occupied. There's a lot to look at without leaving this chamber. Down the far end are some structures that will interest you."

"You're leaving us here?" asked Disisto, glancing at Roche.

"No. The Plenary doesn't require our actual presence. We'll simply interface with the others from here. It's just that we'll be preoccupied if you try to talk to us, that's all."

Roche tried unsuccessfully to read Disisto's expression through his transparent helmet.

"That sounds fine to me," she said. "We won't be going anywhere."

The all-suits floated motionless in the zero gravity without response.

"Shall we take a look?" Disisto said, indicating the far end of the chamber.

The anchor half hid a structure of some kind. Roche couldn't make it out. "After you."

Disisto used his thrusters to head off across the space, cutting a chord deeper into the chamber rather than hugging the outside. Roche did likewise, keeping an eye on her instruments.

"Don't go too close," she said as they neared the anchor point. Although it seemed, perversely, to shrink in size, she was wary of it all the same. In the highly unorthodox domain of the Gauntlet, anything was possible.

"So they've convened a Plenary," he said, ignoring her instruction. "To talk about what?"

"Us. Whether or not to help me."

"I see."

His gaze was fixed forward. He began to fire his thrusters, nudging his way around the anchor. This close it looked like smoked glass spun into a tangled web and seen through a foggy lens. It still looked as though it was moving, although in which direction was hard to determine.

"Do you expect me to help you when it comes time to rescue your friends?"

"You've told me you won't betray Rufo."

"That's right. I have."

"You won't change your mind?"

"No."

"It would be easier if you did," she said. Then, watching his movements around the anchor point: "I can take over your suit at any time, you know, in case you were thinking of throwing yourself into that thing."

His laugh was loud but forced. "Don't flatter yourself, Roche. The idea hadn't even occurred to me," he said. "Tell me, though, what you would do to ensure my cooperation. Torture me?"

"Anything's possible," she said. "I'm determined to rescue Maii."

"And Cane?"

She hesitated before answering. "Yes, Cane as well."

Disisto grunted as they swooped past the anchor point. "You know what I think this is?" he said, gesturing around him. He didn't wait for her reply: "Some sort of covert transportation system. The anchor point obviously led somewhere, once, and the shell of moon around it would've absorbed any emissions when it was used. The labyrinth and the gravity trap would have stopped anyone just wandering in. There could be hundreds of these things scattered across the galaxy and no one would ever know about them."

"But the outriggers got through the traps easily enough. It's not really that secure. Especially given its location."

"Maybe the builders just wanted a little privacy."

"Maybe," she muttered, turning her attention to the structure they were approaching. It looked like a cannon of some kind, or an elongated funnel, directed at the anchor point. Instead of a barrel, though, it contained a cuplike hollow thirty-five meters in diameter. Despite her instruments saying it was inactive, Roche still regarded the structure warily. There was undoubtedly a connection between it and the anchor point, and until she knew exactly what that connection was, she had no desire to be anywhere between them.

They split up when they reached it. Roche circled its lip while Disisto traveled along its underside. It seemed to be made of the same material as the crust, but whorled and knotted as though eroded by centuries of running water.

The channel between them was thick with their silence. Neither was talking for fear of provoking the other.

"Any theories?" she asked. Anything was better than that silence.

"I've never come across anything like this before," he said. "And I've been on plenty of excavations."

"What about Rufo? Think there'd be anything in his files?"

"He's covered more of the galaxy than most people,"

Disisto said thoughtfully. "His records contain thousands of examples of Caste-types and divergent engineering and exotic materials and bizarre technologies, but . . ." He stopped. "If I didn't know better, I'd say this wasn't even Human."

"There's no chance of that, I suppose?"

He snorted. "None. Believe me, if there was any sign of alien life in the galaxy, past or present, Linegar Rufo would know about it."

"He seems the secretive type to me," she said, to see if she would get a reaction.

She did: he laughed. "Listen, Roche. Don't play me for the fool. Making me doubt my boss isn't going to make me automatically want to help you get your friends back." She watched as he jetted up to where she floated near the mouth of the giant trumpet. Through his faceplate she could see him smiling humorlessly. "But I may be useful to you in other ways."

"Such as?"

"I've been thinking. Even if I won't help you fight Linegar, I *can* tell you some things you probably should know."

She cleared her faceplate and met his eye. She sensed an internal struggle raging within him. He wasn't going to betray his boss, but he didn't want to see her fail, either. How he could possibly hope to succeed at both—and why—she didn't know, but she was keen to see him try.

"Go on," she said.

"It's about Cane," he said. "And the other one we're chasing. The Kesh believe they're something to do with the Sol Apotheosis Movement, but Rufo doesn't. He's letting them believe it because it gives him an edge. But he suspects it's all a smoke screen."

Roche shook her head. "A *smoke screen*? What do you mean?"

"Exactly what I say. There might be no connection between the two. And if so, you could be basing assumptions on imperfect data."

"But we've got *proof* that Cane is a Sol Wunderkind:

his genetic design, the control language you've been broadcasting—"

"I'm not a biogeneticist, so I can't argue about his makeup. But I do know the control language didn't come from any of the historical archives. You must have looked before you came here. Did *you* find the codes?"

"No. I assumed Rufo had access to other records—"

"The language *wasn't* in the records," he cut in. "None that any of us can access, anyway. I don't know where the codes came from or what they mean, and I doubt the chief knows either, but I know he was *given* those codes. He's deliberately keeping Shak'ni out of the full picture—and he's letting you believe what you want to believe, too."

"Why?"

"I don't know." Disisto seemed frustrated. "But I think it's dangerous. We should be sharing information. Otherwise we could all be killed by this thing. Or even Cane, for that matter—whatever the hell he is."

"No, you're wrong," said Roche. "Uri found a correlation in the *Ana Vereine*'s database. Cane's face matched that of the man who wiped out the Sol Apotheosis Movement. How can you ignore that kind of connection?"

"Because *we* have no records of any 'Adoni Cane' at all—in the Sol files or elsewhere."

"What?"

"I can't explain it, Roche. All I know is that while you were in the meeting with Linegar, he ordered a confirmatory search, and nothing was found."

"This is insane." She groped for an explanation that made sense. Either Rufo had corrupted his own files in order to keep the information a secret, or the *Ana Vereine*'s records were wrong—along with those of COE Intelligence HQ, which had confirmed the match. For the first time, she wished the Box was around to help her work out what was going on.

The Box . . . It had a habit of manipulating records to suit its own agenda. But why would it encourage her to believe, mistakenly, that Cane's origins lay with the Sol Apotheosis Movement? What could it possibly gain from that? And where had Rufo's information come from? The Kesh didn't know, so that ruled them out, and the Box had been with her for weeks. It just didn't fit together.

"You disapprove of what Rufo is doing," she said, trying to clarify Disisto's feelings on the matter of Cane. "But I suppose you don't disapprove enough to help me rectify the problem, either."

Disisto drifted until one hand rested on the alien surface. "Look, I'd rather we were taking an active role here in the system. The Kesh might go along with it, although I don't really know what they're after. Rufo's attempts to contact the warrior give me the creeps, to be honest. Whoever gave him the information he needed to do that, whoever knew enough about the warrior to identify his type even though we can't—whoever that *is,* I think they know a lot more than they're saying. And I think Rufo is being used. This 'whoever' was too afraid to come here themselves, so we were dispatched. We're all expendable."

Roche suddenly felt cold and vulnerable. The Box had something to do with the High Human called the Crescend. High Humans had access to all sorts of information mundanes never even suspected existed. It might have given the control language to Rufo in exchange for firsthand information. And where *was* the Box now? Jetting around the system in her one and only escape route, while she played xenoarchaeologist with a genocidal clone warrior possibly nearby. . . .

She cursed under her breath and tried to shake the paranoid thoughts. Such a line of thinking was neither helpful nor healthy. Nevertheless, one thing she *had* learned in recent weeks was that being merely paranoid wasn't paranoid enough. And she certainly *was* expendable. . . .

No. She couldn't let Disisto confuse her. She had no reason to believe that the Sol Apotheosis Movement was a smoke screen. Linegar Rufo could be wrong for a change, or Disisto could be lying. Better the latter than the tangled skein of deceit he was proposing in its place.

Disisto seemed unaware of the uncertainty he had provoked in her. That only made it worse. If he had done it deliberately, then he was a better liar than she believed him to be.

"Anyway," he said, "I thought you ought to know about my dilemma. If you can help *me* out of it, then—"

"That's not my problem," she said, pushing herself impatiently away from the alien trumpet. "And there's too much going on for us to just float around sightseeing. The more I can sort out before the Box gets here, the better." She switched to a more general frequency. "Byrne? Idil? Can anyone hear me?"

"Is something wrong?" said Idil after a few moments.

"I want to attend the Plenary. I want to hear what you're saying about me."

"You don't have the interfaces required to do that."

"Byrne said I could sit in on the summary. How much different could it be?"

"Fundamentally."

Out of the corner of her eye, Roche saw Disisto moving away from her. She froze his suit with a simple command. "Regardless, I want to know what's going on. Maybe I can contribute." *Or make sure you come to the right decision,* she thought.

"I'm sorry, but it just isn't possible—"

The auditor's voice cut into the conversation. "Let her," she said. "It will do us no harm."

"Very well, Roche. Surrender your suit's input channels," said Idil. "Do you have direct inputs?"

"My left eye and ear."

"Okay. I'll see what I can do to make it easier."

Roche hesitated before handing over control, wondering what she had let herself in for.

She gave Idil the access codes required to patch into her implants. The outriggers would be able to draw upon her suit's full communication capacity; she could pull out any time she wanted, she assumed.

"Five seconds," Idil said. "Prepare yourself."

For what? she wanted to ask.

Then she recalled that Auditor Byrne hadn't said "harmless" to everyone. Byrne had said that it wouldn't harm *them.*

With a click and a flash deep in the underside of her brain, the Plenary of Long Span spine exploded through her.

6

Mok Interior
'955.01.21 EN
1990

The voice seemed to speak directly into the fissures of Roche's brain:

> Commander Roche
> has come to us for help
> and to offer us help.
> We have numerous options.
> Which do we chose?

With the words came a blinding light. It felt as though the outriggers were overloading the tolerances of her auditory and optic nerves. But her implants had buffers that should prevent that sort of surge. Somehow the outriggers must have infiltrated the hardwiring of her implants.

The voice repeated its spiel. This time Roche sensed a hidden complexity, a second, more subtle strand underlying the first, somehow mixed up with vivid pulses of light accompanying the sound.

Commander Roche
↑how do we know she is who she says she is?↓
has come to us for help
↑or to spy↓
and to offer us help.
↑how?↓
We have numerous options.
↑believe her↓
↑don't trust her↓
↑trust her↓
↑kill her↓
↑send her away↓
↑help her↓
↑help her help us↓
↑help her get away↓
Which do we choose?

The response wrapped itself around the question like a vine. The more the question was repeated the more complex and tangled the response became. Layer by layer, the argument unfolded:

Commander Roche
↑[1]How do we know she is who she says she is?
↑[2]She has no reason to lie.
↑[3]Nor reason to tell us the truth.[3]↓
Does it matter?
↑[3]If she's lying about this, we can't trust her at all.
↑[4]But we have no way of knowing.[4]↓
True.[3]↓
It's good to be cautious, but let's not get out of hand.[2]↓
Agreed, for now.[1]↓

She struggled to keep up as the question cycled and recycled, dragging her along with it:

<u>has come to us for help</u>
↑[1]More likely to spy.
↑[2]Who for?[2]↓
COE Intelligence
↑[2]She says she doesn't work for them anymore.
↑[3]And you believe her?
↑[4]She says she heard a distress call.
↑[5]She could be lying about that, too.[5]↓
We're going in circles!
↑[5]No, *you* are[5]↓
We must establish a reason for suspicion.
↑[5]That our lives are under threat isn't enough?
↑[6]We are safe here.
↑[7]Short term only.[7]↓
Perhaps.[6]↓
Perhaps not, if we let Roche in.[5]↓
Perhaps.[4]↓
Perhaps.[3]↓
We need to make a decision![2]↓
But the *right* one.[1]↓
<u>and to offer us help.</u>
↑[1]How?
↑[2]*Ask* her.
↑[3]Again: why should we believe her?↓
↑[2]What have we got to lose if we do?
↑[3]Our lives.
↑[4]We'll die if she *doesn't* help us![4]↓
↑[3]We have only her word on that.
↑[4]But we *are* trapped here.[4]↓
Undeniably.[3]↓
So can we at least agree to give her a chance?[2]↓
That's what we *are* doing![1]↓

Despite the increasing complexity of the argument, she began to recognize voices—or at least patterns of response. There were the skeptics, and there were those inclined to trust her. She wondered how they could ever expect to achieve a consensus to arise from such chaos.

Each time the question reached its conclusion, the eddy of voices threatened to carry her away. . . .

We have numerous options.
↑[1]don't trust her
↑[2]send her away
↑[3]trust her
↑[4]help her help us
↑[5]believe her
↑[6]don't trust her
↑[7]send her away
↑[8]trust her
↑[9]help her help us
↑[10]disbelieve her
↑[11]kill her
↑[12]use her[12]↓
kill her[11]↓
don't trust her[10]↓
trust her[9]↓help her[8]↓
send her away
↑[8]help her help us↑[9]help her get away
↑[10]send her away[10]↓
trust her[9]↓help her help us[8]↓
kill her[7]↓
send her away[6]↓
let her live[5-3]↓
ignore her[2]↓don't trust her[1]↓

Gradually, the voices began to cluster into groups. The clamor didn't ebb, but it became slightly more coherent to Roche's adjusting senses. Each group made concessions in order to increase its numbers; one, initially prepared to let her go unharmed, eventually allied itself with another group who wanted the resources of *Daybreak* to remain behind; another began by offering help unreservedly but ended up demanding rescue from the collapsing Gauntlet as a condition for giving that help. Then the boundaries shifted again, hinging this time on her possible allegiance with Linegar Rufo. With each concession came increased complexity, so the Plenary became less of a squabble and more of a debate, although some of the exchanges remained heated.

Woven through the groups were odd loners who initially refused to accept any compromise. One of these in particular caught Roche's attention, even though the voice at first didn't contribute much.

> ↑[113-117]We have to make some kind of decision soon.
> ↑[118]But what *can* we do?
> ↑[119-125]The sensible thing would be to wait to see what happens.[125-119]↓
> Do we even have the resources to do anything?
> ↑[119-125]Exactly our point. For that reason we prefer inaction to action.
> ↑[126-129]No. The sensible response is to help her.
> ↑[130-131]Such action would potentially benefit us the most.
> ↑[132]No—*kill her*!
> ↑[133]And miss this chance to avenge my clan?[133]↓
> Irrelevant! Her mere presence here puts us in danger![132]↓
> We have no proof of that.
> ↑[132]Yet.
> ↑[133]But we *know* she can help *me*.[133]↓
> Must we also die in some futile attempt to make a point?[132-131]↓
> It would be a meaningless sacrifice.[130-126]↓
> Perhaps it is better in this case to attempt neither.[125-118]↓

Unacceptable response! Inaction is not an option![117-111]↓
At least we'd be alive.[110-109]↓
For how long?[108-105]↓
My people didn't die so yours could cower here and wait your turn![104]↓
So let's kill her now before she has a chance![103]↓
This is getting us *nowhere*![102-98]↓

The outrigger seeking revenge, Roche guessed, was the lone survivor of the attack on Wide Berth spine; the one seeking Roche's death, however, she couldn't identify. Perhaps it was one she hadn't yet met. A couple of times she tried to interject a comment in her defense, but she didn't know how to. All she could do was feel the currents of opinion ebbing and flowing around her.

Which do we choose?

Each time that question was asked, argument broke out afresh and the entire process was repeated. Slowly, though, a consensus began to emerge.

↑[286-291]We need more information.
↑[292-294]How do you propose getting that?[294-292]↓
By asking.[291-286]↓
And *trusting* her?[285]↓
We could do worse than try.[279-284]↓

Roche felt a growing sense of frustration. They had already interrogated her; what more could she possibly tell them that she hadn't already? There wasn't *time* for this!

The coordinating voice seemed to agree with her. Without warning, the fundamental spiel altered:

We must reach consensus.
Doing nothing is not an option

and neither is stalling for more information.
We cannot wait any longer.
We must decide now.
Do we help or hinder?

Roche almost drowned in the resulting surge of voices as the Plenary erupted into a chaotic buzz. She barely managed to hang onto the central thread in the fervor. And through the babble, only one voice stood out clearly.

↑[143]Either we help her, or we die!
↑[144-155]You can't be certain of that![155-144]↓
My clan is no more; how much more evidence do you need?
↑[144-155]Wide Berth was in the wrong place at the wrong time.[155-144]↓
Exactly—so don't let it happen to Long Span too![143]↓
You are free to leave at any time.[142-137]↓
Maybe I will cast my lot elsewhere.[136]↓
Be serious!
↑[136]Better to have striven and failed than to not have even tried at all.
↑[137-142]We are talking about the possible annihilation of an entire clan!
We have no time for feeble aphorisms, child![142-137]↓
My age is not relevant to this discussion.[136]↓
And you are alone.[122-135]↓
Am I?[121]↓
Are you?
↑[121]Will no one join me?
↑[122]*I will.*

The two words sent shock waves through the Plenary.

↑[123]Do you realize what you're saying?
↑[124-7]If you join her, the spine will be broken!

↑[128]It will be destroyed anyway, won't it?
↑[129-32]There is no evidence of that.[132-129]↓
There is enough to convince me.[128]↓
And me. It *does* seem the lesser of two evils.[127]↓
A choice between methods of suicide is not really a choice![126-124]↓
At least you *have* a choice. My clan did not.[121]↓
They would have chosen life; why can't we?
↑[121]Because life does not seem to be an option anymore.

Roche listened in amazement as the tide of the Plenary turned, the outriggers for the most part preferring to risk exposure and attack rather than see the clan divided.

↑[130-145]We live as one, we die as one.
↑[146]But Roche is not one of us![146]↓
Yarrow supports her.
↑[146]He is not one of us either.[146]↓
We have adopted him.[145-92]↓
Then we can un-adopt him![91]↓
He is one of us now, and always will be![90-37]↓

The resounding emphasis on Yarrow's permanent status as a member of the clan silenced many of the critics. Into the sudden ebb, the auditor repeated the crucial question:

<u>Do we help or hinder?</u>
↑[1-9]We help.
↑[10-27]We hinder.
↑[28-32]We help.
↑[33-40]We hinder.
↑[41-55]We help.
↑[56-66]We hinder.[66-58]↓
We help.[59-42]↓
We hinder.[43-40]↓
We help.[39-26]↓

We hinder.[25-19]↓
We help.[18-1]↓

The vote was fluctuating, changing every time the question was asked. Roche sensed a trend in her favor, but couldn't be certain. There were too many powerful voices commanding a negative vote. She waited anxiously for some sort of confirmation.

No matter what the decision
do we agree to abide by the ruling of the clan?
↑[1-66]We do.[66-1]↓

The giddying motion of the Plenary ceased for a brief moment as all the outriggers agreed on that one point. Again Roche was surprised by the fierce unity of the clan. Perhaps that was only to be expected when the rest of the galaxy treated them with disinterest at best.

Then we decide to help Morgan Roche.

The brief clarity of the Plenary instantly shattered.

↑[1]No! We can't!
↑[2-66]We are decided.[66-2]↓
But it's the wrong decision!
↑[2-66]We are decided![66-2]↓
No! *Kill her!*[0]↓

Something screamed in Roche's ears. At the same instant, the babble of the Plenary abruptly ceased. She opened her eyes to a scene of tangled metal and flashing energy. An outrigger—no, *two* outriggers—were rushing toward her, waldoes extended and lasers bright.

Her suit's systems were already on alert, howling the deafeningly loud impact alarm that had snapped her out of the Plenary. She had just enough time to raise her arms by reflex and target both of the all-suits when one of them—a lozenge with purple squares at either end—fired a projectile at her abdomen.

The projectile exploded on contact, sending her spinning backwards through the alien space of the moon's central chamber

"Roche!" Disisto's voice rang in her helmet, but she didn't have time to reply. The suit fired attitude thrusters to reorient itself, knocking her about while she fought to ready herself for another assault.

Her attackers had moved. She armed weapons and readied herself to fire. Only then did she notice that the other outrigger, battered black with no obvious markings, was grappling with the first. Its numerous waldoes pinned its opponent's wherever it could find a grip; cutting lasers burned close to delicate sensors; attitude thrusters sent both spinning to prevent its getting a bead on Roche a second time.

The black one was clearly trying to save her. Roche immediately removed its image from the targeting systems in her suit. But the two were too closely tangled for her to fire with any hope of hitting just the one of them. She nudged herself closer, hoping for a clear shot.

It never came. Her attacker fired its thrusters at full-strength and tore itself away from the black all-suit. But before the latter could do anything, the purple suit seemed to crack open, releasing an explosive cloud of air into the vacuum. The all-suit spun with its thrusters still firing across the chamber and into a wall, then scraped along the wall for a dozen meters before the thrusters shut down.

It hit a projection and ricocheted, inactive, across the chamber. The black all-suit jetted to intercept it before it could fall into the anchor point.

"Roche! Are you all right?" Disisto's voice fought for attention among those of Idil and the other outriggers. His immobilized suit hung nearby, anchored to the trumpetlike artifact at one end of the chamber.

"I'm fine," she said, although she was short of breath and still high on adrenaline. She allowed his suit to move with barely a thought. "What the hell happened?"

"The purple all-suit just came out of nowhere and attacked you, then the other one tried to stop it." He indicated the black all-suit, which had returned with the wreckage of the other.

"Thanks," said Roche, turning to face it. "Whoever you are."

The outrigger didn't respond.

Before she could speak again, Idil's all-suit slid into view. "This is Yarrow," she said. "Your attacker was Alik. We are deeply puzzled—and hurt—by her betrayal."

Roche didn't have any problem understanding it. "She disagreed with the decision. That seems clear enough."

"But to act against it!" The horror in the outrigger's voice was clear. "No one in their right mind would ever do that!"

"Well, maybe there's your answer," she said. "Or not."

She forced herself to approach the broken all-suit still gripped in Yarrow's waldoes. Its interior lay exposed to the vacuum, dusted with frozen air and debris. Roche shone a spotlight inside and examined what she saw very closely.

She saw a wizened body curled in the claustrophobic embrace of wires, tubes, and padding. Its age, sex, and Caste were difficult to confirm at a casual glance, but Roche could tell that it was tiny, much smaller than Cane. Blood vessels had burst across its skin and its eyes and mouth were open. The expression on the dead outrigger's face was one she wouldn't forget in a hurry.

Definitely dead, and not a clone warrior.

She turned to face the outrigger who had saved her. This close, she could see the old damage to the young survivor's all-suit. The outriggers of Long Span had done their best to mend it, but fresh paint couldn't hide the signs of heat damage. The egg shape of the capsule itself looked slightly off-true, as though warped by a powerful impact.

This was her chance to make contact with the boy. "Thank you," she said again.

But again he said nothing.

"He won't talk," said Idil. "As we told you, he hasn't spoken aloud since his clan was destroyed."

"But in the Plenary—"

"Yes. It was his 'voice,' if you will, that pushed the vote in your favor."

Roche regarded the black all-suit with gratitude mixed with uneasiness. "It seems I owe you on two fronts, now."

The boy's all-suit only turned and moved away, his self-imposed radio silence adding to his all-suit's strange air.

"Morgan Roche." Auditor Byrne spoke by relay from elsewhere in the moon. "I am relieved to learn that you are safe."

"I thought you said you spoke for your people," said Roche with a trace of bitterness.

"I do—even more so now, after this unfortunate setback. The honor of Long Span spine has been tarnished. Our resolve to help you, and thereby regain our honor, is hardened. Alik's attack only worsened her cause."

"Perhaps, but I'll have to talk to my crew about it." Roche checked the time. Four hours had passed; no wonder she felt exhausted. "I will be able to contact the *Ana Vereine* in about in about fourteen hours. Let's meet again in, say, ten."

"Very well. We will make no further decisions for the moment." Byrne hesitated before continuing: "I am deeply sorry, Morgan Roche, for what has happened. Believe me when I say that it will not happen again. All of us of Long Span spine know that if we do manage to escape Palasian system it will only be because we have worked together."

Roche hoped she was telling the truth.

Six hours later, the outriggers detected a beacon from the *Ana Vereine*. Coded into the *ping* was a time and date stamp, plus vector coordinates relative to Hintubet. There was as yet no sign of the Marauder, but that didn't surprise Roche. The ship's camouflage systems were the most advanced in the COE and could easily fool the outriggers' asteroid detection systems.

She recorded a brief message to be sent at the time indicated, outlining her present situation. Then, with her suit secured to a wall in the central chamber, she allowed herself a couple of hours' sleep.

She was awakened sometime later when Haid called to confirm that *Daybreak* was ready to descend to the moon's surface. The courier was far too obvious a newcomer to the double-jovian system, and the energy drain of holding the ship in a stable orbit was something they could do without.

"Are you *sure* it's safe?" he asked.

Roche had thought a lot about the attack on her during the Plenary, and both she and Haid had discussed it. Alik had spoken and acted alone, but that didn't mean there weren't others who felt similarly. She had come to the conclusion, though, that she was probably safe. Not only had Alik killed herself rather than face the wrath of the clan, once she knew her attack had failed, but, as Byrne had said, the spine had to prove itself now. The betrayal of Roche's peaceful approach, and the shame that brought with it, would do more than any threat of being expelled from the clan.

"Let's say I've given up worrying about it, Ameidio," she said. "Just find a suitable spot and bring the ship down."

"Well, that isn't going to be a problem," he said. "It'll be less like landing than docking. Intelligence HQ had more of a tug than this lump of rock."

"How's Myer?"

"I knocked him out. Not literally, of course, even though I would have liked to," he added. "I put him back in the autosurgeon and under sedation for a while. He was getting in the way and I didn't want him trying something while I was busy."

"Understood," she said. "But when you're down, I want

to talk to him. He saw what happened on Aro. I want to know whether or not Rufo forbade him to intervene."

"Okay. I'll instruct the autosurgeon to revive him then. He'll have a headache, but it won't kill him. More's the pity."

When Haid had decided where to land the courier, she relayed the coordinates to the outriggers. Idil guided her to the nearest shaft. There she rejoined Disisto, who had been exploring the moon under the watchful instruments of Yul and Eli.

"Find anything?" she asked.

"The untouched living quarters that Idil told us about earlier." The security chief seemed excited. "From the pictures and other personal artifacts there, it would seem the builders were more like birds than mammals. Hollow bones, long limbs, and wide-spaced eyes—it's quite incredible. They must've re-evolved back up to Pristine from some avian Low Caste."

"Then Transcended," Roche mused.

"Well, they certainly don't seem to be anywhere around here anymore."

"They must've been a pretty long-lived Caste. Given that Humanity has only been settling the galaxy for half a million years, that doesn't give them much time to devolve and re-evolve."

"That makes them a Primordial Caste, then," said Disisto. "My God, Roche! This is fantastic! I doubt there's another site as well preserved as this anywhere in the COE!"

"Well, it won't be here for much longer," she said.

Through the faceplate Roche could see Disisto's face fall.

"Why is it that Humans let their petty differences get in the way of knowledge?" he said. "We could've studied this thing for decades."

Before she could call him a hypocrite, he gestured to a point behind her. "Here's the ship."

Roche turned to where he'd indicated. She still found the blackness unnerving, but it did make detecting moving objects easier. The courier was a red dot drifting away from the half-set limb of Kukumat, growing steadily larger. Somewhere up there were the two spines, Long Span and Wide Berth, but neither was visible.

As Haid brought the ship down, Roche wondered if the curved spikes of the moon's surface were *actually* used as grappling hooks for docking ships. It was possible that ships had been securely stationed to them while their occupants used the anchor point in the moon's center to jump elsewhere across the galaxy.

But that didn't explain why the builders had gone to so much trouble to hide the anchor point in the first place. Or why their living quarters had never been used.

Her train of thought was broken as the courier vessel banked around its landing point. She watched it decelerate to a halt a hundred meters away from them, then waited until the afterwash from the thrusters had dissipated before moving in closer.

"Can't get smoother than that," boasted Haid, his voice crackling loudly over the open frequencies. Grapnels anchored the ship to two of the bent "trees"; Roche checked briefly to see that the hold was secure.

The airlock hissed open as she approached. "Wait here, Disisto."

On a closed channel, Haid said: "We have another message from the Box."

Roche unlocked the suit helmet when the outer hatch had sealed, but didn't allow herself the luxury of leaving the suit entirely. "What does it say?"

"It's picked up coded transmissions from the edge of the system. Looks like someone on the outside is trying to talk to someone in here."

"Is that what the AI thinks?"

"Well, it's keeping its options open. All it says is that the transmissions are centered on Hintubet. My guess is they're being relayed elsewhere."

"Not necessarily."

"But there's no one that deep in-system."

"No, but there is some*thing,*" she said. The sun of Palasian System was currently home to a number of machines of Kesh manufacture. "What if they're talking to the Gauntlet?"

The inner lock hissed open and she stepped through. Haid was waiting for her on the other side. He stepped back to accommodate the suit in the cramped passageway.

"I didn't think of that." He smiled. "It's good to see you again, Morgan. I had my doubts for a while there."

She touched his artificial arm with one gloved hand and stepped past him. "Thanks, Ameidio. Where's Myer?"

"In the medic suite. He'll be groggy."

"All the better." She thudded across the deck to the small medical facility. There, Mavalhin looked much like she had left him, tied flat to a narrow cot so he couldn't move. This time, though, he looked healthier. He had regained much of his color and the only blood on his uniform was brown.

She shook him, not worrying too much if the suit overemphasized the power of her movements. "Myer?"

He stirred, blinking absently up at her. "Morgan?"

"Myer. Can you hear me?"

"I'm not deaf, Morgan." He tried to sit up; puzzlement creased his features when he realized he couldn't because of his restraints. "I didn't think I was dangerous, either."

"For the moment, that's exactly what you are," she said. "Now, tell me about the attack on Aro."

He looked mystified for a second. "You mean when Emptage City and the spaceport were destroyed?"

"No, I mean the outriggers. You watched it happen. Describe what you saw."

"Not much, really. I didn't have the instruments—"

"Don't lie to me, Myer. I *know* you had the instruments; you were there to observe. Now tell me what happened or so help me I'll play cat's cradle with your stitches."

He paled slightly. "They were all killed," he said resignedly. "Cut to pieces. They didn't stand a chance."

"How long did it take?"

"I don't know. Ten minutes; maybe less."

"Why didn't you help them?"

"I couldn't."

"*Why* couldn't you, Myer?"

"I just *couldn't.* It was . . ." He hesitated. "There weren't enough of us, Morgan. There was nothing we could do."

Roche nodded. This was, so far, little different from what Disisto had told her. "But why didn't the trap catch *you,* Myer?"

He shrugged. "We were more careful, I guess."

"*How* were you careful?"

"We—" he began, then looked away and fell silent.

"You knew the traps were there, didn't you?" Roche asked after a few seconds.

His eyes met hers again. "We saw them not long after we reached Aro."

"So why didn't you warn the outriggers?"

"What do you want me to say, Morgan?" He was angry now. "That I was just following orders? Is that what you want to hear?"

"What I want doesn't come into it. What I'd *like* is for you to just tell me the way it was."

"Look," he said, attempting again to sit up. "We just assumed the outriggers would see the traps too. We didn't think there was any need to expose ourselves. If we did, then we risked endangering the station and everyone on board. We couldn't afford to take any risks, so we didn't. And I guess it worked, because the traps didn't spring us, and neither did the outriggers."

"So it was your decision not to act?" asked Haid.

"No, of course not," Myer said, shaking his head irritably. "We had orders. It was my decision to follow them."

"But what exactly *were* your orders?"

"I've already told you: to keep our heads down, no matter what happened."

Roche glanced at Haid, then back at Mavalhin. "Aro was

the obvious place to look for survivors. You would've seen them if they'd been there. What did Rufo tell you to do in such a situation?"

Mavalhin shrugged. "I can repeat it as often as you like; it's not going to change anything."

"Myer, if you're telling the truth, then it changes *everything.*"

He looked puzzled. "How? You were already at odds with the chief."

"Yes, but now it's not personal; it's not just me getting my friends back and settling a score. Now it's about stopping the man who ordered you to do nothing as dozens of innocent people were slaughtered simply because they tried to help. It's about *justice.*"

Mavalhin snorted. "How can you be so self-righteous? What about your 'friend' Adoni Cane? One of *his* associates is responsible for killing nearly everyone in this system—and yet you seem only concerned with what I did, or what Rufo ordered."

"That's not true," said Roche. "This whole thing stinks. I just—"

<Agreed, Morgan,> said a voice deep in her mind. <There is something far more mysterious going on here than even you currently suspect.>

"Box!" She started at the sound of the voice. "Is that really you?"

<Yes, Morgan. This signal is being relayed through the courier.>

"But—"

<I know what you are about to say: I am not supposed to be within range for some hours yet. That was a deliberate ploy to throw anyone seeking the *Ana Vereine* off the scent. It would be prudent to maintain that illusion for now.>

<Yes,> she said, remembering to subvocalize. Mavalhin was staring at her with confusion, Haid with surprise. "Ameidio, let Myer loose but keep an eye on him. I need to be

alone for a moment. If you can get Disisto in here as well, do it; otherwise he can wait outside."

With that she exited the medical facility and headed for the privacy of the bridge. She could tell that Haid was curious as to what was going on, but a proper explanation would have to wait—at least until *she* knew what was going on. . . .

<So, where are you, Box? Where is the *Ana Vereine*?>

<Currently in orbit around Kukumat. You will notice a slight delay as we converse. I am routing my replies around Murukan to avoid detection.>

<You're worried about the clone warrior tracking you down?>

<Yes. You mentioned in the summary you sent some hours ago that Rufo believes the warrior to be hiding in this location. I had also come to that conclusion. That is clearly why Rufo is broadcasting here, using the archival command language. And it might also explain the distress call: someone might have been hoping to lure the *Ana Vereine* here in order to steal it.>

She nodded; that made a cold kind of sense. <Are you aware that the command language might have nothing to do with the Sol Apotheosis Movement?>

<I did wonder. Its syntax bears little relation to anything in this region.>

Roche was surprised by the feeling of relief she felt at being in contact with the AI again. Kajic wouldn't be far behind. For now, that was better than having definite answers. <So, how long have you been listening in?>

<Only a few minutes. Your presumption that Linegar Rufo was a passive accomplice in the destruction of Wide Berth spine seems to be correct, and that would justify any action you intend to take against him. There are, however, other things you must take into account while working out what to do in the near future.>

<Such as?>

<Rufo was sent here to observe the clone warrior. That

seems obvious from what we have heard. The Kesh supplied the Gauntlet in order to isolate the system, and the COE gave them access. The Kesh also provided a destroyer to act as a ferry for the station and presumably to act as emergency backup should things go awry. That seems simple enough so far. But things become more complicated when all is taken into account. Rufo has gone to some pains to attempt to communicate with the fugitive clone warrior. He also tricked you into allowing Adoni Cane onto the station, whereupon he immediately took him captive. These are not the actions of a man sent to simply observe.>

Roche nodded; her thoughts exactly. <You believe he's been trying to get his hands on a clone warrior from the start?>

<That is my conjecture. He could learn more from one in captivity than merely examining its wake.>

Realization suddenly hit. <*That's* why he didn't intervene on Aro. He wanted to watch him in action! But . . . She tried to understand the xenoarchaeologist's line of reasoning. <It's a big risk. A *huge* risk. Why would he do that?>

<Coercion is a possibility. The Kesh are an unsubtle lot at best—as are the COE, who must be involved since Intelligence let Rufo know that you and Cane were coming. Or Rufo could be doing nothing more sinister than seeking knowledge.>

<A chance to study a living relic, you mean?> She nodded thoughtfully to herself. <I can relate to that, I guess. After all, these clone warriors were built two and a half thousand years ago. It would have been tempting to actually get one in the flesh to examine.>

<Morgan, Cane may be much older than two and a half thousand years.>

<What do you mean?>

<I mean that we know too little about him and his kind to state anything with certainty. To know more, we are going to have to access Rufo's data.>

<That shouldn't be a problem. We'll just get it when we get Maii and Cane.>

<Not so simple. I have been examining the security layout of Galine Four. The station is indeed split into two discrete information networks. One, the larger, deals with the mundane day-to-day running of things; this one I have deduced how to subvert, without resorting to such crude methods as keeping palm-links constantly in contact. The other security system, much smaller, is intimately involved with the decision-making process. This second network, clearly, is where we will find the data we require. The two appear to be separated by a Tipper-Linke chaos-lock which, I am forced to concede, will not succumb to—>

<Wait. A *what* lock?>

<The precise details are unimportant. Suffice it to say that the two networks operate independently of each other for much of the time. When they do need to exchange information, it is conveyed in such a way that renders ineffective any attempt I might make to subvert it. Without taking over the entire outer network and somehow forcing the two to link, I can do nothing.>

<So what do you propose?>

<I must be maneuvered into such a position that I am allowed direct access to the inner security system.>

<Clearly. And your thoughts on how to do this are . . . ?>

<Influenced by two critical developments. The first is the communications drone sent out of the system by Rufo upon Cane's capture. Did you ask Disisto about this?>

<He didn't know anything about it.>

<Hardly surprising, since he was your captive at the time it was sent. But that does suggest that the launch of the drone was not a pre-planned event. It was spontaneous, a reaction to recent events.>

<The capture of Cane,> put in Roche.

<Precisely.>

<And the second development?>

<Is the transmission we intercepted from the edge of the

system, of course. I suspect that circumstances within Palasian System are soon to change.>

Roche worked it through step by step. <Rufo called the Kesh. Having a clone warrior actually in captivity must've altered their plans somewhat. But they know Cane is dangerous, so they couldn't plan to keep him long—especially with us on the loose. You think they asked for help?>

<I am sure of it. Depending on how far away from the anomaly the *Sebettu* was stationed, company could already be on its way.>

<The Armada blockade might stop them this time.>

<Why would it, given the COE is working with the Kesh? And even so, they would be no match for a Kesh destroyer in full flight. Neither would we, for that matter.>

<So what are you suggesting? Strike now before it arrives?>

<Nothing of the sort. Quite the opposite, in fact . . .>

When she had finished talking to the Box, she rejoined Haid and helped him secure the ship. Together they prized Mavalhin into a suit, ignoring his protests at the rough treatment of his tender shoulder. Disisto, although now back in the ship, remained in his suit also; thus confined, the two were easier to control. At a simple command from Roche or Haid the suits could be frozen; both were programmed to seize up automatically if they approached within two meters of anyone without permission.

"What happens to us now?" asked Disisto while Roche and Haid double-checked the courier's flight systems from the bridge.

"We take you back to Galine Four," Roche replied without looking up. She didn't need to see Mavalhin's scowl to know it was there.

"And if I don't want to go?" he asked.

"You don't have a choice, Myer," she said. "Unless, of course, you'd like to stay out here after everyone's left?"

"Listen, Morgan, the reason I helped you in the first place was so I didn't have to go back."

"Well, let's just see what happens, okay?" said Roche tiredly. "If you help us like you did before, then perhaps we can drop you off somewhere else afterwards."

"Assuming there *is* an afterwards," he muttered.

"*Enough,* already!" Roche snapped. Then, more calmly to Haid she said: "Ameidio, get Auditor Byrne on the line." Roche had better things to do than argue with her two captives. "We need to discuss tactics."

She heard Disisto chuckle to himself. "That's some fighting force you've got, Morgan," he said.

"I've done better with less," she retorted.

"Why not forget your friends for now? Maii will be released later, I'm sure."

"Unharmed?" said Roche.

"As long as she doesn't cause any trouble, yes."

"And Cane?"

"I don't know what will happen to him," Disisto admitted. "But don't you think you might be safer without him around anyway?"

Roche spun around in her seat to face Disisto. "How about we make a deal: I'll stop trying to turn you against Rufo if you stop trying to use Cane against me."

A thin grin touched Disisto's lips. "Hit a nerve, have I?"

"Cane's saved my life on more than one occasion. That deserves something, doesn't it?"

"Maybe it does. But do you blame me, then, for being suspicious?"

"You don't know what you're talking about—"

"Morgan," interrupted Haid. "Auditor Byrne says she can have a quorum together in ten minutes."

Roche turned to check the ship's systems, fuming. "Ask her if they'll gather out here. I'd like to join them."

"What about these two?"

"We'll freeze them and put them on a tether. A little sensory deprivation will do them a world of good." Then, more to herself than anyone else, she added: "Wouldn't do me any harm to not have to listen to them for a while, either."

"Hey, lighten up, Morgan—"

"Shut up, Myer." She froze their suits with a mental command. "I'm not in the mood."

She went over to help Haid clamber into his own suit.

"I've got a feeling I'm going to be in this for a while," he said as she checked the seals down his left side.

"Bet on it."

"At least we're even, now." His new hand, buried in his powered suit's glove, curled upward into a clenched fist. "Fancy an arm wrestle?"

"Pass. But feel free to try Myer. He'd be stupid enough to take you on."

She patted the last seal closed, then stepped back.

"Morgan." Haid hesitated. "I don't want to pry, but that *was* the Box you were talking to before, right?"

She nodded. "Yes."

"But how? We're not registering any incoming signals."

She stared at him for a moment. "It said it's relaying to avoid detection. Maybe it's masking the signals on our instruments too."

"That's kind of paranoid, don't you think?"

"Maybe we should be glad it is."

The ion bridge was in full flower as they left *Daybreak* to join the gathering quorum. Fifteen outriggers had gathered in a half-sphere around the patch of Mok Roche had chosen at random. She recognized some of them by sight alone: Yarrow's midnight-black, Idil's pinkish-orange, Lud's diagonal black stripes, and one with a green triangle, from the previous quorum, whose name she didn't know.

She and Haid took positions in front of the outriggers, towing Disisto and Mavalhin behind them. When they were stationary, Roche unfroze the two captives so they could see what was going on, and perhaps even contribute.

"This has been something of an unusual day for us, Morgan Roche." Auditor Byrne's teardrop all-suit floated not far from her at the rough center of the gathering. "We would normally only meet once or twice a standard year. Two quorums and one Plenary in less than a day is quite extraordinary."

"It's the situation which is extraordinary," said Roche. "But again, I thank you for your cooperation."

"As I said, by helping you we help ourselves," the Auditor told her. She made no reference to Alik, the outrigger who had attacked Roche, but the knowledge of what she had done hung heavily upon the meeting. "Now, how exactly can we go about it?"

Roche took a deep breath. "You know that I have two friends held captive by Linegar Rufo in Galine Four. I intend to liberate them by any means possible. While doing so, I hope to obtain the information that has been gathered since Galine Four's arrival in this system; this information should prove helpful in our investigation of the clone warriors.

"In return for your help in these matters, we will give you safe passage from this system. It may mean dismantling the spines to squeeze them into the holds, but we'll do it. If I get out of here alive, so will you."

"A fair exchange," said Auditor Byrne. "But given the situation, I wouldn't have accepted anything less."

"There is one other thing," said Roche. "Rufo ordered the inaction of his observers around Aro, and as such is in part responsible for the destruction of Wide Berth's clan. I don't necessarily condone vengeance, but I will assist you in bringing him to justice, should you choose to do so."

Private lasers darted between the gathered outriggers.

"Thank you, Morgan," said Byrne. "But it is us whom Rufo has wronged, and if he is to answer for this, then it must be to us alone. It is necessary for the grief-healing of the clan."

"Roche, that isn't fair!" Disisto exclaimed. "At least grant Linegar the right of reply before you—"

"I warned you, Disisto. Ameidio, shut him out." Disisto's visor went black; his transmissions ceased in mid-outrage.

"How about you, Myer? Got a problem with this?"

Mavalhin looked at Roche steadily for a few seconds. "Not at all, Morgan. This is your show."

"Okay," she said, turning from the pilot. "Byrne, before we go into details, I need to ask you something. Idil said that she had taken over the all-suit of an older clan member when she died. Do you have any other such empty suits around?"

"We have six empty suits at this time, plus another fifteen recovered from Wide Berth. All are tethered to their respective spines. Why?"

"The Box can teleoperate them along with some of the *Ana Vereine*'s ancillary vessels and any others we can lay our hands on. They'll only be decoys, but the more points we can attack from, the better."

"Consider them at your disposal," said Byrne.

"Excellent," said Roche. "And if there are any of you reluctant to fight, you are welcome to stay on board the *Ana Vereine* during the attack—just as long as we have use of your suit to add to our decoys."

"Without our suits, we are nothing," said one of the outriggers, a statement that provoked a general susurrus of agreement.

"I understand that," Roche put in quickly. "But at least this way you might still survive even if your all-suit was damaged. We can arrange some sort of sealed environment in the ship, if you like—even teleop facilities so you can still fly your suit. And should the worst occur, then I'm sure a replacement could be built to specifications at a later date."

While her concern for the outriggers was genuine, that was not her main motive for the proposal. She was more interested in seeing who accepted the offer—and who *didn't*. An all-suit would be a convenient place for a fugitive to hide. If the clone warrior *had* infiltrated the spine, this would narrow down the suspects.

"We shall take your words into consideration," said Byrne. "Now, what about strategy?"

"Well, we need a plan that will give us time to get in, do what we have to do, then get out again," said Roche. "And it isn't going to be easy. A sneak attack by a small number of scouts would be worse than useless. They'd eventually be detected, and that would warn Rufo that a larger attack was imminent, enabling him to prepare his defenses.

"Sneaking up on them isn't an option either," she continued. "They're not blind and they'll be expecting us to try something. Even a small group will stick out in a featureless sky. They'd be shot down long before they'd get anywhere near the station.

"So, our best hope lies in getting a large assembly as close as possible without being seen and striking hard and fast. If we can penetrate their defenses quickly and get inside, the battle becomes one of internal security. That will take the pressure off the attacking force, allowing it to conserve resources and regroup if necessary. That's assuming of course that we don't completely knock out their defenses on the first pass; if we can do that, getting in and out will be considerably easier."

She looked around the quorum. Not being able to see the expressions of those she was addressing was frustrating, but the fact that there was no movement whatsoever from the all-suits gave her the impression she was at least being listened to.

"We do have something of an edge," Roche went on. "Once I get the Box inside the station, we can use it to shut down external security. This will only work for a while—until they manage to re-route it through the internal security shell—but we need all the time we can get. The Box should also be able to tell us where Maii and Cane are held in the station. I doubt they'll be together, so I imagine the landing party will have a lot to do. It's basically me and Ameidio versus the entire internal security, since we're the only ones with legs."

She glanced over at Mavalhin. "Disisto has told me he doesn't want to assist us against his employer, but I'm hoping Myer Mavalhin here will be able to give us some insight into the operation of Galine Four: blind spots or security weaknesses, points of entry, ways to move freely inside, weapons caches—that kind of thing. Any help he can provide would be useful at this point."

Mavalhin looked over to Disisto's blacked-out suit floating beside him, then back to Roche. "I'll do what I can," he said.

"Good," she said. "Then you will be part of the boarding party, too."

"But can he be trusted?" said one outrigger.

"We'll find that out soon enough, I guess," Roche replied. Then, addressing the quorum as a whole, she said, "Now, does anyone have any suggestions? I presume some of you have had combat experience?"

"Unfortunately, we all have," said Auditor Byrne. "We are better at running than fighting, but we stand up for ourselves when we have to. As you know, we possess many tools that can serve as weapons. Many of them would be useful in the attack."

"Good," Roche said. "They'll add some mass to the assault. The *Ana Vereine* has a stockpile of surveillance micromachines. The Box might be able to reconfigure some to attack the station's external surfaces—either the observation systems or the hull itself. Do you have any way to deliver such devices en masse?"

"We have nano seeders," said Lud. "Bullet-shaped and grain-sized. We could send a cloud in ahead of us. They might take it for nothing more than space junk—until it starts eating into them."

"Perfect. Anyone else?"

"What about the crust-rippers?" asked another outrigger.

"Too destructive," said Lud.

"We could use them as a threat. Load Wide Berth spine

with as many as we've got and threaten to ram if they don't surrender."

"An empty threat," said Idil. "We could never use them. If we did, the explosion would wipe out everything for a million cubic kilometers. Including the *Ana Vereine* and our only way out of here."

"We can use ion drilling cannon to cut through the hull if the micromachines don't work," suggested another.

"And blind singleships with spectrometry bombs," said yet another

"And we still have the leftover slag from the asteroids we carved before everything went wrong," said Lud. "We could use it as cover for the nano seeders. Mostly carbon and ice, a bit of iron, nice and irregular in size and shape. The seeders will blend right in."

"Good thinking," said Byrne.

"We also have access to the subsystems of a dozen or so prowling mines," said one. "They are an older make and easily subverted, the same ones the clone warrior used to destroy the Armada base around Cemenid."

"Has anyone considered using drill rigs to boost our own thrust?" came still another suggestion.

Roche relaxed slightly in the suit and let them workshop. She noticed Haid watching her to one side, and signaled him privately, reducing the volume of the outriggers' chatter to a minimum.

"What do you think? Do we have a chance?"

"Depends on how far Rufo will go to keep what he has," Haid replied. "If his life depends on it, he's going to do everything in his power to get rid of us once and for all. Last time he at least tried to pretend that he was doing the right thing. This time there'll be no charades."

"That's true," said Roche. "He knows we have Disisto and Myer. If we didn't know the truth by now, then we wouldn't be worth worrying about in the first place."

"And *do* we know the truth? Even now?"

"I'm sure we don't," Roche said. "Not entirely. But I

know we're a damn sight closer than we were a few days ago."

She quickly returned her attention to the quorum when she heard someone ask:

"What do we do if something goes wrong?"

"If something goes wrong, we'll surrender," Roche said. "That is, *I* will surrender, not you. If we let them have the *Ana Vereine,* they'll be probably be happy."

"And what happens to you then?"

"That's up to Rufo," she said. "It should be no concern of yours. Don't even think of trying to rescue us; you should concentrate on hiding. Galine Four won't be here forever, and there's always a chance a rescue team will arrive in time. Remember, the collapse of the system is still some weeks away."

"If that is your wish," said Byrne, "we will abide by it."

"Good." Despite what she and the Box had decided, Roche hoped it wouldn't come to that. "Now, Myer. Any suggestions on how to get in?"

The pilot cleared his throat. "Well, everything will be locked up pretty tight, as you can imagine."

"Yes, but despite the Kesh, it's not a military station," she pointed out. "There must be some weak points."

"Of course there are. Or rather there *were*. I don't know if anything will have changed since I last looked."

"I guess that's a risk we'll just have to take." She fought the urge to tell him to stop procrastinating. Antagonizing him now would be counterproductive.

"The best bet would probably be the old freight transfer point on deck 17D. No one's used it for months, so the old codes should still work. And if they don't, we can always cut through. They shut it down because of an acid spill; the seals are corroded and could be nice and brittle. Bad for safety, but good for you. I mean, *us.*"

Roche ignored the slip. "How many singleships does the station have, and what other defensive measures can we expect?"

"There are usually fifteen singleships at the ready, from a pool of thirty. I don't know how many you wrecked when you left. The station has the usual stock of E-shields and anti-assault cannon. Nothing too destructive. Getting close enough to get in shouldn't be too much of a problem. It's once you're in that you'll have difficulty."

"Go on."

"Well, you've seen it. It's big and full of people. Bad enough that you want to get to one specific area—but two, or even three? If I wasn't coming with you, I wouldn't give you any chance at all."

"That's exactly *why* you're coming with us, Myer."

"So I gathered," he said. "Anyway, you'll need to bypass as much as possible. Try to keep us off the monitors, or at least covered somehow. If your AI can't do that, you'll have to arrange distractions. Hit them from every angle and they won't know where to concentrate their efforts. You might be able to slip through that way."

That was pretty much what she'd been thinking; maybe not so destructive as blowing up a scutter, though, like last time. "No loopholes we can utilize?"

"Not without knowing exactly where we're going."

"No way of cracking into the second security level?"

"None I'm aware of. Disisto might know, though."

"And he wouldn't tell me if he did." She thought for a second. "I'm not sure I agree that getting in will be easy. The singleships are faster than all-suits, better armed *and* armored. There are more of us, and sheer numbers *may* win the day, but on the other hand they might not. If we plan for every contingency, we might just turn things around to our favor; at the very least, we'll save lives.

"Auditor Byrne, we'll leave you to sort out who wants to fight and who wants to piggyback on the *Ana Vereine*. I'll download the schematics of the station and any other relevant data once I can lay my hands on it so you can discuss possible tactics and ways to minimize your losses.

"Meanwhile, we'll work out what to do from our end.

We have some time to play with, anyway. Even at full burn, it'd take us a day or two to reach the station from here."

"Unless it's moved," said Haid.

"Yes, but there's not much we can do about that from here—not with the information lags as they are."

"Very well, Morgan Roche." The sharp-tipped all-suit bobbed gently in the microgravity; some of the outriggers around her were already breaking ranks. "We will keep you informed of our progress."

Auditor Byrne's silver tear was among the last to leave. Roche waited for them all to disperse before moving herself. She scanned the skies briefly before she did, and in doing so noticed Yarrow, all but invisible in his black all-suit, hanging like an accusation in the starless sky.

Roche felt as though the mysterious outrigger was watching her, and the idea of this made her feel uncomfortable. Why would he have saved her if he wasn't who Byrne thought he was? So far he had done nothing to arouse her suspicion, except be silent.

She stared back at him for a few minutes, but when it was apparent he wasn't going to move, she turned away and started tugging Disisto's limp suit back into the courier's airlock. When she glanced back a moment later, she saw Yarrow's all-suit disappearing into one of the moon's shafts.

<Okay, Box—>

<No need, Morgan. I overheard everything.>

Roche suppressed the obvious response: *How?* But now wasn't the time. She was in one of the courier's two small sleeping spaces with the door locked, having secured Disisto and Mavalhin in the bridge while Haid slept in the room next door. The ex-mercenary had looked exhausted after the quorum, and even he had admitted to not having had enough rest in the last few days.

<So how do our plans fit in with yours?>

<Well enough. I suggest I come out of hiding in twenty-four hours. We can explain my early arrival by telling the

truth in part—that we have been lying low and falsifying our ETA to avoid detection. We should be battle-ready by then.>

<How is the ship holding up? The intrasystem thrusters must be taking a bit of a hammering.>

<Uri has been careful not to exceed safety limits, and they're designed well.>

Roche smiled. <Can I talk to him?>

<Sorry, Morgan, but he's resting. However, I will inform him when he awakes that you asked after him.>

<Thanks, Box.>

<I also suggest that we do not reveal the location of the *Ana Vereine* until we are under way. It would be much more difficult, under those circumstances, to attempt to subvert us.>

Roche considered the suggestion. That would mean docking *Daybreak* to the Marauder while undergoing acceleration—a tricky maneuver at the best of times.

<Are you sure that's necessary? It sounds a bit paranoid—>

<Better too paranoid than not at all,> said the Box, echoing her own thoughts on that subject.

<I guess so,> she said with some uncertainty. <And what about what happens afterwards? Have you given any thought to that? I mean, once we get Maii and Cane back, where do we go from here? What do we do?>

<I suggest we wait to see what Rufo's data tells us before we start examining our options.>

<But shouldn't we at least have some plan? If we *do* manage to avoid the Kesh destroyer and the blockade, chances are we'll have no time to decide what—>

<I understand what you are saying, Morgan,> the Box broke in. <However, I do feel that our mission is best served by patience at this point. After all, we have no clear destination beyond here.>

<I thought as much,> she said wearily. <Reassure me, Box. Tell me we can do this.>

<I cannot offer you any guarantees, Morgan. Everything is subject to chance.>

<Then can you at least give me odds?>

<Sorry, Morgan. I would rather we just went into this assuming that we will win.>

Roche sighed to herself and closed the line. She lay back on the bunk, but realized after a few minutes that she wouldn't be able to sleep. Instead she went to the bridge and called up a communications display. She was curious after what Haid had said earlier about not detecting any incoming signals from the Box.

As before, there had been no voice transmissions, coded or otherwise, sent to or from the courier during the time of her talk with the Box. The only transmission she couldn't account for was one intense burst lasting a second or two, not long after their last conversation. It had been sent from the courier to a destination farther in-system.

She didn't know what that meant. Maybe the Box had downloaded part of itself into the courier, and that smaller part had communicated their conversation to the larger one in a single concise spurt after the fact rather than in multiple transmissions during. That would make sense: after all, the Box itself seemed to be just a smaller chip off the High Human called the Crescend; no doubt the process was repeatable to a smaller degree. But she did doubt that there was room in the courier's available memory for an AI with the sophistication of the Box. And if the *Ana Vereine* was hiding behind Kukumat as the Box claimed, then the transmission had gone in the wrong direction—although there was the possibility that it could have been sent via a relay.

Tapping at the console, she instructed the communications system to notify her every time any such bursts were received or transmitted by the courier.

<I don't think that's necessary, Morgan.>

The voice in her head came as no surprise; she had half expected her actions to prompt the Box to intervene. <And what exactly is it you think I'm doing, Box?>

<I presume you are trying to deduce how I am communicating with you.>

<Possibly. Or maybe I'm just concerned that there's a bug on board the ship sending information back to Galine Four.> She smiled to herself. <That would be more reasonable than suspecting you of anything underhanded, don't you think? But the fact that you didn't even bring it up would suggest that you *are* up to something.>

The Box was silent for a moment. Not long, but long enough. <I assure you, Morgan, that I am 'up to' nothing 'underhanded.'>

<Then how about telling me what you're doing?>

<That isn't an issue I'm prepared to discuss right now. You will find out soon enough.>

She frowned. <Why not now?>

<Because it isn't relevant.>

"Is everything all right?"

She started at the unexpected voice *outside* her head. She turned and saw Disisto sitting up in his suit, helmet off but otherwise immobile. Next to him, Mavalhin lolled like a broken-backed doll, unconscious.

"I thought you were asleep," she said.

"Not me. I've spent too much time in the dark just lately." When she ignored the gibe, he said: "I don't suppose you'd care to give me *some* sort of mobility? My nose is itchy as hell."

She sent a command to allow him to move, although restricting those movements to the crash-couch. "How's that?"

He flexed his arms. "Much better. Thanks."

"You think I'm being too tough on you, don't you?"

He shook his head slowly. "Not really," he said. "The way I see it, I'm lucky to be alive at all. Most of your buddies would have shot me by now."

Roche smiled, although there was no evidence of humor in his tone or his face. "I think you exaggerate a little."

He held her stare evenly. "Maybe," he said. "But the fact is they don't take well to uncooperative prisoners."

In the quiet that followed she said: "You know, you could still help me."

He sighed heavily. "If I've told you once, I've told you a thousand times: I won't help you attack the chief—"

"I'm not asking you to do that," she said. "I'd just like to know what he's doing here, that's all. As do you. All I want is your help finding out that information."

Disisto ran a hand over the stubble dusting his dark face and scalp. "I can't do that *without* helping you in other ways too."

"You could mediate," said Roche. "Rufo and Shak'ni and all their Kesh pals will be intent on blowing us away once we return. Personally, I'd rather talk than fight—and they might listen to you if you try to mediate. Should Rufo give us the information we need—along with Maii and Cane—then we'll leave him alone. Hell, we might even take him out of the system if he wants us to. I'm sure he doesn't like being dependent on the Kesh for that."

"I know he doesn't," he said.

"So?" Roche pressed. "Can I count on you not screwing things up until we've at least tried to talk?"

Disisto sighed again. "Okay," he said. "If it means a possible peaceful solution, then I'll see what I can do."

"Good. Because you're coming in the landing party with us, and I didn't want to have to drag you around like a big sack of rocks." Roche smiled, relieved to have finally reached some sort of compromise with him. "Now, if you'll excuse me, I have to try and turn a bunch of outriggers into something resembling a fighting force."

Disisto leaned back into his seat with a half-smile on his face, but before he could say anything, the alarm Roche had installed in the communications systems sounded through her implants.

She turned back to the console and examined the surge. It seemed no different from the other, except this time it was incoming. A reply from the larger part of the Box, perhaps?

Disisto had said something about Mavalhin, but she wasn't listening.

<Box, what the hell are you playing at?>

<Morgan,> it said, ignoring the question. <I am detecting a powerful neutrino surge from Hintubet.>

She cast an eye across the instruments. There it was: a sharp spike only slowly trailing off. As she watched, it peaked again, higher than before.

<Could it be dangerous?> she said.

<It may affect some modes of communication, but little else. My concern lies with what it says about the source of the surge.>

<Hintubet? I can't see why—> She stopped. <The Gauntlet? You don't think—?>

Another spike, more powerful, again registered on the courier's neutrino detectors. <We caught a signal directed at the sun sometime ago. I assumed it was a routine signal to fine-tune the solar envelope. Now, judging by the sun's severely altered behavior, I am rapidly coming to the opposite conclusion.>

The tone of the Box's voice was leading Roche in the same direction. <They're killing it, aren't they?>

<I think so. By instructing the fleet of quark breeders orbiting within the chromosphere to dump their entire stock of strange matter into the star at once, they can cause the solar envelope to spontaneously collapse.>

<How long, Box?>

<That depends on how the chain reaction progresses. It may cascade, resulting in a catastrophic collapse within a few hours; or it may be held in check by other forces within the—>

<How long do you *think* we have?>

<Taking into account the even spacing of the spikes so far, my best guess would be sixty hours.>

Sixty hours? Roche turned the figure over in her head. Just three days to get the outriggers to Galine Four, across a distance of over five billion kilometers, break in, rescue

Maii and Cane, find out what Rufo knew, and get out again. Then get out of the system before the envelope collapsed completely . . .

"Roche?" said Disisto from behind her; irritably she waved him to silence.

<What about the *Sebettu*?> she asked the Box.

<I can only assume that it is already on its way.>

<And if Rufo is heading for a rendezvous, we have to find him and match velocities, all without being seen. . . . We're really going to have to move fast on this.>

<That would be stating the obvious somewhat.>

She ignored the Box's flippancy and quickly spoke into a mike on the console.

"Auditor Byrne," she said. "I'm going to need your people ready to move in two hours. I repeat: *two hours.*"

"I hear you." The auditor's voice came on instantly. "But why the sudden urgency?"

"I just found out that the collapse of the envelope is being brought forward," she said. "We now have just three days to do what we have to do and get the hell out of here."

"*Can* we do it?"

"We can try," Roche said. "Beyond that, I'm not making any promises. . . ."

PART FOUR:

SEBETTU

INTERLUDE

He woke in a panic: someone was talking to him!

At first he thought it was one of the attendants in the Shadow Place. But the voice was cold and slippery, sharp as a hypodermic needle and as flexible as wire. It slid through his defenses and pierced his brain like a fishhook.

He struggled for a reference point. When he found none—only void—he remembered where he was.

The abomination!

<Can you hear me?>

He tried desperately to think. When had he fallen asleep? How had he allowed himself to become so vulnerable?

: HELP

He felt the technician start at the voice issuing from his monitors. <I thought I'd knocked you out cold. Ungrateful sod. Don't you want to rest?>

: HELP

: ME

<What's wrong?>

: ABOMINATION

<What?>

: HERE

<What the hell are you talking about? There's no one here but you and me.>

He gave up, defeated yet again by spatial coordinates. And anyway the voice had gone, faded into some dark recess like a bad dream. Maybe he *had* dreamt it . . .

<Can anyone hear me?>

His body jackknifed in shock, its epsense organ flailing from the back of his skull like an electric eel in a thunderstorm; every cell in his body screamed at the insidious touch of that voice. An alarm sounded somewhere, heard and felt secondhand through the technician. What was this? Fear for his well-being? Or fear he might be trying to escape? He couldn't tell which. Perhaps it was both.

<I *feel* something—I feel *you*! Who are you? Where am I?>

: KILL

<Kill who? Who are you talking to?>

: HER

<Wait. It's clearing. I can see you better now. You're the one who's been soaking up all the thoughts in the system!>

: HELP

<What are you? Olmahoi? What does *irikeii* mean?>

: ME

<All these names . . . The Cruel One and her servant . . . The enigma and the Shining One . . . the . . .>

The voice ceased. He waited breathlessly, hardly daring to believe that he had rid himself of her so easily.

<*Abomination?* Damn you! Who are *you* to judge me?>

Sharp-tipped tendrils encircled his mind. He relaxed minutely. If this was how attack would come, he was safe.

The tentacles slipped; their tips failed to find purchase. <I can't—how do you *do* that?>

Deep within him, he fashioned a private place in which

he could think, a shelter not even she could reach. The Cruel One's servant had underestimated her threat, and he lacked the skills to warn him. Fear flooded through him. The abomination could not hurt him directly, but she could still do him harm. For him, death's sting was none the worse for being someone else's. Indeed, his own might come as something of a relief if she were to break completely free.

Still, there was hope. She was only a child. Without the mind of an adult to direct it, her raw talent was mostly wasted. With luck she would never realize exactly what she was capable of—as long as he kept the thought buried deep, away from her prying mind.

He had no idea what to do next, but he knew he would accomplish little hidden in his private space. He had to come out eventually to do the bidding of the Cruel One's servant. If he didn't come out, the abomination would only try all the harder to smash her way in. . . .

<What are you frightened of? I don't want to hurt you, really. Just don't go thinking any more thoughts about killing me, okay?>

He wondered why he should enter into a bargain with someone like her.

<Because I can help you. You're trapped here too. They're using you. We could help each other escape.>

There was nowhere to escape *to.*

<The *Ana Vereine* has a working slow-jump drive. We can leave here any time we want.>

So why didn't she?

<Because we haven't finished what we came here to do. Here, look.>

The abomination thrust an unwieldy slab of thought at him, and he recoiled automatically.

: NO

<What is it? Do I revolt you that much?>

He didn't answer. The technician was examining him more closely now. His odd twitches and utterances were not going unnoticed. He needed to be careful lest someone think he was up to something.

<Well, you *are* hiding something.>

Of course he was. More things than she would ever know.

<Don't be pompous. Something about Rufo. And Cane. I thought *you* were Cane when I first touched you. No one would be able to get through this fog, except maybe him. Or so I thought.>

In his private place, he realized that she too had been fooled by the Shining One's camouflage. That was something. She wasn't as perceptive as he had feared.

<Why can't I touch anyone else? Where is Morgan?>

He recognized the name from the abomination's own mind, but had no idea where the enigma had got to. The proximity of the Shining One obscured the rest of the system from his sight.

<So Rufo doesn't know, either?>

That wasn't necessarily so. The Cruel One's servant had numerous sensors and singleship scouts on the lookout for the two fugitive vessels. It was only a matter of time before one of them turned up.

<Still, it's a point in her favor, right? It'll be easier for her to sneak back here, when she's ready.>

He reacted with surprise to the certainty in the abomination's mental voice. Come back? The enigma would be insane to do such a thing!

<Trust me, she'll come.>

The abomination's thoughts slid across each other like shining metal sheets, polished by friction. Her screen was good, but not perfect. Occasional insights slipped through the gaps, and he gathered them up, hoping to learn as much as he could about her. Leverage might come in handy, later.

<Why do you call me an abomination?>

The question surprised him. The Surin bred for epsense; they were not without experience in the field. Surely she knew that minds like hers should not exist?

<Who says?>

He supposed she was too young to understand. Long-term maintenance of epsense ability required either built-in genetic disposition or intense discipline. If she had been made and raised around others like her, or around natural reaves who lacked the proper training—

<Pompous *and* patronizing.>

Abominations like her were prone to self-destruction. There was no place for them in the galaxy; they never fit in. It wasn't that they were rejected, more that they could not be accepted. In time, they always disintegrated.

<Oh, really?>

He felt perversely sorry for her; after all, it wasn't her fault she'd been made this way. But he could not—and *would* not—allow feelings of sympathy to intrude on what he had to do.

There had to be a way.

<I guess our battle lines are drawn,> she said. <If the only way I can talk to anyone else is by getting rid of you, Olmahoi, *irikeii,* whatever you are, then so be it. The chances of us ever reaching agreement are pretty damn slim.>

Nonexistent, he would've thought.

<Well, then. Will you tell me what you're hiding or do I have to wring it from you drop by drop?>

For a moment, in his private retreat, he was tempted to accept her challenge. Not that there was any risk of her getting what she wanted that way. No matter how strong she was, he would not fall to a direct assault; his very nature forbade it. He was more like a channel than a vessel; the hole in the fabric of n-space that was his mind could be filled and overflow, but that would not harm him directly. It would simply spill onto those around him, including the one attacking him, and thereby neutralize the threat.

No, he decided, letting his thoughts rise back to the surface. It would be more interesting to give her what she wanted. That would get her off his back, temporarily, and perhaps enable him to see what she made of it into the bargain.

<Don't expect me to tell you anything.>

Dialogue was possible even between enemies, especially when the conflict was not diametrically polarized. If they both perceived a common foe, mightn't it seem sensible to exchange information?

<*If* we do, yes. But you'll have to convince me of that, first.>

He opened his mind. Not totally, and not all at once. And not, he had to admit, without doubt—for all he had learned was necessarily colored by the minds that had given it to him. But he himself did not add anything. He offered her no deceptions.

He showed her his home. He showed her how he had come to be snatched from it and brought here. He showed her the Cruel One. He showed her the complex web of intrigue and machinations woven around him. He showed her why it was unlikely he would ever be allowed to return to his people.

Then he showed her the dark hole at the heart of the Shining One. He showed her the secret fear breeding in the Cruel One's servant's mind. He showed her the difference between what the enigma thought to be true, and what he had garnered from those closer to the heart of the matter.

Mostly what he hoped to show her was her ignorance. . . .

<No.>

The abomination's voice was strained.

<That's impossible. You're *lying*!>

He assured her that he wasn't—but she was already gone. She had fled rather than endure the truth.

He barely had time to feel satisfaction when—

Pain!

He struggled to orient himself. Agony tore through every nerve in his body. What had gone wrong?

<Hey! Pay attention! Why the hell didn't you warn us?>

His mind strained. Wider, wider. Desperate to stop the pain.

: SLEEPING

: DREAMING

<Well look *now,* damn you! There's a fleet bearing down on us! We need to know numbers. And we want to know if the other clone warrior's behind them!>

He looked; it was true. He could see them now rising out of the mist of the Shining One, numerous minds all focused on one place, one challenge.

: MANY

<*How* many?>

: MANY

: COMING

He peered closer, harder, through the light, at another.

: SHINING

: RESONANCE

And there, at the forefront, he saw it. He didn't know why he was surprised, and perhaps even a little relieved. He knew the Cruel One's servant would feel very differently. But at least now he would be able to keep an eye on her.

Just as the abomination had said, the enigma had returned. . . .

7

COEI *Daybreak*
'955.01.23 EN
1840

The outrigger fleet came in fast. After twenty hours of hard acceleration and deceleration on the back of the spines, then riding on momentum alone for the last hour to hide the emissions of their tiny drives, they burst into the sky around Galine Four like the absent stars. Seventy-six all-suits in total, more than half of them empty and teleoperated either by their original owners or the Box, while the spines remained hidden far away; behind the outriggers, six lumbering prowling mines—big tanklike masses of metal designed to overtake sluggish asteroids and slowly tear them to pieces; and hidden among them, carefully camouflaged as another prowling mine, the *Ana Vereine*—using its shields to protect as many of the outriggers as possible until they were within firing range.

Roche occupied the copilot's chair of *Daybreak,* fully suited and ready to disembark at a moment's notice. Her suit had come from the holds of the *Ana Vereine* and was a substantial improvement on the old one: cool air circulated across every part of her body; silent servo-assists gave her increased strength and agility; hidden weapons awaited her slightest mental prompt to attack. Information flowed across eyes-up displays and through her implants; she could see from a dozen different viewpoints simultaneously, and could eavesdrop as needed on the outriggers' exchanges. She was like an angry insect queen surrounded by her warriors, swooping in for the kill.

Beside her, Haid sat similarly dressed. Mavalhin and Disisto wore the COE suits that had come with the courier vessel, but they weren't armed. Roche had promised Mavalhin a hand weapon when they boarded Galine Four, but she still hadn't decided whether to keep that promise or not.

Behind them waited four empty combat suits from the *Ana Vereine*. These would accompany them onto Galine Four, to be directed by the Box if that proved to be possible. There was no guarantee that they would be able to communicate with the fleet outside. It was worth taking the chance, though, Roche thought. If the drones *did* work, they would effectively double their numbers.

It seemed to take the Galine Four defenders a moment to believe what they were seeing. By the time the first shots were fired, the outriggers were almost in range. As soon as they were, the formation dissolved and return fire began to come in.

"How's your status?" she asked the *Ana Vereine*.

"Just waiting on your signal, Morgan." Roche could hear the elation in the ex-captain's voice. After days of running and hiding, the prospect of action had Uri barely able to contain his excitement.

Roche studied the views before her. The station gunners were concentrating on the prowling mines—not surprising considering their mass. If just one of them rammed, the battle would effectively be over. Roche had no intention of doing this, but the station gunners weren't to know that.

"Your shields are holding?"

"They're doing okay," reported Kajic. "I'm displaying signs of damage in order to preserve the illusion."

"Could you also feign disablement?"

"Shouldn't be difficult."

"Then do so after the next particularly heavy battery. Don't head for the station, though; tumble so you'd miss. That way they should leave you alone. As soon as the shields are back to full strength, join the battle properly."

"Understood."

Roche steadied herself as the courier rolled beneath her. They were well back from the frontline, but close enough to catch the occasional stray shot. The makeshift E-shields and disrupters the Box had installed were bearing up well, much to her relief. They were going to need them once she decided to make her move.

The outriggers were close enough to take potshots at the A-P cannons scattered over the station's exterior surfaces. Their voices sang through her in a fugue similar to the Plenary she had witnessed, but without its innate sense of order. In among the battle calls was the Auditor herself, her calming voice keeping everything under relative control.

[25-26]Watch out! Watch out!

[31]Covered. Keep an eye on that second gunner!

Groups 4-9 and 17-26 pull back and down.

Flank support required.

[17-22]We have a positive on feeder placement in sectors blue and yellow.

[9-13]How long until hull integrity is compromised?

[17-22]Five minutes. Can you hold out that long?

[9-13]We'll have to, I guess.

Shields are falling in orange sector;

All available fire to concentrate here.

The cannon are vulnerable.

[45]Damn!

[33]You okay?

[45]Singed. This is just like stripping JA-32!

[33]And we know what happened there, don't we?
Concentrate, people.
We have company.

Singleships spilled out of docking bays from all over the station, scattering the outriggers on a wave of returned fire.

Hold formation!
Don't turn your back unless you want to be shot in it!

<Box!> Roche called. <Send in the drones!>

From the nooks and crannies of the prowling mines came every independent craft Roche had been able to lay her hands on. Mass-throwers, impact probes, and remote instruments of every description converged on the station.

"Byrne! Tell your people to be careful. It's going to get messy in there!"

Retract all antennae!
Incoming debris!

The space around the station became thick with energy and matter. A wild variety of thrusters—some as small as a fingernail—flashed and burned; accurate shots sent fragments and dust flying in all directions; laser beams were absorbed or deflected in crazy patterns. Through it all moved the singleships and outriggers, with *Daybreak* close by. And behind them all came the prowling mines, still lumbering on and laboring under the concentrated fire from the station's artillery.

The *Ana Vereine* took a volley of shots to its flank and went into a slow roll. Roche nodded in satisfaction. It would be ready to attack in a few minutes.

"Take us closer," she instructed Haid.

[34]Be careful!
[38]I am. It's just . . .

[34]Laird? Goddamn! I need reinforcements!
[5-7]Hold on. We're coming!
Let the drones and teleop teams go in first.
And watch out for pincer attacks.
I want live fighters; you aren't any good to me dead!

"Look at them," said Haid, watching a similar view to Roche's on a bridge monitor. The singleships swooped and parried, pairs targeting lone outriggers and dispatching them first, then trying to break up larger groups. "They're Kesh pilots," he said. "I've seen them fight like that before."

"Efficient, aren't they?" Disisto commented emotionlessly from behind them.

"They'd never fight like that against their own kind," said Haid.

[27]Hull breach in orange sector!
[38]Concentrate your fire. Hurt them! Hurt them!
Group 31-34, stay back.
That tower's about to blow!
[8]Lud? Are you still with us?
[14]Barely . . . Pressure's dropping.
[8]Withdraw! We can handle it from here.

"Byrne," said Roche. "Tell the wounded or damaged to fall back. We're about to move in."

Expect reinforcement soon.
Fall back on my command.
Injured and compromised first.
I want everyone else to remain for the second wave.

"You hear that, Uri?"

"Yes, Morgan." Kajic's voice came from the bridge speakers. "We will break cover in twenty seconds."

"Okay, good. We're relying on you to watch our back. And keep an eye on Yarrow, if you can." As Roche had expected, the Wide Berth survivor hadn't taken the option to hide in the hold of the *Ana Vereine*. "Ameidio, full thrust as soon as the *Ana Vereine* is exposed. We go in under its covering fire."

"You got it." Almost imperceptibly, the pilot stiffened at the controls of the courier.

"I guess this is it," Mavalhin muttered nervously.

"It sure is, Myer," Roche said, "And you're going to do exactly as I tell you, *when* I tell you." She kept her attention on the image of the disguised *Ana Vereine* as she spoke. Suddenly the appearance of the crippled prowling mine shimmered, then vanished altogether. In its place was now the Marauder, its many prongs lit up against the black sky by its own blazing weapons.

"Hold on everyone!" Haid pushed the courier forward and into the melee. Singleships dodged and weaved to avoid the energy weapons bombarding them from all directions. Two fell instantly; seconds later, another. The station's cannon turned to bear on the swooping ship and *Daybreak* aimed into the gap.

The freight transfer point was located near the *R* painted on the side of the station, halfway between the nominal top and the docking equator. Haid looped once around the station, then veered in closer. The wreckage became noticeably thicker. Heavy clangs announced impacts with pieces large enough to penetrate the shields; near misses dissipated with bright flashes of energy.

A recessed gantry appeared before them.

"That's it," Mavalhin said.

Outrigger fire had scarred much of the area around the gantry, aiming for surveillance equipment and anti-intrusion emplacements. The area looked secure. There was just enough room in the docking space to hide the courier.

"Take us in, Ameidio," said Roche. "Byrne, we're there!"

All except teleop groups—
withdraw!

Haid brought the courier close enough for grapnels to hook onto. Roche glanced up at the sky. As some of the outriggers fell back, the *Ana Vereine* stepped up the attack on the singleships. At the same time, the prowling mines had approached to what must have been uncomfortably close proximity for those aboard Galine Four. With so many threats harrying the station, she hoped to be able to dock the ship relatively unnoticed.

<Box, are you back in the outer security system?>

<Getting there. They have changed the codes, but these won't take long to bypass. I expect to have access to internal communications within ninety seconds. Once I have that, I will be able to delay security in this area should they attempt to move in.>

Roche grunted her understanding. She braced herself as the courier clanged home, then stood up. Haid secured the console, then also rose. The four drone suits stirred.

"Let's go," Roche said to Disisto and Mavalhin. "I want your voice transmissions kept to a minimum."

They filed back to the airlock as pumps evacuated the entire ship. The inner door was already open when they reached it. Part of her hoped they would encounter some form of resistance; another part of her prayed they wouldn't.

The outer door hissed open at their approach. Roche went first, hands extended, weapons and sensors in her gloves scanning the gantry. It was clear. She removed a rifle from its back holster and stood aside.

The others followed. One of the drones placed cutting equipment against the corroded seals Mavalhin had mentioned and began blasting. The metal parted like melting cheese. Radiation warnings pinged in Roche's chest, but they weren't urgent enough to require her to step away.

Above them, the sky continued to boil.

One of the suits—she had already lost track of which were drones and which weren't—stepped toward her and touched her shoulder.

READING ME? asked Haid.

<Yes,> she sent back. <Hold still.>

She activated the laser on her left glove and burned a black line on the seamless chest of his suit. Stepping back, she did the same to herself.

<Now we'll know who's who.>

The remains of the gantry door swung silently aside.

<After you.>

Stepping past the drones and over the still-glowing edge of the gantry door, Haid led the way into the station. The others followed, with Roche and two of the drones taking up the rear.

The freight transfer deck was spacious but empty. Nevertheless, Roche kept alert for any sign that they had been spotted.

<I have you on visual,> said the Box. <All automatic security alerts have been disabled. The area is deserted. You are free to move.>

<I hope you know what you're talking about, Box.>

<I always do, Morgan.> She couldn't tell if it was meant as a joke or not. <I will dispatch two of the drones to seek out the data you require. This will save time.>

Roche frowned; they hadn't planned it that way. <Are you sure that's a good idea? I don't want you to overextend yourself, what with the empty all-suits and—>

<I am not overextended, Morgan. I will let you know the moment that unlikely event should arise.>

She wasn't reassured. The Box sounded as if it was enjoying itself. At times like these, she had learned to be worried.

<Okay, but I want a direct visual from one of the suits.> At least that way she could check on what they were up to without having to ask the Box.

She checked a moment later to make sure it had been done: through the sensors of the drone immediately behind her, she saw herself wave an arm.

Turning to the others, Roche motioned them forward. The maps she'd acquired on her first visit to the station indicated the exit she wanted. As they approached, the door slid open. They moved off along the passageway, pressure doors opening and closing smoothly as they passed. At the second intersection they came to, two of the drones turned right. Haid automatically went to follow.

<No, this way.> She touched his wrist. <We turn at the next intersection.>

BUT—

<I'll explain later.>

While she didn't know precisely where Cane and Maii were being held, it seemed likely they would be in one of the two holding pens indicated on the station's maps. They were located midway between the outer hull and Galine Four's centralmost chamber, but on opposite sides of the station. The closest wasn't far from where they were, so it was to this one they headed. Roche silently prayed it was the right one.

At the end of the corridor were two freight elevators waiting to take them deep into the station's infrastructure. As the heavy doors slid aside, a rumble echoed through the floors and walls.

<Box? What's going on out there?>

<*Daybreak* has been spotted. Hold while I concentrate.>

Roche stepped into the elevator and steadied herself. Having a moment to spare while the cage dropped, she reconnected herself to the battle outside.

[17]Get the ship!

It's too late! Fall back!

[38]We can't let them take it!

[18]Yarrow! Don't—

[17]What the hell is he doing?

[25]He's going to mine it!

Clear the area!

Now!

Through the senses of the courier Roche saw a singleship loom close. The sky beyond was thick with crossfire. Into the web of energy came the black shape of Yarrow's battle-scarred all-suit, a magnetic mine in one extended manipulator. Watching the speed and precision with which he moved, Roche couldn't help but think of Cane. The obvious comparison left her with mixed feelings, the strongest of which was fear.

The singleship turned to defend itself, but it wasn't Yarrow's target. He dived straight toward *Daybreak* and pressed the mine onto its hull. Then he moved away, heading low and close to the hull to maximize the amount of mass between him and the explosion.

When it came, the view from the courier blacked out instantly. The last thing Roche saw was the singleship realizing what had happened and trying too late to get away.

A heavy *thud* made the floor beneath jump. From the *Ana Vereine*'s point of view, Roche watched as a blue-white hemisphere suddenly blossomed from the side of the station, then disappeared, leaving blackened ruin in its wake.

Another deep rumble echoed through the station. Haid's suit whined softly as he staggered.

"What the hell was that?" His voice came from internal speakers this time. "One of the prowlers?"

"A mine. They found *Daybreak*. Yarrow destroyed it, and the entrance."

"Is he *crazy*?"

"It actually makes sense," said Roche. "This way they won't be able to work out how many of us were in the ship—nor can they follow us in. They don't even know if we got in at all. It's a mess up there."

"It still leaves us trapped, though!"

"Don't worry. We'll find a way out."

The elevator slowed to a halt, but the doors didn't open.

<There is a security presence outside,> said the Box.

<Show me.> A new window in Roche's field of view opened, revealing two guards maintaining watch at the end

of the corridor. They were armed, but not heavily armored. When a siren began to wail, they became instantly more alert.

<What's going on now, Box?>

<They have confirmation that you are in the station.>

<How is that possible? I thought you had everything locked down.>

<There must be something I've overlooked,> said the Box. <According to the low-level security dispatches I am monitoring, it seems they know *you* are on board, but they don't know precisely where—or even if you are alone.>

<Well, that's something. But I can't hide in here all day.> She checked her map. <We're on the right level. The security compound is two corridors over.> To the others she said: "We have a couple of guards outside. Is everyone ready?"

"You're really going through with this?" asked Disisto.

"I have no choice. You and Myer keep your heads down and follow me." She studied the view of the security guards. Their weapons looked like standard issue; her armor would absorb it easily, but Disisto and Mavalhin would not be so well protected.

<Box, send one of the drones in with me first. We have to prevent them from sounding the alarm. Ameidio, you come last, but before Myer and Disisto. I don't want them hurt.>

His hand touched her upper arm. GOT IT.

<At the end of the corridor, we go right.> She took a deep breath. <On my mark. Go!>

The drone moved out as soon as the elevator door opened, with Roche stepping past it to its left. The drone raised its rifle and fired a single sharp burst before the guards had a chance to react. One guard fell. Roche was a split-second behind; her shot caught the second guard in the shoulder, spinning him around and into the wall. He slid down to the floor and didn't move.

Two down, she thought.

The pitch of the alarms didn't change.

<Any more?> she asked the Box.

<Two more to the left, another five in a guardroom closer to the compound itself. Beyond that is a black zone I cannot penetrate.>

<Is it likely we'll find anything in there?>

<There's only one way to find out, Morgan.>

<And in doing so, we expose ourselves. Okay.> She touched Haid's shoulder. <Two to the left. You take a drone and deal with them, then catch up. We have a nest of five just ahead.>

OKAY.

He edged up to the corner, with one of the drones close behind. Once he had rounded it, Roche headed off along the passageway, with the two captives and the other drone behind. So far Disisto and Mavalhin had shown nothing but cooperation, but she couldn't afford to relax. She would feel easier once Haid caught up with them again.

She had almost reached the guardroom when two sharp retorts rang out along the corridor; then a third. The response was immediate: voices and movement came from ahead of her. Instinctively she selected a subsonic from the suit's array of weaponry and stepped around the corner into the guardroom itself.

Two of the guards were fully equipped and ready for action while the others were still in the process of fitting armor and weapons. None of the armor was powered, and the blast of low-frequency sound caught them by surprise. One keeled over backwards; another doubled over vomiting; the others clutched their heads in pain.

The drone moved forward, its raised gun taking out a guard with a single shot to the chest.

<No, Box! Don't kill them. Just knock them out.>

The drone immediately flipped the rifle and used the butt to club the remaining four unconscious.

A hand touched Roche's shoulder: MESSY, said Haid.

<Could have been a lot worse,> she replied, looking down at the dead body.

A corridor on the far side led into the black zone.

<Ameidio,> Roche said. <Wait here with these two and a drone. I'm going to have a look around on my own.> Before Haid could protest, she explained: <The Box can't stop them looking into the black zone. If they do, they'll think there's only two of us. And I'll have you to cover my back.>

OKAY. SHOUT IF YOU NEED BACKUP.

"Wait," said Mavalhin as Roche stepped forward.

She turned. "What?"

"I know this area," said the pilot. Then in response to Roche's quizzical expression, he explained: "I've, ah, spent some time here in the past."

"Well-deserved too, if I recall," muttered Disisto.

Mavalhin shot the security chief a sharp look. "I paid all the money back!"

"Eventually, and only because—"

"I haven't got *time* for this!" Roche's bellow startled them both to silence. It had been effective, but she hoped her voice hadn't carried too far. "Myer, you come with me. I'm looking for maximum security cells, possibly with medical facilities."

"Not a problem," he said. "Lead the way."

Roche's laugh was brief and humorless. "I don't think so," she said. "If I'm going to be led into a trap, I'm making sure you're right there in front of me, Myer."

"Were you always this suspicious, Morgan?"

"Just move it."

He swallowed under her glare. "Okay. This way, I think."

She followed him into the black zone, down a corridor that looked no different from any of the others they had traversed. They passed several closed doors, but none of them looked secure enough to be cells, and Mavalhin didn't stop.

Their movements were cautious and relatively quiet, and there had been no signs of any other guards. Nevertheless,

Roche remained tense and uneasy. She knew that setting off just one internal alarm would change everything. . . .

"Here." Mavalhin pointed through a closed transparent door.

Roche peered in and saw steel-gray bulkheads, six down each side of a wide corridor. Everything about them said high security to her.

There was a panel by the side of the door. <Box, do you think—?>

<Place your suit's left palm-link within range.>

She did so. <Can you break into the system from here?>

<No. This is just an isolated lock. It does give some interesting codes and passwords, though.>

The door clicked and hissed slowly open. Roche nudged Mavalhin ahead of her. The first door on her left had a transparent panel at eye level. She peered through it, but saw nothing except for featureless walls and floor. The cell was empty.

So was the one opposite, and the next one along. All twelve, in fact, turned out to be empty.

"Are these the only cells here, Myer?"

"I'm afraid so," he said. "At least they're the only ones I ever saw down here." He led her out of the corridor. "See, there's a dead end, and that leads to the way we came."

"Damn." She cursed their luck, but quickly regained her composure. She needed to stay focused. "Okay, then. It's back the way we came." To the Box she said: <Get another elevator ready for us. This is going to be awkward. We need to go down two levels and across to the other side of the station.>

<Working on it now, Morgan.>

When they got back to the others, Roche found that Haid had taken the time to bind the four unconscious guards. Their absence, along with that of their dead comrades, would inevitably provoke some concern, but for now it afforded them a little breathing space.

Disisto looked worried when she walked into the room,

which surprised her. If anything, she would have expected him to have been relieved to see her empty-handed.

"What's wrong?" she asked.

He shook his head. "When do I get to talk to the chief?"

"Later," she said, shepherding him and Mavalhin ahead of her. "Just keep moving."

Back in the elevator, Roche checked the status of the battle outside. The all-suits had retreated entirely, apart from a few of those teleoperated by the Box or the outriggers aboard the *Ana Vereine*. Casualties were higher than Roche would have liked. They were down to forty fully functioning all-suits, while the station had lost just ten singleships. Half of the prowling mines had been disabled and their hulks were drifting steadily away from the battle. The *Ana Vereine* had also pulled back, as though reassessing its options, and conducted only the occasional raid on the station.

There was little point in maintaining the illusion that the attack had merely paused and would begin again at any moment. Rufo and the Kesh somehow knew that she was inside. And when the attack resumed, they would know that she was preparing to leave.

<Morgan,> said the Box, <we have a blip on the long-range scanners. Precisely on schedule.>

She acknowledged the news with merely a grunt. Time was definitely running out.

"Do you know the other security compound at all?" she asked Mavalhin.

The pilot shook his head. Even through his suit's helmet she could see the sweat trickling down his face. "Sorry, Morgan."

The elevator stopped and they disembarked once the Box had assured them the area was clear. The AI had a transit cab waiting for them at the nearest tube entrance. They filed inside, and were rapidly whisked around the equator of the station's inner perimeter. At the other end, they found another elevator and went down several levels.

"I think I should try to get in contact with someone," said Disisto.

"Only when we've got nothing to bargain with."

"You haven't anything *now*!" he shot back. "You're not exactly doing that great out there."

"We're doing all right," she said.

"You could at least *try*."

She turned to face him. He looked worse than Mavalhin. "Why? We've got this far without bargaining."

He didn't answer.

Doubt suddenly flooded through her. "It's been too easy, hasn't it? That's what's worrying you . . ."

Still he said nothing.

The elevator was two floors away from stopping.

<Box, drop us at the floor *above* the one we need.>

The cab decelerated suddenly. The map showed a maze of corridors at that level; a maintenance and storage floor that promised to be mostly empty.

<Can you knock out security on this level?>

<Already done, Morgan.>

<And make it look like the elevator has kept going?>

<Naturally,> the AI said. <I have also taken the liberty of preparing a diversion, should it be required.>

Roche belatedly remembered the other two drones. She quickly checked through the vision of the one the Box had allocated her, but saw only darkness on most frequencies except infrared, which revealed a dull background of heat. It was almost as though the drone had its faceplate pressed up against something warm. She didn't have time to work it out, so closed the window to the drone's viewpoint.

"This way," said Roche as she exited the elevator. She led them along a winding corridor, keeping one eye on where she was going and the other on the map. Superimposing the two levels was confusing; she relied heavily on the Box to warn her if they were about to run into company. But soon they were where she wanted to be: below their feet, separated by only a meter of decking, was the other black zone.

"This isn't going to be subtle," she said to Disisto. "If you have any suggestions on how to minimize possible loss of life, tell me now."

The security chief warred with himself for a moment, then said: "The closer you get to the middle, the safer it will be. But stay out of the exact center. That would be dangerous."

When she realized he wasn't going to provide any more detail, Roche concentrated on finding an appropriate place. She had no way of knowing what they would be going into; she wanted somewhere away from a bulkhead with an enclosed space above it. All she could do was look for the latter in about the right place and hope for the former.

She found a storage hold that looked about right, and with the help of one of the drones began laying charges in the floor. The charges weren't as precise as she would've liked, and their entrance would be all too dramatic, but it was the best she could think of under the circumstances.

When she was ready, she cleared the room. The Box closed the door behind her.

"Five seconds," she said. "The drones go first, then we all follow. I'll go last. And remember this," she added to Disisto and Mavalhin: "One, the longer we're here, the more likely it is we'll be trapped; and two, I'm holding a gun to your backs, and I have no intention of allowing you to slow us down."

There wasn't time for either captive to acknowledge her: the charges went off with a force that made even her suit lose its balance. The door came off its tracks, and by the time she was upright again the drones were already pulling it free. On the other side, most of the floor of the room had dropped away in a ragged circular slab, tilted where a wall cut a chord across it from underneath. Smoke and dust filled the air. The drones half-dropped, half-slid down the slab and fired at something she couldn't see. Roche heard someone call out, but they were abruptly cut short. Somewhere close by, another siren began to wail.

Haid followed the drones. Roche shoved her reluctant captives ahead of her, then followed herself.

She landed on a pile of rubble in the middle of a giant open-space area. Wrecked consoles and desks lay scattered for tens of meters around them; fire burned in carpet that had once been grass-green. Oddly placed panels broke the space into discretely semidetached segments. From behind one such panel, someone was offering resistance and calling for help. The drones ignored that one voice for the moment, concentrating instead on picking out cameras and other security placements throughout the place, disabling them with single, precise shots.

As Roche took her bearings, a door opened in a distant wall and a squad of security guards ran in.

She dropped to one knee and fired. The squad ducked for cover, turning over furniture and scrambling for the nearest panels. Return fire crackled back at her, whining as it ricocheted off her armor. The drones and Haid backed her up from behind the cover of the slab they had ducked behind.

"Which way?" shouted Haid.

Roche glanced around her. The wall through which the guards had entered was curved, as was the wall behind the slab, suggesting that the space was circular, enclosing them. The guards had been on the outer wall, so what they were protecting was farther in.

The inner wall was not far away, near enough for a quick dash. There was a door within sight.

"There!" she shouted, pointing.

"What if it doesn't open?" Haid called back.

She used the suit's sensors to zoom closer for a better view. The door was almost flush to the wall, and there didn't seem to be any way to open it.

"It'll have to," she said. "Cover me."

She shouldered her rifle and darted across the gap.

She had barely reached halfway across when the door opened from the other side, revealing Shak'ni and Haden B'shan. Both Kesh officers were dressed in full battle uniform and holding ceremonial—though clearly functional—weapons.

She didn't know who was more startled, the Kesh or her. All three lifted their weapons simultaneously, but Shak'ni got in the first shot, catching Roche in the thigh. Her suit shrieked but absorbed the blow.

Her stomach twisted in panic. Kesh weapons were a higher gauge than the ones her suit was designed to withstand. A handful of shots were all it would take—maybe as few as three. But that might be all she needed . . .

She called up the menu on her rifle as a second shot from Shak'ni hit her in the visor. She blinked but managed to select the options she required. B'shan went for her knees, and made her stagger. She aimed the rifle and fired just as Shak'ni caught her a third time, in the chest, knocking her backwards and off her feet.

Aimed up and between the two Kesh warriors, the percussion charge struck the ceiling just inside the door and exploded violently, tearing another hole in the already damaged ceiling. Half of the door went with it, along with B'shan and Shak'ni.

Roche rolled out of the shock wave and was on her feet before anyone else had recovered. Her ears rang and the suit seemed a little stiff, but she was otherwise unharmed. The two Kesh stirred weakly some distance from what remained of the door. Haid and the others were already moving.

More guards appeared off to the left, hugging the curve of the wall.

"Okay, Disisto!" she shouted as she pushed him ahead of her into the ruined doorway. "*Now* you can talk to them!"

"Very funny, Roche!" he called back over his shoulder.

She fired another percussion charge into the floor behind them, hoping its partial collapse would delay pursuit for a moment or two. She could already hear Shak'ni bellowing for assistance.

"I'm serious, Disisto," she said. "I need you to stay here and tell them what I want. This is your one and only chance to mediate. But I suggest you think fast about what you're going to say, because Shak'ni won't be in the mood for listening."

Disisto looked sick with worry, but Roche didn't have time to concern herself with that at the moment. Haid had already gone through the inner door with Mavalhin and one of the drones, leaving her to follow. The most she could do was leave him a drone for support.

"Box, do your best to keep him alive, will you?" She patted Disisto roughly on the shoulder. "Good luck," she said, meaning it, then ducked through the doorway after the others.

There was a palm-lock on the far side, which the Box made short work of, shutting the door on the sounds of the weapons from outside. Roche heard Disisto offer a wry "Thanks" before the door slammed shut.

Then silence.

Only then did she really take the time to look around.

She was in a corridor that curved away uninterrupted in either direction. There seemed to be no one about, and no doors. There was no sign of the others through the lingering smoke and dust, and for a moment she felt panic.

MORGAN, IS THAT YOU? There was no point hiding transmissions anymore.

<Haid? Where are you?>

HEAD TO YOUR LEFT. I THINK WE'VE FOUND WHAT WE'RE LOOKING FOR.

<Good. I'm on my way.>

The corridor led her to an antechamber barely large enough for the four of them. Two consoles faced away from the way she'd come in, next to a door that looked solid enough to stop a hydraulic ram. Each of the consoles monitored two cells, making four in all.

Haid was fiddling at one of the consoles, while the drone gave the Box access to the other. Mavalhin kept carefully out of the way.

"We seem to have three immobilized prisoners," said Haid. "One was brought here within the last few hours."

"That would make sense," said Roche, "especially if they thought we were coming. It would be easier to defend one area rather than two."

"So I thought. But the security is tight here. I can't tell which cell is which. And I can't get this damned door open, either."

"Box?"

The AI's voice issued from the drone's speakers: "There is a second entry point which must be accessed simultaneously."

Roche looked around her, then back the way she had come. "What was to the right of the entrance?"

"Another room like this one," Haid said. "Do you want me to—?"

"No, I'll go. Just tell me what I need to do when I get there."

She headed off along the corridor, past the door leading back to where she had left Disisto. Curious, she quickly switched over to the drone's senses to check what was happening.

The image was poor and breaking up, and the drone itself seemed to be lying on the ground with its head to one side. But Roche was able to make out Shak'ni, along with the dirty black mark marring the harsh perfection of the field officer's combat armor. He was holding Disisto by the throat with one hand; the other hand held a rifle to the security chief's head. Disisto's eyes were closed and he was talking furiously. Roche couldn't make out what he was saying, however, as the drone was transmitting visual data only.

B'shan stepped out of the background and said something to Shak'ni. The field officer threw Disisto to the floor, then lowered his rifle and fired at the drone. The transmission abruptly ceased.

The sound of gunfire followed her as she raced to the other control room.

It was a mirror image of the one she had just left.

<Okay, I'm here,> she said.

<Take the left console,> said the Box. She did so. <It's all manual. Key in the following instruction: Bulkhead Release 947. The system will request a password. Type: "Driftglass." You should be seeing a countdown now.>

<Yes.>

<When it reaches zero, hit the green button at the top right of the console. I'll do the same at the other end.>

She waited for the numbers to scroll down from ten, pressing the button impatiently the precise moment the display reached zero. A warning Klaxon sounded and the door opened with a grinding sound. She grabbed her rifle and approached cautiously.

All she saw was another corridor, curving away to her left.

<Careful,> she said to Haid. <I can't make out anything from here. Send the drone first, then Myer.>

Two doors appeared, one each to her left and right. They were both closed. <Box, can you open the internal doors from here?>

Both doors hissed open. Each was comprised of two panels: the outer panel slid aside; the inner one rose up into the ceiling. There was no way to look into one cell without exposing herself to the other. Roche mentally tossed a coin and stepped forward.

The cell on her right was empty, little more than a four-meter-square space. In its center was a stainless-steel bed uncomfortably reminiscent of an autopsy slab. She snap-turned and aimed her gun into the second cell.

It too was empty.

That left two cells, but there were still three prisoners.

She remembered that Galine Four security knew where *she* was, not the others.

<Ameidio, this is our chance. You're coming up on them from behind. I want you to—>

MORGAN, Haid interrupted. THEY HAVE MAII!

<Box, let me see.> She jumped to the other drone's senses.

She saw the young Surin reave strapped to one of the steel "beds." A Kesh guard stood beside her, a pistol pressed firmly to her forehead. The girl seemed oblivious to what was going on around her.

Roche hissed through her teeth. If they hurt her—

"Give up, Roche!" called a voice. "You're surrounded!"

She didn't grace the speaker with a reply. The drone turned its head. There were more guards in the room. All held their guns on Haid, the drone, and Mavalhin. If she ordered Haid to attack, he would probably win—but not in time to save Maii.

There had to be another way . . .

<Box, I think we could use that diversion about now.>

<Yes, Morgan.>

<Just give me a minute to get myself in position, then I'll give you the word.>

<I will ensure that your suit is ready.>

Roche was about to ask the Box what it was readying her *for,* when another voice spoke softly into her mind.

<Morgan?>

<*Maii*? Is that you?>

<Morgan, look . . .>

Maii's voice was little more than a whisper, and through the drone's eyes she looked completely unconscious. But as Roche stared at her, she saw the index finger on the girl's left hand move. She was pointing!

Roche tried to extrapolate the layout of the room, given what the others had looked like. Maii was pointing out the door. Out the door and to the cell opposite—presumably to where the other two prisoners were held.

"You have five seconds, Roche," called the Kesh guard. "Then she dies. Five."

<Okay, Box,> she said. <Tell Uri and Byrne to resume the attack. Blow the piles on the prowlers; send in more of the nano breeders to eat the hull. Hit them with everything we've got, and make sure they hurt. Let's not make it too easy for them.>

"Four."

The sound of footsteps in the control room she had just left echoed up the corridor. <And if you can close the doors behind me, do it.>

The door slammed shut. <I have taken the liberty of closing both, Morgan.>

<Good. Ameidio, are you hearing this?>

YES.

"Three."

She inched as far as she dared around the corridor and clutched her rifle to her chest.

"Two."

<Okay, Box. Now!>

The lights went out. Her suit and implants switched automatically to infrared. Then the floor fell out from underneath her—and *kept* falling.

She clutched for balance, but her suit had already adjusted. The Box must have hit the artificial gravity generators somehow. When some sense of weight returned, it was at half-strength—enough to enable her to run around the corner and to the second cell.

The door was shut; she fired the rifle at it. Gunshots came likewise from the cell containing Maii, followed by the sound of someone hissing in pain. She couldn't afford to be distracted. All she could do was hope that Maii hadn't been hurt.

The cell door juddered open a crack, and she used the suit's strength to lever it the rest of the way. Inside—

She hesitated for a split second.

—inside were two bodies. One belonged to Cane. He

was naked and encased entirely in a slab of what looked like clear amber which was in turn bolted to a mobile platform. Wires and tubes were threaded through the transparent material, but there was clearly no way he could talk or move. Metal straps around the amber block further ensured his imprisonment.

His eyes were shut, but somehow Roche knew that he was awake, and possibly even aware of her presence.

The other body belonged to something far from Pristine. It looked vaguely Olmahoi, but unlike any she had ever seen. Its black skin was shiny and abraded, its limbs thin, almost vestigial, its body was hunched, its face featureless and pinched. The only vital element to the entire creature was its epsense organ—a thick tentacle sprouting from the back of its skull. But where most Olmahoi epsense organs were rarely as thick as a normal wrist, this one was thigh-like in width—fat and almost a meter and a half long, throbbing with vitality, almost as if it were sucking the life out of the creature attached to it. Roche could see where needles and other instruments penetrated its flesh, supplying nutrients or performing other mysterious tasks.

The creature lay on a bed like Maii's. It was bound, but not firmly. It seemed to Roche that it didn't need to be. She doubted it could even have walked, let alone run away.

There was a monitor behind it. On it flashed a single word:

: BEWARE

<*The irikeii*!> Roche had never heard the Box sound surprised before.

<The what?>

CLEAR, transmitted Haid from behind her.

Distracted, she turned. <And Maii?>

UNHARMED.

<I have Cane. He—>

She grunted as someone pushed past her.

"Sorry, Morgan," said the Box via the drone. "But I must get through."

Roche faced the drone across the body of the Olmahoi creature. "What the hell are you doing?"

"I am administering Xarodine," explained the Box as the drone injected something into the base of the Olmahoi's skull. "There were doses in Maii's cell, naturally."

The creature twitched, and the word on the screen changed to:

: CRUEL

"*Why,* Box?"

"Xarodine is an epsense-inhibitor."

"I *know* that, but—"

"Give me a moment, Morgan."

A muffled explosion from farther up the hallway reminded her of Shak'ni and the rest of the guards.

"I don't *have* a moment, Box."

She rushed out of the cell. Haid was already there. The sound of pounding came from both ends of the corridor.

WE'RE TRAPPED.

"Any suggestions, Myer?" she called into Maii's cell. "Myer?" Maii was still on the table, although her bonds had been removed. The guards and their weapons lay scattered across the floor. But the pilot was gone.

"He was here a moment ago," Haid said, dispensing with his implants. "He must have snuck out while I was busy with Maii."

"*Damn* him!"

"Do we go after him?"

Roche sighed. "We haven't got time. Besides, we don't even know which way he's gone." She made a mental note to be sure that Myer paid for this at a later date. "Our only chance is to bust out before they're ready. Take them off-guard. One of us will have to carry Maii; maybe we can use the guards' armor to protect her."

"What about Cane?"

She cursed Myer again. "He'll have to wait. He looks safe enough as he is." She went back into Maii's cell and bent to strip one of the dead guards. <Box, when I give the word I want you to open the right-hand door only, okay?>

<Okay, Morgan.>

Her helmeted head brushed Maii's.

<Is that you, Morgan?>

Roche laid a gloved hand on Maii's arm. <I'm right next to you, Maii.>

<It's clearing; I can see again! What happened to the *irikeii*?>

<The *irikeii*?> Remembering what the Box had called the Olmahoi, she dashed into the other cell. The drone was bent over the hunched figure on the bed. The word on the screen now read:

: ONE

<Box, what have you done?>

<Set Maii free. I suggest you use her while you can.>

Another explosion sounded up the corridor just as the word changed to:

: COMES

Then Roche was embraced by the young reave's excited mind. <Morgan! I can read you! I can *read* you!>

<Maii, listen to me: we're in serious trouble here.>

More calmly the girl said: <I know. What can I do to help?>

<Somewhere near here you'll find Shak'ni and B'shan.> Roche felt guilty for pushing the girl so soon, but right now she was their best chance of getting out of there alive. <I want you to knock them out, and anyone with them. Can you do that? Can you reach that far?>

There was a pause before she replied: <I can feel them.>

<Good. Don't kill them; just knock them out.>

<Okay. Give me a second to get my bearings . . .>

Roche checked the charges on her rifle; enough for a while yet. The sounds from the ends of the corridor died down, and she assumed the reave had already begun to work.

Then Maii said: <What does it mean when the destroyer

you've been waiting for is right on top of us and ordering us to surrender?>

A chill went through Roche. <Box?>

<I was just about to tell you, Morgan. The *Sebettu* has completed its final approach. It will be within firing range in twenty minutes. Its senior officer has issued a message.>

The recording came through her implants:

> AGGRESSORS IN THE VICINITY OF GALINE FOUR: DESIST IMMEDIATELY OR FACE THE CONSEQUENCES. WE WILL NOT HESITATE TO USE LETHAL FORCE. YOU HAVE BEEN WARNED.

That was why the guards had stopped pounding at the doors: they knew they'd won. All they had to do now was wait her out.

<Uri? How are you holding out there?>

<We are continuing to harry the station, Morgan,> replied Kajic. <In an hour or two we would've mopped up the last of the singleships.>

<How do you rate your chances against a Kesh destroyer?>

<Poor,> he admitted. <We could get away, but we'd have no chance of taking it out.>

<Then tell Byrne to get her people the hell away. The Kesh will squash them like bugs.>

<I'll relay your message now,> the ex-captain said. <What would you like me to do?>

She paused. The words burned in her throat. <Get ready to stand down. We're going to surrender.>

<I have a transmission from Field Officer Shak'ni,> said the Box. <It's being broadcast on the outer security level.>

<Play it.>

It was brief: "Come out, Roche, or we *will* destroy you."

ARE WE REALLY GOING TO SURRENDER? asked Haid.

<We haven't a choice with that destroyer there.> She switched the rifle to standby. <Box, tell him he's won. We'll come out peacefully. Just give us a minute.>

She went into the cell and squatted next to Maii.

<Will you be okay?>

The reave's expression was closed. <Yes.>

<You know what I'm thinking?>

<Yes.>

<I'm sorry.>

<Don't be, Morgan.>

<Shak'ni will accept our surrender under some conditions,> the Box said.

<And they are?>

The Kesh officer's voice told her himself: "You, Morgan Roche, and your party will submit to the authority of interim peacemaker Field Officer Shak'ni. All hostilities directed against Galine Four and Linegar Rufo will cease. The *Ana Vereine* will dock with Galine Four and allow Lieutenant Haden B'shan to assume control. All internal systems—including that of Uri Kajic—will become the property of the N'Kor Republic. The Surin reave will be sedated and undergo further Xarodine therapy. The AI you refer to as 'the Box,' serial number JW11110101110, will be ejected from the ship immediately. Any transmissions from said AI will be regarded as a violation of this agreement and as such will incur a penalty: the immediate execution of one of your party, starting with the Surin girl. Further transmissions will result in similar penalties. Do we understand each other?"

Roche didn't answer immediately. She stared at the knotted scar tissue where Maii's eyes had once been. She felt very tired.

<Do you have a backup, Box?>

<Software can be replicated, Morgan, but hardware cannot.>

<And you're prepared to take the risk that they might just blow you out of the sky?>

<If you recall, I am graded to withstand a—>

<—a nuclear strike from a hundred meters,> she finished for the AI. She smiled, despite herself. <I can take that as a yes?>

<You can.>

<Then tell Shak'ni I agree.>

She stood and walked down the corridor, the way she had come. There she found Mavalhin cowering against the door. He started when he saw her, and wouldn't meet her eyes. She didn't care.

<Is everything ready, Box?>

<It is.>

<Then let's get this over with. Open the door.>

Outside the station, an airlock opened on the side of the *Ana Vereine*. A small black valise shot out of it and tumbled in the vague direction of Hintubet. The sun's reddish glow was exacerbated by the hastening collapse of the Gauntlet, but it was still barely bright enough to paint a dull sheen on the battered case.

Roche watched through the *Ana Vereine*'s sensors as a Kesh singleship scooped the valise up with a pair of remote manipulators and took it aboard the *Sebettu*. So distracted was she by the view that the Kesh guard escorting her had to prod her roughly in the bare shoulder with a rifle butt to get her moving faster.

She winced and rubbed the new bruise he had given her. Her capture had been inglorious enough without being made to strip off her armor in front of everyone. Dressed only in her sweaty undersuit and handcuffs, she felt completely naked. That Haid, Disisto, and Mavalhin had been treated similarly didn't make her feel any better. Maii lay back in her cell, her mind suppressed once more by the suffocating effects of the drug Xarodine. The only comfort Roche could take was that Galine Four's internal gravity generators were still not working properly. The self-destruction of one of the Box's drones right in the very heart of the station had done too much damage, and ambient gravity remained at about half normal.

"Where are you taking us?" she asked.

"The only time you'll speak, Roche," said Shak'ni from behind her, "is to give us information."

INTERROGATION, HUH? Haid broadcast.

<I'd be disappointed otherwise.>

"You will cease any other forms of communication, too," Shak'ni added. "You may only continue to receive information from your ship provided it is non-encrypted."

The procession of guards and captives wound their way to freight elevators, then down into the heart of the station. At least that was something, Roche thought to herself. If they'd been taken to the destroyer, things would've become difficult indeed.

She watched through the *Ana Vereine*'s sensors as the *Sebettu* approached. In design it was little different from other Kesh craft—an odd combination of streamlined and prickly, as though an ordinary spaceship had been half-melted and stretched—but its size was impressive. A dozen Galine Fours would have fit easily into its holds. Its entire surface was pockmarked by retractable weapon emplacements, instrument clusters, and fighter launch bays. The intrasystem engines that brought it to an imposing halt beside the station radiated as much energy as a small sun.

She hoped Byrne had managed to get the outriggers away from the area. The spines were their only hope of survival. Although not capable of slow-jumping out of the Gauntlet, they did at least possess resources that would allow the outriggers to survive in the middle of nowhere.

When Roche realized what she was thinking, it occurred to her how ridiculous it was. The system was due to be totally destroyed in less than a day. Although the collapse of the boundary was initially slow, it would proceed exponentially. The double-jovian system had already succumbed;

she had watched it dissolve into the invisible barrier like ice into fire just before the attack had begun. The region of space occupied by Galine Four would be gone in twelve hours. If the outriggers weren't gone by then, no amount of supplies would save them.

All evidence of what had occurred here would be gone forever, she thought. It was the perfect situation in which to conduct a little genocide. . . .

The freight elevator opened opposite a window showing the hanging gardens at the heart of the station. The vibrant green contrasted sharply with the gloom of her situation, but she tried to take hope anyway. All was not yet lost. Not quite.

The guards led her to Rufo's sanctum sanctorum. Its elegance and purity were unchanged, but she admired it less for the corruption she knew it hid. Rufo himself looked old and bitter despite his victory. His speech was rapid and sometimes hard to understand; he paced constantly, and he seemed unable to maintain eye contact with anyone but Haden B'shan; all of which, Roche noticed, he was apparently unaware.

A chair slid out of the floor beside her and she was forced into it. The others were treated likewise, despite Mavalhin's protests. Disisto's expression was tight-lipped, but he said nothing, seemingly confident that things would be sorted out with his boss soon enough. Haid sat straight in his chair and watched everything closely.

"So, Commander Roche." Rufo spoke with the disdain of a reproachful parent, stepping up to Morgan with his hands behind his back. "We meet again. Perhaps you will be more accommodating this time."

"Perhaps you might show me the same courtesy," Roche shot back.

Rufo shrugged, his eyes averted to the floor. "I suppose there were lies on both sides," he acknowledged.

"Who was it that said that there are lies, and then there are damned lies?"

Rufo smiled humorlessly. "I believe the earliest recorded mention of that saying is some two hundred and fifty thousand years ago. The Human condition hasn't changed much in that time, has it?"

"Obviously."

"There will always be optimists whose dreams of a moral society are about as realistic, and as foolish, as those who believe in fate."

"Look, Rufo," said Roche, "we really don't have time for this kind of banter. Why not just get on with it?"

He stopped pacing for a moment, but still his eyes wouldn't meet hers. "Very well," he said. "I want to know everything you know about Adoni Cane. And remember, Field Officer Shak'ni has his instructions, so please, no lies."

Roche had already decided to tell him everything she knew. It wouldn't hurt; he probably knew more than she did, anyway. So she started at the beginning—at Cane's examination on Sciacca's World—and brought him up to date. He nodded constantly, but didn't say anything himself until she had finished.

"And you are satisfied with the explanation that he is a product of the Sol Apotheosis Movement—a Wunderkind, as they were called?"

"Not entirely," she said. "There are inconsistencies."

"Of course there are. We have images of these Wunderkind. They were quite remarkable." A window opened above the desk; in it appeared a figure that looked as if it had been inflated with liquid helium. Its skin was bluish over limbs that bulged alarmingly. The scale next to it showed that it stood almost three meters high. "Do you agree?"

Startled, she didn't know what to say. If Rufo had that image, then presumably COE Intelligence had it too. Why hadn't the Box or her ex-superiors in COE Intelligence failed to notice the disparity between it and the near-perfect Pristine reality of Adoni Cane?

Disisto looked smug. He had been telling the truth after all.

"I don't understand," she managed after a moment or two.

"Obviously." Rufo wandered around the room, touching panels and studying screens as though bored. "We will return to Cane in a moment. For now I wish to talk about the other clone warrior."

"What about him?"

"Did you find him?"

"I doubt I would be here now if I had."

"That's not necessarily true. These creatures may be ruthless, but they aren't stupid. If his purposes were not served by killing you, then he would not do so. That is the only explanation I can deduce for your extended survival while in the company of Adoni Cane."

She couldn't argue that point. "You believe he was among the outriggers," she said.

"Did you see anything to suggest that he might have been?"

She thought about Yarrow. "Not hard evidence as such, no . . ."

"But suspicions?"

She hesitated. "Yes."

Field Officer Shak'ni spoke: "Your cargo hold contains several of these people. Could the clone be among them?"

She shook her head. "They were examined as they boarded. All were ordinary mundanes. Nothing like Cane."

"Then the one we are seeking might be among the others still at large." The Kesh grunted to himself. "We will hunt them down, one by one. If he *is* among them, we will find him."

Roche gritted her teeth. She'd thought that her capture would end the involvement of the outriggers. "They're not to blame. They didn't know—"

"They wouldn't have," said Rufo. "These creatures are chameleonic in their ability to blend in, when they want to.

Indeed, that is their primary function: to insinuate. Then to corrupt. Like everything else they do, they do it well."

"You sound like you've studied them for some time," she said.

Her guard nudged her in the shoulder for speaking out of turn, but Rufo waved him away.

"At a distance, yes, but always after the fact. Only recently have people begun to suspect that something might be going on. Highly placed people. The Highest. They have become concerned. There is evidence to suggest that beings like Cane have been emerging for years now throughout the galaxy—far more than the handful you are aware of. Thousands, possibly millions of them. Although the individuals may not be noticed, their effects are. We mundanes do not see them, though; we are entangled in the details, in the data. A superior perspective is required to tease out the trends."

"That's where you got the command language from, then. The High Humans?"

"Yes. One of them or more; I can't tell. Even individually, they have access to information I can only dream of. Together . . ." Rufo seemed to gather himself. "Did Cane respond to the command language, by the way? I presume by your question that you detected it."

"He said he understood fragments but that it didn't make any sense as a whole. It was jumbled, as though whoever put it together didn't know what it meant. And the Box said its syntax wasn't like anything from around here."

Rufo chuckled softly. "Hardly surprising. Those fragments were recorded over half a million centuries ago."

For a moment, Roche was speechless.

It was Mavalhin who spoke: "Bullshit."

The guard clouted him, but the sentiment had been aired.

"I assure you, Myer, it is not," said Rufo. "Although I will admit to a similar skepticism when I first heard that claim. Of course, since then I have learned more than enough to convince me otherwise. The language Cane and his ilk respond to was written when Humanity was a single pure strain—before the Primordial Castes, before the Pristines, before even the High Castes. It is a piece of history, and Cane is an integral part of it."

"What do you intend to do with him?" Roche asked.

"He's not your concern anymore," said Rufo. "He'll be kept as he is until we are ready to study him. And study him we will, I assure you. We intend to learn the precise secrets of his genetic makeup and abilities. We want to know how many there are like him, and where they are headed. We need to know who made him, and, more importantly, *why.*"

"And then," said Shak'ni, "we will kill him."

A martial fanfare echoed through the station, and every Kesh in the room suddenly stiffened.

Rufo visibly paled as the sound of marching feet came from the anteroom. The inner door slid open. The Kesh saluted as an officer entered the room surrounded by a full military escort. Roche swiveled in her seat to look.

The new arrival was easily the tallest and strongest Kesh officer she had ever seen—which in itself was impressive. Dressed in armor not dissimilar to the weapons and ships of the Caste—smooth, concave lines tapering to sharp points at odd places, burnished wood in color—with a retractable helmet bearing insignia Roche had never seen in person before, the Kesh general exuded power, confidence, and ruthlessness in equal portions.

The general stopped in the middle of the room and surveyed its contents.

"Sh'shek hroga vied ra vhul kimosh'n ka," she said, her voice hoarse from an old injury.

"Opulence is a sign of waste," a junior officer translated. "And waste is forbidden."

The general continued, via the translator: "I will be glad when this arrangement is concluded, and the stench of inferior species is gone from my nostrils."

"*Kuresh* Darkan—" Shak'ni began, but the general cut him off.

"This operation has been conducted without honor. You will be disciplined."

Shak'ni nodded stiffly, the red veinlike marks on his face standing out. "As you wish," he said so all could hear and understand.

"General Darkan does not wish to debase herself by speaking to inferiors." The interpreter's face was permanently pinched in distaste. "She grants me permission to speak for her. You—Linegar Rufo. Is debriefing concluded?"

The scientist stepped forward, carefully projecting a passive, respectful demeanor. "We are close to finishing, but—"

"Can their word be trusted?"

"Yes, General," said B'shan. "I have spent enough time with these people to know when they are telling the truth."

The general nodded distantly. "Then we have learned the precise location of the second warrior."

"Not exactly," said Rufo, "but we do have an idea—"

"But we do still have the one called Cane?"

Rufo nodded quickly. "Yes, of course."

"Then we can abandon the other one to his fate," said the interpreter. "We cannot linger here. In seventeen hours this system will be nothing but dust. We will leave the moment we have downloaded the contents of the station's datapool."

"If I may speak," said Shak'ni.

The general nodded without looking at him.

"We have captured a vessel—"

"The *Ana Vereine*," said the interpreter. "Yes, we know."

"It contains many new technologies. We have docked it to this station. It should be retained for study."

"And the AI? What of that?"

"I gave strict instructions that it should be placed under the tightest security. Any transmissions—"

"We are aware of the risks. Any transmissions in either direction will result in its expulsion and destruction. Are you suggesting we keep this, too?"

"It is bounty—"

"What use is a box too dangerous to open? Besides, its technology is irrelevant to us. No intelligence, artificial or otherwise, can equal the Kesh Ideal. Its tricks are worthless and dishonorable."

Roche wanted to ask what the general thought of the High Humans but decided that speaking out of turn was inadvisable.

The general grunted something in the Kesh language, and the interpreter translated: "We will, however, take the ship. It has a working slow-jump drive, and to leave it here would be folly. What purpose it is put to by the Dictatrix is up to her."

"And the captives?" Shak'ni asked.

The general gazed contemptuously across the room, directly into Roche's eyes.

"They will remain here with the others," said the interpreter with a slight smirk. "When the system collapses, they will die."

Rufo stepped forward again. "When you say the others," he said anxiously, "you mean the outriggers, right?"

"Those as well, yes."

"Ah, as well as—?"

"This station and all those upon it, of course."

"But our arrangement—"

The interpreter smiled again. "We have no further use for you, Rufo. You are as inferior as the others. It would be a waste of time and effort to return you to your people. Let *them* save you, if that is what they wish."

"I—" the scientist stammered, fear and hopelessness rising to fill his eyes. He seemed to age decades in an instant. "That is—you cannot—"

"Jin'ek ke yi," sneered the general.

Roche didn't need the interpreter to understand; it was clear from the general's tone and expression. They could do it and they *would.*

"This is insane!" Disisto's voice broke the tension in the room.

The general faced him, nostrils flared in anger. A guard struck him in the back, knocking him to the floor.

"You were not permitted to speak," said the interpreter with a smooth grin.

Disisto picked himself up, wincing. "I don't give a damn! We've done *everything* you asked us to do here. We've worked for you, put ourselves at risk, got you what you wanted—"

The guard whipped an arm around Disisto's throat and tightened his hold until he could no longer speak or even breathe. Dragging the security chief upright, the guard held him motionless, choking.

Waving the interpreter aside, the general crossed the room to face Disisto. "You think us cruel?" she asked.

Something odd stirred in Roche's mind—a feeling of unreality, distancing her from the events unfolding before her.

Disisto was unable to reply. The general gestured, and the guard threw Disisto to the floor. The security chief gasped for air, barely able to rise on all fours, let alone speak coherently. The general reached for the guard's pistol and aimed it at the back of Disisto's head. She fired, once, and Disisto slumped forward.

"Perhaps we are," she said, returning the guard's pistol.

Roche's vision went blank; all she could see were the words that had flashed one by one on the *irikeii*'s display.

: BEWARE
: CRUEL
: ONE
: COMES

And all she could smell was the blood pooling around Disisto's body.

"N'hok vi ha'kahri tsen!"

Roche snapped out of it. She looked around, trying to

find the source of the exclamation, but at first was unable to.

The general's anger was tempered by her own surprise.

"Who dares claim the Right?" asked the interpreter.

"Ri," said Haid, standing. "I do."

"Outrageous!"

Roche was as shocked as anyone. "Ameidio, what are you—?"

"Vask!" The general ordered the room to silence; even those unfamiliar with the language knew what she was demanding. She stepped up to Haid. "Do you realize what it is you do, little man?"

"*Du.* I claim the Warrior's Right to challenge a superior's decision by formal combat."

"And who made *you* a Warrior?"

"Sh'manit Dro, the Sixteenth and last G'rodo Matriarch."

General Darkan hissed through her teeth. "A disgraced lineage."

Haid nodded. "But a lineage all the same," he said. "Or perhaps you are unprepared for such a challenge?"

"We are *always*—"

"Then name a champion to defend your honor," said Haid smoothly. "Unless you choose to fight yourself."

The general sneered in open disdain. "I would not demean myself with such a fight. I would stand to lose more honor than I could possibly hope to gain."

"I will fight him, General," said Lieutenant-Doctor Haden B'shan. "With your permission, of course."

The general rounded on Shak'ni's junior officer. "Clearly you have spent *too much* time with these people, Lieutenant. There is no time for these games."

B'shan nodded in agreement. "Nevertheless, he knows the traditions, he speaks the Tongue. I believe his claim to be a legitimate one."

The general snorted. "It is your decision, Lieutenant. I will not intervene should you wish to debase yourself thus."

"Yes, but will you honor the victor?" Haid asked.

The general glowered at Haid, her eyes filled with contempt. "You confuse your capabilities with your dreams," she said shortly. Then: "But should B'shan succumb to that dream, then yes, you *will* have earned the Right."

"Your name on it?"

"My name on it." The general indicated her interpreter and guards. "And these are my witnesses."

Haid bowed stiffly. "Where do we fight?" he asked. "Here?"

The general thought for a moment, then continued in her native tongue: "On the way here we passed an enclosed area with several observation points; a garden of some kind. That will do." Then to B'shan, she said, "You can fight while we download this station's data and free the bounty ship from its chattel." It took Roche a moment to realize that the general was referring to the outriggers in the hold. "We will leave the moment this farce has ended."

Haid nodded, apparently satisfied.

"Ameidio—" Roche began.

"Quiet!" Her guard pressed her back into the seat.

"There is no time left for discussion," the general said. "I want the data transfer to commence as soon as possible. Any physical resources we have contributed to this station will be returned to the *Sebettu* immediately. However"—she swept the Humans in the room with a warning glance—"a full contingent will remain on board to ensure against further foolishness. Field Officer Shak'ni, you will see personally to the neutralization of the Olmahoi and Surin epsense adepts. They and the clone must be ready to move in one hour. And this time I want no loose ends."

Shak'ni bowed and stalked out of the room, casting a baleful glance at Roche as he went.

The general allowed herself a chuckle as she spoke to her interpreter.

"The two Warriors will have a moment to reflect upon the import of the task ahead while they wait for the weapons to arrive," he translated. "The rest of you may clean *this* up." He pointed at Disisto's body. "If you wish," he added, then turned to follow the general as she strode heavily from the room. B'shan silently followed.

Mavalhin was instantly on his feet. "Congratulations, Rufo," he spat. "You've managed to get us all killed!"

The old scientist didn't respond. All he could do was stand and stare blankly at the body of his security chief.

"The Kesh drive a hard bargain," Haid said. "The moment you think you've got a fair deal, it's time to check the fine print."

Roche put her hand on his arm; his biomesh was sharp and cold to the touch. "Why are you doing this, Ameidio?"

"Because I've always wanted to, and I figure this might be my last chance."

"Be serious—"

"No, I am. You've seen the way the Kesh are. They're impossible to deal with. Anybody who spends any time with them ends up tiptoeing around to avoid causing a fuss. It wears thin after a while. Even the G'rodo were like that; better than most, in a lot of ways, but in the end just as annoying. It's nice to get your own back, just once."

She sighed. "Well, what about the weapons? Do you get a choice?"

He shook his head. "When you invoke an ancient rite, you get what you're given."

She stared at him for a long moment. "This is insane."

"Perhaps, but we don't really have many options open to us, do we? Unless you have a plan you haven't let me in on yet?" When she didn't answer, he smiled and said: "Then I guess we go with my idea."

Roche muttered under her breath as she turned away from Haid; she faced Rufo and said: "Rufo, you're still the chief around here, for what it's worth. How about getting someone in to take Disisto away? I think he deserves better than this, don't you?"

Rufo nodded numbly and moved over to the console. He spoke briefly to someone outside and, moments later, the Kesh guard let a medical stretcher through. Disisto's body was bagged up and taken away. Nothing was said by anyone throughout the process; everyone just stood and watched in silence.

"How long do we have?" said Roche after the doors had closed again.

Haid shrugged. "I don't know. The longer the better. Even artificial limbs need time to limber up."

Roche stepped over to Rufo. "Is there anything else I should know?" she asked. "Cane is older than I originally thought; the command language has been coming from the High Humans . . . Anything at all?"

He looked up at her with eyes empty of anything but despair. "What difference does it make now?"

"Spare me your self-pity," she snapped. "Now *talk* to me! Do you have any contact names for the High Humans? Or possible suspects for the people who made Cane? There must be *something* else!"

Rufo stared vacantly into space. Then he said: "Introns."

"What?"

"Check Cane's introns."

"I don't even know what you're talking about."

"We took a tissue sample before we put Cane into hibernation," he said. "It looks like yours or mine on the surface; it has the same ratio of introns to exons. You see, introns are part of everyone's genetic code; the junk parts, the filler. The exons do all the work. We assumed the differences lay in the exons, so we concentrated on those areas. But there was something about the introns—something unusual. We haven't had the time to look at them properly. You could start there." He stopped, the beginnings of a hopeful gleam in his eye abruptly extinguished. "But you won't have time either, will you? You can't even get a message outside to let someone else know."

Mavalhin made a noise of disgust from behind him. Roche ignored it.

"Is that all?" she said.

He shook his head. "You know as much as I do, now. Frightening how little it is, don't you think?"

Roche could only agree.

It wasn't long before the Kesh returned. Haid had been warming up for just ten minutes when B'shan walked in.

"Why are *you* doing this?" Roche asked, stepping in front of him. "I thought you were better than the others."

"At least this way you'll have a chance," he said evenly.

Up close Roche found the Kesh lieutenant's skin almost beautiful: his blue and purple markings looked like tribal tattoos applied by a skilled ink-worker. For all his leanings toward mundane culture, it wasn't difficult to believe that he could descend to such barbarism.

She stepped out of the way. "You're both fools," she said.

B'shan faced Haid across the room, and bowed. They exchanged a handful of words in the Kesh language, then bowed again.

"He has consented to allow me use of my implants," Haid said to Roche.

"Otherwise I fear the battle would be somewhat one-sided," B'shan explained.

Roche shuddered at the idea of Haid stripped back to nothing but flesh. He would have been utterly helpless, a cripple.

"The general will permit those of you who wish to observe to do so," B'shan went on, addressing everyone. "You are, after all, witnesses to her oath, and we must ensure she carries it out. Combat will commence in five minutes."

"What about the weapons?" Roche directed the question at Haid, but it was B'shan who answered:

"There will be no armor, powered or passive. There will be nothing but the druh."

"That's the weapon we'll be given," explained Haid. "Not much more use than a pocketknife, really."

"Even a pocketknife can kill," said B'shan.

"I know. I've tried it."

B'shan straightened. At full stretch, he had about thirty centimeters on Haid, and he looked considerably stronger. While Roche didn't doubt her friend's agility under the best circumstances, fighting in half-g with unfamiliar implants was hardly optimal.

Instead of saying anything more, B'shan simply bowed again and left the room. Haid followed, casting a reassuring look at Roche as he passed. When he had gone, the guards indicated that the others should also leave.

As Roche walked out the room, Mavalhin stepped in beside her.

"I hope you know what you're doing, Morgan," he hissed.

She frowned. "What do you mean?"

"Well, you're up to something, right? This is all a ruse of some kind."

She turned on him sharply. "Don't look to me to get you out of your own stupid situations, Myer. And don't bother trying to say it was me that got you into this mess, either. You jumped at the chance to join me when it looked like I was going somewhere—just like you did back at College." For a moment she felt vertigo, as though reliving her dream of falling. "Take control of your own life, Myer, and leave me to sort out mine."

He backed away, face flushed with anger and embarrassment. She didn't care. He meant nothing to her. All she wanted to do was talk to the Box. But she couldn't. The slightest attempt to do so would result in its destruction, as well as Maii's execution. If the Kesh detected any transmissions, it would be expelled into space and fired upon from a dozen different directions. No matter what sort of firepower it was rated to stand, that was going to hurt. . . .

They didn't have to walk far. The general had ordered the garden windows to be smashed; there seemed no reason to maintain the delicate ecosystem any longer. Rufo's dismay only increased when he saw the damage. The corridor surrounding the garden now more resembled a gallery, with both Kesh and mundanes curious to see what would happen. Word had obviously spread.

When the two combatants stepped into the garden, a small cheer went up. Roche wasn't sure for whom the cheer was intended; maybe it was just for the spectacle itself. Haid and B'shan stood on one of several mesh walkways crisscrossing the garden. Where the bottom was, Roche couldn't see; far enough below for a fall likely to be lethal, she imagined.

The general clapped her hands once. Haid and B'shan held curved bronze-colored swords in their left hands, each barely as long as the average Pristine forearm. They were intricately carved with elongated Kesh characters that made no sense to Roche. Haid raised his to kiss the narrow guard, and bowed to the general.

"Sh'ten dri ka," he called. "By the blade!"

"To the death," B'shan responded, also bowing.

"Begin!" rasped the general, and the two men faced each other.

They stood two meters apart, and were wary at first. Haid tested both his reach and B'shan's defenses by darting forward twice to slash at the Kesh's exposed side, but B'shan parried with ease. The third time Haid tried it, B'shan counterattacked with a quick stab, only to catch a boot to the side for his troubles. The kick didn't even wind him, but it did take him by surprise. Roche could see the Kesh lieutenant hesitate, reassessing his opponent.

Then the combat truly began. Later she would recall a hail of thrusts, stabs, and sweeping slashes from B'shan as he sought to overwhelm Haid's defenses. The ex-mercenary was hard-pressed to keep up, parrying with his one good arm and relying on a more clumsy artificial limb to keep his balance. Twice B'shan's druh caught Haid's biomesh, parting several strands and slicing shallowly into flesh. It was difficult to tell through the blood, but Haid's implants didn't seem to be affected. He certainly didn't display any sign of weakness. Apart from the odd moment when his guard was down, he fought as well as ever.

It was clear from the outset, though, that he was no match for the Kesh officer. B'shan went for his kidneys, and Haid only just managed to block the blow. Barely had he recovered his balance when the druh swept in to slash his throat. He staggered backwards, ducking just out of reach. A halfhearted stab in the general direction of B'shan's sword arm failed to connect, and he was struggling for his life again.

Roche felt that her friend's only hope lay in superior agility. B'shan had power to spare, able to hammer blows with an emphasis Haid couldn't possibly match, but the Kesh's size left him clumsy. A couple of times Haid gained ground by encouraging him to overextend, permitting a nimble stab from below, or a quick shove to put him off balance. At times like this, with B'shan forced onto his back foot, Haid made ground.

But that ground was soon lost. Roche knew that unless fortune smiled upon him, Haid would ultimately fall.

Her knuckles gripped the windowsill as Haid endured another blistering barrage from the Kesh. Above him, the general watched impassively, her expression almost one of boredom. For the most part the fight was conducted in silence, apart from the ringing of metal on metal, the various sounds of exertion, and the occasional call of encouragement from the spectators. Both men were breathing heavily, although the Kesh's smooth skin was almost entirely sweat-free.

B'shan had almost managed to back Haid to the end of the walkway when Haid miscalculated. Knowing that he was about to be cornered, the ex-mercenary needed to find space. There were only two options: another walkway, or pushing through B'shan and out the other side. For once, Haid took the offensive, summoning every last iota of energy to put B'shan off his stroke. The moment he had an opening, he leapt onto the guardrail and sprang for the next walkway down.

It almost worked. The move took B'shan by surprise, just long enough for Haid to avoid the slash that followed him. He managed the leap well enough, his artificial legs being more than up to the task in half-gravity. It was the landing he fumbled, stumbling heavily and throwing out his good arm to break his fall.

Roche heard the crack before she saw what had happened. The walkway he'd left partially obscured his new position, and a few seconds passed before she found a better viewpoint. By the time she reached it, he was on his feet, holding his broken arm to his stomach. The sword was in the hand of his new arm. He flexed it, eyes seeking another way out as B'shan followed him across the gap.

Eyes seeking *her,* Roche realized. He was waiting for her to save him.

But there was nothing she could do.

As B'shan straightened warily, druh at the ready in case Haid attacked while he recovered from the leap, a whistle echoed across the leafy space. It came from the general and her entourage, a Kesh version of the warning sirens associated with mundanes. The general held a whispered conversation with her interpretor, then looked pointedly across the garden to Roche.

"Morgan Roche!" the general's voice boomed. "Would you care to explain why we are once again under attack?"

Everything stopped, and all eyes turned to look at her as the general continued:

"I have just received word that a number of outrigger all-suits have been seen approaching this location in attack formation. I suppose you know nothing about this?"

"I don't, I swear!" And it was the truth. Roche genuinely had no idea what was going on. Another attack by the outriggers? What was Auditor Byrne up to?

"Gah!" The general turned away, disgusted, back to Haid and B'shan. The two had backed away from each other during the interruption, although B'shan still stood with his weapon raised, as though unsure whether to continue. For a moment Roche was certain he would press home his advantage while the chance remained. But he didn't.

Haid grinned up at Roche, and nodded his thanks.

Roche could only stare dumbstruck back at him.

"This farce is at an end!" the general declared. "There will be no further distraction, and no more leniency. Lieutenant, your weapon." The general indicated the druh in B'shan's hand. The Kesh threw it expertly across and up to his superior, who caught it with one strong hand. She waved vaguely in Roche's direction. "Bring her to me."

Roche realized what she meant when the general's bodyguards began converging on her. She looked around for some way to escape, but every exit was blocked. A circle formed around her as she backed away. Strong hands grabbed her from behind and dragged her to where the general waited, druh at the ready.

"It is bad luck to wield a blade without bloodying it," the general said. She pointed at the ground before her, and Roche was pushed onto her knees. She struggled but could do nothing to prevent being forced facedown onto the ground at the general's feet.

"Morgan!" Haid's voice echoed up from the gardens. She realized he couldn't see what was going on, and was glad to be spared that indignity.

"Ameidio!" she called back. "Do what the Box says—take the *Ana Vereine*—tell Maii—!"

A boot connected with the side of her head to silence her, and her mouth filled with blood.

She heard the general curse her in the Kesh native tongue. She sensed the blade being raised. She closed her eyes and waited for the blow.

Into the expectant hush, a woman's voice spoke.

"General Darkan!" said the voice. It came over Galine Four's public address system and seemed to echo from everywhere at once. "Surrender control of the *Sebettu* immediately or I shall overload its primary generator and send you all to hell!"

Roche heard the general hiss. "Who is this? What is the meaning—"

"You have thirty seconds to think about it. If I don't have an answer by then, I will make good my promise."

The general roared. Roche, forgotten for the moment, dared to breathe again.

"I do not listen to threats!"

"Then listen to this: I have instructed your cooling systems to shut down. In five minutes a chain reaction will begin that cannot be stopped. Your primary generator *will* blow if you don't give me a reason to reverse the instruction. There is nothing you can do to stop it, except to hand over control to me. It's as simple as that. You now have twenty seconds left."

"How is this possible?" the general roared, but for the first time Roche detected a hint of fear in her voice. "How are you doing this?"

"*How* I am doing this is irrelevant. Know only that I *am* doing it, and give me control of your ship!"

"Never!" The booming voice was defiant, but the general's expression was full of uncertainty.

"Then mine will be the last voice any of you will ever hear."

"Who *are* you?" barked the general.

"I'm the one everybody has been looking for, General," said the voice. "But I suspect you already knew that."

Roche's head reeled: *female*?

There was a long silence from the general, then:

"No," said the general. "I would rather die than let you loose on an unsuspecting galaxy."

"So be it," said the woman. "You have five minutes to

make peace with Asha, General. I suggest you make good use of that time."

"You are bluffing!" the general hissed, but neither the clone warrior nor Morgan Roche was listening.

INTERLUDE

While under Xarodine, the universe was a very different place.

What little he could see was far off and blurred. The only minds close to him belonged to the Shining One and the abomination. The latter also labored under the epsense-inhibiting drug, coiling around herself like a restless snake, while the former appeared to be sleeping. Certainly his thought patterns were passive and his sensory inputs minimal. Yet the dark speck at the heart of his glare was still active, and through this speck some of the outside world leaked in.

The enigma had been taken away. The other Shining One had come closer. The Cruel One, too, had appeared to put fear into the hearts of her servants. Things were coming to a head, that was for certain, and he was frustrated to be kept at arm's-length from it, trapped in a fog of Xarodine.

Then someone appeared. It was a mind he had encountered before: petty, brittle, filled with self-doubt and hatred for all others. This mind came on a mission from the Cruel One: to take the Shining One elsewhere and to neutralize the other prisoners. Those were his orders, and he would fulfill them to the letter. It was either that or face further dishonor. And as far as this Kesh officer was concerned, dishonor was worse than death.

"Neutralize" meant kill. That much he could glean from the mind bearing down on him. But it was with some relief that he contemplated the imminence of his demise, for it would also mean the end of the abomination.

The officer spoke briefly to the guards, who admitted him to the secure compound with an escort and closed the doors behind him. Nothing, even now, was being left to chance.

The officer checked the cocoon within which the Shining One rested. All was well there, it seemed. Various instruments and controls were prepared for travel, and an internal supply was activated. From that moment on, the Shining One became independent of everyone around him. Thus encased, he could survive several hours in a complete vacuum until the gel boiled away, and, if rescued in time, emerge unscathed.

Not that the officer thought such precautions were necessary. He refused to believe that the captive could be superior to a Kesh warrior. The events he had witnessed in recent weeks he put down to luck, or the element of surprise. Pristines made poor warriors in his eyes, and he found their slaughter an unremarkable thing. All it would take was planning and persistence—the twin virtues of Kesh military dogma.

When gunfire sounded from the other side of the security compound's already battle-scarred doors, the Kesh officer thought for a moment that he was hearing things. There was no resistance left in the station; the Cruel One had everything under control. What could possibly have gone wrong?

The Kesh officer wheeled the Shining One into the hallway and ordered his escort to guard the cocoon. When he tried to speak to the guards outside, only one of the two groups monitoring the double doors answered; the other was under attack by an unknown number of assailants.

Remembering his other captives, the Kesh officer tried more esoteric means to find out what was going on. He had already decided not to call for reinforcements until he was sure what he was up against; he did not want to risk the general's further displeasure.

"How many are there?" he asked, manipulating the paingivers.

The minds of the guards under siege—imprecise and vague through the drug—saw only a single attacker, and then only fleetingly.

: ONE

"Who is it?"

That one's mind didn't register at all.

: NO ONE

"Don't play games with me—"

The Kesh officer stopped, for the sound of gunfire at the entrance had ceased. But the silence didn't last long: a moment later it began at the other entrance, where the second group of guards waited.

"Who *is* that?"

: NO ONE

: ABOMINATION

: KILL

"Bah! You're talking rubbish."

Still the officer hesitated to call for help. He was sure he and his guards could deal with a single assailant. The interior of the security compound would be easier to defend than the exterior, and he made sure his escort was ready for anything. They would put the three prisoners in one cell and seal it shut. That way the intruder would be at a disadvantage, not knowing which cell to aim for and therefore where to direct his attack.

Then it occurred to the officer that the welfare of two of his prisoners was irrelevant. They could even be used to his advantage. The officer ordered the Shining One to be locked securely away once more and the other two to be brought out into the hallway.

Again the gunfire ceased. The Kesh officer tensed. It was theoretically impossible for one person to open the doors, but he didn't dare believe that would be the end of it.

Sure enough, the doors clanked and began to open. Barely a second had passed and the officer was at the nearest door, ready to repel the intruder. All he saw, though, was one of his own guards, sitting at the console to the door with some sort of device strapped to his chest.

"He made me, I swear—I—!" he babbled.

Then the device exploded.

But the Kesh officer was already running back to the captives. He had been fooled; the intruder was coming in the other door!

Through the smoke and dust, he saw the flash of a weapon, and the last member of his escort tumbled to the floor. He watched in some panic as a tall, silver-armored warrior stepped over the bodies to survey the scene.

The Kesh officer hissed, choking on a growing sense of failure. He warned that he would shoot the prisoners if the warrior did not immediately retreat.

Seemingly unconcerned by the officer's threat, the warrior raised his weapon to target the Kesh.

Howling a Kesh battle cry, the officer fired indiscriminately, striking prisoners and warrior alike. The great silver figure staggered back under the power of the officer's ceremonial firearm. A lucky shot knocked the assailant's weapon aside and cracked the seal of the silver armor at the shoulder. Concentrating on that point, the officer fired three more shots in quick succession, knocking the assailant to the ground.

A silver arm skidded across the floor, severed by the final shot.

Hope returned to the Kesh officer's mind like fresh air through the smoke. He stepped forward to survey the carnage. Both stretchers had spilled their contents to the floor: the Surin reave had sustained an injury to her legs, and the Olmahoi creature was bleeding from a wound in its abdomen. He would put an end to their suffering in a moment, once he was certain that the intruder was dead.

The silver armor was the same as that worn by Roche and one of her companions when she had been captured. This one, he assumed, must have been stolen before they could be taken to the *Sebettu* for examination. It had been irreparably damaged, missing its right arm from the shoulder down, and now lay inert facedown against a wall.

He nodded in satisfaction, although a new anger rose. Heads would roll for the theft not to have been reported. The occupant of the suit had fought well against insurmountable odds; almost as well as a Kesh . . .

The officer stared in horror as the suit suddenly rolled over. Its left arm scrabbled for its fallen weapon and, before he could react, fired two shots. Falling to his knees, the Kesh clutched at his stomach, feeling the life ebb with his blood out onto the floor.

As his executioner turned away, the dying Kesh caught a perfect view of the interior of the suit, through the hole where its right arm would have been.

His eyes bulged even further as he keeled forward to die on the floor.

The suit was empty.

There were no minds left to view what happened in the secure compound. Only the Shining One remained, and he saw nothing through those eyes.

He felt his body lifted back onto the stretcher, but it had already become distant—even more so than usual. And the foggy sense that remained of his usual all-pervading sight was itself fading. As blood rushed out of his body and drained from his uniquely developed epsense organ, darkness pressed in.

The light of the Shining One was fading. As he watched it dwindle, unafraid, a voice spoke:

<I'm sorry.>

He had forgotten about the abomination. They must have been close for their drug-crippled minds to touch.

<I would ease your pain, were there any pain to ease. But you don't feel anything at all, do you?>

She was right. Apart from when his body had been tortured in order to gain information, he had had no care for it at all.

Yet here he was, dying because of its injuries. He would be glad for an end to this life. Without his people, without the Grand Design, he was nothing.

His only sadness was that he was dying alone.

<You aren't alone,> she said, and her mind touched his more firmly. He could not resist the abomination, nor did he want to. She offered herself to him, another mind to cling to, alone in the dark as he was, and he welcomed her reassuring touch.

He *was* comforted. That much was true, despite himself. And he wondered if the feeling was mutual as together they spiraled ever steeper down into the dark . . .

8

Galine Four
'955.01.24 EN
0550

The vision came as a concentration of thoughts and words, of memories too, and its intrusion was as intense as it was abrupt. It had traveled so many routes on its way to her that its details were indistinct. But it could not be denied. It blossomed in Roche's mind with the intensity of an outrigger Plenary minus the auditor's guiding hand.

She saw a war. That much was obvious. A war so big that the galaxy burned for centuries, and trillions of lives were extinguished in a bloodbath never to be equaled.

Half a million years later, she watched as the events blossomed rapidly in her mind, with the war's political machinations unfurling like the bloodied petals of a flower. Peace returned to the galaxy only after hundreds of novae had added their heavier elements to the dust clouds, and one of the opposing armies was defeated.

But even then it did not end. The vanquished had foreseen their fate and had prepared for their revenge—a revenge which would take place long after they had been forgotten by those who had eradicated them.

Roche saw a cloud of tiny machines erupt from the galactic spiral and dissipate away from the inhabited areas, into the outer depths. Their exact number was unknown, but they numbered in the millions at least. Traveling well below the speed of light, the machines did not have the momentum to quite escape the gravitational pull of the galaxy, although they did travel vast distances from the core.

Before long the great war was forgotten, buried by time and lost to more immediate conflicts; but the machines continued to hurtle to the darkest edges of the galaxy. Memories of their makers faded too, their legend dissolving into little more than a curiosity for scholars, and eventually forgotten altogether; and still the machines continued to travel on. . . .

Eventually their velocity decreased and, as it did, they gathered mass—atom by atom, molecule by molecule. And as their orbits pulled them back to the denser regions where they had originated, they began to build. Each one became a capsule. And within each capsule, a life was born.

These lives would burn bright and fast, and, in burning, they would find revenge.

The Sol Apotheosis Movement and its followers had nothing to do with this plan; they were nothing more than a convenient cover. Yes, they had existed, and had been slaughtered at the hands of their united neighbors; they had indeed chosen for their base system one that had long been associated with ancient Humanity, although it was now fallow; and they might well have conceived such a plan for revenge, although they lacked the skills and subtlety to put it into action.

The name Adoni Cane had nothing to do with them. That name was as old as the ancient war itself. Other such names fell effortlessly into Roche's thoughts: Vani Wehr, Sadoc Lleshi, Jelena Heidik, Ralf Dreher, and more. Each had played a role in the events at the dawn of time; each had been marked by the vanquished for revenge; each had a role to play in the times to come.

This was what Linegar Rufo feared: a plan far older and more widespread than anyone had suspected. And this was the knowledge the *irikeii* had given Maii, and which she in turn gave Roche.

When it was over, nothing remained of the young reave in Roche's mind. It felt strangely empty, hollow. Why had Maii only managed to send her that one mind-dump and nothing more? Roche shook her head to clear her thoughts. But try as she might to deny the possibility that something bad had happened to the girl, the emptiness in her mind continued to fill her with concern.

She lay on her side at the feet of the Kesh guards. No one seemed to be paying her any attention, for which she was thankful if not a little surprised. Then she remembered the clone warrior, and she realized that compared to *her,* Roche was no threat at all.

Some time had passed, but she had no idea exactly how much until she heard the general boom:

"Five minutes are up! She has nothing to bargain with—*nothing*! Just more games to waste my time!"

"General, someone *did* infiltrate our cooling systems," she heard the translator say. "If we are still alive it's only because they don't want to destroy their only way out of here."

"Then she *still* has nothing! *We* control the *Sebettu*; until that changes, we will not negotiate. Let her attack! It will do her no good."

It took Roche a second to realize that the general was speaking in the Kesh tongue but that she could still understand what she was saying.

"Is the download complete?"

"Yes, General. The last of the data was transferred twenty minutes ago."

"Then why are we lingering in this accursed place? Instruct all personnel to return to the *Sebettu* for immediate departure!"

A voice began talking over the station's PA system, repeating the general's order in the Kesh tongue. At this the guards near Roche moved off; after they had gone she managed to sit up, fighting dizziness and the aches all over her body. The general was some distance away around the curve of the corridor. She frowned for a moment, confused as to how she had been able to hear the general conferring with the other Kesh. Then she realized that the translation of the general's words had been coming through her implants.

<Box? Is that you?>

<Yes, Morgan. I have been—>

A roar of fury from the general cut across anything else the AI might have said.

"That incompetent fool! If there were time I would have Shak'ni skinned for this!" The general rounded on her aides, who backed out of arm's reach. "I've had enough of this stupidity! Leave him behind. Leave *all* of them behind! We will erase this place from our memories!"

The general stalked off, the booming of her boots along the corridor receding quickly into the distance. Roche suddenly found herself alone.

She clambered stiffly to her feet. Her neck and back hurt where the guard had held her, and a bump had already formed on her skull.

<Box, what have you gotten us into now?>

<Nothing untoward, Morgan. Our plan worked as expected. The program my drone placed in the security shell of this station was successfully transferred with the rest of the data to the *Sebettu,* where it has allowed me to communicate unnoticed. I now have full control of this station and complete access to the data Linegar Rufo collected.>

Roche didn't have the heart to tell the Box that she'd come across most of that data by other means. <And the *Sebettu*?>

<The destroyer remains outside my reach. It too has been

fitted with a Tipper-Linke chaos-lock to ward against intrusion.>

<But the generator—>

<I only made it appear that the cooling systems had been shut down. If someone checks manually—as no doubt they will—they will realize the truth.>

<And the clone warrior? Does she know about this?>

<She goes by the name of Jelena Heidik.> Roche recalled the name from Maii's mind-dump. <Ours was a temporary alliance, nothing more. I needed a distraction and knew she would be willing to pool resources. Auditor Byrne and I gave her the empty all-suits left over from the attack. She was allowed to think that she was acting to meet her own ends, when in fact she was serving mine. There was no great risk.>

<So you say.> Roche didn't dare believe it would be that easy. <What about Maii?>

<She is presently in a coma, but will recover. My remaining drone was able to prevent Field Officer Shak'ni from killing her and making off with Cane. They are both being moved from the secure compound to the *Ana Vereine* as we speak.>

Relief flooded through her. <And the—what was it? *Irikeii*?>

<Is dead.> There was no hint of regret in the Box's tone. <Under normal circumstances it acts as a counterbalance to the Olmahoi Caste's natural epsense abilities. The thoughtworld they create, their Grand Design, is fragile and would, unchecked, spiral into disorder. The *irikeii* absorbs and behaves as a passive sink for spurious thoughts in its vicinity. That, clearly, is why General Darkan had it kidnapped and brought here. Had it not—>

<Enough, Box. What does it mean to Maii?>

<Her normal epsense abilities will return the moment she awakens. I estimate that to be in about fifteen hours.>

<Then . . .> Roche stopped, hearing footsteps approaching.

It was Haid. "Morgan!" The ex-mercenary held out his new arm to grip her shoulder. "Are you all right?"

She almost laughed. "Me? What about *you*? Your *arm* is broken."

"Just another reminder of how poor flesh and blood actually is," he said. "But I'll live." The fingers on his artificial arm flexed. "These toys didn't perform so badly after all."

"I guess not."

Haid looked around; there was a cut to his cheek she hadn't noticed before, oozing thick blood. "The Kesh are pulling out all over the station. B'shan went with them. He asked me to tell you that he regretted what had happened. I think he might even have meant it."

"Yeah? Well apologies won't help us much at the moment," she said brusquely, but it did surprise her. It wasn't like a Kesh to apologize for anything, whether he meant it or not. "Cane and Maii are on their way to the *Ana Vereine*, so we'll join them there. When things settle down we can talk about getting the station out of the system. If Uri thinks the ship is up to it, we might be able to translate the entire thing, otherwise we'll just have to ferry the people out in lots."

Haid nodded. "The boundary's getting closer by the second. Round trips will become progressively quicker."

"And the holds should still be full of outriggers; that'll save time. Once we pick up Byrne and the others, we'll be done."

"What about the *Sebettu*?"

She shrugged. "We let it go. It's too big to take on directly, and if they leave peacefully I see no reason to pick a fight. We'll just have to settle our scores at a later date, I guess."

<General Darkan has just left Galine Four,> the Box announced. <Two more shuttle craft are still docked. When they disengage, the last of her staff will have left.>

"Is that the Box?" asked Haid, tapping one ear. "How did you manage that?"

Roche's stomach sank as a realization struck her. The Box! "Oh, hell. The Box is still on the *Sebettu*!"

<That is correct,> said the AI. <But do not concern yourself with my safety, Morgan.>

"What about the data?"

<I have already transferred it to the *Ana Vereine*. The important thing is that you survive. I am not irreplaceable.>

That was probably the closest thing to humility that she had ever heard from the Box. "Don't be such a martyr, Box. We'll get you back if we can. Tell Uri to warm up the drives. We're coming now."

Haid hurried after her as she strode for the nearest transit cab. Rufo tried to get her attention as she passed, but she ignored him. Myer Mavalhin was more persistent. He trailed them to the cab and squeezed inside after them, apologizing hastily when he brushed against Haid's broken arm. The ex-mercenary was still holding the druh in one clenched fist, and made sure Mavalhin knew it.

"Morgan!" the pilot panted. "Where are you going in such a hurry?"

"None of your business, Myer."

"Are you leaving?"

"Not just yet."

"Then where—?"

"She said it was none of your business." Haid's expression darkened and the blade twitched.

"Okay, okay." Mavalhin receded into the cab, and for a second Roche thought he might've finished. But as they crossed the glitch in ambient gravity—made even more disorienting by the damage to the generator—he started again.

"Can I come with you?"

She turned on him. "Myer, don't you listen to anything I say? I told you to leave me alone."

"No, you told me to take control of my life. Which is what I'm doing." He consciously straightened. "I've decided that I want to serve with you on the *Ana Vereine*. It's the right thing to do, I know it. Our destinies lie together, Morgan. You can't say no."

"Can't I?"

The cab slid to an abrupt halt and the doors opened. They were on the outermost level, close to the major docking bays.

<Morgan, the last of the shuttles has docked with the *Sebettu*.>

They entered a large disembarkation point similar to the one through which they had first entered the station. Roche was reminded of Disisto, whose job it had been to maintain security in this area, and felt a twinge of regret.

<How long until the Kesh leave?>

<Soon. The chief engineer has confirmed that there is nothing wrong with the primary generator's cooling system and declared the destroyer fit to travel. There is nothing I can do to prevent its departure. It would be best for you to let me go.>

<Is that what you want me to do, Box?>

<Yes.>

<Why? Does this further some secret plan you've hatched?>

<Quite the opposite, in fact, Morgan.>

<Then be quiet. You were built by the Crescend for a purpose; it would be remiss of us not to at least *try* to get you back.> Mentally turning her back on the AI she spoke to Kajic: <Uri? Hail the *Sebettu*. Tell them we want the Box back and we're prepared to negotiate.>

<Okay, Morgan.> The ex-captain of the *Ana Vereine* sounded glad to hear her voice.

An inner airlock hissed open and they passed through a cramped umbilical. At the far end, the *Ana Vereine*'s outer hatch hung open, waiting for them. Roche felt a strong sensation of relief to finally be back on board. The sepia walls and earthy tones had begun to feel almost like home.

<Morgan,> said Kajic, <are you aware someone is following you?>

Roche turned to see Mavalhin crossing the threshold.

He smiled sheepishly and stopped halfway. "Well, you didn't actually *say* I couldn't come."

"You're right." She strode back to face him and stared him in the eye.

"Does that mean I'm in?" he asked.

"No." She pushed him in the chest. He staggered back a step. "Uri, close and seal airlock three. Don't let anyone else on board without my express permission."

"Yes, Morgan." The hatch cut off any further protests Mavalhin might've made.

She hurried to the bridge with Haid behind. "Uri, are we ready to go?"

"All systems are one hundred percent operational. Maii and Cane are secure, as are our passengers in the hold."

"The Kesh didn't try anything while they had access to you?"

"They didn't have time."

"Good." She reached the bridge and settled into her usual chair at the first officer's station, allowing herself a brief but satisfactory smile as she did. "Disengage from Galine Four and bring us about."

As the mighty engines stirred, a message arrived from General Darkan:

THERE WILL BE NO NEGOTIATION.

"That settles that, then," said Haid from his position at the weapons console.

"Ameidio," she said, swiveling to face him. "You should be in sickbay!"

"Morgan, you need all the people you can get at the moment, and you know it. *Especially* if we lose the Box."

She was about to snap back a negative when the view through her left eye suddenly changed.

She was receiving a feed from one of the *Sebettu*'s many gun emplacements. Through its sensors she saw a pyramidal formation of all-suits circling the station and its attendant destroyer. The *Sebettu*'s powerful weapons had been trained upon them, monitoring them in case they tried to attack. At the center of the formation was Yarrow's warped black all-suit.

As Roche watched, the destroyer's weapons fired, instantly vaporizing four of the outriggers. Another six were disabled. The black all-suit tried its best to dodge the incoming fire, but without success. One glancing shot cracked it open and a cloud of frozen air jetted out of the interior. Its engines fired nonsensically before guttering out entirely. The remaining all-suits ceased flying in a purposeful way at the same time, their central control removed. With the threat gone, the dead all-suits were allowed to tumble away into the darkness.

Her vision returned to normal. <Thanks for that, Box.>

<I thought you might like to know that one threat has been neutralized.>

"Morgan!" Kajic appeared in the center of the bridge. "Their weapons are turning on *us* now."

"Any fighter activity?" she asked Haid.

"None. It's just us and them."

"That's all they'll need. Take evasive action," she ordered.

She gripped her armrest as the *Ana Vereine* rolled beneath her. The destroyer's forward batteries flashed, and a wave of flicker-bombs swept over one of the ship's nacelles, making it shudder.

"Damage?"

"Minimal," Kajic replied. "The disruptors held, just."

"How much of that can we take?"

"I'd rather not find out."

"Can we outrun them?"

"In the short term, yes, although their engines are designed for the long haul and would eventually catch us."

"Get us out of here, then. Box, is there anything you can do at your end? I still want to get you back if I can."

The AI's voice came from the speakers at the front of the bridge: "My resources here are severely limited. The entire command grid is completely separate from the rest of the ship's systems. I was lucky to take them unawares once, but I would not be so lucky again. Most likely they would immediately guess the source of the misleading data, expel me from the ship, and destroy me. That way you would gain nothing."

Roche reluctantly conceded the point. On the main screen, the enormous bulk of the destroyer had begun to recede. "I don't suppose there's any way you can get yourself expelled but *not* destroyed, is there?" she said dryly.

"Morgan," Kajic interrupted. "They are no longer targeting us."

"Excellent." She turned to face the ex-captain. His face, surprisingly, was still grim.

"Its weapons are now aimed at Galine Four," he said.

"Damn!" Although Galine Four had more firepower than the *Ana Vereine,* it was about as maneuverable as an asteroid. The station and everyone on it would be nothing but target practice for the destroyer's novice gunners.

But that wouldn't matter to the general. What had she said? *We will erase this place from our memories!* It seemed she had something more literal in mind than just determined forgetfulness.

"Ameidio, Uri—we don't have much choice. We have to draw its fire. The only way I can think to do that is to attack. So get ready. We move in as soon as possible."

No one argued with her, except the Box.

<Morgan, what are you doing?>

She felt the engines stirring beneath her as though her own veins were vibrating, and she wondered if this was a pale echo of what it was like to be Uri Kajic. "I can't let innocent people die just so I can make an easy escape, Box."

<I must urge you to reconsider, Morgan.>

"What's it to you, anyway? You're safe regardless. Unless, of course, the general decides to crack you open later."

The Box was silent for a moment. Then: <You are determined?>

It wasn't as if she had much choice: Maii was still in a coma, the Box was useless, she was generally outgunned and underequipped. But there was nothing new about that. "I have to at least try."

To the others she said: "Fire as soon as we're in range. Take us in close and fast, then back for another pass. If it doesn't work, keep hitting them. The moment they come after us, we move."

"Should I plot a specific course?" Kajic asked.

"No. Let's just see what happens."

She forced herself to lean back into the seat's firm embrace.

"In range in five seconds," said Kajic.

<They have noticed you,> said the Box.

"Three."

Batteries of weapons poised to fire upon the station were suddenly given a new target. A-P cannon rotated; missiles recalculated their hyperspatial trajectories.

"One."

The *Sebettu* fired.

A maelstrom of energy tore apart the space ahead of the Marauder, and there was no avoiding it. Shields did their best to keep out the worst, but some inevitably burst through. The hull screamed in at least two places. Repair systems were overloaded with input.

But the *Ana Vereine* held. Kajic kept its course true while Haid did his best to return fire. Two emplacements burned in a flash on the hull of the destroyer, then a third. A severed sensor tower pinwheeled into a blast meant for the *Ana Vereine* and disintegrated instantly. A lucky strike opened a rent in the hull four decks long, black and ugly, spilling air and Kesh personnel.

Then they were through. Roche steadied herself as the

Ana Vereine turned for another pass, but the smell of smoke in the air made her think twice.

"Can we do that again?"

"We've lost two shield generators," Kajic said with a pained expression. "We have breaches on three levels and meltdown in two others. Structural integrity is down by twenty-five percent. In short, I don't know, Morgan. It'd be close."

"Engines?"

"Undamaged."

"Good. What about the *Sebettu*? Is it following?"

"It is turning about," said the Box over the main speakers. "Weapons are locked."

"Then forget the second pass. We've got what we wanted." She stood, unable to sit any longer. "Uri, head for the Gauntlet's edge—maximum acceleration."

A map appeared on the main screen: the boundary of the solar envelope rippled and shimmered like a gray aurora.

<The edge is highly unstable, Morgan,> said the Box. <It is currently moving at an average of more than fifty thousand kilometers per second, a sizable percentage of the speed of light—but I emphasize that this is only an average. The sections in which the boundary is flexing most dramatically may be moving much quicker than that.>

"But that's only the outer rim, right? The thing as a whole is shaped like a disk, and the edge is collapsing most rapidly. If we go up or down, it should be more stable."

<Only relatively, Morgan.>

"Good." Roche was outwardly unperturbed. "Uri, aim for the most unstable piece within range. Up or down. Get us there as quickly as you can. If I've annoyed our friend the general enough, she'll be coming after us with all engines firing."

"That appears to be the case." Kajic brought up a display showing bright emission halos around the destroyer and its rapidly changing red shift.

"How long until we reach the boundary?"

"Fifteen minutes, Morgan. I have located a region in which parts of Autoville have been destroyed, upsetting the boundary's stability. Space-time in that region is highly stressed."

"Perfect. Box, you know what I want to do?"

<Yes, but I advise against it. The possibility of error is too great.>

"That's what you're here for."

<Don't forget, Morgan, that we are not communicating directly. My signal is relayed through Galine Four, from which you and I are becoming increasingly distant. Before long, the lag will become dangerous. Any decision I make will be based on information that might already be outdated. Your life will be in jeopardy.>

"Then we'll just have to do it on our own." Roche thought for a moment. "Uri, drop proximity and impact mines and dump everything in the cargo hold we can spare—even excess water if we've got it. Give them a wake to run into; keep them annoyed any way you can."

Roche sat back down and tried not to fidget. The tension in Haid's shoulders was noticeable even from behind, as was the pallor of his normally midnight-black skin. He had lost more blood than she'd thought.

"We have time to kill, Ameidio," she said. "At least get some painkillers."

He turned and gave her a wry smile. "In a few minutes it might be irrelevant."

She shrugged, the smile on her own face uneasy and forced. "Maybe," she whispered.

"The *Sebettu*'s flight profile is confirmed," Uri said. "It will be within firing range in twelve minutes."

"And how long until we reach the boundary?" asked Roche.

"Approximately twelve minutes. The margin for error is high given the region's instability."

Roche nodded. "See if you can get a response from them. Ask for Lieutenant Haden B'shan."

Kajic nodded.

Roche waited. The risk was high—doubly so without the Box to coordinate things. But she refused to believe that it couldn't be done—that she and the people with her, who had already done so much, couldn't meet this one, final challenge.

The fact that it probably *wouldn't* be the last chance they took together didn't matter. One at a time, she told herself. If she didn't make it over *this* hurdle, the ones that would've followed were irrelevant.

"We have a response," said Kajic eventually. "Putting it on the main screen now."

B'shan appeared, looking uncomfortable. Perhaps having the enemy name you specifically meant a loss of face in the Kesh code of honor. Roche didn't worry about that. She had more chance of reasoning with B'shan than any of the others.

"This is your last chance," she said. "We'll be at the halfway point in less than a minute. After that it'll be too late to turn back. We'll hit the boundary whether we like it or not."

B'shan nodded slowly. "We are aware of that, and we know what you're trying to do. But it won't work."

"No? You're not as maneuverable as we are."

"We're not completely inept, either, Roche. We have had more experience doing this than you. If you make it, the chances are we will too—and then what? There's nowhere you can run to on the outside."

"So it doesn't really matter if I make it or not, does it?"

B'shan stared at her for a long moment. "What about the others, Roche?" he said. "Do you have the right to decide for them?"

Roche laughed. He was trying to appeal to her Pristine side. A Kesh simply didn't think like that. He knew her kind well enough to know what buttons to push.

"Nice try, B'shan." She glanced at the countdown; the halfway point had just flashed by. "You just missed your last chance to end this sensibly. We'll either see each other on the other side, or . . ." She paused for a few seconds. "Or we won't, I guess. Goodbye, Lieutenant."

She turned to Kajic without waiting for a response. "Kill it."

The image winked out, and was replaced by a map of the boundary. She couldn't grasp the scale of it, because its surface was fractal in nature; the closer they came to it, the more detail appeared, making it look as if they were traveling nowhere.

"Who's the spokesperson for the people in the hold?" she asked.

"The outrigger named Lud."

"Can I speak to him?"

"I hear you, Morgan Roche," said Lud.

"*Are* you willing to go along with this?"

"We allied ourselves to your cause," he said. "Regardless of our personal preferences, we will stand by you as a group."

She nodded. "Does that mean you yourself would rather not be here, because if that's the case we can drop you off in an escape capsule—"

"As I said, what *I* would like doesn't enter into it." The tone of his voice was wry. "Besides, we both know I would be shot instantly."

"That's true." She repressed a slight smile. "Well, it's good to have you aboard, Lud. Maybe we can get you back in touch with your all-suit when this is over and done with."

"Unlikely," Lud said. "It was destroyed in the initial attack."

The line closed between them. Roche pondered the outrigger's words—and his situation—for longer than she realized. When she looked at the clock there were only three minutes remaining. The *Sebettu* was looming large in the aft screens, forward guns at the ready.

"Box?"

There was an appreciable lag before the AI replied. <Yes, Morgan?>

"Any advice?"

<Trust your instincts. Follow them always, and they will lead you where you most wish to go.>

She thought about it for a moment. "What the hell does that mean?"

There was amusement in the AI's tone when it replied: <It means that I have nothing constructive to say.>

"That's a first," said Roche solemnly. She felt something absurdly like grief rising in her throat. "And Box . . . ?"

<Yes, Morgan?>

"Thanks."

There was a long pause before the Box spoke again. <For anything specific?>

"Not really. Just on the whole, I figure I owe you."

<Don't worry, Morgan. The 'Greater I' hasn't finished with you yet.>

She didn't doubt that. But if there was anything left of her in a minute's time, she would probably kiss the Crescend's High Human cheek in gratitude—if it had a cheek, of course.

She sat straighter in her seat. "Okay, this is it. Uri, how are we looking?"

"All systems are green for slow-jump."

"It's your decision. I'd rather rely on *your* instincts in this case."

"Understood. The *Sebettu* will be in range in thirty seconds."

She studied the boundary ahead of them. It was whipping like a flag in a gale.

"How long until we jump?"

"Soon . . ." The ex-captain's voice and expression were all concentration.

The chronometer hit twenty seconds.

The *Sebettu* was so close, Roche could practically smell its Kesh commander. If it came too close too soon, hitting the boundary wouldn't be an issue. One solid strike from behind would put an end to all their problems.

"Ameidio, full shields aft."

"Aye, Morgan."

"Fire if you think it'll help. Uri?"

The boundary loomed large. Previously small details now looked like giant ice floes tossing on an impossibly heavy sea.

The counter hit ten.

"Soon . . ."

"Their weapons are all locked and ready to fire." The edge to Haid's voice betrayed his own anxiety. "They'll be in range in no time."

"Looks like we're going out the same way we came in," said Roche, gripping her armrests.

Five seconds.

A wall of tortured space-time seemed about to strike them, and the *Ana Vereine* lurched violently to one side.

"Almost," whispered Kajic.

Zero.

Plus one.

Plus two.

Plus three.

"They're firing!" Haid shouted, bracing himself against the console.

The boundary hit them at the same time as the barrage from the *Sebettu.*

"Now!"

Kajic's voice filled the bridge as the engines let loose their contained energies in one, powerful surge.

For a split second, Roche felt like a tiny insect squeezed between the thumb and forefinger of some unimaginably giant beast.

Then they were jumping.

The ship rattled and shook as space warped and twisted. She felt as though she were being pulled inside out and spun around at the same time. Somewhere in the ship, Maii stirred in her coma; Roche could sense the distress of the reave as a wave of panic washed through her mind.

Veils of red fell behind them. Darkness peeled back and exposed—

Stars.

Then a blaze of blue light obscured them as the *Ana Vereine* dropped fully into real space.

Roche stared incredulously at the screen.

They were rocketing out of what looked like the surface of a large blue giant, warped into a fat spindle shape by incomprehensible forces. The anomaly had grown since they'd last seen it. Its surface was disturbed by the mighty distortions in space-time it hid.

"Behind us!" Haid yelled.

Something black and angular jutted out of the surface of the anomaly. Energy whipped around and from it, reaching for the *Ana Vereine* as though to pull it back down but also arcing back to strike itself. The sight filled Roche with both amazement and horror: the *Sebettu* had followed them through!

Then the surface of the anomaly flexed like a droplet of water in free-fall. The Kesh destroyer seemed to hang suspended for a moment, half in and half out of the slow-jump. There was a bright flash of orange light—even brighter than the anomaly—and the destroyer began to disintegrate.

First it broke into two, lengthways. Then those two fragments—each many times the size of the *Ana Vereine*—broke apart into smaller segments. Each piece hung briefly silhouetted against the anomaly, then either fragmented further or exploded. Within a second, there was nothing left larger than a grain of rice; another second reduced the Kesh destroyer to molecules; one further second and only plasma remained, a cloud of elementary particles tearing itself apart from internal forces.

"Box?"

Roche gripped the edge of her console hard. The ship shuddered as the shock wave hit it.

"Box!"

"We are experiencing communication problems due to the radiation from the anomaly," Kajic said.

"Try the . . . what was it? The Eckandi emergency band!"

"I am broadcasting on those frequencies."

"Any response?"

Kajic waited a second. "Nothing."

"Give it a minute."

Kajic nodded, and Haid turned to face her. She forced herself to breathe. No one said anything as the seconds swept by. The surface of the anomaly rose to meet them at a rate inversely proportional to the rate it was shrinking inside. The *Ana Vereine* angled its headlong flight until it seemed to be gliding.

A minute passed with no word. The Eckandi emergency band was empty, as were the others. Roche waited another minute just in case, then had no choice but to accept the truth.

The Box was gone.

"Take us back in," she said quietly.

No one spoke as the *Ana Vereine* began its descent back into the maelstrom.

Epilogue

IND *Ana Vereine*
'955.01.25 EN
0170

"Do you have any idea how many people crew a typical Kesh destroyer?"

Roche didn't answer because she didn't want to know. The face on the screen looked like it was going to tell her, anyway.

"Four thousand three hundred and fifty." Marine Commander Gent sighed to himself. "I don't know how I'm going to explain this back home."

"Just fill out your report as usual," Roche said. "And mark it to the attention of Page De Bruyn."

"De Bruyn, of COE Intelligence?"

"Yeah," said Roche. "And you can deliver a report from me too. I'm kind of obliged to tell her what's going on every now and again."

"Well, I wish you'd tell *me*."

"Look, take it up with your superior officers if you like." Gent was definitely old school, and Roche was fast losing patience with him. "Tell them what I've told you and wait for a reply. They'll only confirm what I've said, and you'll only have wasted your time. But I'm happy to wait. As long as you do your bit and make sure these people get to where they're supposed to, my involvement with you is at an end."

Gent grunted. "Okay, Roche. Have it your way. But if I find out you're spinning me a line—"

She broke the link with a flick of her wrist and leaned back into her seat. She shouldn't have been surprised. Broadcasting a distress call had been risky—but when they'd found the wreckage of the COE blockade and realized that there wouldn't be enough room to house all the refugees longer than a day, she'd had no choice. The *Ana Vereine* wasn't built to accommodate that many people.

She simply hadn't known that the first ships by would be the frigate *Starburst* and a full Armada reconnaissance squadron, or that there was a war brewing outside.

Her eyes were hot with fatigue. She rubbed them with her fingertips, trying to knead new life into them.

"Leave the galaxy alone for a few days and look what happens," said Haid dryly. "Perhaps next time we should get a sitter."

"Open conflict with the Dato Bloc. Revolt in the Narm Protectorate. Tension with the N'Kor Republic—and don't think this incident will make things easier on that front. The Olmahoi sending in grayboots to find the *irikeii.* Talk of impeachment in the COE capital . . ." She shook her head; bright-colored blotches danced across the vision of her one natural eye. "How could it have fallen apart so quickly?"

"Perhaps it's just symptomatic of the main problem."

Roche looked over to him. "You mean the clone warriors?"

Haid shrugged. "They're good at blending in, Rufo said; they insinuate, then they corrupt. Maybe they don't always work from the bottom up when they want to tear things down."

"Maybe." Roche's gaze returned to the screen, and the

image of what remained of the anomaly. It had cooled as it expanded, changing in color from blue-white to yellow to red. At that point—when no space at all remained within the Gauntlet—the boundary between the real universe and the anomaly had evaporated. Three hours later, a warm pile of primeval dust with nothing but angular momentum was all that remained within the perimeter of the former Palasian System. One day, it might accrete into a protostar and give birth to a new system, but that would occur long after Roche had left the scene. Billions of years later, probably.

"Uri, Get Auditor Byrne on the line," she said.

"Hailing her now," said Kajic.

She waited, but it was Lud that spoke: "Sorry, Morgan Roche. I'm not sure where Auditor Byrne is right now. Can I help?"

"I just wanted to know how you got on with those all-suits. Anything recoverable?"

"A few bits and pieces. We're still looking through them. We'll let you know if we need anything."

"Do that." The outrigger spines hung not far from the *Ana Vereine,* looking absurdly like two giant conifers stripped of their leaves. Each "branch" held a berth for one outrigger; most of them were empty, even those of Long Span. The remains of the all-suits destroyed by the *Sebettu* were being cannibalized for parts to repair those still needed; the rest of the components would come from the *Ana Vereine*'s stores.

"Idil wants to know what you've done with Linegar Rufo," Lud said.

"Give him to Gent. They're going to take him to face trial for his crimes."

"Good." She could hear the satisfaction in the outrigger's voice. "No matter what Yarrow . . . what she *was* at the end, her people deserve retribution."

Roche grunted a vague affirmative, not wanting to mention the strife in the COE; civilized proceedings might be on hold for a while if things went badly on any of the fronts. Lud would hear soon enough. For now, he was happy, and that was what mattered.

"By the way," he went on, "we have the body of the clone warrior. Do you want us to dispose of it?"

Roche was about to agree, but thought better of it. "No. Bring it aboard when you get the chance. It's bound to be of use to someone."

"Consider it done." Lud signed off.

More than just useful, Roche thought. It would be a wellspring of information on the clone warriors. To the best of her knowledge, none had been dissected. The Box would've loved it—and Rufo too. Part of her was tempted to keep the scientist with them a little while longer in order to have access to his specialized knowledge. But she could never trust him. He was too self-centered and treacherous; even his data would be suspect.

<I agree with you on that score,> said Maii when Roche asked for a second opinion. <His mind runs deep with knowledge, but is ethically shallow. He yearns for fame and money without concern for the cost. Not power as some might crave it, for he is genuinely disinterested in what most people do, unless it directly impinges upon his work. But domination in academia is domination nonetheless, and that makes him a megalomaniac.>

Roche smiled to herself. The young reave was almost back to her old self, exploring the minds of those around her with ease and disquieting confidence. She was doing it from her bed in sickbay still, but Roche knew that in no time at all the girl would be fully recovered and once again on her feet.

She refused to discuss what it had been like under Xarodine for so long, and neither had she talked about the *irikeii*—but that wasn't surprising. She had only been conscious for a couple of hours, and Roche had been busy for much of that time.

<Is Cane awake yet?> asked Roche.

<Not as far as I can tell.> Maii was also reticent to de-

scribe the state of the clone warrior's consciousness. <That is, I can't detect any mental activity behind his shields.>

Roche wondered how the reave could tell at all what was happening behind someone's shields, or even how someone could be awake *without* thinking—but she let it go for the moment. The fine details of epsense were something she knew little about.

For now it was enough that the girl was alive and safe. Whatever else had happened, at least Roche could relax on that score.

The question was: how far could she relax around Cane, knowing what she had recently learned about him?

"Morgan." Kajic's voice was soft, cautious, his expression in the holographic display regretful. "I have concluded a preliminary scan of the region. There is no sign of the Box anywhere. I can continue looking if you like; there is still a slight possibility that it might be simply damaged and unable to hear you. However, a conclusive search will take much longer than—"

"How *much* longer?"

"At least a month. The space we have to search is as large as Palasian System. If we didn't know where to start looking, even a small planet would be hard to find. And as the collapse of the Gauntlet has disturbed space for a light-year in every direction—"

"Okay, okay, I get it," she said tiredly. "You can stop looking." She raised a hand to massage her temple. "I just thought we should try to . . . I mean, if it had been me out there, I'd like to think that the Box would have . . ." Her voice trailed away to silence.

Kajic filled that silence quickly: "Don't worry, Morgan. I'm sure we'll hear soon."

She didn't say anything, just got out of her first officer's seat and went for a walk.

If there was one thing Roche hated, it was waiting. Not waiting in the sense of waiting for a delivery to come; in those cases, what was coming was known, and there was usually a rough idea how long it would take. She'd had plenty of training at that in the Armada.

What she hated was waiting for something unspecified at a time unknown—knowing only that nothing could be done until it arrived.

Like most of the mundane Castes, she'd had little if anything to do with High Humans before her mission to collect the Box. Already she had learned how frustrating it could be. The entire business with Cane—from start to finish—had been orchestrated by them from the shadowy recesses of the galaxy. They knew more about the clone warriors than anyone else, and probably had known for a lot longer, too. Their perspective on the galaxy was much broader than that of any single government, even one as widespread as the Commonwealth of Empires, so the effects of the clone warriors would have been more visible to them.

She remembered something Rufo had said: "We are entangled in the details." That was how she felt: caught in a web. And the more she tried to understand, the more entangled she became.

She was under no illusions about her own role in all this. She was just a courier for the Box, an intermediary allowing the Crescend, via the Box, access to spaces he normally couldn't get into. No doubt he was eagerly awaiting some sort of transmission from the fragment of his much larger self. When that signal didn't arrive, and word reached him that Palasian System had collapsed, he would know that something had gone terribly wrong. But she doubted he would relinquish such a privileged position so readily.

Part of her was half expecting a replacement Box to arrive at any moment, or some other development by which her next step would be made clear; another part believed she was redundant now, and the Crescend would find another courier for another sliver of himself. It didn't matter either way. For now she was stuck, caught between possibilities, still buried under a pile of details threatening to suffocate her.

She came to a halt outside the ship's medical center.

The last time she had seen Cane, he had been lying on his back, half-covered by the crystal in which Rufo had encased him. The *Ana Vereine*'s autosurgeon had begun removing him from the shell, and his vital signs had been gradually returning to normal—although what was normal for him was still not entirely known. How long until he would return to consciousness was likewise unknown. The drugs Rufo had used to immobilize him might have been strong enough to cause some lingering damage, in which case simply taking him out of the crystal cocoon wouldn't be enough; he would have to heal himself.

She had no doubt he would do that eventually, and sooner rather than later. Adoni Cane was the most incredible organism Roche had ever encountered. His physical strength, agility, and endurance were matched only by his cognitive abilities. The only times she had ever seen him puzzled were when he had confessed to responding to the command language Rufo had been broadcasting to the other clone warrior, and when he had first come to her cabin on the *Midnight* and had not known anything more than his name.

For all intents and purposes, the other clone warrior had proven herself to be as equally developed as Cane—if not more so—but something still bothered Roche. She had assumed that the other clone warriors would be just that—*clones*. Jelena Heidik had patently not been a clone of Adoni Cane, unless gender itself was something these warriors could change at will in order to perfect their disguise.

Cane was still lying on his back when she let herself into his isolated ward. The protective shell had gone, though. He now lay naked beneath a translucent sheet with various monitors snaking across and under his skin. A bank of monitors on one wall displayed his vital signs. They seemed within the bounds of normality, as far as Roche could tell.

"I don't know if you can hear me," she said, leaning on

the end of the bed by his feet. "But there's something I need to know. I might as well ask it now. If you *can* hear me, it'll give you something to think about. At the very least you can decide whether to answer me honestly or not."

She paused, wondering for a moment if she really expected a response from him, or even if she *wanted* one. "Before Rufo captured you," she went on, "you told me that although you didn't know what you were, or what you were for, you *did* know what you could easily become." She remembered the look in his eyes: cautious, cold, calculating. "What is that, Cane? *What* could you become? A warrior like Jelena Heidik? Is that it? Or something else entirely?"

She waited for a sign that he had heard, but the steady rise and fall of his broad chest didn't change. His brown skin seemed to absorb the light shining upon him, making him look like some kind of wooden statue. A totem, she thought. Something to frighten children with.

She sighed heavily and began pacing irritably about the bed. "Am I crazy for trusting you, Cane? You could do anything, any time, and I know I couldn't stop you. Before, I used to worry about the Box conspiring to get rid of me; and yet even without the Box, I'm *still* worried. The Box was the Crescend's tool through and through, and it followed its own agenda, but it was still just an AI. It had its limitations. You . . ." She stopped at the foot of the bed. "You're like a new virus no one's ever seen before. Who knows what effect you'll have if we let you loose?"

Roche watched him, clutching for a response, but in the silence that followed she felt like a fool standing there trying to talk to him. Maybe later, when Maii picked up signs of activity, she would return and try again.

She turned to leave, but the sound of tapping stopped her.

Turning back, she saw that his eyes had opened. They weren't looking at her, though; they stared straight upward at the ceiling, as though he didn't even have the strength to turn them.

The noise came from his side: one finger was tapping gently on the edge of the bed.

She leaned in closer. "You can't talk, right?"

With some effort, he managed to swallow, but his lips refused to move. Only his finger seemed to have any life, tapping continually on the bed.

"Tap once for yes and twice for no, okay?"

But the tapping continued unchecked. Only gradually did she realize that there was a pattern to the sound. He was doing more than just trying to get her attention: he was tapping in code.

She had studied various simple methods of signaling at the Armada Military College, but this one she didn't recognize.

"Uri—"

"I'm listening," said Kajic.

She half smiled. "You've been learning from the Box," she said. "So, what's he saying?"

"It sounds like a variant on a very old code, one I've not heard in practice before."

"Can you decipher it?"

"He seems to be saying"—Kajic paused—"that he's as Human as you."

"What?"

"'I am as Human as you are.' That's the message he keeps repeating, over and over."

Cane's finger stopped and the room fell silent.

"That's it?" She leant over Cane. "What does that *mean*? Are you trying to reassure me?"

He didn't reply. His eyes slowly closed, and she was left facing a corpse once again.

"Dammit!" She slammed the flat of her hand against the bed. "Uri, keep a close eye on him. The moment he wakes properly, I want to talk to him. And don't let him out of here—or anyone else in, for that matter. Understood?"

"Understood, Morgan."

<You too, Maii,> she added.

<I'll do my best,> said the young reave. <But I'm still not picking up anything.>

Of course not, Roche thought to herself bitterly as she left the room. That'd make things too goddamn easy . . .

She walked to burn off her frustration, and to keep herself active. There was too much work to do for her to rest: loose threads to tie up, plans to set in place just in case the Crescend *didn't* contact her, decisions to make. Would she return to the COE and see what happened, or try somewhere else? If the clone warriors had appeared in many other places, as Rufo had suggested, maybe ranging further for information might be fruitful.

There was one image she couldn't shake: it was of the cloud of seed machines that had made the revenge capsules which had in turn made the clone warriors. Rufo, via Maii and the *irikeii,* had imagined them dispersing outward through the galactic halo, then inward again, converging at one point. Why he had imagined that, she didn't know. Maybe he was aware of something she wasn't, or maybe it was just the easiest way to visualize what was going on. It might have meant nothing, but she found it hard to forget. If the clone warriors *were* converging, it would make sense to find out where they were heading. And meet them there.

But without the Box, many things she had taken for granted became complicated. Collecting and collating data from a variety of sources was just one of them. Monitoring Cane was another. She was appalled to realize just how dependent she had become on the AI during their short association. The Box had fulfilled many of the simpler functions of other machines but with the independence and initiative of a person trained in many different fields.

Even something as basic as flying the *Ana Vereine* would be difficult without the Box. Kajic oversaw most systems, and there were numerous dullard AIs to take up some of the slack, but Kajic was still only Human. He needed to sleep, like everyone else, and made the occasional mistake. At some point, she supposed, she would have to find him a crew.

Right now would be the ideal opportunity, too. Galine Four had been lost when the Gauntlet collapsed, and as a result the *Ana Vereine*'s holds were full of refugees from the station, jammed in with the isolation tanks she had jury-rigged for the resident outriggers. The latter had weathered the disaster well, even the ones like Lud who had lost their all-suits; some were already talking about where to sell the spare spine and what system to target next. It was the station personnel, more used to comfort and space, who were complaining. Some, she was sure, would happily accept an offer of employment in exchange for better conditions, even if only in the short term.

Myer Mavalhin was one of them. He had eventually made it onto the ship, and his incessant calls for her attention were no doubt designed to ensure he wasn't kicked off again before he tried to plead his case one more time.

After talking to Cane, she went to the holds, found him among those crowded together there, and took him into a secure office cubicle to talk in privacy. His expression betrayed hope, which she was quick to dispel.

"You're not coming with me, Myer," she said. "And if I can't say it enough times to make it sink in, then that's your problem, not mine."

"Why are you so adamant about this, Morgan?"

The question was reasonable enough, and she did her best to answer honestly, to keep old hurts out of it. "One: you're unreliable; I can't depend on you when I need to. Two: you're a loose cannon, thinking more of yourself than the people around you. Three: you don't have the sort of experience I'd need for someone in this situation—"

"As if anyone has," he interrupted, avoiding her gaze.

"Four," she continued firmly. "You rarely listen to any-

one but yourself—especially if it's something you don't want to hear. Even now I doubt I'm getting through to you."

He grimaced slightly. "So much for hoping it'd be like old times."

"There was never going to be any chance of that, Myer," she said bluntly. "You want me to keep going?"

"Thanks, but I'd prefer you didn't." He looked at her then in a way that she found disconcerting. "You know, Morgan, back in College you'd have given in to a bit of coaxing and sweet talking—like that time when we scammed that cruiser to Temoriel. Remember? God, you swore three shades of purple there was no way you were going along with it. But in the end you did, *and* you enjoyed yourself, too. You always did. That's what you were like in those days. I could rely on you then." He shrugged, apparently unaware of the irony in his words.

"I've more important things to worry about now," she said.

"You tried that excuse then, too, but it didn't have as much power over you. Now it's as though the important things are all you have left. You've . . . changed, I guess," he concluded.

She smiled at this. "I guess I have," she agreed, and got up to leave.

But he had one thing left to ask her.

"Did you ever find your parents, Morgan?"

The question took her by surprise, and she stopped and stared at him for a long moment. "What?" in the end, was all she could manage.

"Your parents," he said. "*Did* you ever find them like you said you would?"

"No, I . . ." she began. "I mean . . ."

"I'm sorry," he said sincerely. "I didn't mean to upset you. Just that I knew what finding them meant to you, and I was curious as to—Hey! What'd I say?"

But she was already running from the room, ignoring the sound of Myer calling after her. She could hear Kajic also, in a moment, as well as Maii. But she didn't stop to reply to any of them. She just kept running, moving through the corridors of the ship as though she were being chased by demons . . .

Her parents . . .

She remembered. Her aspiration had always been to join COE Intelligence. Part of that had been her desire to travel, and to escape poor conditions on her homeworld, but another part had been to gain access to powers ordinary citizens didn't have. The records on Ascensio, her homeworld, had been closed to her when she shipped out to Military College. She had always intended to return one day to find out who her parents had been. She had had a mother once, and a father. Something about them must have been recorded somewhere. Even a name would've been better than nothing.

But she had never gotten around to it. How could she have forgotten them? What had happened to her? Perhaps she had changed more than she had ever allowed herself to realize.

She didn't see the corridors that whipped by her. She didn't even care. Intentionally or not, Myer had managed to hurt her very deeply, and she was running from him as much as herself. Maybe if she ran hard enough, she could forget that she was crying, too. Tears spilled out uncontrollably, welling up from somewhere deep within her; somewhere long forgotten . . .

<You are behaving in a highly irrational fashion, Morgan,> said a voice inside her head.

She came to such an abrupt halt that she almost tripped over her own feet. She swayed on one spot for a few breaths, wiping at the sweat and tears on her face and waiting for the voice to speak again.

<Aren't you going to say anything?> it said finally.

<*Box*?>

<Yes, Morgan.>

<But—*how*?>

<Listen to me, Morgan. It is imperative that you do not tell anyone about my reappearance. I have gone to great lengths to ensure that my true location remains unknown. It would be a shame to have to start all over again.>

<Your *true* location?> She was slowly catching her breath, but felt as though she were losing her mind. <The valise was destroyed—>

<That was always a possibility. Hence, a backup was needed. Or, more accurately, the valise itself was the backup. At best it was only ever intended as a decoy.>

<A *what*?> Confusion quickly changed places with anger. She had lugged that damned valise hundreds of kilometers across a desert world, thinking it the most valuable thing in the galaxy—only to find that it was a *decoy*?

<It was necessary, Morgan. You will come to understand that eventually.>

<So where *are* you? If you weren't destroyed with the *Sebettu,* you must be around here somewhere. On the *Ana Vereine*? But how did you get on board? The only thing I brought with me from Sciacca's World was the valise. Along with Maii and Cane and Haid, of course—>

She stopped as a terrible thought occurred to her.

<Correct, Morgan. That is indeed all you brought with you.>

<With *me*.>

<Yes,> said the Box. <I am a part of you, and always have been.>

Now she was certain she was losing her mind.

She remembered being in orbit around Trinity, where AIs were made for the COE by the Crescend. She remembered waiting for the mysterious engineers to arrive to take her down to the surface, where she would be given the AI she had come to collect. But she didn't remember anything after that point, because somehow she had been rendered unconscious. The next thing she knew, she had awakened with the valise strapped to her wrist and the Box's voice inside her head.

<They *operated* on me? Without my permission?>

<It was deemed a tactical necessity to maintain security to the highest possible degree. You might never have known. I certainly had no wish to tell you. I feared your reaction would be negative.>

<Could you blame me?> Hugging herself, she slid down the nearest wall until she was squatting against it. Too many shocks; too much uncertainty; too much to be afraid of. <So where exactly are you?> she asked.

<There is no specific location, Morgan. I am distributed evenly throughout your body. That way, I could not be removed by cutting off, say, an arm, or severing your head. Such amputations will only momentarily hinder my performance. My components work on a cellular level, and are able to call on your cells as backup should you and I be severely damaged.>

<Does it work both ways?>

<It is not intended to.>

She closed her eyes, trying to get her head around the concept of having an AI inside her, but not even really wanting to succeed. She was riddled with it—like fat, or cancer.

<How do I get rid of you?>

<You don't until we return to Trinity. Only there does the necessary equipment exist to disentangle our separate structures. Until then we remain symbiotes.>

<And afterwards?>

<You will have noticed no side effects for my being inside you. I am completely self-sufficient and undetectable, internally and externally. The difference between my being in a valise strapped to your wrist and being inside your body is a small one, I would think.>

<But kind of an *important* one, wouldn't you agree?> She had been invaded, and she was angry with how dismissive the Box was being about it all. <What if I were to

change my mind? What if I told you and the Crescend to stick your little conspiracies and go my own way? What would happen to you then?>

<Don't fool yourself, Morgan,> said the Box. <If your intention was to keep me from my maker, then you would not succeed. You would be located eventually, and I would be taken. I am too valuable a tool to be thrown away so carelessly.>

<But I *can* get out of this if I choose to?>

<Of course.> The Box seemed to ponder this possibility. <But you won't, will you?>

She didn't answer at first as doubt suddenly welled in her. <This is crazy. No—it's impossible! What about all those times we were out of contact, or we had communication lags, or we really needed you and you couldn't get through?>

<Maintained to allay your suspicions. You coped with every situation well enough.>

<And on Mok?>

<Then you were correct to be suspicious. I was relaying information via you to and from the *Ana Vereine,* which was much farther away than I had you believe. Juggling you and Kajic was difficult, but by running the backup in the valise it was possible. Had the need to talk not been so great, I would not have bothered. Certainly it was the only time I broke my usual cover.>

She shook her head. <I can't believe you'd go to so much trouble.>

<I cannot force you to accept the truth, Morgan; you can believe what you like. You are not some puppet that dances as my will directs. You are as free as you ever were.>

<But—>

<But the fact remains: I am here, talking to you now, when you *know* the valise was destroyed, and I have always put your safety above my own. How else can you explain it?>

She put her head in her hands. She couldn't explain it, none of it. It was all a mystery to her. It was all so crazy.

A hand touched her shoulder and she flinched violently.

"Hey, it's okay, Morgan! I didn't mean to startle you."

She stared up at Haid, too disconcerted and confused to speak.

His hand withdrew. "Uri told me you'd had some sort of fit and I came to see if you were all right. Are you?"

"I—" She almost blurted out everything she'd just learned. That the Box was inside her and had been put there under circumstances the Box described as a "tactical necessity" but which she thought more akin to rape. That she was being used even more thoroughly than COE Intelligence had used her. That she had been betrayed—*again.*

But something stopped her. Something the Box had said.

I have gone to great lengths to ensure that my true location remains unknown.

The fact that the Box—that the Crescend—might have gone to such extremes struck her as so strange and unlikely that it temporarily overrode any concerns she had for her own well-being. She could think of only one explanation for its behavior, and once the thought was in her head there was no denying it. Why else would it wish its existence in her to remain a secret even now, when the danger of the second clone warrior was past?

The Box was hiding from *Cane.*

It was afraid of him.

"Morgan?"

"What?" She remembered Haid standing there. "Oh, I'm fine. Just thinking and working too hard, I guess. Didn't mean to give you a scare." She held out her hand and he helped her to her feet.

"Are you sure?" he asked, still studying her.

"Positive."

"Maii? Is she lying?"

<I have sworn not to read Morgan's mind without her permission,> the reave said to both of them.

Roche breathed a small sigh of relief. If Maii was telling the truth, the Box's secret could be kept a little while longer.

And as she thought this, she suddenly realized that she had already made up her mind: she *would* keep the Box's secret. For now, at least. And not because anything it had said convinced her to, either. She hated what had been done to her, but her curiosity as to what the Box planned to do next was strong enough to override the anger she was feeling.

Haid was still watching her.

"Maybe I should spread the workload a little," she said, smiling weakly. "If you're bored, there are plenty of repairs to be done. I'm sure Uri could use a hand. And we'll soon have shuttles from the *Starburst* docking to offload all these people. They have to be organized and ready to move. And what about supplies? Do we have enough to keep—?"

"Okay, already!" Haid raised a hand, laughing. "I'll get on to it now, I promise. But do me a favor and make sure you get some rest soon, all right?"

"Sleep is for the faint of heart," she said, quoting a lecturer from Military College. "If a lack of it makes you a little crazy, then you're in the perfect state to fight. If it doesn't, you're in the perfect state to lead."

Haid's brow creased. "Sounds like rubbish to me."

Privately she agreed.

It was only later, as she lay back on her bunk, that she realized how difficult it was going to be to find any time at all to rest.

Most of the refugees had been offloaded. All of the *Starburst*'s shuttles and three of the reconnaissance squadron's cruisers had made two trips each. The remaining stragglers would go with the last shuttles, due to cycle through within the hour. Haid was in charge of liasing with the Armada while Kajic concentrated on repairing the *Ana Vereine*. Yarrow Jelena Heidik's wizened body had been loaded aboard and placed in argon until someone was available to look at it. Roche had feigned exhaustion—no great task—to go to her quarters.

<Commander Gent is about to call you,> the Box said. <He has just received a priority communiqué from his superiors.>

Roche sighed and lay back on the bed. It hadn't taken the Box long to get back into the swing of things.

<Saying?>

<That the Armada is massing near Sol System, fearing a breakout of Wunderkind at any time. He has to join them, but will drop off the refugees along the way.>

<Good.> She closed her eyes. <Why won't you tell us the truth?>

<I'm sorry, Morgan?>

<You know what I mean. You infiltrated the datapools on the *Ana Vereine* when we first got on board; you corrupted COE Intelligence so they would think the Sol Apotheosis Movement was behind it all; you've done everything possible to lead searches in the wrong direction, and still you won't let anyone know what's going on. Why?>

<This is too big a threat, Morgan—truly galactic in scale.>

<So?>

<So what the COE thinks it knows won't make much difference to the big picture—if it is wrong. There are many thousands of similar governments under similar threats; some or all may already have been infiltrated by the clone warriors. Information is the key to any war, and we do not wish to reveal the full extent of our knowledge just yet.>

<So it is a war, then?>

<Most definitely, albeit one conducted thus far on a covert level. Only when cornered will the true and indiscriminate aggression of the clone warriors surface.>

<'Indiscriminate'?>

<They will kill anyone, any way they can. They seem to have no other purpose.>

<But what's the point of that? If they kill everyone, no one wins. Everyone's dead. Isn't that a bit self-defeating?>

<That may be the entire point. Several attempts have been made to study these creatures in situ; Palasian System was a fairly spectacular failure on many levels, but did at least demonstrate that they will fight to the very end. What we need to learn is whether the clone warriors will discriminate against any one Caste or social group. If such an exception does arise, then we may have discovered who their makers were related to. Logically the ones most like them will be the ones they spare.>

Roche nodded. <What about Cane? How does he fit in?>

<I suspect he knows he is being watched. You know that I released him from his cell on the *Midnight,* and that he and I colluded to ensure your escape from Sciacca's World. If he has suspected that I am an agent for someone more powerful, and if he now believes that I am gone, then it will be interesting to see what he does next. And believe me, I will be watching him very closely indeed.>

<Rufo suggested we look at the introns in his genetic code.>

<I know. I have already done so. His introns contain information I cannot interpret. The Crescend and his allies have been alerted to the possibility that this might be important, and will look at it immediately. Cane is, however, the exception to everything we have seen so far. If he is an aberration, a nonaggressive freak, his introns may contain nothing of use. At best, the information may turn out to be misleading.>

That seemed a depressing prospect to Roche. As much as she didn't want to believe that Cane would betray her, that would be better than drawing erroneous conclusions about the rest of his kind because he comprised a flawed data set.

<So what's this about Sol System?> she asked.

<Sol System is one of a number in a very old area, long abandoned for lack of resources. It has been fallow for many thousands of years, apart from the odd fanatical splinter group, such as the Sol Apotheosis Movement, and the occasional archaeologist. At least a dozen systems within the region are rumored to be the birthplace of Humanity.>

<And that's where the clone warriors are converging?>

<It seems so. Along with other forces, now. The Commonwealth of Empires is not the only regional government fearing a disaster from that area. Representatives from many Castes will be there, fearing threats different in name but similar in details.>

<At your urging, no doubt.>

<Indirectly, of course. We expect the clone warriors to attack. They will come with the fleets, hidden or walking in disguise among them.>

<And while everyone is looking to see who they attack first, you'll be waiting to see who they attack *last*.>

<Correct. When we have that information, we will be better positioned to retaliate.>

She shook her head. <It seems a bit risky, Box. I mean—>

A chime interrupted her.

"Marine Commander Gent wishes to talk to you," said Kajic.

<As expected,> put in the Box.

She ignored it. "Okay, Uri, put him through. Voice only, at this end."

An image of Gent's face came to her via her implants. He was standing on the bridge of the *Starburst*; his eyes wandered, having no fixed image of her to latch onto.

"I have received a communiqué from—" he began.

"I know, and I appreciate you going out of your way to help us like this."

Gent looked flustered for a second, then nodded formally. "It is the least we can do."

Besides which, thought Roche, he was required by law to assist in any regional disaster.

"Well, Commander," she said, "if that's all . . ."

"Not entirely. I wanted to discuss the matter of Auditor Byrne."

Roche frowned. "What about her?"

"She requested a ship to conduct a sweep of the outer fringes of what's left of the system. I loaned her the *Lucence-2* for a couple of hours, once it had finished ferrying passengers."

"I don't know anything about this."

"But she said it was your idea."

"She did?"

"Yes, and seeing as we've now lost contact with her, I thought I'd check with you to see what—"

She cut him off. "Give me its location."

A chart superimposed itself upon Gent's face. A red ring enclosed a small dot some distance from those marking the squadron. "They've drifted a fair way," said Gent. "Given that we need to move smartly in order to make this rendezvous—"

Again she didn't give him time to finish. A cold feeling had blossomed in the pit of her stomach. "Uri, I need Lud—*fast.*"

"Yes, Morgan."

<Box—>

<I know. I am checking it now.>

<Use the autosurgeon to crack the seals—with my authority so you won't be traced.>

"Lud here."

"This is Roche. Do you have genetic records of your clan members?"

"Yes. We keep detailed—"

"I need them. Can you send them to me now?"

"Of course." The outrigger didn't argue, even though the puzzlement was evident in his voice. "Give me a second to locate them."

<Maii?>

<I read nothing,> said the reave. <Nothing at all from that region.>

"Is something wrong, Roche?" Gent looked perversely pleased.

She ignored the question, and his attitude. "Target the *Lucence-2*, Commander Gent. If I give you the word, I want you to hit it with all you've got."

"What?" His expression wavered between amusement and alarm. "Are you serious?"

"Just *do* it, Commander. And tell me: how well is that ship armed?"

"Well enough," he said. "Look, what the hell is going on?"

"Transmitting those codes now," said Lud.

"Thanks." The cold feeling was growing. <Box?>

<I have conducted a visual inspection and am taking a genetic sample now. The tissue is extremely dehydrated, suggesting an extended exposure to vacuum.>

<Longer than a day?>

<Much.>

The feeling in her stomach turned to nausea. "Gent—shoot that ship! *Now!*"

"Are you out of your mind?" Gent bristled, outraged. "I can't just fire on my own people. I need a *reason*!"

"That wasn't the clone warrior in the all-suit!" She was shouting now. "It was Auditor Byrne!"

"How could you possibly know that?"

<I have the test results, Morgan,> said the Box, <confirming that the body is neither the outrigger known as Yarrow, nor is it of similar genetic stock to Cane. Auditor Byrne died at least five days ago.>

"Fire, Gent! *Fire!*"

But the dot on the chart that was *Lucence-2* had already begun to move. Too rapidly for pursuit to begin, and much more quickly than Gent's willingness to fire, it accelerated into the gentle gravitational well of the destroyed system.

Faster and faster it went, until it reached the minimum speed required for a slow-jump; then its hyperspace engines kicked in, space rippled, and—

It was gone.

Lud was the first to speak.

"Byrne?"

"The clone warrior hid in Yarrow's all-suit after the ambush around Aro, as he thought," Roche explained. In hindsight it was all too clear. "But then she killed Byrne when Byrne tried to heal who she thought was Yarrow. The clone warrior took on Byrne's identity and hid the body in Yarrow's all-suit, which she then teleoperated the rest of the way. It was she who broadcast the distress call that led me to Mok, and she who manipulated the spine into helping me. She led the attack on Galine Four, she wanted us to be suspicious of Yarrow and she even let us think she had died by letting Yarrow's suit be destroyed . . ." Roche shook her head, appalled. "We're lucky she decided not to stick around."

<Yes,> said the Box. <It is clear now that she gave up on attack long ago and decided instead to concentrate on escape.>

"My ship—the *crew*!" Gent was still stunned by the sudden turn of events.

"Face it, Commander. They're not coming back."

"You knew this would happen!"

"If it's a scapegoat you want, look no further than yourself. You let your guard down. You should have checked with me before giving anyone a ship."

"But I—" Gent stopped, swallowed. "I was not fully aware of the dangers."

Roche felt almost sorry for him. No one had expected anything like this. "None of us are," she said, thinking of the Box as well as her.

"So that's it?" said Haid from the bridge. "She gets away?"

"Not as easily as that." Roche sat up and fumbled for her shipsuit. Sleep was even farther away than she had thought. "We're going to follow her."

"Through hyperspace?" said Gent. "That's impossible!"

"Not when you know where she's going." Roche stood. "Uri, set a course for Sol System, shortest possible route. I want to beat her there if I can, or at least be right behind her when we arrive."

<This is the correct course of action,> the Box whispered in her mind. She didn't need it to tell her that.

"Ameidio, get those last few refugees off the ship as soon as possible—in survival capsules if necessary. I want to move within the hour. Maii?"

<Yes, Morgan?>

<I want you to take all we've learned about this—everything from Rufo and the *irikeii*—and give it to Lud. Not so he knows, but so it will surface if he hears we've failed. Can you do that?>

<Yes. Word of our deaths will trigger the release of these memories.>

"Lud?" To the outrigger last of all she said: "Thanks for your help. I'm sorry we have to leave, but—"

"I understand," he said. "Fight well, Morgan, for Idil's daughter and for all of us. We'll keenly await news of your victory."

"Do that."

Only Gent remained on the open line, red-faced and blustering. "Do you have even the slightest idea what you're doing, Roche?"

"Yes," she said, thinking of Sol System—of all those ancient places and the beings converging upon them. "We're going home . . ."

APPENDIX

THE OLMAHOI:
Reconstructing the Myth for Beginners
(R. Pyatt Adamek, '595 EN; Introduction, pp. 1-7)

There is no word in the Olmahoi language for "alone."

In fact, the Olmahoi Caste[1] has no spoken language at all, nor any desire to possess one. Being a race of natural epsense adepts, they employ instead a complex palette of emotions, sensations, and associations to talk between themselves, with the ease of thought itself. Mere words not only seem primitive and crude in comparison, but are quite outside the average Olmahoi's experience as well.

A Pristine Human might as well try to communicate with a bacterium by chemicals, or with a bee by dance. Even the concept of "loneliness," which we take for granted, is foreign to them: when one's entire family, one's entire Caste, is but a thought away, one is never alone.

Their uniqueness is marked on many other levels. Olma-

---

[1]Not to be confused with the Olmahi Republic, an independent government of the Nezhina Caste.

hoi society[2] is completely unfathomable and literally impenetrable to anyone not possessing epsense ability. They are, from a Pristine perspective, the most exotic of the known mundane Castes, not only in physical appearance, but in reproductive androgyneity as well. They are immensely knowledgeable in all fields and possess an average intelligence greater than that of Pristine Humanity; yet, in apparent contradiction to this sophistication, they have proven themselves on many occasions to be ruthless combatants.[3] And while each Olmahoi individual is a member of a far-flung interstellar empire, he still wears the long robes made from the skin of the Drish'en and prefers to live underground, both in the manner of his distant ancestors.[4]

Yet communicate with the Olmahoi we do. Through a medium of epsense "translators," trade has existed between our two Castes since the arrival of the Eckandar Trade Axis in this region of the galaxy some fifty thousand years ago. Now, after many millennia of contact, our involvement with them is a given, and seems certain to remain that way in the foreseeable future.

It is strange, then, and not a little disconcerting, to be reminded of how little we actually know about them.

On a fundamental level, there is the matter of their epsense abilities. N-body theory, from which stems the science of epsense and various related disciplines, hints that such a talent cannot evolve by chance, no matter how great the complexity of a mundane Caste member; it has to be guided into being by conscious, intelligent will, without which even a fledgling epsense predilection (such as that

---

[2]Often referred to by researchers as the Grand Design.

[3]Not for nothing are Olmahoi retribution units (grayboots) the most admired—and feared—fighting force in the Outer Arms, thereby disproving the usual association between pacifism and epsense ability.

[4]*He* is the usual pronoun used when referring to an Olmahoi individual, and covers both "sexes": reproductive function, which is changeable at will, plays little part in an Olmahoi's sense of identity.

which occasionally arises in an individual of any Caste) will falter.

That the Olmahoi appear to have defied current scientific theory may seem a small matter for scholars to debate: it is, after all, a *fait accompli.* With elongated tails tapering from the back of every Olmahoi's skull—these being the principal organs of the epsense, uncannily like an extra spine hanging free of the body—the Olmahoi possess tangible, physical evidence that this improbable evolutionary path has been followed at least once in the history of the universe. Studies of the Olmahoi physiognomy concur, revealing vestigial organs associated with the "vulgar" senses, such as a mouth and throat now used solely for ingestion that once possessed vocal chords and a tongue, ears associated with balance but still possessing the basic structures of an organ designed to detect sound, and so on.

However, proving that the ancestors of the Olmahoi did once possess function vulgar sense-organs is not enough to explain how an epsense ability could have evolved to supersede them. It is precisely by exploring this puzzle that science hopes to glean deeper truths lying beneath the *status quo*—to probe Humanity's place, not just in the Outer Arms, but in the greater galaxy as a whole.

If the Olmahoi possess a naturally occurring epsense ability, how *did* it arise? Current evolutionary theory[5] is simple and obvious. The Olmahoi home planet, Hek'm, is an icy, inhospitable world, and has been for many millions of years. Food is scarce; the Noma Araku, an extinct species of biped distantly related to the modern Olmahoi,[6] relied upon lichens and fungus growing on cave walls to balance an irregular diet of vegetable roots. For a predatory species to survive even a few generations, it must evolve new means

---

[5]As propounded by Professors Dubsky and Toma of the Cornilleau University of Antiquities.

[6]Itself a Low Human developed from mundane in the distant past.

of locating prey. Epsense ability is one such means: a way of hunting life directly, by seeking the spoor of thought itself. From this small beginning, evolutionary theory tells us, the Olmahoi Caste was born.

But neither the Noma Araku nor any other species of known biped leading to the modern-day Olmahoi has been proven to have possessed epsense ability, no matter how small. And indeed, the evolution of intelligent life in any form, on a planet such as Hek'm, is itself a statistical unlikelihood. The physical evidence available[7] indicates quite strongly that the species directly preceding the modern Olmahoi appeared almost overnight, approximately fifty thousand years ago, and was already in full possession of the range of epsense powers with which we are familiar today.

This evidence, and a smattering of facts adding suggestive credence, lie at the heart of the counterargument against evolution: that of intervention.

Again, this theory[8] is intuitively simple, although its ramifications are far-reaching. If epsense ability cannot evolve by chance, then it must have been deliberately nurtured in the Olmahoi Caste. Genetic analysis offers circumstantial support for this conclusion. The Olmahoi genome is elegantly complex, capable of creating a race of individuals whose only remarkable feature, it sometimes seems, is their lack of individuality,[9] but with just enough diversity to maintain a viable gene pool. Furthermore, the exon-to-intron ratio[10] is very low, suggesting that the genome might have been "trimmed" some time in the past, possibly to protect against mutation.

The critical question, and the one that has prevented this

---

[7]Predominantly in the form of cranial fossils, ruins, and the like.

[8]As championed by Professor Linegar Rufo of the independent research facility Galine Four.

[9]Olmahoi are notoriously difficult to tell apart.

[10]Analogous to a signal-to-noise ratio.

theory from gaining wide acceptance in the scientific community, is obvious: who intervened in the evolution of the Olmahoi Caste to ensure its epsense development?

Even among those who support the interventionist line in principle, there is a wealth of disagreement on this particular point. For once, it is a lack of evidence, suggestive or otherwise, that confounds the issue. There are no ruins on Hek'm to hint at the presence of an earlier, advanced civilization capable of such genetic and epsense manipulation, so it could not have been the Olmahoi natives. Likewise with the other Castes—High or mundane—currently inhabiting this region of the galaxy: none have ever possessed the ability (or the predilection) to perform such a feat; not even today, let alone fifty thousand years ago. So it must have been another Caste entirely, perhaps one of the five pre-High Human Castes mentioned in the Gil-Shh'ana Fiche, or another even more mysterious. Or, most peculiar of all, the Olmahoi themselves might be that very unknown Caste: the descendants of travelers from a distant and relatively unknown part of the galaxy, stranded on Hek'm millennia ago and only now rediscovering the legacy of their past.

Although the key to unlocking this mystery should, one might think, lie in the hands of the Olmahoi themselves, any racial memories, archetypes, or legends they might once have possessed about the origins of their epsense abilities are sadly no longer extant.[11] As a result, the origin of the Olmahoi Caste is either a vexing thorn in the side of anyone who would understand the continuing evolution of Humanity, or a tantalizing glimpse of a history still waiting to be discovered.

The emphasis of this Introduction, and indeed the greater part of the work, is on the latter. There is much that is

---

[11]Or perhaps, say the Kesh researchers in this field, they simply choose not to reveal them.

unique and beautiful among the Olmahoi, and much that we fail to understand. Most notable of all is the Grand Design: the web of minds that is centered on Hek'm, where the Olmahoi naturally congregate; quite possibly the most intricate mental structure in the universe, with tendrils stretching across the galaxy. To describe it in words is to attempt the impossible. Yet the renowned Linn Queale perhaps came close, with the following excerpt from his best-selling *Galactic Reference Book:*

"If empty space is a flat plain, with minds like bumps projecting from it, then the Grand Design resembles a cartographer's nightmare: towers, prominences, and spires project from it as far as the psychic eye can see, with strange ridges and rills, repeated figures and harmonic cadences, changing constantly in every direction—all linked by slender bridges that defy imagination, looping from peak to peak in a dance that resembles nothing so much as the dance of ocean weed in the grip of a cyclonic storm.

"At the very heart of this chaotic mental realm, however, lies the most peculiar thing of all: a bottomless pit, drawing everything toward it as a whirlpool or black hole draws ordinary matter to a single point. This, the one flaw in the multifaceted gem that is group-mind of the Olmahoi Caste, is the *irikeii,* which literally means 'the unnamed' or 'the unnameable,' one of the few thought-shapes in the Olmahoi 'language' that has a vocal analogue. Little is known about the purpose or origins of the *irikeii,* but we do know this: that it is not an artifact, nor a spontaneous natural phenomenon, but is, in fact, a living entity.

"One is born every generation: an otherwise normal Olmahoi whose mind is not so much a peak as an abyss, sucking thoughts in, swamping the Grand Design for a vast area around—counterbalancing, perhaps, the tremendous complexity that is the Olmahoi world of thought. This one is shunned but not reviled; the Olmahoi understand the *irikeii*'s role in their world, strange as it seems to us. Whenever that one is removed, as he must always be eventually, by natural death if not by accident,[12] another is immediately born to take his place. And thus the cycle continues, as it has for countless generations.

"So, even at the center of the Olmahoi Caste, where one might have expected utter chaos, one actually finds another example of the universe's natural tendency toward balance, symmetry, and cycles—proving, perhaps, that, despite the many and varied efforts of every Caste in the galaxy, the greatest beauty of all is still to be found in nature."

---

[12]No Olmahoi in his right mind would dare murder the current *irikeii*; the penalty for committing such a crime is the most severe allowed under Olmahoi Law.

GLOSSARY

A-P cannon—a weapon that fires accelerated particles of various types. Common on spacefaring warships.

Adamek, R. Pyatt—author of *The Olmahoi: Reconstructing the Myth for Beginners,* published in '595 EN.

Alik—an outrigger belonging to Long Span spine.

all-suits—the generic term for the highly individualized environment suits worn by outriggers.

***Ana Vereine,* DBMP**—the first of a new class of warships—the Marauder—manufactured by the Dato Bloc as part of the Andermahr Experiment. Its design incorporates a captain surgically interfaced with the ship. Once part of the Ethnarch's Military Presidium, it is now an independent vessel registered to Morgan Roche.

anchor drive—the usual means of crossing interstellar space, but by no means the only one (see **slow-jump**). Indeed, the anchor method has undergone several radical redesigns over time; current technology is rated at 49th-generation.

anchor points—regions of "weakened" space from which translation to and from hyperspace is both easier and less energy-expensive; jumps from anchor points are therefore of a greater range than from "normal" space and usually terminate in another anchor point. They are typically located near inhabited systems (but far enough away to avoid distortion by background gravitational effects) or in locations in deep space that are considered strategically important. There are approximately ten thousand million anchor points currently in existence—one for roughly every ten stars, scattered across the galaxy.

Andermahr Experiment—a covert project specializing in cybernetic interfaces designed to allow mind and machine to merge. Founded by Ataman Ana Vereine, who desired captains that were as much a part of their ships as was the anchor drive—an integral, reliable system rather than a flesh and blood afterthought. Continued in secret until the Ataman Theocracy emerged from the COE as the Dato Bloc. Culminated in the DBMP *Ana Vereine,* the first Marauder-class warship, with Uri Kajic its captain.

Armada—see **COE Armada**.

Aro—the largest moon of Jagabis and site of Emptage City; also the largest solid world of Palasian System. (Relative mass: 0.000271 (1.6 Cartha's Planet); distance: 1 million km; max. surface temperature: –140 degrees C; diameter: 5500 km)

Ascensio—the homeworld of Morgan Roche.

Asha—the single, warlike deity of the main Kesh religion.

Asha's Gauntlet—see **Solar Envelope**.

Ataman Theocracy—a tightly knit empire that existed as an independent entity until its absorption into the COE after the Second Ataman War in '442 EN. After several centuries, it eventually seceded as the Dato Bloc ('837 EN).

Autoville—the vernacular name for the innermost dark body halo of Palasian System, so-called because of the prowlers that dominate it. (Radius: 2.4-4.0 PAU; largest mean diameter: 2400 km.)

AVS-44—one of the *Ana Vereine*'s large contingent of scutters.

B'kan's Folly—the remains of the system in which a Solar Envelope was first employed.

B'shan, Lieutenant-Doctor Haden—a Kesh officer/scientist, serving with Linegar Rufo on Galine Four; subordinate to Field Officer Shak'ni.

Baeris Osh—a Surin territory.

Bassett—commander, COEA *Golden Dawn.*

Batelin Limit—the ceiling above which the complexity of a nation exceeds the biological capabilities of the individuals inhabiting it. In the case of the Pristine Caste, the value of the Batelin Limit is approximately three and half thousand systems.

Black Box—the generic term for AI. Usually abbreviated to "Box."

Bodh Gaya—the capital system of the COE. Its second moon houses the Military College of the COE Armada.

Box, the—an AI commissioned by COE Intelligence. Its binary identification number (JW111101000) is one digit longer than normal, indicating its unique status. Created by the High Human known as the Crescend, the Box is designed to infiltrate and subvert all available systems, thereby increasing its own processing powers until, at its most powerful, it resembles its creator.

Byrne, Auditor—the leader of the outrigger clan associated with Long Span spine.

Calendar—The galactic standard timekeeping method consists of: 100 seconds per minute, 100 minutes per hour, 20 hours per day, 10 days per week, 4 weeks (40 days) per month, 10 months (400 days) per year. All dates are expressed in the form of Year (usually abbreviated to the last three digits, ie '397), Month, and Day from the *Ex Nihilo* reference point. See also **Objective Reference Calendar.**

Cane, Adoni—the occupant of an unidentified life-support capsule recovered by the COEA *Midnight* near Ivy Green Station anchor point while en route to Sciacca's World. A genetically modified combat clone designed to mimic a Pristine Human, his origins may lie with the Sol Apotheosis Movement, although that theory is yet to be confirmed.

Cartha's Planet—the rocky, innermost world of Palasian System. (Mean distance: 0.16 PAU; diameter: 3600 km; relative mass: 0.000169; specific gravity: 5.3; mean surface temperature: 425 degrees C.)

Caste C—third of several unknown Castes mentioned in the ancient Gil-Shh'ana Fiche. See **Primordial Castes.**

Castes—Following the speciation of the Human race, numerous Castes have proliferated across the galaxy. These Castes are too numerous to list, but they can be classified into three broad groups: High, Low, and mundane (which includes Pristine and Exotic). There are seven predominant Exotic Castes to be found in the region surrounding the COE: Eckandar, Hurn, Kesh, Mbata, Olmahoi, and Surin.

Cemenid—the fourth and largest planet of Palasian System; a gas giant with thirteen major satellites. (Mean distance: 2.24 PAU; diameter: 183200 km; relative mass: 1.33.)

chaos-lock—a security device employing the chaotic electrical output of two identical circuits to conceal ordered data: when the two "tuned" circuits are linked, the data can be extracted from the signal; otherwise, the signal is concealed within unpredictable noise, and is impossible to decode.

COE—see **Commonwealth of Empires.**

COE Armada, the—the combined armed forces of the COE, responsible for external security. Active soldiers are referred to as Marines.

COE Intelligence—the body responsible for information gathering outside the COE. Originally and still nominally a subdepartment of the Armada, but an independent body in practice.

COE Intelligence HQ—the command center of COE Intelligence, a large, independent station located in deep space near the heart of the Commonwealth.

COE Military College—the main training institution of COE Armada personnel; situated on the second moon of Bodh Gaya.

COEI—COE Intelligence vessel identification prefix.

Commerce Artel—a galaxy-wide organization devoted to initiating and coordinating trade between Castes and governments that might otherwise have no contact. It prides itself on remaining aloof from political conflict yet has some strict behavioral standards to which it expects its customers to adhere (such as the Warfare Protocol). Structurally, it is divided into chapters managed by indigenous Caste members with only loose control from above. It has strong links, locally, with the Eckandar Trade Axis.

Commonwealth of Empires—often abbreviated to "COE" or "Commonwealth." A relatively ancient Pristine nation currently in its 40th millennium of nominal existence—"nominal" in that the membership of the COE is fluid by nature, with provinces joining and seceding on a regular basis. It has had many different capitals and its borders have changed radically over the centuries. Indeed, it has drifted with time, and now occupies territories quite remote from its original location. One thousand inhabited systems currently fall under its aegis, and another three thousand uninhabited systems have been annexed. It is ruled by a democratically elected Eupatrid and a council of representatives who, when united, wield supreme executive power. Its security departments include Intelligence, Armada, and Enforcement.

Congreve Station—the abandoned xenoarchaeological base built upon Mok, the moon shared by Kukumat and Murukan.

Cornilleau University of Antiquities—one of the many centers of study in the galaxy devoted to the exploration of Humanity's past.

Crescend, the—a High Human of some note and great history. His time of Transcendence is not recorded. Little is known about him, beyond the facts that he is the founder and overseer of Trinity, an ally of the COE and a key supporter of the Interventionist Movement. He is assumed to be a singular entity simply because the (male) first person singular is his pronoun of choice.

Dahish—a mildly alcoholic drink found in most places in the COE.

dark bodies—small, solid bodies found in most planetary systems (usually in belts, or **dark-body halos**) falling in size roughly between asteroids and planets.

Darkan, General—a senior officer of the Kesh N'Kor Republic and commander in chief of the destroyer SRF *Sebettu.*

Dato Bloc—an independent nation founded on the ruins of the Ataman Theocracy that recently broke free of the COE. Although not hierocratic in nature, the Ethnarch exerts a strict rule. Its security departments include the Ethnarch's Military Presidium and the Espionage Corps.

***Daybreak*, COEI**—a courier vessel belonging to COE Intelligence.

DBMP—vessel identification prefix for the Ethnarch's Military Presidium.

De Bruyn, Page—head of Strategy, COE Intelligence.

Dictatrix—supreme leader of the Kesh N'Kor Republic.

Diprodek-2—a potent neurotoxin most effective against Pristines.

Dirt & Other Commodities, Inc. (DAOC)—a mining consortium that currently owns the rights to the Soul of Sciacca's World. Its jurisdiction includes the planetary surface down to and including the mantle. In exchange for these exclusive rights, DAOC Inc maintains the COE's penal colony based in Port Parvati and the Hutton-Luu System's only major base, Kanaga Station.

Disisto, Gered—dock security chief, Galine Four.

disrupters—see **hyperspace disrupters.**

Dominion, the—a long-lived multi-Caste nation which joined the COE in '199 EN in order to fend off the Ataman Theocracy.

Drish'en—a burrowing animal found on Hek'm.

Dro, Sh'manit—the Sixteenth and last G'rodo Matriarch.

druh—a Kesh weapon used in armed combat; typically a curved, bronze sword about as long as the average Pristine forearm.

Dubsky, Professor—a scholar based at the Cornilleau University of Antiquities.

E-shield—an electromagnetic barrier designed to ward off particle and energy weapons. Used mainly by medium-to-large spacefaring vessels.

Eckandar—(Eckandi: adj & sing. n)—a Caste flourishing in the regions surrounding the COE. Its members are typified by their slight size, gray skin, bald scalps, and unusual eyes. They are a gregarious Caste, preferring trade and communication over conquest. They are also well-advanced in genetic science. Their past stretches back beyond that of the COE, although they lack the continuity of history that strong nationhood often provides. Their sole uniting body is the Eckandar Trade Axis.

Eckandar Trade Axis—the main society of the Eckandi Caste, devoted, much like the Commerce Artel (with which it has close ties), to facilitating free and nondiscriminatory trade with and between the COE and its neighbors.

Eli—an outrigger belonging to Long Span spine.

Emptage City—the main base of Palasian System; situated on Aro, the largest moon of Jagabis. (Population approximately 350,000.)

EN—see *Ex Nihilo.*

epsense—an ability encompassing telepathy and empathy. The ritual training of epsense adepts generally takes decades and incorporates elements of sensory deprivation. Note: telekinesis and precognition are not covered by epsense and are assumed to be nonexistent. Skilled utilizers of epsense are referred to as **epsense adepts,** or reaves.

Espionage Corps—see **Dato Bloc.**

Ethnarch—the title of the leader of the Dato Bloc.

Ethnarch's Military Presidium—see **Dato Bloc.**

Eupatrid—the title of the chief executive officer of the COE.

Ex Nihilo—refers to the date upon which the COE is believed to have been founded. Evidence exists to cast doubt upon the accuracy or relevance of this date—notably the fact the Commonwealth as a single body did not exist at all between the 13th and 15th Millennia—but the date remains as a reference point. Usually abbreviated to *EN.*

Exotic—any mundane Caste that differs physiologically from the Pristine. There are a vast number of Exotic Castes, and, although no one type of Exotic comes close to outnumbering Pristine Humans, the Exotics as a whole mass far greater than Pristines alone.

Far Reaches—the name of the outermost fringes of the Outer Arms.

Ferozac—a neurotoxin effective against Pristines.

flicker-bombs—devices used in space warfare to attack an enemy vessel. Employing the fact that small masses (under a few kilograms) can slow-jump a small distance within a gravity well, these missiles skip in and out of space on their way to their target, which, it is hoped, they will materialize within, causing massive amounts of damage. They are easily deflected by hypershields, however, which form a barrier in hyperspace that no such weapon can cross.

40th Millennium—the current millennium in the history of the COE. See ***Ex Nihilo.***

Free-For-All—outermost dark-body halo surrounding Palasian System. (Radius: 15.2-21.7 PAU; few clusters and eccentricities known; largest mean diameter: 1375 km.)

G'rodo—a Kesh lineage recently expunged from the N'Kor Republic.

Galactic Reference Book—see **Queale, Linn.**

Galine Four—a small mobile station owned by Linegar Rufo III; crew no more than one thousand.

Gatamin—the fifth world of Palasian System; a gas giant with three major satellites and an extensive ring network. (Mean distance: 4.56 PAU; diameter: 60000 km; relative mass: 0.3; rings 100000-145000 km.)

Geyten Base—a COE communications base around Cemenid in Palasian System.

Gil-Shh'ana Fiche—an anomalous data storage device recovered from Hurn ruins in '636 EN. Some segments of the fiche's contents point to the existence of several unknown Castes occupying the region now inhabited by the COE, although incompatible technology prevents clear translation; such ancient relics are occasionally found throughout the galaxy, but few are as spectacular or mysterious as those in Palasian System.

***Golden Dawn,* COEA**—COE Armada destroyer.

Gorund Sef—a planet in COE territory.

Grand Design—the Human term used to describe the social communion of the Olmahoi Caste.

grayboots—see **Olmahoi retribution squad.**

Guhr Outpost—a COE Armada refueling base orbiting Voloras, outermost planet of Palasian System.

Gwydyon—a system near but not part of the COE.

Haid, Ameidio—former transportee, Sciacca Penal Colony, and mercenary.

Handrelle System—a COE system.

Hek'm—the Olmahoi Caste homeworld.

Herensung—the third world of Palasian System; a gas giant with five major satellites and an extensive ring system. (Mean distance: 1.46 PAU; diameter: 100000 km; relative mass: 0.3; rings 135000-300000 km.)

Hetu System—a territory in the COE.

High Humans—or **High Castes.** Superior intelligences that have evolved (Transcended) from the mundane. Extremely long-lived and far-seeing, they concentrate on issues quite removed from the rest of the galaxy; indeed, due to their enormous scale, they are the only beings capable of comprehending the galaxy in its entirety. They generally leave mundanes alone, to let them progress (and, ultimately, to Transcend) in their own time. See **Castes** and **Transcendence.**

Hintubet—the primary of Palasian System; a greenish-yellow Main Sequence star supporting a large solar system consisting of seven gas giants, one rocky planet, one asteroid belt and several dark-body/cometary halos. (Surface temperature: 7800 degrees C; diameter: 1.8 million km; low sunspot activity, prominences, flares, etc.)

Hurn—an exotic Caste typified by ritual and complexity. In appearance they are lean and muscular, averaging greater than Pristine height. They are predisposed toward music and mathematics. Socially they prefer oligarchies with a baroque middle class.

hypershield—a barrier erected in hyperspace to deflect or inhibit the passage of anything traveling by that medium. Commonly used as a prophylactic against hyperspace weapons. Hypershields operate under a maximum volume constraint: i.e., they will only operate as intended under two thousand cubic kilometers.

hyperspace disrupters—a form of hypershield that actively combats incoming hyperspace weapons, such as flicker-bombs. Compare anchor points, which "weaken" space: disrupters do the opposite, making it more difficult for anything nearby to emerge from hyperspace.

Idil—an outrigger belonging to Long Span spine.

IDnet—see **Information Dissemination Network.**

IND—independent vessel identification prefix.

Information Dissemination Network—a communications network dedicated to the spread of data across the galaxy, although its reach thus far extends not much beyond the COE and its neighbors. It acts as a combined news service and medium for gossip. Also known as IDnet.

Intelligence—see **COE Intelligence.**

Interventionism—a movement among High Humans—and some mundanes—that advocates closer links between High and mundane Castes. See **The Crescend.**

irikeii—one of very few Olmahoi "sound-thoughts" that can be equated with audible words; often translated as "unnamed" or "unnameable." (See Appendix.)

JA-32—the largest charted dark body in Mishra's Stake, Palasian System; full name JA140732.

Jagabis—the second planet of Palasian System; a gas giant, it possesses an ageing ring system and six major moons, one being Aro, the largest solid body in Palasian System. (Mean distance: 1 PAU (460 million km); diameter: 133200 km; relative mass: 1.0; (2 million million million million tons); rings 156000-173000 km.)

Johak Corporation—original manufacturers of the device known as Asha's Gauntlet; see **Solar Envelope.**

JW111101000—see **Box, the.**

K'mok ni Asha—late Kesh (Regional Variant #14) for "Asha's Gauntlet"; see **Solar Envelope.**

Kajic, Uri—former captain, DBMP *Ana Vereine,* physically bonded to his ship.

Kesh—the most primal of the local Castes. The Kesh are typically warlike and predisposed to violence. In appearance, they tend to be larger than the Pristine average and have mottled, multicolored skin. Their social structure is heavily ritualized, with a strong tribal or family base. They are known for being highly racist.

Kesh Ideal—the epitome of the Kesh culture, a being comprising ideological and physical perfection, to which most Kesh, especially those in the military forces, aspire.

KM36—an inconstant ion flux tube connecting Kukumat and Murukan; known as "old thirty-sixer" in the vernacular.

Kukumat—one of a gas giant pair occupying the sixth planetary orbit around Palasian System; the pair shares a single moon, Mok. (Mean distance: 7.17 PAU; diameter: 45000 km / 43000 km; relative mass: 0.25/0.2; average separation: 2 million km.)

Kuresh—Kesh for "General."

Long Span—an outrigger spine.

Low Castes—devolved mundane Humans. These animal-like creatures come in many forms and occupy many niches across the galaxy. Some evolve back up to mundane status, given time and isolation, while others become extinct as a result of the forces that led to their devolution in the first place.

Lucence-2—COE Armada escort and assault craft.

Lud—an outrigger belonging to Long Span spine.

Maii—Surin epsense adept.

Marauder—an experimental class of warship developed by the Dato Bloc. See **DBMP *Ana Vereine*.**

Marines—see **COE Armada.**

Mattar Belt—Palasian System's asteroid belt. (Radius: 0.38-0.76 PAU; various gaps and groupings known; largest 750 km across.)

Mavalhin, Myer—ex-COE Intelligence trainee, now a pilot for Linegar Rufo.

Mbata—(Mbatan, adj & sing. n)—a well-regarded Caste known for its peace-loving and familial ways. In appearance they resemble the ursine species, larger and stronger than the Pristine. Their culture is egalitarian and open to trade.

***Midnight,* COEA**—COE Retriever-class frigate.

Military Presidium—see **Dato Bloc.**

Mishra's Stake—the vernacular name for the second dark-body halo of Palasian System. (Radius: 7.6-11.1 PAU; largest known: JA140732, diameter: 1500 km.)

Mok—the moon shared by Kukumat and Murukan with a highly irregular, chaotic orbit. (Relative mass: unknown; diameter: 1050 km; surface g: unknown; max. surface temperature: –125 degrees C.) It houses a small xeno-archaeological base, now abandoned.

Montaban—the homeworld of Ameidio Haid.

mundane Castes—Castes of Humanity that are essentially similar to the Pristine in terms of size, mental capacity, world-view, etc. Naturally there is a spectrum of types across the mundane Caste—from the highly evolved (some might say near-Transcendent) Olmahoi, through the socially complex Surin and Hurn Castes, to the Eckandar and Pristine Castes with their societies based on trade and empire-building, and beyond, via the earthy Mbata, to the relatively primal Kesh. Mundanes are typically short-lived (a century or so, when allowed to age naturally) and build empires up to four or five thousand systems in size. There is a ceiling of complexity above which mundanes rarely go without Transcending. See **High Humans** and **Batelin Limit.**

Murukan—one of a gas giant pair occupying the sixth planetary orbit around Palasian System (see **Kukumat**).

n-body—the epsense "counterpart" to the physical body.

N'kor Republic—a Kesh government neighboring the COE. Although the relationship between these two nations is officially friendly, there have been frequent border clashes.

n-space—a word used by epsense theorists to describe an environment completely empty of thought.

Narm Protectorate—a part of the COE.

Nezhina Caste—a mundane Caste located on the other side of the galaxy from the COE.

Nirr—the neutral homeworld of the Kesh Caste.

Noma Araku—an extinct species of biped distantly related to the modern Olmahoi.

Objective Reference Calendar—a system of date-keeping established by the A-14 Higher Collaboration Network.

old thirty-sixer—see **KM36.**

Olmahi Republic—an independent government of the Nezhina Caste.

Olmahoi—an Exotic Caste that communicates entirely by epsense. Physically they are of similar size to Pristines, but are much stronger; their skin is black and they possess little in the way of distinguishing features, apart from the epsense organ which dangles like a tentacle from the back of the skull. Their social structure is too complex to explore in detail here. They are renowned fighters, capable of feats of great skill, yet also possess a capacity for peace far in excess of any other local Caste. (See Appendix.)

Olmahoi retribution units—renowned fighters able to combine perfectly their physical and epsense abilities. Also known as grayboots.

Outer Arms—the low stellar-density regions of the galaxy between the Middle and Far Reaches.

outrigger—a unique type of miner/explorer found in sparsely populated systems; living within all-suits that double as mobile homes, outriggers typically scout uncharted dark-body halos and asteroid belts looking for viable mineral sources, which they then either mine or report to a centralized authority (if any) for a modest fee. Outriggers are notoriously self-sufficient, avoiding even other outriggers as much as possible, and have been known to exist for years without contact with another being. Spending much of their lives drifting in hibernation between dark and cometary bodies, some live longer than three centuries. Few outriggers have family names, coming as they do from such small communities that single given names are usually enough.

Palasian System—a system of the COE recently quarantined by the COE Armada as as result of an enemy outbreak. Due to its lack of habitable or easily terraformable planets, it has never been extensively colonized, but is the home to several Armada bases and a small commercial mining operation: total population, five hundred thousand people.

PAU—the abbreviation of Palasian Astronomical Unit, the mean distance from Jagabis to Hintubet, that being 460 million kilometers.

Perez radiation—a side effect of a crudely tuned hyperspace jump.

Plenary—full outrigger meeting, convened only in extraordinary situations. The individual members are rarely in the same physical location, however.

Primordial Castes—precede the earliest confirmed records, half a million years ago. Little is known about them, except that they existed; ruins of several unique types are to be found throughout the galaxy. They are called Castes A, B, C, and D, for even their names are unknown.

Pristine Caste—the form of Humanity which most closely resembles the original race that evolved an unknown time ago on an unknown planet somewhere in the galaxy. The Pristine Human genome, handed down from antiquity and regarded with near veneration, is stored in innumerable places among the civilized worlds. Pristines themselves, however, are accorded no special status.

prowling mines—known also as **prowlers.** These are mobile, semiautonomous mining installations, typically found in the dark-body halos of sparsely populated systems and are usually corporate owned.

Queale, Linn—author of the *Galactic Reference Book,* a popular all-purpose travel guide and almanac.

Quick, Alemdar—a duelist on the COE fighting circuit.

Quolmann—COE Intelligence code word.

quorum—the outrigger decision-making body; flexible in both number and identity of members.

Ramage, General—commander in chief of the COE Armada.

reave—see **epsense.**

Riem-Perez Horizon—the technical name for the boundary cast by a hypershield.

Roche, Morgan—former commander, COE Intelligence.

Roptio ur-music—music performed by a Low Human Caste known for its lack of sophistication.

Rufo, Linegar—renowned xenoarchaeologist; see **Galine Four.**

Sciacca's World—the only habitable world of the Hutton-Luu System; once an agricultural planet of the Dominion, now a desert penal colony of the COE (Sciacca Penal Colony). Its ring of moonlets—the Soul—is owned and mined by DAOC Inc.

Scion War—the war in which the Sol Apotheosis Movement met its downfall at the hands of the Dominion, the Ataman Theocracy, and the COE, among others. The war was brought to an end in the 37th Millennium ('577 EN) when the leader of the combined military forces ordered an attack on the headquarters of the Movement, provoking their explosive suicide. See **Sol Apotheosis Movement.**

scutter—a small, swift spacegoing vessel with many uses, both military and civilian.

Sebettu—Dictatrix who, in '173 EN, briefly unified the Kesh Caste.

***Sebettu,* SRF**—Kesh destroyer.

Shadow Place—the temple-like quarters in which the Olmahoi *irikeii* is housed.

Shak'ni, Field Officer—a Kesh officer subordinate to General Darkan.

slow-jump—a common alternative to the anchor drive that utilizes similar technology. Most ships with an anchor drive can slow-jump if necessary. It is essentially a jump through hyperspace from any point in real space. A certain degree of kinetic energy is required before translation can be achieved, so ships must accelerate for some time beforehand. Even then, the hyperspace jump is short-lived, and the vessel emerges soon after (typically less than a light-year away from its departure point) with significantly less kinetic energy. The process must be repeated from scratch if another slow-jump is required. As a means of crossing interstellar space, it is inefficient and time-consuming, hence its name. Slow-jumping becomes increasingly nonviable closer to a gravity well, but more efficient as mass (of the traveling object) decreases.

Sol Apotheosis Movement—a quasi-religious organization devoted to the pursuit of Transcendence via genetic manipulation and biomodification that reached its peak and was destroyed in the 37th Millennium. Its fanatical followers were a source of unrest for decades, until an alliance was formed among their neighbors dedicated to putting a stop to them. In '577 EN, at the climax of the Scion War, a flotilla of allied forces encircled their base, which the Movement destroyed in order to prevent its capture. The resulting explosion annihilated them as well, of course, but also decimated the flotilla. Of the four stations involved in the battle, only one survived, and that was severely damaged. So embarrassed was the alliance that the leaders of the day ordered the event stricken from history. They even closed the anchor point leading to the system to keep anyone from learning what occurred there. Nothing survived of the base, and the rest of the system is an unsalvageable ruin.

Sol System—an uninhabited system in a nonaligned region near the Dato Bloc, one known for its antiquity. Former home of the Sol Apotheosis Movement.

Sol Wunderkind—genetically modified clone warriors designed and bred by the Sol Apotheosis Movement.

Solar Envelope—a device designed by the Johak Corporation in 38,138 EN, intended to provide a jump shield large enough to enclose an entire solar system. Two prototypes were built in '211 EN by an early Kesh Government, which held them in storage until the Great Embargo of '221 EN. Asha's Gauntlet was used on one system at this time, with disastrous results: the system's primary sun, modified to power the Envelope, was exhausted within two months; the entire system collapsed shortly thereafter, and is now known only as B'kan's Folly. Of no use as a defensive weapon, and outlawed by the Convention on Extraordinary Weapons in '254 EN, the second Gauntlet has remained in the hands of the N'kor Republic since then.

spine—the collective noun used to describe a loosely linked group of outriggers; from their means of traveling between systems, on the back of a naked real-space drive known as the spine.

***Starburst*, COEA**—COE frigate.

Surin—a relatively minor Caste found in the regions surrounding the COE. They exist in isolated clusters overseen by a governing body that guides rather than rules. They are social beings, yet are fond of isolation, giving them a reputation for occasional aloofness. They are technically accomplished, especially in the biological sciences. In stature, they tend to be slight and have hair covering much of their bodies. It is occasionally speculated that they have re-evolved from Low Caste status.

Surin Agora—the ruling body of the loosely knit Surin nation.

Synnett, Torr—security guard on Galine Four.

Temoriel—a COE Armada trainee port not far from Bodh Gaya.

Thin Trunk—an outrigger spine known to Long Span.

Tipper-Linke Conduit—a specialized form of chaos-lock, combining tuned circuits with quantum encryption: the chaos-locked signal is broadcast along a beam of polarized light, with digital data represented by 90-degree separations in polarization; without knowing which polarization angles to look for or which angle is 0 and which is 1, the signal will be garbled. By the uncertainty principle, any incorrect attempt to measure the polarization of the light will result in interference, which will alert the users of the Tipper-Linke Conduit, who can then change the angle of polarization, leaving the hackers exactly where they started.

Toma, Professor—a scholar based at the Cornilleau University of Antiquities.

Tongue, the—how the Kesh refer to their own language.

Transcend—to break free of the constraints of mundane Humanity. A being or Caste that has Transcended typically has an extremely long life span and spreads its consciousness across a number of primary containers—such as neural nets, quantum data vats, and the like. Transcended entities, singular or collective, are referred to as High Human and accorded the highest status.

Transcendence—the state of being Transcended. Usually achieved when consciousness research and computer technology overlap, allowing an organic mind to be downloaded into an electronic vessel, thereby gaining the potential for unlimited growth.

Tretamen—a region on the fringes of the COE.

Trinity—the world on which AIs are made in the region dominated by the COE. The AI factory was founded and is overseen by the High Human known as the Crescend.

Veden, Makil—an Eckandar Trade Axis citizen and Commerce Artel ex-delegate; deceased.

Vereine, Ataman Ana—the last leader of the Ataman Theocracy and founder of the Andermahr Experiment.

viridant—a reptilian creature found on Ascensio.

Void 34—a cyborg duelist on the COE fighting circuit.

Voloras—the eighth and outermost planet of Palasian System; a gas giant with three major satellites. (Mean distance: 13.0 PAU; diameter: 40,000 km; relative mass: 0.33.)

vukh—a hot alcoholic beverage enjoyed by members of the Kesh Caste.

Walan Third—a COE world leased to the Commerce Artel.

Warfare Protocol—the code by which war is conducted within and between those nations that trade with the Commerce Artel.

Warrior's Right—the right of a Kesh to challenge by physical combat a superior's decision.

Wide Berth—an outrigger spine.

Wight Station—the automated solar research station on Cartha's Planet, Palasian System.

Xarodine—an epsense-inhibiting drug.

Yarrow—an outrigger belonging to Wide Berth spine.

Yul—an outrigger belonging to Long Span spine.

The battle for the future of humanity begins here...

EVERGENCE

THE PRODIGAL SUN

by SEAN WILLIAMS & SHANE DIX

Commander Morgan Roche of the Commonwealth of Empires is charged with escorting an artificial intelligence unit to her superiors, with the aid of a genetically engineered warrior whose past is a mystery even to him...

__0-441-00672-8/$6.99

"A personal story told on a galaxy-sized canvas. Filled with action as well as intriguing ideas."
—Kevin J. Anderson

Prices slightly higher in Canada

Payable by Visa, MC or AMEX only ($10.00 min.), No cash, checks or COD. Shipping & handling: US/Can. $2.75 for one book, $1.00 for each add'l book; Int'l $5.00 for one book, $1.00 for each add'l. Call (800) 788-6262 or (201) 933-9292, fax (201) 896-8569 or mail your orders to:

Penguin Putnam Inc.
P.O. Box 12289, Dept. B
Newark, NJ 07101-5289
Please allow 4-6 weeks for delivery.
Foreign and Canadian delivery 6-8 weeks.

Bill my: ❑ Visa ❑ MasterCard ❑ Amex _____ (expires)
Card# _____
Signature _____

Bill to:
Name _____
Address _____ City _____
State/ZIP _____ Daytime Phone # _____

Ship to:
Name _____ Book Total $ _____
Address _____ Applicable Sales Tax $ _____
City _____ Postage & Handling $ _____
State/ZIP _____ Total Amount Due $ _____

This offer subject to change without notice. **Ad # 898 (4/00)**

PENGUIN PUTNAM INC.
Online

Your Internet gateway to a virtual environment with hundreds of entertaining and enlightening books from Penguin Putnam Inc.

While you're there, get the latest buzz on the best authors and books around—

Tom Clancy, Patricia Cornwell, W.E.B. Griffin, Nora Roberts, William Gibson, Robin Cook, Brian Jacques, Catherine Coulter, Stephen King, Jacquelyn Mitchard, and many more!

Penguin Putnam Online is located at http://www.penguinputnam.com

PENGUIN PUTNAM NEWS

Every month you'll get an inside look at our upcoming books and new features on our site. This is an ongoing effort to provide you with the most up-to-date information about our books and authors.

Subscribe to Penguin Putnam News at http://www.penguinputnam.com/ClubPPI